An Unsuitable Marriage

Colette Dartford

ZAFFRE

First published in Great Britain in 2017 by

ZAFFRE PUBLISHING
80-81 Wimpole St, London W1G 9RE
www.zaffrebooks.co.uk

This is a work of fiction. Names, places, events and
incidents are either the products of the author's imagination or
used fictitiously. Any resemblance to actual persons, living or dead,
or actual events is purely coincidental.

A CIP catalogue record for this book is available from the British Library.

ISBN: 978–1–785–76053–2

Also available as an ebook

1 3 5 7 9 10 8 6 4 2

Typeset by IDSUK (Data Connection) Ltd
Printed and bound by Clays Ltd, St Ives Plc

Zaffre Publishing is an imprint of Bonnier Zaffre,
a Bonnier Publishing company
www.bonnierzaffre.co.uk
www.bonnierpublishing.co.uk

For my husband, Trevor, and our children, Charlotte, Matthew and Nicholas

Prologue

It was Olivia who found the boy. She only went to the changing room because she thought that was where she had dropped her keys, and there he was, suspended from a coat hook, a black leather belt round his neck. At that moment she knew why people claimed not to believe their eyes. It seemed an odd expression, implying one's eyes had the capacity for deceit, but now she understood it completely.

His face was ashen – a greyish sort of white – his lips tinged with blue. Olivia clamped her hand over her mouth to stifle a cry. She wanted to call the boy's name but was too shocked to remember it. Instead she lunged forward, grabbed his legs in a kind of bear hug and took the weight of his body in her arms. The obvious thing was to shout for help, but the changing rooms were out of bounds after supper so nobody would hear. She released her right arm, taking all his weight in the left, reached up to the metal buckle and pulled it undone with a hard tug. The boy slumped forward over her shoulder. Freddie Burton. Of course.

Olivia laid him on the bench that ran under the row of hooks and felt his vividly bruised neck for a pulse. New houseparents had to take a first aid course, otherwise she wouldn't have known that the carotid pulse can be felt on either side of the windpipe, just below the jaw. It was weak and faint, barely there.

'Freddie,' she said, her voice artificially calm. 'Freddie, it's Mrs Parry. You're going to be fine.'

She didn't know if that was true but it seemed the right thing to say. As gently as she could, she manoeuvred him into a sitting position and from there managed to roll him over her shoulder. His build was as stocky as hers was slight, and he felt awkward and heavy as she carried him, fireman-like, along the dimly lit corridor and out into the deserted quad. His bony shoulder pressed painfully into hers. She breathed through the pain, the way she had when Edward was born.

A biting wind whipped fallen leaves into a frenzy. Its ghostly howls drowned Olivia's pleas for help and she braced herself to scream. From the pit of her stomach she released a shrill, desperate sound, bringing Leo Sheridan, Freddie and Edward's housemaster, to the dorm-room window. He flung it open and shouted down to her.

'Olivia? What's going on?'

'Ambulance. Call an ambulance.'

Seconds later Leo was in the quad, dashing towards her. Explanations could wait. He relieved her of the boy and carried him into the school building, up the wide stone staircase and past the girls' dorm to sickbay, where Matron was waiting, her face slack with shock.

'I've called the ambulance and Martin's on his way,' she said, helping Leo lay the boy down on a narrow metal-framed bed. Olivia hated the sickbay beds. They had something of a mental asylum about them: austere, cold, frighteningly functional.

Matron checked the boy's pulse and respiration while Olivia recounted how she had found him, but then Martin Rutherford, the headmaster, rushed in, panting as if he had run from his house at the end of the long driveway, and she had to repeat it all again. He put his hands to his forehead, almost covering his eyes, and shook his head.

'I don't understand.'

Olivia summarised. 'He tried to hang himself.'

'Good heavens,' gasped Martin. 'Is he going to be all right?'

'He's breathing,' said Matron, 'and there's a faint pulse. The ambulance will be here soon.'

Martin's sickly pallor was now strikingly similar to Freddie's. 'I should call his parents,' he said. 'Burton, isn't it?'

'Yes,' said Leo. 'He's in my dorm. The parents are divorced so there are two numbers.'

Martin ran a hand through his thinning hair and pulled himself up into headmaster mode. 'Fetch those numbers, would you, please,' he said. 'And don't say anything to the other boys yet. This needs to be handled sensitively.'

Olivia didn't envy Martin the task of breaking the news to Freddie's parents, a thought interrupted by the piercing scream of approaching sirens, and then everything happened very quickly. Two paramedics checked Freddie's vital signs, put a collar round his neck and whisked him off to hospital with Matron by his side. Martin and Olivia watched in silence as the ambulance sped away, its flashing blue lights fading into the inclement night.

*

In the tense weeks that followed, an ominous cloud of rumour and disquiet descended on St Bede's. The press relished an opportunity to engage in a bit of finger-wagging, vilifying those callous parents who 'farmed out' the care of their offspring to expensive boarding schools. They dragged up cases where deviant adults had sought out such establishments in order to gain access to vulnerable children. Martin attributed these articles to resentment about perceived privilege and elitism, but it didn't help that Freddie's father, Toby Burton, gave an interview citing the school's 'near fatal neglect of his son's welfare'.

It was Freddie who set the record straight. He had lingered in a coma for five agonising days before the prayers offered up at morning chapel were finally answered. He explained that he had hung himself from a coat hook as an early Halloween stunt, his sole intention being to 'scare the shit' out of his friends. Freddie was well known as an attention seeker, a serial prankster, but even for him this seemed extreme. Didn't he realise how dangerous it was, that he could have died? This, Martin confided to Olivia, is what he had asked when visiting Freddie in hospital, but the boy had shrugged and blamed it all on his friends. They were supposed to meet him in the dark and spooky changing room after supper, where they would have found him *pretending* to be hanged. He had stressed that, Martin said, because he was fed up with being asked stupid questions about whether he meant to harm himself. Olivia was surprised when Martin said that Freddie blamed Edward in particular, because he was the one who had piped up that *Doctor Who* was about to start, prompting Freddie's friends to forget him altogether.

'Let's hope he never does anything like that again,' said Olivia, to which Martin replied, 'Amen.'

It was a relief when October half-term arrived and at chapel, on the last day of school, Martin urged staff and pupils to pray for a return to normality. They had just stood for a hymn – three rousing verses of 'Give Me Joy in My Heart' – when the strangest sensation of dread crept over Olivia. Not a premonition as such, but an inexplicable sense of foreboding. At least that's what she claimed later, although she had no more inkling than anyone else that before the year was over, another boy would be discovered close to death, and this time she would know his name.

One

The prospect of ten days at the Rectory was about to test Olivia's resolve to make the best of a bad situation. As she packed her bag – a suede Gucci holdall that reminded her of more affluent times – she tried to focus on all the things she would do with Edward, on long country walks with the dogs, on having Geoffrey's warm body next to her in bed. Sleeping alone was one of the many changes she had been forced to make when she swapped the luxury of a listed farmhouse for a cramped little flat above the science block at St Bede's. She shook that thought from her head. No, she refused to dwell on it now.

Edward arrived as she zipped up the holdall. He had Geoffrey's strong jaw and broad shoulders, her mop of unruly blonde hair. He ran his hand over the top of his head, flattening the curls as best he could, but they sprang back, thick and determined.

'You ready, Mum?'

No, not really, but until this whole mess was sorted out they had to spend school holidays in the guest room at the Rectory, Edward in Geoffrey's childhood bedroom, Rowena smug with the pyrrhic victory of having got her precious son back home. Olivia stopped herself right there. No unkind thoughts about Rowena. The pair of them proved the cliché that mothers-in-law and daughters-in-law harboured thinly concealed resentment towards each other, but whatever their history, Rowena was recently widowed and for that, Olivia was genuinely sorry.

Wine would help. She hoped Geoffrey had remembered to buy some. Nothing decent of course – that would be extravagant under the circumstances. Cheap supermarket plonk would be fine.

She glanced round her unlikely refuge and threw Edward a reassuring smile. 'I'm ready.'

*

It had been six weeks since Olivia left Compton Cross in the shimmering heat of an Indian summer, Geoffrey at the wheel of her Land Rover, the boot crammed with bags and boxes. They hadn't talked much. What was there to say? He was driving her away from the life they had built together but which he had single-handedly dismantled. When he reminded her she had a choice, that it wasn't too late to change her mind, she had looked out of the window because she didn't want to look at him.

What were her choices, exactly? Live at the Rectory with Geoffrey and his mother or take a job as houseparent at St Bede's. Their own house – Manor Farm, their home – was about to be repossessed by the bank. Tucked away at St Bede's, she would at least be spared the shameful spectacle of their belongings being packed up and driven off to the self-storage unit Geoffrey had rented on the Mendip Industrial Estate. Downings Factory was on the estate too. How was that for irony? He must have read her mood because he had stopped talking and turned on the car radio.

Edward did the same now – found a radio station playing a Coldplay song that reminded Olivia of boozy nights with Johnny and Lorna, the sort that leave you with a pounding headache and queasy stomach. In the morning you wish you hadn't drunk so much but as the day wears on and the hangover wears off, you remember how much you laughed, how free you felt. Was their friendship spoiled too? She drove past the row of thatched cottages where Johnny and Lorna lived, the twins' bikes in the front garden, lights on inside even though it was early afternoon. She would call Lorna tomorrow. Definitely.

The lane was thick with tractor mud that splattered the Land Rover in sticky clumps. Countryside and clean cars didn't go together. Over the summer Edward and the twins went from house to house offering to wash cars for five pounds a time. They didn't make much money.

'You OK, Mum?' he said.

Olivia realised she was frowning and forced a smile. 'Uh huh.'

'You're quiet.'

'Is that a bad thing?'

He curled the corner of his mouth into a half-smile, exactly like Geoffrey did. Was it a mannerism Edward copied or something imprinted in his DNA? Usually she pined for him during term-time, the house so empty and still without him. The silver lining to her houseparent storm cloud was that she saw Edward all the time at school. It wasn't the same, though – she had to learn a whole new set of rules. He called her Mrs Parry, pretended he hadn't seen her if he was with his friends, recoiled in horror if she went to touch him.

One night she committed the heinous crime of wandering along to his dorm to say goodnight. He was sitting in front of the television with the other boarders, the buzz of easy banter all around them, when Freddie Burton spotted her loitering in the doorway and announced in a loud, theatrical voice, 'Your mummy's here, Parry.' Edward turned round, his face crimson with shame, and glared at her. She knew instantly she had transgressed. 'Doesn't matter,' she said quickly and retreated to sounds of mocking and laughter. Not a mistake she would repeat. When she saw him in chapel the next morning they didn't acknowledge each other. She sat four rows behind him, the back of his head as familiar to her as breathing, everything else disturbingly different. The melancholy hymn didn't help. 'In Christ Alone' – Martin Rutherford's idea of being modern. Ten minutes later, as they all filed out, Edward offered a conciliatory smile. Nothing obvious, but enough to know she had been forgiven.

She glanced at him in the passenger seat, so smart in his burgundy blazer, white shirt and black trousers. His profile was changing, becoming less soft and childlike, more angular and adolescent. He caught her staring and said, 'You seem a bit weird.'

She raised her eyebrows. 'Only a bit?' She turned it back on him. 'Are *you* OK, darling?'

He bobbed his head, more to the beat of the music than in response to her question. She had thought the thirty-minute drive would be a good opportunity for them to talk but he seemed happy and relaxed and she didn't want to spoil that.

A city girl born and bred, Olivia had been wary of moving to Compton Cross. So much grass, so few people. She drove slowly through the narrow lane that skirted the village green, recognised the scatter of vehicles parked outside the Lamb and Lion, waved to a fellow dog walker whose name she could never remember and then turned into the Rectory. The gate was open, Geoffrey's silver Mercedes in the driveway, its personalised plate a source of chronic embarrassment: GP 007. Olivia complained it was crass – *you're not a doctor or a secret agent, you own a factory* – but he pointed out they were his initials and anyway, it was a collector's item: a good investment. He never told her how much the coveted number plate had set him back, no matter how many times she asked.

She turned off the engine and sat for a moment. Edward undid his seat belt and looked at her, waiting. Was he really that resilient? He had lost his home too.

Geoffrey opened the front door and Edward jumped out to greet him. Their manly hug was a pleasure to watch – lots of back-slapping and that boxing thing where they pretended to spar with each other. When Geoffrey looked in Olivia's direction he offered a faux frown and tilted his head to one side. Thirteen years together – she could read him so well. His look said: sorry about all this shit, I know I've screwed up, please be nice. She got out of the car and walked over to him as Rollo and Dice bounded out of the house, tails wagging, wild with excitement. They leaped up at Edward, lashing his face with their rough pink tongues. A cacophony of barking accompanied the reunion: a picture of innocence and joy that eased Olivia's trepidation about the days ahead.

'It'll be fine,' said Geoffrey, reading her mind. 'I promise.'

*

Don't make promises you can't keep.

Geoffrey showed Olivia to their room, its musty odour clinging to them like a damp shroud, and put her holdall on the bed.

She thought he might make a lame joke – tell her not to get too excited, or 'it's not exactly the Ritz, is it?' – but he didn't. All he said was that his mother had made lunch and she could unpack later.

Olivia followed him to the kitchen – large, old-fashioned, redeemed by the warmth of a bottle-green Aga – where Edward was already sitting at the long pine table, chomping on an apple, the dogs curled obediently at his feet. Rowena, busy slicing a loaf of home-made bread, put down the knife and wiped her hands on her apron.

'There you are,' she said. 'I was expecting you earlier.'

The first subtle barb of the day. By implication Olivia was late, even though she had said she would arrive around two and it was ten minutes past. In her head she heard Geoffrey tell her not to be so sensitive, that it was a perfectly innocent comment and his mother didn't mean anything by it, but Olivia felt that she absolutely did.

They took a few steps towards each other until they were close enough to peck cheeks. Rowena's signature scent – dough, Jeyes fluid, a hint of lavender soap – stirred a deep-seated sense of grievance. Olivia had been judged and found wanting and however many years had passed, Geoffrey could not persuade her that was then and this is now. Get over it, move on, were his stock pleas when she complained about his mother's slights. Did he genuinely not see them, or did he choose not to see them? Or maybe he was right and Olivia took offence where none existed.

Rowena looked the same as she always did: tallish and straight-backed, weathered face, devoid of creams or cosmetics, steel-grey hair pinned into a loose low bun. She wore a long woollen cardigan over a blouse, buttoned to her throat, and a calf-length pleated skirt. There was no outward sign that just three months ago she had lost her husband of forty-five years, but she must surely be in pain. Olivia resolved again to make a special effort, although it wouldn't be easy. Two women under one roof? They had both run their own homes, managed their own families, lived separate but intersecting lives until Geoffrey's financial problems changed everything. Homelessness had imposed a sense of humiliation that unbalanced the scales in Rowena's favour. Olivia was unsure of her status, her role. Should she treat the Rectory as her home, come and go as she pleased, have a long lie-in if she felt like it, invite friends over for coffee and a chat? Or would she fall foul of the tacit set of rules that the Parrys instinctively understood but Olivia had never quite figured out?

'Are you hungry?' Rowena asked, picking up the bread knife again. 'I'm making sandwiches.'

Ah, this rule Olivia was familiar with. Refusing food went against the Parry code of conduct. She had discovered this early on in her relationship with Geoffrey, when they first moved to Compton Cross and she was pregnant with Edward. They were often invited to the Rectory for lunch or afternoon tea; occasionally dinner on a Saturday night. Olivia had been laid low with a vague but persistent nausea that lasted well into her sixth month and however much Rowena tried to coax her, she simply had no appetite. This became an unnecessary bone of much contention, Olivia made to feel ungrateful, difficult to please, a generally rather awkward girl. You're not *made* to feel like that, you just do, was Geoffrey's analysis.

Nevertheless, it prised open a rich seam of innuendo: about Olivia's lean figure (*We didn't have eating disorders in my day*), her domestic failings (*Shop-bought is fine if you don't have time to bake*), her general contrariness (*You must make me a list of all the things you won't eat so I don't forget*). Geoffrey insisted she had the habit of taking general and innocuous comments and applying them to herself, hearing criticism that wasn't there. But irrespective of who was right and who was wrong, Olivia had tired of fighting a battle on two fronts. Easier to go along with whatever was required, which today was to sit round the table, eat sandwiches and play happy families. That Olivia's stomach churned and she didn't think she could eat a thing was neither here nor there.

She looked at Geoffrey and made a little gesture with her hand, bringing an imaginary glass to her mouth. Wine at lunchtime would be a rare but much appreciated treat. Alcohol wasn't allowed on the premises at St Bede's and on the few occasions she had craved it, she realised it wasn't the wine she missed, but the ritual of selecting, uncorking, pouring, sipping. It seemed very grown-up, very civilised: a reminder of the life she and Geoffrey used to have. And a small glass of wine might help calm her gnawing apprehension; wash down the unwanted but obligatory sandwich.

Geoffrey produced a bottle of Chablis from the fridge and rummaged around the cutlery draw for a corkscrew – the sort waiters use in good restaurants.

'Would you like a glass, Mum?' he asked, deftly opening the bottle.

'No, thank you,' she said, 'but you two go ahead.'

Olivia ignored the tone of permission having been granted and asked if there was anything she could do.

'All done,' said Rowena, placing the sandwiches on a large oval plate and ushering Olivia over to the old church pews on either side of the table.

She slid along next to Edward, who had discarded the apple core and was now peeling a banana. He offered her a satsuma but she declined in favour of a deep drink from her glass. Olivia was impatient for the wine to do its job and damp down the panicky feeling that this was all wrong. It wasn't her life; it couldn't be.

Edward filled a tumbler from the tap and topped it up with orange squash. Rowena put the platter and a pot of tea on the table, took off her apron and sat down.

'Well, this is nice,' she said, passing round white cotton napkins. 'Have you unpacked, Edward? You know that used to be your father's room?'

Edward nodded – he wouldn't speak with food in his mouth. When he finished chewing he said, 'There are ten of us in my dorm so it's nice to have a room to myself.'

'And what about you, Olivia?' said Rowena. 'I don't want you to feel uncomfortable.'

Being told not to feel uncomfortable was itself uncomfortable. Olivia took another hit of wine.

'I'll try not to,' she said, then noticed the way Geoffrey was looking at her. 'Thank you,' she added.

Conversation turned to the incident with Freddie Burton, Rowena asking Edward why a child would do such a silly thing; such a dangerous thing. Edward shrugged in an exaggerated way and said Freddie was always doing stupid stuff, that he was a bit of a show-off.

'Is he a friend of yours?' Rowena asked.

Edward thought about it for a second. 'Sometimes,' was his answer.

Olivia had no wish to compound her uneasiness by being reminded of that dreadful night, so moved the conversation in a different direction.

'I thought we could take Rollo and Dice for a walk when we've finished.'

Rowena turned round so she could see out of the window. 'It's raining,' she said.

'Still,' said Olivia, 'Dalmatians need a lot of exercise.'

'We always had terriers when Geoffrey was a boy,' said Rowena, selecting a cheese and pickle sandwich. 'Very easy little dogs. No trouble at all.'

Olivia heard this as criticism and looked at Geoffrey, willing him to wade in and defend their canine preferences. He pretended not to notice and reached for another sandwich.

'I don't mind getting wet,' said Edward, refreshingly oblivious.

'Me neither,' said Olivia, looking straight at Geoffrey.

*

Their walk had been a miserable trudge. Edward wore a pair of Geoffrey's wellingtons, two sizes too big, because

God knows where his were – packed up and put into storage, no doubt. Geoffrey said he would have gone but had important emails to attend to. Olivia hadn't exactly hidden her disappointment but he pretended not to notice that either. Pretending was one of his skills.

She regretted the wine, how tired and irritable it had made her. Manor Farm came into view from the crest of the hill. Home. The hot sting of tears were another side effect of the wine. She wiped them with a gloved hand before Edward noticed.

When they got back to the Rectory she had excused herself saying she needed to unpack, but what she really needed was to lie down. She had drifted into a three-glasses-of-Chablis sleep – so much for one small glass to settle her nerves – and when Geoffrey had gently roused her at seven for supper, she told him she couldn't face it. It was a mistake for him to say his mother had gone to a lot of trouble, roasted a chicken, baked an apple and blackberry pie, and couldn't she just make a bit of an effort? In retrospect, yes, Olivia could have been less vehement in her response, but come on. *A bit of an effort? Are you serious? Every day is an effort. What more do you want from me?*

So often the thing you're arguing about isn't the thing you're arguing about. It's a proxy for all the grievances that accumulate throughout a marriage: the things never quite resolved, never quite forgiven. Geoffrey had shaken his head and retreated downstairs, leaving Olivia curled in the foetal position, dry-mouthed but too lethargic to go to the bathroom and fetch a drink of water.

16

He woke her again when he came to bed – told her it was ten o'clock and she should probably get undressed. It took a few moments to register where she was, that she had missed dinner, that her stomach was empty and rumbling. He took off his clothes, tossed them on to a chair by the dressing table, put on his pyjamas (he never wore pyjamas at home) and went to the bathroom, the creak of floorboards marking his every step.

Olivia produced a dressing gown and toilet bag from her unpacked holdall and shivered as she pulled her jumper over her head. The radiator was stone cold. A draught from the window moved the flimsy curtains to a flutter.

Geoffrey returned and, without a word, slipped under the icy sheet, the itchy woollen blanket, the pink candlewick eiderdown seen only on the beds of those aged seventy and over. Olivia took her turn in the bathroom, quickly brushed her teeth, splashed her face with tepid water and had a much-needed pee. On her way back along the landing she checked on Edward, fast asleep in Geoffrey's old single bed, his golden curls illuminated by a thin slither of moonlight. She tiptoed over and kissed his forehead like she used to when he was small. *Sorry*, she whispered, knowing he wouldn't hear, but needing to say it anyway.

When she got under the covers next to Geoffrey, he didn't move. She lay on her back, rigid, and stared into the darkness. So much for making the best of things. Day one and she had already screwed up. Guilt pressed down on her. She imagined the scene at supper, Edward asking where Mum was, Geoffrey making some thin excuse. Worst of all, she had played right into Rowena's hands. How often would she be reminded of the afternoon she drank too much and had to sleep it off instead of joining the family for a roast chicken supper, cooked especially because it was her favourite?

*

The next morning a mug of steaming tea and plate of toast had mysteriously appeared on the bedside table. Olivia propped herself up on the pillows and sipped gratefully from the mug. Geoffrey's side of the bed was warm but empty. Memories of yesterday eked into her consciousness; ill-fitting pieces of a depressing domestic jigsaw. How could she face Rowena? Or Geoffrey. And what about Edward? Her stomach wafted between hunger and nausea. She started on the toast, hoping it would make her feel better. It galled her to admit it, but Rowena's bread was delicious: light wholemeal flour with mixed seeds and a good crust. Butter too – none of those bland low-fat spreads. Geoffrey arrived with his own tea and toast and a sheepish look she knew all too well.

'Feeling better?' he asked, setting his breakfast down on the dressing table.

'Feeling stupid and embarrassed,' she replied.

He came over and perched next to her. 'Don't. It's my fault we're here. It won't be for long, I promise.'

Another promise he couldn't keep. He had no way of knowing how long it would be before they had a home of their own again. The uncertainty was frightening; having no idea what lay ahead. If she thought about it she panicked, so she forced herself not to.

Geoffrey tentatively stroked her hair, as if to gauge her mood. Hard to believe they had spent their first night together in weeks and had barely touched each other. She leaned her head on his hand. So many nights, as she lay alone in her bed at St Bede's, she had thought about Geoffrey holding her, making love to her, but now that the moment presented itself, she was distracted by the musty smell, the faded floral wallpaper, the heavy mahogany furniture that made the room appear smaller and darker than it was. If she moved his hand away, however gently, it would seem like a rejection so she closed her eyes and imagined they were in their bedroom at Manor Farm, with its huge four-poster and thick cream carpet. No, that didn't work. All it did was make her miss their home more keenly.

She switched to a different image: her thirtieth birthday at the Four Seasons in Mexico, sun beating down on her tanned bare breasts. OK, that worked better. She relaxed into the sensation of Geoffrey's lips on her neck, his breath warm on her skin. He slipped his hand under her T-shirt and she arched her back in response. He put his mouth on hers, a vague taste of marmalade on his tongue. She lay back down, eager to feel the weight of his body on hers, and ran her fingers through his tangle of wavy hair. They locked eyes, the anticipation building, when Rowena's voice brought them bolt upright.

'Breakfast, Edward. It's on the table.'

Olivia and Geoffrey froze, like a couple of teenagers caught doing something they shouldn't. They waited, motionless, as Edward bounded noisily down the stairs, sending Rollo and Dice into a barking duet. Geoffrey took a long breath in through his nose and held it for a moment before he exhaled.

'That's that then,' he said.

*

Olivia wanted to call Lorna but worried about how much could be read into a tone of voice, how the most casual comment, the wrong inflection on a word, a pause where a pause shouldn't be, might so easily be misinterpreted. Better to send a text – brief and to the point – but Edward beat her to it. After breakfast he had called Josh and arranged to cycle over there. At first he refused Olivia's offer of a lift, preferring to make his own way on his much prized mountain bike, but when a search of the garage and garden shed proved futile, Geoffrey admitted it might have gone into storage by mistake. Sorry – he would go over and retrieve it later.

Edward wasn't in the mood to wait so accepted Olivia's offer after all. She couldn't say why she didn't text Lorna to let her know she was coming, except that the same creeping sense of unease stopped her. Not on a conscious level – she wouldn't allow herself to admit it – but it nagged her, like a tiny ulcer on her tongue. She sent Edward to the village shop for a bag of chocolate eclairs while she dressed and put on a bit of make-up. Geoffrey loitered, as though he wanted to say something but wasn't sure how. He thought the shift in her friendship with Lorna was down to him. He had said it before and depending on her mood, Olivia either denied it (if she was feeling kind), or agreed with him (if she wasn't). And yes, it was largely Geoffrey's fault that Johnny was out of work, that he and Lorna were struggling to pay the bills. How could that not impact on their friendship? But it wasn't the whole story. There were things Geoffrey and Lorna didn't know, things Olivia had promised to keep from them.

This morning she was feeling kind. She kissed Geoffrey lightly on the mouth and he pulled her up against him, his hand firm on the small of her back. Edward bounced in with the eclairs, saw them and covered his eyes.

'Get a room,' he said with mock disgust.

Geoffrey whispered in Olivia's ear. 'I wish.'

*

Johnny and Lorna's cottage nestled in the middle of a row of five – all identical and picture-perfect until you had to live in one of them. Thatched roofs that needed replacing every twenty years (theirs was overdue), low beams Johnny had to duck, small rooms, big spiders, one bathroom between four, no downstairs toilet. The Grade One listing meant planning for an extension would be denied, but Johnny was adamant he would never move. He had been born in that cottage, in the bedroom he now shared with Lorna. What was it about men and their childhood homes?

Olivia parked on the lane and walked up the garden path with Edward, her heart pattering like rain against glass. Lily opened the front door wearing skinny jeans and an oversized hoodie, straight auburn hair falling like curtains around her pretty face. Such a shame Edward and Lily would never be more than friends. Too familiar – that was the problem. They had known each other all their lives, Lily like the sister Edward never had. Olivia and Lorna had spent many a happy afternoon fantasising about a

Parry–Reed marriage: sharing grandchildren, being family as well as friends.

'That's mine,' said Josh, tugging at Lily's hood, and then to Edward, a matey, 'All right?'

'Nice to see you too, Josh,' said Olivia.

'Are those for us?' he asked, relieving her of the bag. He peered inside. 'Chocolate eclairs. Thanks, Olivia.'

Edward kicked off his trainers and followed the twins into the kitchen but Olivia hung back. If Lorna was home she would have come and said hello. No Benji either – she must be walking him. The children's chatter spilled out of the kitchen, comforting and familiar. Olivia popped her head round the door.

'Will Mum be long, do you think?'

Lily turned to her with a mouth full of eclair and shrugged. The boys hadn't even registered the question. Olivia couldn't decide if she should wait. That was the problem with secrets. They disrupted the natural flow of things, rendered the simplest decision laden with meaning only you understood.

Perhaps she should come back later, but would Lorna be upset knowing she had been here and left without seeing her? Olivia was wrestling with this when the back door opened and Benji ran in wearing the leather-studded collar Olivia had bought him as a joke a few Christmases ago. A Jack Russell who thought he was a pit bull: snarly, snappy, full of attitude. Lorna had her back to the door, prising off her muddy Hunters with the boot pull. When she turned and saw Olivia, it was a fraction of a second before she smiled.

'Hello, stranger. When did you get back?'

'Yesterday. I was going to call but Edward needed a lift.'

It wasn't clear how Edward needing a lift prevented Olivia from calling, but they moved swiftly past it.

'Cup of tea?'

The children piled out of the kitchen – something about a wicked new computer game – leaving Olivia and Lorna alone.

'Love one. I brought cakes.' Olivia looked in the paper bag. 'Sorry, there's only one left. We'll have to share.'

'Home-made?' asked Lorna, filling the kettle.

The tension floated away.

'Of course,' said Olivia, mimicking Rowena's cut-glass accent. 'One can always find time to bake.'

Lorna chuckled. 'How is the dowager Parry?'

'Missing Ronald, I imagine. I promised myself I would be sympathetic but failed abysmally.'

'Oh?'

'I lived down to her expectations last night – drank too much wine and slept through supper.'

Lorna made an 'ouch' face and poured boiling water into a china teapot. Nothing but loose-leaf tea would do. She considered tea bags the devil's work: expensively flavoured dust. Olivia sat down at the table and cut the eclair in half. The children's rough and tumble thumped on the heavily beamed ceiling and Olivia realised how much she'd missed this. If she couldn't be in her own home, this was the next best thing.

Lorna gave the tea a stir and then poured it into two man-sized mugs: 'World's Greatest Dad' on one, 'Keep

Calm and Drink' on the other. She sat down and took her half of the eclair.

'Now tell me everything.'

Olivia outlined her six weeks at St Bede's: the moment she found Freddie Burton (*God, that must have been awful. It was all over the news*), the fallout (*baptism of fire for the new head*), how onerous the responsibility of looking after a dozen girls (*one is bad enough once the hormones kick in*), how hard it was to treat Edward like a pupil and not a son (*I can't imagine*). Olivia was about to ask what had been happening with Lorna but that would lead to talk of futile job-hunting, money worries, having Johnny under her feet all day, so she carried on with tales from the Rectory. Olivia versus Rowena; reassuringly familiar territory.

Rowena was the reason Olivia had disliked Lorna before she even got to know her.

They were pregnant at the same time, Olivia recently having moved to Compton Cross, friendless and home-sick for Reading, an admission too embarrassing to share with anyone but her mum and dad. She and Lorna had spoken a few times when their paths crossed in the village but severe pre-eclampsia meant Olivia spent the last weeks of her pregnancy in a hospital bed, lonely, frightened, mind-numbingly bored. Edward had to be delivered by Caesarean section at thirty-five weeks, weighing roughly the same as two bags of sugar. Rowena had peered into his hospital cot and announced that Lorna Reed was along the corridor, twins safely delivered, both a healthy six-and-a-half pounds. Oh, and she managed a natural birth. Olivia was left in no doubt whatsoever she had let the side down; failed in some grievous yet unspecified way. Unable to carry a baby to term. Unable to produce a strapping baby. Unable to push said baby out of her vagina. The same vagina that had trapped Geoffrey into an unsuitable marriage. Her vagina, it seemed, had a lot to answer for.

Once home, Olivia's mum had come to stay – a protective buffer between her and Rowena. When they spotted her walking up the path, her mum would usher Olivia upstairs and choose from a list of pre-prepared excuses: catching up on a bit of sleep, taking a bath, settling Edward down for a nap. Out of politeness Rowena would stay for a cup of tea before making her own excuses to leave.

Becoming a mother made Olivia feel like a child again. Being responsible for another human life terrified her. With Olivia, Edward tended to fuss and cry, but with her mum he always settled. When the time came for her mum to go home, Olivia pleaded with her to stay. She knew she was being whiny and unreasonable, putting off the inevitable moment when she would have to cope by herself, but whenever she imagined being alone with a fractious baby, her stomach clenched. *I have to get back to work, and to your dad and Sam. You'll be fine, darling – it's always hard at the beginning.*

The day her mum left, Geoffrey came home from the factory to find Olivia sobbing on the sofa. He hated it when she cried. *What do you want me to do?* A question that only made her cry harder. He did the worst thing possible and called Rowena. An epiphany, as it turned out. Olivia finally realised what she was up against. Put simply, Geoffrey was clueless when it came to dealing with the messy business of emotions, so outsourced the problem to his mother, who was no expert herself. Olivia felt her difficulties with home-sickness and motherhood were viewed not with sympathy, but as a sign of weakness. Geoffrey insisted this wasn't the case, that Olivia had a chip on her shoulder and it was up to her to get over it.

So be it. She washed her face and brushed her hair so that when Rowena arrived, expecting to have to step in for her useless daughter-in-law, she was greeted with a cheery smile, an offer of tea and cake – her mum had rustled up a Victoria sponge before she left – and Edward asleep over Geoffrey's shoulder. This was Olivia's new strategy. If she was right and Rowena took perverse pleasure in seeing her struggle, Olivia would simply deny her that pleasure.

Easier said than done. In her capacity as vicar's wife, Rowena took it upon herself to visit new mothers and regaled Olivia with glowing reports of how marvellously Lorna Reed was coping with twins: how healthy she looked, how bonnie the babies, how they fed and slept without so much as a murmur. This in contrast to Edward – a diffi-cult, colicky baby who never slept more than two hours at a time. Olivia neglected to wash her hair and wore the same shapeless tracksuit for days on end, the shoulder crusty with dried baby sick. Geoffrey called Olivia's mum, who took another week off work and returned to Compton Cross. Her advice was that Olivia should try to get out more, mix with other new mums, make some friends. Great in prin-ciple, but Olivia had little energy and even less confidence, so launching herself on the mother-and-baby scene – if such a scene even existed – was unthinkable.

The week flew by and when her mum's bags were packed, Olivia was five years old again, clinging to her at the school gates. They stood by her red Fiesta, both of them trying to be brave, when Edward's piercing screams forced Olivia back inside. She climbed the stairs, gathered him up in a heap of blankets, went to the window and watched her mum drive away.

Olivia came to detest Rowena's tales of Lorna bloody Reed and her perfect bloody twins until one afternoon Lorna dropped by unannounced, a present for Edward in her hand, Josh and Lily asleep in the car. Olivia stood aghast, wholly unprepared to come face to face with her nemesis. It was a moment before she could speak. *Would you like to come in?*

Two hours later they were the best of friends. Over tea and cakes, helpfully supplied by Lorna via the village shop, they compared notes. The saintly twins, it transpired, weren't saintly at all. As soon as one stopped crying the other one started. Josh had squirmed so much when Lorna tried to nurse him, she feared permanent injury to her nipples and had put him on the bottle. To Olivia, still valiantly struggling under the tyranny of 'breast is best', this was a revelation. *Can you really do that?* Apparently you could. It didn't mean you had failed, that you didn't love your child, that you were selfish and inadequate; it just meant your baby did better on formula milk. Lorna had two bottles of formula in her bag. Always carry a spare – excellent advice.

Edward was squirming in his Moses basket, his face screwed up and an angry shade of puce. Lorna offered Olivia one of the bottles. She hesitated, unsure if this really was allowed or if Lorna, in cahoots with Rowena, was trying to trick her, but Edward emitted such an ear-splitting scream that she grabbed the bottle and shoved the teat in his mouth. He sucked so hungrily she wondered if she had been starving him all along. When he had finished every last drop he fell into a miraculously sound sleep. A blissful six hours had passed before he woke. Olivia remembered weeping with gratitude.

'What are you smiling about?' asked Lorna, licking eclair from her fingers.

Upstairs, music blared, Lily belting out a pop song in a terrible singing-shouting voice.

'I was just thinking about the first time we met properly, when you came over with that blue bunny for Edward and a life-saving bottle of formula.'

'God, you looked a state. I had half a mind to call social services.'

Olivia laughed. The boys joined in the singing and Benji tried to burrow inside the fleecy cover of his bed. Lorna stood up and went over to the sink.

'More tea?'

Olivia was about to say yes when Johnny opened the back door. The kitchen seemed to shrink around him – Gulliver arriving in Lilliput. Newly acquired flecks of grey threaded through his ebony hair. They looked at each other, their expressions somewhere on a continuum between good surprise and bad surprise, before they put on their game faces and smiled like the old friends they were.

'Boots off,' said Lorna. 'I'm just putting the kettle on if you want a cuppa.'

He set about unlacing his boots, the heavy-duty type labourers wear on building sites.

Olivia grabbed her coat from the back of the chair. 'I should make a move. I promised Geoffrey I'd go to the storage unit with him and get Edward's bike. OK if I leave him here?'

Did it seem too abrupt? Afterwards Olivia thought maybe it did, but she hadn't prepared herself for Johnny.

When he dropped Edward off later, he didn't come in. Geoffrey saw him from the study window, pulling up on the lane and then driving away. He reported this to Olivia as she peeled potatoes, Rowena next to her, rinsing vegetables in the cavernous Butler sink.

'I can't believe he's turned his back on you,' said Rowena crisply. 'So much for loyalty.'

Olivia had nothing to add. She was grateful when Edward breezed in and asked about his mountain bike. Tomorrow, promised Geoffrey, without fail. He went to the fridge, got himself a beer and sank dejectedly into the rocking chair by the Aga. It was wrong to let him shoulder all the blame but the truth wouldn't make him feel better. Quite the contrary. Olivia cut a Maris Piper in half and plunged it into boiling water.

No, it had to be this way.

Two

It was a bit early for the pub but Geoffrey hoped he might see a friendly face, have a chat over a couple of pints – something to lift his spirits. He had walked four miles to the industrial estate, spent an hour searching through the container – their belongings hidden under acres of bubble wrap in floor-to-ceiling boxes – before he finally found Edward's mountain bike and cycled it back to the village.

Downings hadn't been on his itinerary but it was right there opposite the storage unit. A heavy-duty padlock secured the main door; smaller ones on the side doors. All the windows had been boarded up, several broken as if pelted with stones. Graffiti defaced the walls – the usual obscenities, a drawing of a giant erect penis, the start of an anti-war slogan the author had changed his mind about, or maybe he'd been chased away by a security guard. Geoffrey stood for a long time, staring at the empty building, not quite able to believe his years of hard work had come to this.

'You all right, mate?'

One of the uniformed guards had been about twelve feet behind him, a walkie-talkie in his hand. He hung back cautiously at first but then recognised Geoffrey and strode confidently towards him. The last thing Geoffrey needed was to have to explain himself to the man who used to wave at him each morning, admire his brand-new Mercedes, regard him with a satisfying conflation of envy and respect. Geoffrey raised a hand in acknowledgement, got on Edward's bicycle and pedalled hard in the opposite direction.

When did he get so unfit? He changed down to a low gear but still the incline towards the village brought him out in a sticky sweat. He used to play rugby every weekend and train at least one evening during the week. Yet another casualty of his financial demise. Downings had sponsored the local rugby team so when the factory went, so did the sponsorship. Geoffrey played on for a while but sensed a difference in the way his teammates treated him. Olivia said he was being oversensitive. No one had ever accused him of that before.

A few familiar vehicles were parked outside the Lamb and Lion – mud-encrusted Land Rovers mostly. The mid-day sky was a metallic grey but it looked like the inevitable rain would hold off for a while, so Geoffrey propped the bicycle up against the back wall.

It had been years since smokers were forced to indulge their habit at the mercy of the elements, but the latent stench of stale tobacco lingered. Geoffrey missed his twenty-a-day habit, something he was shamed into giving up when Olivia was pregnant. He was often tempted to sneak the odd cigarette – fantasised about pulling the sharp smoke into his lungs and holding it there for a few heady moments before releasing it through pursed lips.

'Pint of my usual please, Bert,' he said, taking a handful of change from his trouser pocket.

When Geoffrey and Olivia first dated, she had refused to kiss him if he'd had a cigarette. Bert enquired after her.

'Oh, she's fine. She and Edward are home for half-term, actually.'

Bert set Geoffrey's pint on the bar. 'Well, I'll leave you to it.'

Geoffrey wasn't sure what he was being left to, exactly. Solitude? Even more time to dwell on his long list of fuck-ups and all the people whose lives had been ruined?

When it was clear Bert wasn't coming back for a chat, Geoffrey took a seat by the inglenook and sank half his pint in two gulps. Nothing quenched his thirst like a cold beer. A copy of the *Western Daily Press* lay on the table, an unwelcome reminder of when the closure of the factory had occupied the front pages day after day: job losses, pauperised villagers, mismanaged finances, etcetera. Three former employees came in but didn't acknowledge him. Bert appeared from the back and greeted them warmly. He said something Geoffrey didn't catch and they all laughed.

Being ostracised was a new and withering experience. He had always been so popular. Olivia said it would blow over in time, that he needed to be patient. He closed the newspaper, finished his pint and left.

On a whim he cycled to Manor Farm. It upset him to see it but he couldn't help himself. It drew him to it, as though if he stared at it long enough, he would work out a way of getting it back.

The grass needed a cut. An estate agent's board had been hammered into the verge: 'Fine Period Farmhouse'. He and Olivia could have stayed longer but Geoffrey believed that moving out on a date of his own choosing, rather than complying with the bank deadline, exerted some element of control. Olivia and Edward had decamped to St Bede's; he to his childhood home. So much for control. His phone beeped – a message from Olivia. *What are you doing?* He had no idea.

One of the hardest things was having nothing to occupy himself. Since the summer of his graduation, when his parents had persuaded Bob Downing to give him a job, the factory had taken up all of Geoffrey's time. Working there had been the last thing he wanted but as Olivia had pointed out – and everyone else who felt entitled to an opinion – he was about to become a father, with responsibilities and obligations and no say of his own, apparently.

It wasn't even a good fit. His degree was in civil engineering – building roads, dams, bridges – and Downings was a mechanical engineering factory specialising in stainlesssteel fabrications. Geoffrey hadn't wanted to be an engineer anyway, although he could see how his degree may have given that impression. Mediocre A-levels meant universities weren't exactly clamouring to have him on board, but his father had put in a good word with the admissions tutor at Reading – lay preacher, met on some diocesan awayday – and the only course that would have him was civil engineering. He regretted it almost immediately – had little aptitude and even less interest – but what could he do? Penury limited his choices. He couldn't see himself in some dreary, dead-end job, so engineering it was.

Downings had been a family business, Bob having taken over from his father and Downing senior from his father, but Bob's own son had eschewed sheet-metal fabrication in favour of a career in social work. *Can't understand the appeal*, Bob would confide to Geoffrey, *but you have to let them follow their own path.* If only. Geoffrey's path had been mapped out with minimal input on his part.

After a hastily arranged wedding, he and Olivia had moved into a rented stone cottage with four pokey rooms and a narrow strip of grass. Geoffrey was expected to go to church on Sundays, something he hadn't done since he'd left for university. Olivia had never been a church-goer but had quickly taken to it: the rituals, the hymns, his father's sagely sermons. The small but loyal congregation roped her into their do-gooding and she had taken to that too once Edward started school. A photograph of him had taken pride of place on Geoffrey's desk, swamped by a blazer big enough to grow into, proudly wearing his first pair of lace-up shoes.

The other day, when Edward got out of the car, he had looked tall, solid, his jaw and shoulders already broaden-ing out. Not once had he complained about having to give up his home, his bedroom, its walls plastered with post-ers of sporting heroes and the red Ferrari he would buy when he was older. When Geoffrey and Olivia had sat him down and explained why they were moving to the Rectory, Edward said they could have the birthday and Christmas money he had saved, if that would help – one hundred and fifty-seven pounds. Geoffrey remembered the pride he felt at having raised such a good son, and the shame he felt at having let him down.

An approaching car made Geoffrey duck for cover behind the high privet hedge that ran the width of the front garden. Bad enough to lose your home – worse still to be found loitering outside like some sad fucking stalker.

*

The scene that greeted him at the Rectory made him wish he had stayed at the pub. He heard activity in the kitchen and found Olivia in her Hunters and Barbour, snapping leads on to the dogs as his mother looked on, tight-lipped. He was about to mention that it had started to rain and maybe she should wait a bit, but remembered the controversy of a few days before and held his tongue.

Olivia left with a terse *See you later*. If she had asked he would have gone with her. He had so looked forward to her visit – although was it a visit when strictly speaking, the Rectory was now her home – to having his wife back again, but she was pent-up and distant, bristling with the effort of not saying all the things she wanted to say. And they hadn't made love – the thing he had looked forward to most of all.

'I simply asked if a shopping trip to Bath was a good idea?' said his mother.

Olivia had mentioned she and Lorna planned an afternoon in Bath and would have taken his mother's remark as alluding to their dire financial straits: the suggestion she was spending what they didn't have.

'She's a bit sensitive about the whole money thing.'

'I can't pussyfoot around her. Not in my own home.'

His mother picked up a Brillo pad and set about scrubbing a roasting tin. The quickest way to bring a cessation to hostilities was for Geoffrey to apologise for Olivia, a course of action not open to him if Olivia had actually been present. But since she wasn't –

'Sorry, Mum. I'll talk to her.'

She rinsed the roasting tin under a torrent of scalding water and wiped it dry. 'Would you? I don't want an atmosphere.'

Her shoulders rose and dropped as she exhaled. When she pulled a tissue from her sleeve Geoffrey thought she might cry. It tore him up to see his proud, stoic mother reduced to tears.

'Since your father—' Her voice trailed off as she dabbed her eyes.

'I know,' said Geoffrey, putting his arm round her. 'I know.'

He thought the ache of missing his father would have dulled with time, but it hadn't. Shock had rendered him numb from the feet up and when it wore off, a dark emptiness had taken hold that he just couldn't seem to shake. His mother blew her nose and put the tissue up her sleeve.

'Good,' she said, fixing a clip that had come loose in her hair. She wiped her hands on her apron and went to the fridge. 'I'm making steak and kidney pie for supper,' she said, a little brighter now. 'So nice to have people to cook for.'

*

In his father's study, Geoffrey poured himself a small Scotch and tried to see a way of smoothing things over between Olivia and his mother. He hated being caught in the middle, having to negotiate their moods and sensibilities. Yes, his mother could come across as a bit judgemental and her views on most things were laughably outdated, but she was a product of her age and background and she certainly wasn't going to change now. He had learned years ago there was no point upsetting her, that it achieved absolutely nothing.

This nugget of knowledge had been passed from father to son like a faulty gene. His mother being upset meant meaningful looks and long chilly silences and when normality was restored – randomly, after an arbitrary amount of time served – the relief was palpable.

Geoffrey had never given much thought to any of this – things were the way they were – and then one evening, just before he went off to university, his father took him to the Lamb and Lion. Geoffrey had made some silly comment about Mum having him all to herself now, but instead of the resigned smile he expected, his father embarked on an uncomfortable account of why his mother sometimes seemed to be on the periphery of the family rather than at its heart. It struck Geoffrey as an odd thing to say, but then his father went on to talk about them being married for ten years before he came along, and how they got used to it being just the two of them. Geoffrey squirmed at references to them having tried for a family and almost giving up hope. The thought of his parents having sex was beyond hideous. His father concluded with a comment about how his mother sometimes felt a bit left out, at which point Geoffrey nodded and steered them towards an entirely different topic of conversation.

He had forgotten all about it until Olivia mentioned something his mother had said after Edward was born. She couldn't remember it exactly – she likened sleep deprivation to having her head stuffed full of cotton wool – but it was along the lines of Olivia having to share Geoffrey now that he had a son, especially if Edward turned out to be a daddy's boy like Geoffrey was.

Geoffrey had never thought of himself as a daddy's boy and was surprised to hear that his mother did. But then these past weeks she had spoiled him in her brisk, vaguely detached way. She missed having someone to look after and cooked his favourite foods, brought him tea and sandwiches on a tray in front of the television, washed, pressed and put away his laundry. He was a bit ashamed of how much he enjoyed being taken care of and intended to play it down if Olivia noticed. So far she hadn't, but then she was in a strange mood.

The trouble with Olivia was that she bore each of his mother's perceived slights as though they had happened just yesterday, the wound still fresh and oozing. On one occasion she told Geoffrey that his mother was passive-aggressive. He had no idea what that meant but had taken the line of least resistance and agreed. Then a few weeks ago, when he was slumped in front of the old television set hidden away in the snug like a dirty secret (oh, how he missed Sky Sports), a pretty blonde psychologist appeared on the screen and perked him up a bit. In a voice far too authoritative for one so young and sexy, she described the characteristics of a passive-aggressive personality: sulking, being cryptic, playing the martyr, the silent treatment. Well, what do you know? The hot little blonde had described his mother to a tee.

*

Edward was delighted to get his mountain bike back, so at least Geoffrey could do something right. He hoped they might spend a bit of time together – kick a ball around, maybe go fishing for the afternoon – but Edward had made plans with the Reed twins and cycled off down the lane with a cheery wave.

It was dusk before Olivia got home. She had texted saying she intended to drop in on some book-group friends, but more likely just wanted to stay out for as long as she possibly could. He decided not to take it personally. It was his mother she didn't want to be around, and the inescapable air of formality.

Supper was a turgid affair, more so because Edward had decided to sleep over at the Reeds' and it was just the three of them. The steak and kidney pie was mouth-wateringly good, but Olivia hardly touched it. She said Ellie Thornton had offered afternoon tea and she hadn't wanted to appear rude. Being rude to his mother obviously didn't count. *Sorry, I probably should have called, said not to bother with supper for me.* You think? If Geoffrey had been stupid enough to comment, he would have said yes, she should have let his mother know that yet again, her culinary efforts were wasted on an inconsiderate daughter-in-law. Christ. Olivia banged on about his mother but she could be just as bad.

He swallowed his opinion with the last of the Merlot. Mission Marriage was his objective tonight and to that end he insisted on clearing up while Olivia took a nice long bath. When she stood up, leaving her plate on the table but making sure to take her wine, Geoffrey's mother huffed in a theatrical show of disbelief.

'Well,' she said, grabbing Olivia's plate and noisily scraping its contents into the dogs' bowls. 'I fail to see why you have to pander to her, Geoffrey.'

'I'm not *pandering*,' he said. 'She works hard at St Bede's – why shouldn't she have a bit of rest and relaxation?'

His mother stood waiting for the sink to fill with hot water, her foot tapping impatiently on the quarry tiles. That Olivia earned a living and Geoffrey didn't was something it was impossible to argue with. He wondered if it contributed to his alarming lack of libido – emasculated him on a subconscious level? He blamed the sexless debacle of her first night home on the stress and strangeness of it all. The second night it was he who had succumbed – crushed by the sight of Johnny driving away, proof that his friend held him responsible for his loss of livelihood. Tonight would be different. Tonight he and Olivia would hold each other, kiss and make love. Afterwards he would confide how derelict the factory looked, how he couldn't keep away from Manor Farm, how he hated drinking alone.

Once the dishes had been washed and dried, the work surfaces wiped down and the tablecloth and napkins folded, Geoffrey's mother said she wanted to turn in early and could he please check that the bathroom was free. Ridiculous that such a large house had only one bathroom. Geoffrey's parents had never felt the need to convert one of the five bedrooms to a second bathroom for the comfort of guests. When he checked on Olivia, she was already in bed, reading.

'Back in a minute,' he said, before rushing downstairs to tell his mother the bathroom was all hers.

She made a fuss of locking doors and turning off lights, reminding Geoffrey to lock the back door again after he had put the dogs out. He nodded patiently, gave it fifteen minutes and then went up.

Olivia, still in her dressing gown, put her book on the bedside table. She never wore her dressing gown in bed at home. If she wore anything at all it was something slinky with lace and thin little straps.

'I'm sorry about all this,' said Geoffrey, glancing round the unappealing room.

She rolled on her side. 'I'm tired, you're tired. Let's hope to God your mother is tired, not lying awake listening for the bounce of bedsprings.'

The thought repulsed him. 'I drugged her cocoa.'

'Tomorrow, will you drug mine too?'

Sense of humour intact: an encouraging sign. He stripped down to his boxers, male pride telling him to keep them on until he warmed up a bit.

'No pyjamas?' said Olivia as he climbed in next to her.

He lay on his side facing her. 'Thought I'd sleep naked tonight.'

He pulled her towards him until their bodies pressed together.

'Not quite.' She pinged the waistband of his boxers.

'I've missed you,' he whispered, slipping his hand inside her dressing gown. Her firm little breast fitted perfectly in his palm. He kissed her for a long time, only mildly concerned that the message didn't seem to be getting from brain to groin. Even when Olivia reached for him – boxers now discarded – nothing much happened. She peeled off her dressing gown with all the tease of a stripper, and kissed her way down his body. It wasn't until she took him in her mouth that he sprang to life at last. He gasped as she worked her magic, but when she moved to straddle

41

him, he shrivelled. Olivia sat back and looked at him, her expression a mix of hurt and surprise.

'Sorry,' mumbled Geoffrey. 'Don't know what's wrong with me.'

'I thought you'd be raring to go after all these weeks of celibacy.'

He glanced down at his flaccid penis. 'Despite evidence to the contrary, I am.'

She flopped on to her back and studied the ceiling. 'Not the most conducive of surroundings,' she said, her voice flat.

They lay in silence, Geoffrey consumed by failure and frustration. It was a while before he stopped thinking about himself and turned towards Olivia.

'Sorry,' he said.

'You have to stop saying that.'

'I'll stop saying it when I stop feeling it.'

Olivia made no comment. She looked beautiful lying there naked: lean, taut, the only blemish on her skin a faded Caesarean scar. When he ran his fingers over her belly, her hips rose to his touch. He nuzzled her neck as she guided his hand to the soft, warm flesh between her thighs. He kissed her deeply, his fingers mirroring the same rhythm, until her breath quickened and he knew she was about to come. She arched her back, lips parted, eyes closed, and then the toilet flushed. They froze – barely dared to breathe until his mother's bedroom door shut with a judgemental click. Olivia covered her face with her hands.

'Did you?'

She shook her head.

*

The male ego was a fragile thing. This was the conclusion Geoffrey came to after hours of obsessive rumination as to why, night after night, he was unable to make love to his wife. So fragile in fact, that an isolated failure was enough to derail a healthy libido and place an otherwise virile thirty-five-year-old among the sad ranks of those who suffered from erectile dysfunction, performance anxiety, impotence – all male problems, he noted sourly.

On one of his and Olivia's long dog walks he listed the litany of horrors that had beset him in recent months – the factory going bust, his father's heart attack, losing their home to the bank, losing her to St Bede's – pointing out that none had rendered him impotent. Sure, their sex life had waned but at least he could still do it. *I don't understand what's happening*, was his pathetic and frequent lament. Olivia suggested that perhaps the accumulation of events had finally taken their toll. Not helpful. She warned that fixating would only make things worse, but how could he not? He was in unchartered waters and struggling to stay afloat. She blamed the atmosphere at the Rectory, their very presence there a reminder (as if they needed one) of everything they had lost. *You just need to relax. Dinner, candles, nice bottle of wine.* Geoffrey had gone along with it – Edward happy to be packed off to the Reeds' again – hopeful his mother would take the hint and make herself scarce too. She hadn't. Her comment on the provenance of the wine was the finishing blow: *2008 Burgundy?*

Olivia had become more creative after that. They drove to a quiet spot outside the village and pulled off the road.

Things had started well, Geoffrey aroused by teenage memories of fumbling in the back seat of parents' borrowed cars, when a curious dog walker appeared and put him off his stride. Olivia tried to turn it into a positive – something about voyeurism and exhibitionism being quite a turn-on – but the damage had been done.

The following afternoon, during a dog walk of their own, she suggested a bit of al fresco fun and had playfully pulled Geoffrey to the ground. It was wetter than it looked – too wet, in fact, for any sort of fun – and they struggled to their feet, clothes smeared with mud. Back at the Rectory, his mother had taken one look at them and wanted to know what on earth had happened.

'Nothing,' said Olivia tersely. 'Nothing at all.'

*

It started innocently enough, or at least that's what Geoffrey told himself. True, innocent wasn't a word usually associated with pornography, but his motives were pure. It was as much for Olivia's benefit as for his. He needed to break this cycle of failure and God knows nothing else had worked.

His mother had gone to bed early and Edward, dressed as a zombie, was at a Halloween sleepover. Olivia had read for a while before drifting off, at which point Geoffrey crept out of bed and downstairs to the study, where his laptop was charged and ready for him.

Before he touched the keyboard he closed his eyes and tried to empty his head of every impediment to sexual satisfaction: his father sitting at that very desk, writing his sermons in longhand, the cold war between his mother and his wife, the son he had disappointed but who was too kind to complain. Christ, was it any wonder he couldn't get it up. The combined efforts of his family had fucking neutered him.

He went to the sideboard and poured a small whisky from his father's heavily depleted decanter, and downed it in one. The sour heat made him grimace. He sat down again and took another approach – slow deep breaths like he'd seen Olivia practise on her yoga mat. It took a few minutes but between the breathing and the whisky his head was now light and blissfully clear.

OK, he was ready.

Even googling the words brought a frisson of excitement: girls, sex, sluts. He had given a lot of thought to 'sluts'. He didn't want the girls too young or too wholesome and 'sluts' seemed to strike the right balance. The sheer variety available at the mere touch of a button made him reel. His first hit was too graphic – spread legs and gaping mouths from the outset. He wanted to be teased, his excitement building slowly.

The second hit was even more graphic – filthy might be a better word – and he wondered if he deleted 'sluts', would the material be more to his taste? It was. A new search brought tamer options – attractive young women undressing for him, shyly touching themselves and inviting him to touch himself too. They weren't caked in make-up – he loathed false eyelashes and slippery wet-look lips – with pumped-up breasts. They looked real, the sort of girl you might see shopping in Bath or Bristol.

The intensity of his orgasm took him by surprise. All that frustration released in one soaring gush of ecstasy. He basked in the aftermath for a while before going back upstairs and sliding into bed. Olivia didn't stir. For the first time since she had arrived, Geoffrey fell into a deep and unbroken sleep.

Three

Going back to school a day early was Olivia's idea – her escape plan. She told Geoffrey that Martin Rutherford liked houseparents to arrive a day before the pupils and it wasn't an outright lie. Martin preferred houseparents to arrive early but it wasn't compulsory. Truth was, Olivia couldn't endure another day of Rowena, or, more worryingly, of Geoffrey.

Like lovers in a French farce, they might have had a bit of fun avoiding Rowena – a quick and quiet exit on hearing the squeak of her sensible shoes, stifling their giggles as they hid from her, their clothes dishevelled – but such behaviour would have been wildly inappropriate. Ronald's absence bore down on them all. Olivia half expected to see him behind his desk, peering at her over his half-moon glasses. He had always been so happy to see her, so interested in what she had to say. She overheard Rowena tell Edward how proud of him his grandfather had been, before she suddenly became tearful and apologised. Instead of being embarrassed – Olivia was sure that would have been the reaction of most twelve-year-old boys – Edward had given Rowena a hug and then handed her a wodge of tissues.

At moments like that Olivia's heart did go out to her, but then she would see the cloying way she doted on Geoffrey and feel something akin to contempt. If Rowena had any tact at all she would have understood they needed time alone and absented herself for the occasional afternoon, like Edward had. Instead, she always seemed to be lurking.

Their bedroom should have been their sanctuary, the one place where Rowena couldn't intrude, but just knowing his mother was asleep in the next room (or not – Geoffrey was convinced she would be awake, listening) was enough to render him impotent. Olivia was understanding at first, coaxing him, teasing him, stroking his ego and his unresponsive manhood, all to no avail.

A lack of sex quickly translated into a lack of intimacy – no handholding, no kissing, no snuggling up in bed. Physical contact entailed the threat of sexual failure, so was diligently avoided. They slept back to back, doing their best to limit movement. A stray foot might find its way on to an unwilling calf, an innocent hand on to a tense thigh. Bed, their natural habitat, had become unnatural.

Olivia wasn't sure which scenario was more disturbing – that she was unable to arouse her husband or that her husband was so cripplingly cowed by his mother. There were other factors too, of course, although Geoffrey was convinced that his mother and the Rectory were at the root of the problem. But what did it say about the fabric of their marriage that it so easily unravelled under Rowena's critical gaze? And what did it say about Olivia that a small, vengeful part of her relished Geoffrey's suffering?

'Good break, Olivia?'

She spun round, startled. For such a tall man, Martin Rutherford moved quietly, as if apologising for occupying more than his fair share of physical space. When he had learned that his nickname was the BFG, he said he was touched to be viewed as a much-loved figure from children's literature.

'Martin – sorry, didn't see you there.'

'I would have knocked but the door was open.'

'Of course. Yes, very good break. You?'

'The girls kept us busy – day trips, cinema, that sort of thing. Edward not with you?'

'Geoffrey's bringing him tomorrow.'

Martin nodded and struck his signature pose: bent index finger on his top lip, chin resting on his thumb. It afforded him a pensive air – complimented his measured, rather deliberate way of speaking.

'Look, why don't you join us for supper this evening – get to know Ruth a bit better? Nothing special. Spag bol, I expect. The girls' favourite, but I'm sure we can rustle up a decent bottle of red.'

Olivia had been looking forward to an evening on her own: time to decompress after the suffocating atmosphere of the Rectory. And once the boarders were back, she wouldn't have a moment to herself. But Martin seemed keen for her to accept and she hated to disappoint.

'If you're sure it's no trouble.'

'No trouble at all.'

*

The path between the main school building and the Rutherfords' house was poorly lit. No light pollution in rural Somerset, just an ink-velvet sky and a showy dazzle of stars. A thin wet fog hung stubbornly in the cold night air, the only sound gravel crunching under Olivia's boots.

She had no idea what sort of evening she was walking towards. Martin had only been appointed head towards the end of the previous school year, when Teddy Clarke-Bowen was taken ill. Teddy had been head when Geoffrey was at St Bede's. Olivia thought it sweet that even as a parent himself, Geoffrey had still called him 'sir'. Olivia was fond of Teddy too, the way he encouraged a shy Edward to shine: praised his achievements, however small, knowing this was the way to nurture greater achievements. The school choir sang so beautifully at Teddy's funeral, even a few of the male teachers had shed a tear.

After serving as his diligent deputy, everyone expected Sheila Fitzwilliam to step up as head, but the governors wanted a man. They still thought of St Bede's as a boys' school, even though girls had been admitted several years before. True, boys were still in the majority but did that mean there couldn't be a female head? Unofficially, yes, it did. Sheila was spirited away into early retirement and then Martin Rutherford appeared. Much younger than Teddy – mid-forties perhaps – the general consensus was that he lacked his predecessor's charm and charisma. Olivia felt sorry for anyone who had to step into Teddy Clarke-Bowen's shoes.

Olivia and Geoffrey's first encounter with Martin had been at the end of school year celebrations: Sports Day, Speech Day, Leavers' Tea. He smiled patiently as he shook hands with the throng of curious parents, introduced himself to each set individually, enquired after their child's name and year. She overheard someone asking about his wife, and his reply that she and his daughters were looking forward to joining him in September. Olivia certainly hadn't imagined she would be living at St Bede's by then and on her way to have supper with them.

Alice and Maisie must have been keeping watch because the front door swung open just as Olivia arrived.

'Hello, Mrs Parry,' they chimed in unison.

Their first few weeks in Olivia's dorm, she struggled to tell them apart. Both were long-limbed and fair-skinned, their eyes an extraordinary limpid blue. But as she got to know them better she realised that though Maisie was a year younger than her sister, she was more confident, more inclined to push her chin up when she spoke, tilt her head to one side when she listened. Alice lowered her eyes when asked a question and answered in a whispery voice that you had to strain to hear.

'Can I take your coat?' asked Maisie with a toothy grin. Her new front teeth seemed too big for her mouth.

Olivia slipped off her full-length shearling and handed it to her. 'Thank you, Maisie,' she said in her jolly, St Bede's voice, and to Alice, 'Are you looking forward to going back to school tomorrow?'

Alice stared at her shoes and nodded.

Ruth trundled down the stairs, damp hair loose around her shoulders, not a trace of make-up. The tracksuit and bare feet were rather more casual than Olivia had expected. When their paths crossed at school, Ruth looked considerably more polished.

'Olivia,' she said, air-kissing her on each cheek, 'so nice to see you not up to your elbows in boarders. Martin's in the kitchen.' She led the way. 'I left him in charge of proceedings while I took a quick shower.'

Martin was stooped over the sink, draining spaghetti into a colander. Olivia had never seen him in casual clothes: beige cords, checked shirt, navy jumper. On his feet he wore brown moccasins that could have been either shoes or slippers. As always, his trousers were an inch or so too short and, as always, he sported a pair of brightly coloured socks – on this occasion, red with yellow spots. A constant source of speculation in the staffroom, the consensus was that his quirky socks represented eccentricity, rebellion, an unlikely hint of zaniness lurking beneath the staid suits and conservative ties.

Ruth poured a glass of red wine and handed it to Olivia. There was another one on the table, almost empty.

'We started without you,' said Ruth, picking up the glass. She drained it in one gulp and pulled out a chair for Olivia.

'Top me up, would you?' she said to Martin.

The bottle was right in front of her. Heat tinged Martin's sallow complexion. He seemed to be weighing up his options before he responded. 'I'll leave it here, shall I?' he said, moving the bottle an inch closer to Ruth.

Their eyes met for a moment before she refilled her glass and sat down, gesturing to Olivia to do the same. She looked in Martin's direction, her offer of help batted away by Ruth.

'Sit, sit.' She sounded like Rowena commanding Rollo and Dice.

'Have the girls washed their hands?' Martin asked Ruth.

'Have you washed your hands, girls?' Ruth asked Alice and Maisie.

A quick glance at each other and they ran off to the bathroom.

'Thank you so much for inviting me,' said Olivia.

Ruth shot Martin a censorious look that Olivia pretended not to see, and she thought of lunch at the Rectory, the first day of half-term. She sipped her wine in silence as Martin seasoned the bolognese sauce. Ruth rummaged noisily in the cutlery draw and dropped a scatter of knives, forks and spoons on the table. The tension only dissipated when the girls reappeared, Maisie chatting excitedly about a trip they had taken to Weston-super-Mare and how Alice had cried when a dog barked at her.

'Now, now,' said Martin gently. 'Don't be unkind to your sister, Maisie.'

'It's not unkind if it's true, is it, Mummy?'

Ruth was too preoccupied spooning out spaghetti bolognese to bother with a reply. She spilled a splodge of sauce on the tablecloth and rubbed it aggressively with a napkin.

'Darling, I think you might be making it worse,' said Martin. 'I'll get a cloth.'

'It was a big dog, wasn't it, Mummy?' said Alice shyly.

Ruth didn't seem to register any of this.

'I'm sure Mrs Parry doesn't want to hear about the dog,' said Martin, dabbing ineffectually at the spreading stain. 'Now, who would like to say grace? Olivia?'

Even at the Rectory they didn't say grace, but Olivia put her hands together and closed her eyes. 'For what we are about to receive, may the Lord make us truly thankful.'

On opening her eyes, Olivia caught Ruth refilling her glass, clearly thankful for the wine, at least.

It was a very British evening. Olivia and Martin chatted politely, skilfully avoiding any acknowledgement that

Ruth was drunk. They regarded her as one might a difficult relative – talked about nothing more controversial than the weather, school news, parish business. Ruth sat heavy-lidded with boredom, her meal hardly touched, the wine bottle now conspicuously empty. Olivia wondered how much Ruth had had to drink before she arrived. Maybe Martin had suggested a shower in the hope she might sober up.

The girls seemed oblivious, happily twirling spaghetti round their forks, implying that this somewhat disturbing family scene was not at all unfamiliar to them. Olivia recalled one of her first nights as a houseparent, going from bed to bed saying goodnight and God bless. When she had reached Alice's bed, she found her curled up, crying softly into her teddy. Olivia hesitated. Matron had warned her about homesickness, especially among the younger girls. Olivia remembered how homesick she herself had been when she first moved from her parents' house in Reading to live in Compton Cross with Geoffrey. How much worse must it be for such a young child? After a moment Olivia had asked Alice why she was sad. At first she said nothing, just sniffed and sucked her thumb. Olivia had been about to walk away when Alice rolled on to her back and looked straight up at her. *I don't like it when Mummy shouts.*

Ice cream followed the pasta, with a cheese option for the adults. Olivia declined both, explaining she wasn't quite ready for tomorrow's influx of boarders and still had a bit to do. She offered to help clear up but Martin wouldn't hear of it. Ruth's ambivalence suggested no strong feelings either way. Martin rummaged around under the sink for a torch and insisted he walk Olivia back to school.

The fog had become dense and eerie, giving Martin and Olivia further scope on the safe topic of weather. It wasn't until they reached the quad, and Olivia thanked him one last time for supper, that he dropped the pretence. The way he looked down as he spoke reminded Olivia of Alice.

'I'm sorry about Ruth.'

'Please, you don't need to—'

'It's been difficult.' His long, laden sigh hinted at troubles too private to share. 'Ruth's finding it difficult.'

Olivia didn't know what to say. They weren't equals, strictly speaking. Martin was her boss. Anything she said, however well intentioned, could be held against her. Never get involved in other people's marriages – her mother's advice, religiously adhered to.

'Don't give it a second thought,' was the best she could come up with, but hated to end the evening on the subject of marital discord. 'The girls are delightful – a credit to you both.'

Martin looked relieved at the implied promise of her discretion. 'You're very kind,' he said, nodding to underscore the point, and despite her own marital discord, Olivia couldn't help but feel a pang of pity.

She made her way into the main building and up the stairs to her quarters, weary but grateful for a bit of time to herself. After a quick wash she got into bed wearing her fleecy winter dressing gown and a thick pair of socks. She tried to read but found herself drifting off and without

Geoffrey's lugubrious presence, Olivia managed a surprisingly good night's sleep.

She rose early and went for a brisk run round the grounds. What a contrast to the Reading comprehensive she had attended: grey concrete playground, intersecting white lines for netball, football and hockey; all very confusing. Shared playing fields were over a mile away and littered with dog mess. She still recalled the misery of those long, rain-soaked trudges and then, when she was older, the usual excuses to avoid games altogether. Shame really. Olivia had been good at games.

A circuit of the cricket pitch and rugby field, twice along the driveway, then she was done. She stretched out before a quick shower – hot as she could stand – and felt ready for the day ahead.

*

The dorm hummed with returning boarders and their families. Parents greeted Olivia warmly, their daughters polite but apprehensive until they spotted their friends and then skipped off, chatting excitedly, the way children do.

Ruth Rutherford arrived late with Alice and Maisie, hair tied back in a neat ponytail, make-up discreet but effective, casually smart in a crisp white shirt and black jeans. If she had a hangover, it didn't show. She greeted Olivia with a peck on both cheeks and set about making up the girls' beds. Olivia felt she should thank her for supper but wasn't sure she would want to be reminded of it. She was mulling it over when Ruth jumped in.

'Sorry about last night.'

OK, they were going to talk about it; clear the air. Having endured years of Rowena's carefully camouflaged put-downs, Olivia welcomed the candour.

'Martin can be such a bore,' said Ruth, rolling her eyes. 'Going on and on like that.' She grabbed Alice's duvet and gave it a good shake. 'He means well,' Ruth concluded, now making hospital corners with Alice's pink and yellow striped sheet. For a second Olivia was stumped.

'I had a lovely evening,' she said pleasantly, once she had regrouped. 'It was kind of you to invite me.'

Ruth waved a dismissive hand. 'Come on, girls,' she said, tossing their bags on their beds. 'Let's get you unpacked.'

Maisie and Alice meekly complied, Ruth assuming a supervisory capacity rather than actually helping them. One by one the other mothers approached her, eager to befriend the headmaster's wife. Before long Ruth was completely surrounded, the main topic of conversation the Alpha meetings she was supposed to host but which were yet to materialise. *Next week*, she promised. *I'll get the school secretary to email the details.* Her foot tapped impatiently as she fielded the host of questions being thrown at her, but her smile never faltered. Olivia was helping one of the older girls with her trunk when some latecomers arrived with animated accounts of roadworks and endless motorway tailbacks.

'Are you lost?' said Ruth, and Olivia turned to see Geoffrey loitering by the door wearing his charm-offensive smile.

'Geoffrey Parry – Olivia's husband.' He toned down the smile when he looked at Olivia. 'Just dropped Edward off. Thought I'd come and say hello.'

'Come in,' said Ruth, excusing herself from the gaggle of mothers.

She introduced herself and offered Geoffrey her hand. Olivia was surprised to see him in a suit and wondered if he had a meeting; something about the factory or another telling off at the bank. He took a long look around.

'This was a boys' dorm in my day,' he said.

'Oh, were you a pupil here?' asked Ruth.

'For my sins,' he replied. 'Although I never rose to Edward's stellar heights. The most I could manage was milk monitor.'

Ruth's giggle was both girlish and flirtatious.

'Any chance you could spare Olivia for five minutes?' asked Geoffrey. 'Just to walk me to the car.'

'Of course,' said Ruth, clearly won over. 'I'll hold the fort here.'

The car park was full: lots of Range Rovers and hybrids and the odd Volvo estate. Geoffrey's Mercedes looked pristine, as though just driven from the showroom. Olivia knew how much that car meant to him; how much it would mean to lose it. He opened the passenger door for her and then walked round to the driver's side.

'Are you going to kidnap me?' she said lightly.

'Wish I could,' said Geoffrey.

He squeezed her hand. 'I'm sorry about everything. I know I haven't been much of a husband lately.'

Olivia had neither the time nor the appetite for a heart-to-heart about their marriage. 'I had dinner at the Rutherfords' last night,' she said sunnily. 'Ruth was actually quite drunk.'

'Really? That must have been a fun evening.'

'Hardly. I felt sorry for Martin.'

'How much did she have?'

'I think she was drunk when I got there. She polished off the best part of a bottle over dinner.'

'Is she a happy drunk?'

'She seemed more bored than anything.' Olivia thought for a moment before adding, 'Marriage is hard sometimes.'

They left it at that. After the briefest of kisses, she got out of the car and hurried back to the dorm. It was the closest she had felt to Geoffrey in a while.

*

Olivia was still learning the protocols. Teaching staff should be addressed by their surnames when pupils were present, Christian names when they were not, but Martin was always 'Headmaster'. Ancillary staff formed something of a grey area. Dinner ladies seemed to like being called Mrs, the caretaker was Mr Hill and the groundsmen were young Tom and old Tom. Old Tom wasn't old at all, just older than young Tom, who was barely out of his teens. He caused quite a stir at the beginning of term when he took off his T-shirt to mow the cricket pitch.

Early September had been searingly hot and the sight of his lean, muscled torso didn't go unnoticed by a group of top-form girls, en route to play tennis. They quickly forgot all about tennis and formed an excited huddle in the pavilion where they could spy on him as he worked. It was like that Diet Coke ad on the telly, Lisa Pearce had said in the staffroom later. Olivia was sorry she'd missed it, although she did hear about it in great detail in the dorm: the eagle tattoo across his back, the fashionable absence of chest hair. Olivia wondered about young Tom's motives. Was it really so hot he had to discard a flimsy bit of cotton, or was he showing off, preening and posturing for girls too young to understand the power of their allure? Either way, she felt for the Tom fan club. How could anyone forget the intensity of those first crushes, the agony of unrequited love, the heartbreak when the object of your desire was oblivious to your existence. Who would want to be a teenager?

Soon it would be Edward's turn, his thirteenth birthday just a few months away. Olivia was sad to think of her sweet boy succumbing to the unruly surge of hormones. Lorna said it had already happened with Lily: periods, a proper bra, mood swings, the lot. Olivia's reply probably hadn't helped. *It'll be boys next.*

They had gone window-shopping in Bath, its cobbled streets teeming with tourists, performance artists, homeless people with dogs. There was no money for actual shopping as Rowena had so considerately pointed out. When they stopped for coffee Lorna paid for the cappuccinos, Olivia for the carrot cake. She wanted to dissect the disturbing phenomena of Geoffrey's impotence, compare notes, ask if it had ever happened to Johnny, but couldn't risk going where that might lead.

They had headed towards the new Southgate development, an area they used to avoid because it was rough and ugly; a blight on an otherwise glorious Georgian city. Olivia loved coming to Bath. Lorna said she could take it or leave it. The city's obsession with Jane Austen was something that particularly irritated Lorna. If anyone in the book club chose a Jane Austen novel, Lorna would groan and put her head in her hands. They stopped to watch a clown on a unicycle fire-juggling outside the Pump Rooms and threw a pound coin into his upturned top hat on the pavement.

Nearer the abbey, an old man singing 'What a Wonderful World' had sounded just like Louis Armstrong. Olivia gave him a pound coin too because the song reminded her of her grandparents dancing together, her grandmother's head resting on her grandfather's shoulder.

Even though it was October, some of the shops already had Christmas trees. God knows where they would find the money for presents this year. Edward wouldn't go without; that was the most important thing. Olivia and Lorna headed back to the car empty-handed as the afternoon sky had begun to darken. At the entrance to the multi-storey a young woman sang opera. Lorna gave Olivia her 'what did I tell you?' look. *Even the buskers are posh.*

When Olivia dropped her off, Lorna had invited her in for a glass of wine. The battered Land Rover she and Johnny shared was parked outside. 'Best not go back smelling of booze', was the excuse Olivia had offered.

*

Life can turn on a sixpence; that's what Olivia's grandmother used to say. She had a saying for most occasions; pithy aphorisms that warned what might happen if you dared to get too comfortable, like 'when money flies out the window, love goes out the door'. Was that what was happening with Geoffrey? Olivia had been too busy to dwell on it but now the boarders were asleep and she was alone in her flat, it preyed on her mind. Clips of the last months kept flashing into her head. A montage of difficult times in a healthy marriage, or the final gasps of a dying marriage?

She longed to sit down with her mum and have one of their heart-to-hearts over a pot of tea and a packet of Hobnobs. One of the reasons Olivia could so readily empathise with Alice Rutherford was because she missed her mum too. At Manor Farm, their night-time routine had been that Geoffrey would take Rollo and Dice for a walk before bed and Olivia would give her mum a quick ring that usually lasted half an hour. It wasn't the same on Skype. With the eleven-hour time difference between the UK and Sydney, and unpredictable Wi-Fi in her flat, conversation felt a bit like dancing out of sync to music. Olivia always pretended to be chattier, happier, more positive than she was because if her mum suspected how she really felt she would have been on the next plane home.

Her parents hadn't been sure about leaving in the first place, what with the factory closing down and then Ronald dying so suddenly. It took a lot for Olivia to persuade them it was too good an opportunity to miss. They had worked hard all their lives and six months visiting Sam in Sydney would be a terrific adventure. Olivia said she was worried about her little brother, all alone on the other side of the world. She wasn't. Whenever she managed to log on to Facebook it was clear Sam was having a blast, but Olivia didn't want her troubles to rob her parents of a once-in-a-lifetime trip.

She checked her watch: eight thirty in the morning in Sydney. As she opened her laptop, she pushed her hair behind her ears and practised her happy smile. When the Wi-Fi kicked in and Skype connected, it lasted just long enough for Olivia to see her mum's suntanned face, before it was gone again. Two more attempts and Olivia gave up. Even if she did manage to get a good connection, she wasn't sure she could have kept faking her happy smile.

*

Olivia had jumped at the chance to escape to St Bede's. Rowena was helping pack up Manor Farm when she mentioned that a houseparent had been asked to leave quite out of the blue and the new headmaster was in a bit of a bind. *Claire Heather said it was a clash of personalities with the head's wife, but that's just between you and me. Goodness knows how they'll find someone now term has started.*

Claire Heather: the font of all school gossip. Not only the headmaster's secretary and close friend of Rowena, but her husband had been a bookkeeper at Downings. The interconnecting tendrils of life in a rural community. Olivia had stopped packing books into a cardboard box and gave Rowena her full attention. The houseparent looked after the girls' dorm; only twelve boarders. That was all she had gleaned before Rowena set about wrapping a stack of dinner plates, noting that one or two were chipped.

Olivia had phoned the school the following morning, went in for a chat that afternoon and had the job by the time she got home. Martin's email had been waiting in her in-box. As she read it, heart pumping uncomfortably hard, she began to understand the enormity of what she would be committing to. Not just taking responsibility for the pastoral care of a dozen young girls, but living apart from Geoffrey. Shards of resentment stabbed at her when she thought about the mess he had made of everything.

They were all condemned to live with the consequences of his decisions – decisions she was never consulted about. If taking the job at St Bede's upset him, then too bad. She had trusted him with their future and nowhere in that future did she imagine living with her mother-in-law. At least she would be spared that at St Bede's. Olivia wrote a two-line acceptance and pressed Send. So her grandmother had been right. Life really can turn on a sixpence.

*

Olivia shivered in the few square feet of quad where you could get a phone signal. Two bars, three if the wind blew in the right direction. She wanted to catch Geoffrey before the staff meeting, ostensibly to remind him about Edward's rugby game, but really just to talk to him – be *normal,* whatever the heck that was these days. With each unanswered ring she felt her muscles tighten. The easy rapport she and Geoffrey once shared was already frayed round the edges, but the strain of half-term had pulled at all manner of loose threads. Olivia felt a flicker of relief when the call went to voicemail and signed off her bright and breezy message with a quick 'love you'. She slipped the phone in her coat pocket and hurried back inside.

*

Mornings and evenings were her busiest times, when the girls were in the dorm, vying for her attention. They were so different from boys: inclined to talk rather than play, form cliques and alliances, easily crushed by any perceived slight. Edward and his friends were refreshingly straightforward. Give them a bit of space to run around, a ball to kick, a tree to climb, and they amused themselves for hours.

Olivia was the only houseparent who didn't have teaching duties as well, so was called upon in a variety of ways: to listen to the younger children read, stand in for absent teachers, help out with plays and concerts. She found it made the day go faster, all this extra-curricular activity. And if her willingness to muck in improved Edward's chance of a scholarship, then it was well worth the effort. As an existing pupil he had been awarded a bursary for reasons of 'financial distress', but he would lose that at the end of the year when he went up to the senior school. *If* he went up to the senior school – without a full scholarship, they had no hope of paying the fees. That thought was all the motivation Olivia needed to be as helpful as she possibly could.

*

Martin had called a staff meeting and would have looked quite smart if the trousers of his dark grey suit had been just a tad longer, and the diamond-patterned socks just a tad less colourful. Brown lace-ups weren't the best choice either, but eight out of ten for effort. Olivia got the impression he tried a bit too hard, that if he relaxed and was more himself, he might emerge from the long shadow cast by Teddy Clarke-Bowen.

The main piece of news was that the French student from the Sorbonne would be leaving at the end of term but a replacement would follow in January. *I'd like to thank Monsieur Dubois for all his hard work and wish him the very best in his future endeavours.* Hugo Dubois ran a hand through his well-groomed hair and offered a quick nod in Martin's direction.

Olivia hoped his replacement would take an interest in Edward the way Hugo had. French was Edward's worst subject – lack of interest the probable cause – but he'd been doing better under Hugo's tutelage. It helped that Hugo coached rugby too, so he and Edward had something in common. Olivia would ask him to set extra French for Edward over the holidays – something to do with rugby perhaps, so he wouldn't get too bored.

Lisa Pearce tapped Olivia on the shoulder as they filed out of the staffroom.

'Well that's a blow,' she said under her breath. 'Do you think the next one will have Hugo's dashing good looks?'

Olivia smiled. 'You're old enough to be his mother.'

Lisa affected grievous hurt. 'I most certainly am not.'

She stood a little taller and pulled her shoulders back, which only accentuated her fulsome bosom and apple-shaped figure. 'Age shall not wither her, nor custom stale her infinite variety.'

Lisa's fondness for quoting Shakespeare rather baffled Olivia. She taught history, not English. Edward complained that she dished out too much homework but he said that about all his teachers.

Lisa had made a big fuss of Olivia when she started at St Bede's, always seeking her out in the staffroom and sitting down next to her during lunch. Olivia, desperate to make a friend, suppressed the suspicion that Lisa's interest had a prurient quality and decided to take it on face value. Drawn in by Lisa's natural exuberance, she confided the occasional snippet about her and Geoffrey's situation. Where was the harm? Then three weeks into the term,

Olivia overheard Lisa telling one of the other teachers something she had told her in confidence, and realised how gullible she had been. She didn't let on she knew – she might not have made an ally but she certainly didn't want to make an enemy – and was still friendly towards Lisa, but now knew better than to trust her. If Lisa sensed that Olivia was less forthcoming than before, she never mentioned it. And she was certainly right about Hugo – the place would seem a little duller without him.

He appeared to have usurped young Tom as the school heart-throb, the onset of winter necessitating Tom hide his light under the proverbial bushel, or rather an oversized hoody and grubby wax jacket.

Hugo exuded Parisian style: hair just long enough to suggest youth and virility, athletic build hugged by well-tailored jackets and slim-legged trousers. Waistcoats made the occasional appearance, as did a mocha turtleneck that Olivia felt sure must be cashmere. A casually draped scarf added the final touch of panache. *It's Somerset, not bloody Paris,* commented Rudd Lender, the testy maths teacher Edward often moaned about. He had a point, though. Compared to the young Frenchman, the other teachers looked a shabby old bunch.

During morning break Olivia tried to call Geoffrey again. Hard enough living apart without the added strain of not being able to talk to each other. She got her coat and headed towards the cricket pitch, eyes fixed on her phone, willing those elusive bars to appear. She almost fell over Hugo, sneaking a cigarette by the cluster of horse-chestnut trees between the school and the pitch. His phone was in his hand too.

'Have you got a signal?' asked Olivia hopefully.

He shook his head and showed Olivia the dark-haired beauty that filled the screen. 'My girlfriend.'

'You must miss her.'

He threw his cigarette on the ground and mashed it with the sole of his highly polished shoe. 'Désolé,' he said, pushing his hands deep into his trouser pockets. 'I try to give up.'

He looked frozen, his tweed jacket clearly more for fashion than for the British winter. A flaying wind hit Olivia face on. She pulled her collar up as high as it would go and turned her back to it.

'Actually, I wanted to talk to you about setting some holiday work for Edward.' She pointed to the shelter of the cricket pavilion. 'Do you have a minute?'

They jogged across the spongy grass, the far-off smell of burning wood stirring memories of log fires and Christmas.

A wooden veranda bordered the pavilion, five shallow steps leading up to the door. Olivia followed Hugo inside but he stopped so abruptly she almost fell into him again. He smelled of damp wool, cigarettes, musky cologne. It took a second for her to see what he had seen: what had, quite literally, stopped him in his tracks. Young Tom was on his back, jeans around his ankles, a half-naked Ruth Rutherford astride him, skirt bunched up, breasts free and ample. For the second time in her short St Bede's career, Olivia could not believe her eyes. Nobody moved – the scene immortalised in freeze-frame. It was Hugo who took the initiative and excused himself with another curt 'Désolé'. Tom was on his elbows now, looking rather pleased with himself. Ruth turned towards Olivia, her face flushed and shiny.

'Can I help you?' she asked.

Olivia stumbled down the steps and bolted towards Hugo, who stood quite calmly on the grass, holding a pack of Gauloises. He fished a lighter from his trouser pocket, lit a cigarette and then offered one to Olivia. Despite her hatred of the habit, if she had thought it would relieve the mortifying embarrassment that consumed her, she would have taken one.

'We shouldn't say anything,' she managed when she caught her breath. 'It's a private matter – nothing to do with us.'

Hugo shrugged. 'Of course.'

Olivia realised how provincial she must have sounded. Hugo was clearly far too sophisticated to be troubled by the adulterous inclinations of consenting adults. He took one last long drag before discarding his cigarette into the hedge. Olivia watched him walk away, apparently unfazed. She, on the other hand, was gut-wrenchingly fazed. And shaking. She forced herself to take long, slow breaths that pulled winter deep inside of her.

The sound of the bell made her stomach flip. How could she go back and face everyone? How could she face Martin? She had promised to help him with the Christmas newsletter. He would be waiting for her in his office. She was already carrying one ugly secret and now she was burdened with another. The weight of silence didn't ease with time; it became heavier and harder to bear. She felt it already, with each step she took back towards the school.

Four

The thud of mail hitting the flagstones sent a bolt of dread through Geoffrey.

He didn't rush to fetch it. If his mother saw he was anxious she would ask questions he didn't want to answer. The novelty of being the sole recipient of her attention was wearing gossamer thin.

'Is that the postman?' she called from the kitchen.

The absence of a reply brought her into the hallway. Geoffrey popped his head round the study door, his mother's back to him. She scooped up the scatter of letters, leaflets and a large glossy catalogue, and set about sorting them out.

'Anything for me?' he enquired with as much nonchalance as he could muster.

She handed him two official-looking envelopes and the catalogue – a sleek new Mercedes on the front cover – and held on to the rest.

'I keep telling him not to push junk mail through the letterbox—' She waved a handful of flyers before disappearing back into the kitchen. 'And yet.'

Geoffrey went to the study, dropped the letters on the desk and paced: desk to window, window to door, door to desk. He had to brace himself for the contents of those letters; prepare for the inevitable bad news. Too early for a drink. Pity.

The first letter was from the administrator who had been appointed to deal with the liquidation of assets. Creditors would be paid with the proceeds and the shortfall covered, in theory, by Geoffrey's personal guarantees, which the bank had called in. That was the second letter. The bank had assigned him a 'relationship manager', a misnomer if ever there was one. A weaselly little man called Fredericks, with lank hair and waxy skin, had set out in writing what they had already discussed in person the afternoon Geoffrey had dropped Edward off at St Bede's. He had intended to tell Olivia about the meeting when they snatched a few minutes together in the car, but lost his nerve. She was already doing so much – he couldn't burden her with more. And how could he tell her that the bank had drawn up a draconian schedule of repayments and that if he didn't make those repayments, they would file for bankruptcy.

It was hard for Geoffrey to make the connection between that one word and his ruined life. The punishment seemed so much harsher than the crime. Was it his fault that the economy had bombed, that competitors in the Far East could undercut his prices, that manufacturing depended on investment in the latest equipment and technologies and it was all so fucking expensive?

It sickened him to think what Bob Downing would have said. Geoffrey hadn't only let down his own family, but Bob's family as well. Three generations of Downings had built the factory into a thriving business – not *Sunday Times* Rich List, but one of the largest employers in the area. It had taken Geoffrey just five years at the helm to destroy all of that.

He had joined the ranks of Downings reluctantly. After university he'd planned to backpack through the rugged and exotic landscapes of South America, not take a job in an industrial park four miles outside of Compton Cross. Edward's conception meant Geoffrey had to forgo his youthful dreams: be a grown-up, get married, go to work, fall asleep at night fantasising about all the adventures he had missed out on. Sometimes when he woke, it took a moment to remember why he was lying on a lumpy mattress and not basking on a white-sand beach, a cold beer in his hand, bikini-clad beauties splashing playfully in the surf.

What had made it bearable – apart from Olivia, whom he grew to love, and Edward, whom he loved instantly – was Bob Downing. It was as if Bob understood that Geoffrey was living the wrong life – the price he paid for having done the decent thing. Bob made it his mission to teach Geoffrey everything about the business; not just all the technical stuff, but how to find satisfaction in doing a job well. It took a few years, but it happened. No 'eureka' moment when it all came together, but gradually Geoffrey found himself looking forward to work.

Sales were his forte. He was good at negotiating – putting deals together. Signing up a new client excited him. He likened it to pursing a woman: the flirtation stage (friendly but casual, coffee, drinks maybe); the courtship stage (attentive, supportive, eager to please); and, finally, sealing the deal. Truth be told, he had more experience in business than he had with women, but he liked the analogy – found it raised a chuckle when he delivered it in his legendary sales masterclasses. It had been Bob's idea to call their monthly meetings over tea and biscuits 'masterclasses'. Geoffrey was flattered. Masterclasses. Who would have thought?

From his glass-fronted office on the mezzanine that overlooked the factory floor, he would watch people going about their business, proud that his ability to secure new orders kept them all in a job. In those early years, when Downings held little interest for Geoffrey, he never imagined he would come to enjoy working there.

Every Friday evening Bob would take him to the Lamb and Lion for a few pints and a chat. Work featured heavily but they talked about other things too, personal things. Bob was Geoffrey's only real confidant. He had friends, of course, mostly to do with sport – the guys he played rugby with, the village cricket team, a few old university friends he skied with for a week in January – but their relationships hummed along at a superficial level. He had been close to Alex, his best friend from school and best man at his wedding, but he bought a vineyard in France and since he'd moved out there full time they spoke infrequently and kept it light, chatty – more of an update than anything else. Nothing too heavy, nothing too personal; that was the unspoken rule. But with Bob, Geoffrey could get to the heart of things.

It had been another ordinary Friday in the pub when Bob broke the news of his diagnosis. Non-Hodgkin lymphoma – a type of cancer. Even now, more than six years on, Geoffrey could feel the stab of disbelief. It must have shown in his face because Bob patted him on the shoulder and gave him a bit of time on his own. *I'll get us another pint.* Geoffrey watched him at the bar, unable to take it in. He looked fit and well, fifty-two years old, his hair not yet grey. Never smoked, never had more than three pints. How could he be ill?

He was ill, though – very ill. That was why Geoffrey bought him out of the factory, so he could spend his final months with his wife and son, doing the things they had always talked about doing, the way you do when you think you have all the time in the world. *Are you sure you want to sink your whole trust fund into the factory? Isn't there something else you would rather do with the money?*

His trust fund (courtesy of his maternal grandparents) amounted to twenty thousand pounds – not nearly enough to buy the factory. He knew he'd have to supplement it with bank loans but didn't need to worry Bob with the details. Geoffrey hadn't had access to the trust until his thirtieth birthday, three months after Bob had first broken the news. By then he'd had chemotherapy – looked older, thinner, moved more slowly, struggled to manage the stairs. *I'm sure.*

Geoffrey had done the right thing by Bob but looking at this morning's letters laid out on the desk, he shook his head in despair. The right thing had somehow become the wrong thing and Geoffrey still didn't understand quite how that had happened.

He was too dejected to answer his phone when Olivia called. He let it go to voicemail and listened to it later, when he had a drink in his hand. Olivia telling him not to forget about Edward's rugby match tomorrow. Hardly. The highlight of an otherwise dire week.

*

Geoffrey got to St Bede's early, relieved to have an afternoon away from the oppressive atmosphere at the Rectory. His mother looked to him for the companionship his father had provided. She expected Geoffrey to sit with her in the kitchen and listen to Radio Four; watch *Songs of Praise* with her on Sunday evenings; reminisce about people he hardly knew.

There was something profoundly wrong with a grown man living with his mother. With very few exceptions – a temporary arrangement while your expensive house was being renovated, an unexpected time lag between selling one expensive house and buying another, serious illness on either side – nothing screamed 'loser' more loudly. Except bankruptcy of course – descent into a growing underclass deemed too feckless to manage their own affairs. If the bank followed through with their threats he would be denied even the most basic bank account, a credit card or a mobile phone contract: all the trappings and necessities of adult life. Stigmatised and punished – treated like a recalcitrant child. He shook his head. It might not happen. He had to believe it might not happen.

Fine drizzle thickened the air. It blurred the familiar outline of the main school building, the central archway with castellated wings on either side; East Wing and West Wing, just like the White House.

Geoffrey had happy memories of St Bede's: of sport and chapel and horsing around with his friends. He wandered from the car park towards the main building, hoping to bump into Olivia, but bumped into Martin Rutherford instead, moving at a slow jog, a stack of files under one arm.

His gait had an air of clumsy campness. The way his legs splayed out slightly from the knee made Geoffrey think of Bambi. And why did he wear such loud socks? Did he imagine he was being cool? Geoffrey hadn't made up his mind about Martin Rutherford, but Teddy Clarke-Bowen he was not.

After a quick exchange of pleasantries Martin excused himself and rushed off, leaving Geoffrey alone in the quad. He hung around for a few minutes and was about to give up on Olivia and head over to the rugby pitch when she appeared in a doorway and gestured for him to come over. Her waist looked tiny in a belted grey dress, her legs slim and shapely in black tights and ankle boots.

'Let's go up to the flat,' she said, her manner faintly conspiratorial.

'Is that allowed?' he said, equally conspiratorial.

'No,' she said, and grabbed his hand.

Maybe sneaking into Olivia's quarters would be the boost Geoffrey needed. Was it too much to hope he could do there what he hadn't been able to do at the Rectory? Her eagerness boded well. He followed her brisk pace along the central hallway where he used to get told off for running, and up the wide stone staircase that led to the boarders' quarters. Olivia's flat was at the far end. The sitting room seemed smaller than when Geoffrey had helped her move in.

That had been one of the bleakest days in months of bleak days. Watching her unpack the few belongings she had brought from home provoked a sinking sense of failure. He helped her make the bed with their five-hundred thread Egyptian cotton sheets, but everything was too big for the ugly double divan. They had luxuriated in a king-sized four-poster at Manor Farm, and this was what she was reduced to. They stood looking at the fitted sheet that didn't fit, the duvet cover that drooped to the cheaply carpeted floor, and all he wanted was to take her home.

Olivia had barely uttered a word during the whole depressing process. As she looked around for somewhere to put a framed photograph of the three of them on holiday in Snowdonia, Geoffrey finally caved and felt the sharp sting of tears. Christ, things were bad enough without Olivia seeing him blub like a baby. He had quickly retreated to the bathroom, grabbed a handful of loo roll and rubbed his eyes like they were the enemy. *Pull it together*. Deep breaths and a splash of cold water on his face restored a semblance of dignity. In the absence of a towel he had pulled more loo paper from the almost empty roll and noticed there was no bath, just a cheap plastic shower stall squeezed into a mildewy corner. Olivia loved a long, lingering soak. She'd light candles, get a glass of wine, put on some Norah Jones. He'd get home from work and like a horny bloodhound, blindly follow the scent. *Join me*, she'd say, her face glistening with tiny beads of sweat. He'd strip off there and then, throw his clothes across the bidet they never used and lower himself into the sea of bubbles. They'd talk, drink wine, kiss, make love. And now he had to leave her here, all alone in this shitty shabby flat.

'Something's happened,' said Olivia, snapping him back.

'What?'

'You're not going to believe it. I caught Ruth Rutherford and one of the groundsmen in the cricket pavilion.'

She paused for his reaction.

'Doing what?'

She stood askance, palms open, signifying the answer was surely too obvious to have to spell it out.

'Having sex,' she said in a theatrical whisper.

'Sex?'

'Shhh, someone might hear you.'

He lowered his voice. 'They were actually having sex?'

'He was on the floor, she was on top, skirt up around her waist, boobs in his face.' Olivia's expression was one of disgust, as though she had bitten into rotten fruit. 'Not a pretty sight, I can assure you.'

'I don't believe it. Ruth Rutherford?'

'Ruth Rutherford. I'd gone there with Hugo to talk about setting some holiday work for Edward, and we walked in on them.'

'Who's Hugo?'

'French exchange student. You know – coaches rugby.'

'I thought Leo Sheridan coached rugby.'

'He does. Hugo helps out.'

'Right. Sorry – why did you go to the cricket pavilion?'

'I told you – to talk about Edward.'

'But why the cricket pavilion, why not a classroom or the staffroom?'

She huffed, clearly irritated that they were getting off topic. 'I was trying to get a signal so I could call you and I bumped into him sneaking a cigarette.' She shook her head. 'Doesn't matter. What matters is what we saw.'

'She must have been mortified.'

'Actually, no. I don't think she was.'

'What did she say?'

'Can I help you?'

'Can I help you?' Geoffrey laughed, clearly not the reaction Olivia was hoping for.

She shushed him again. 'It's not funny.'

'Well, it sort of is. Plummy Ruth Rutherford. Who would have thought? Must be awkward when you run into her.'

'That's just it. Once I'd got over the shock I went up to the house to see her. I told her not to worry – it was none of my business and I wouldn't breathe a word, and she gave me this strange smile.'

'Strange how?'

'I don't know, like she wasn't worried, but maybe I should be.'

'Huh?'

Distant voices got closer; girls talking, laughing. Olivia put her index finger to her lips and stayed very still until the voices faded. All this cloak-and-dagger stuff seemed faintly ridiculous.

'I don't understand why you're the one that should be worried.'

'Me neither, but then yesterday Peter Havant—'

'Peter Havant?'

'Geography. He made a comment about me and the handsome Hugo—'

'Handsome, eh?'

She ignored that. 'It was the way he said it, like he was implying there was something going on.'

Geoffrey took a moment to process this. Not that he had ever actually read one, but he imagined this was the stuff of Jilly Cooper novels – bonking and infidelity among the upper-middles.

'So let me get this straight. You and the French student caught the headmaster's wife and the groundsman at it in the cricket pavilion and now there are rumours about you and the French student.'

Maybe more D. H Lawrence than Jilly Cooper – definitely shades of Lady Chatterley.

'Basically, yes.'

'And you think Ruth Rutherford started those rumours?'

'I do.'

'But why would she?'

'In case I said anything about her and young Tom.'

'Young Tom?'

'The groundsman.' Olivia gave him an exasperated look, as if expecting him to be au fait with the cast of players at St Bede's.

'Not sure I follow.'

'Think about it. If people hear I'm having some sort of relationship with Hugo, then anything I might say about Ruth will look like I'm trying to deflect suspicion away from me and no one will believe a word of it.'

'So tell her you're not going to say anything.'

'I've already done that. Weren't you listening?'

He hated to see her pretty face pinched with worry. When he enveloped her in his arms she resisted, but that just made him hold her harder. She gave in and rested her cheek against his chest.

'I'm sure it'll blow over,' he said, kissing the top of her head.

She pulled away, unconvinced. 'Remember how this job came up suddenly? I think Ruth Rutherford had something to do with the other houseparent leaving.'

'I don't follow.'

Olivia ran her fingers through her hair, the way she did when she was frustrated. 'Oh, I don't know, but I can't lose this job, Geoffrey. We need the money and I can't live with your mother. I'm sorry, I just can't.'

She looked like she might cry. Geoffrey put his arms round her again. 'No, it's me that should be sorry – sorry you have to put up with this shit. It's all my fault.' On this occasion, she didn't argue. 'Look, just keep a low profile for a while.'

She pulled away again, smoothed her hair and took a deep breath. A cleansing breath, she called it – something she learned at yoga. Her voice was composed when she said the match was about to start and they should get moving. She opened the door a few inches and peeked along the corridor before she beckoned him to follow.

*

Geoffrey never felt more proud of Edward than when he watched him play rugby: his speed, his courage, the way he motivated his team. Geoffrey had been captain of rugby in his final year too, and remembered his own father on the touchline, cheering him on, his face beaming. Geoffrey didn't want to taint that memory with the disappointment he brought later. His father had been proud of him. He had.

The match was against Kings Broughton, one of their players almost six feet tall. It often happened at that age: some boys still children, others already in the throes of adolescence, their bodies strong and angular. It made Olivia nervous to watch Edward play against much bigger boys. She covered her eyes when he went in for a tackle, turned away when he crumpled to the ground. On one occasion Geoffrey had to stop her running on to the pitch to make sure Edward wasn't hurt. Not that Geoffrey liked seeing him take a knock, but it was all part of growing up, toughening up. Olivia could be very overprotective.

The French student seemed to be standing in for Leo, giving the team some last-minute encouragement. He patted Edward on the back and sent the boys on to the pitch.

*

St Bede's three: Kings Broughton twelve.

You could judge a school by the calibre of its match tea. Even the gloom of a trouncing like the one they'd just had was alleviated by a hearty selection of sandwiches, scones and home-made cakes. Some schools had started doing hot food – pizza and jacket potatoes – but Geoffrey was a traditionalist. St Bede's was known for putting on an excellent spread.

Olivia had been roped into helping out so had left the match at half-time, which was just as well because the Kings Broughton six-footer had Edward in his sights as the one to bring down. Geoffrey made his way over with the throng of parents commiserating about the score. The consensus was that St Bede's hadn't played badly; they had simply been outclassed by a far superior team. Leo Sheridan's whereabouts remained something of a mystery and the young French guy – Hugo, did Olivia say? – was clearly out of his depth. It was Edward that Geoffrey felt sorry for. Despite Kings Broughton's nine-point lead, he had battled on to the bitter end. Such a mild-mannered boy by nature but on the pitch he showed gladiatorial spirit: fearless, determined to win. He had scored St Bede's only try – had a terrific game, considering. Geoffrey wanted to go over and tell him so at the final whistle but the French guy got there first. He watched him put a consoling arm round Edward's shoulder and wondered what he could say that would make Edward feel better? Nothing, probably. Edward hated losing.

They filed into the library where match tea had been laid out on a series of trestle tables draped with white cotton tablecloths bearing the school's coat of arms and motto: *Laudare, Benedicere, Praedicare – Praise, Bless, Preach*. Behind one of the tables stood Ruth Rutherford and Olivia, busily dispensing hot drinks. Geoffrey thought humour might diffuse any tension between the two and asked Olivia for a pint of his usual. She responded with a weak smile and a cup of tea.

'Nice to see you, Geoffrey,' said Ruth. 'Good game?'

He expected her to be embarrassed. She must have known Olivia would have confided in him, that he would be exempt from her oath of silence. No sign of it, though.

'Disappointing score. Edward played well.'

'Not that you're biased,' she said, flicking her hair off her face.

He saw her in a completely different light now. Hard to imagine her bare-breasted, slumming it with the lower orders. Young lad as well, Olivia had said. Geoffrey sneaked a furtive glance at her breasts as he sipped his tea. Impressive.

He considered her passable in the looks department –
not too fat, not too thin, not too tall, not too short. Her
hair, skin and eyes were pale, affording her a lissom, slightly
ethereal air. She had the sort of mouth that looked better
when solemn. Her top lip vanished to a thin line when she
smiled. What distinguished her was her poise. She exuded
the innate confidence of a woman who knew that she was,
in some indefinable yet utterly irrefutable way, better than
her peers. The rules that governed their mundane lives did
not apply to her. If she wanted to get drunk, she would get
drunk. If she wanted to fuck the groundsman, she would
fuck the groundsman. And woe betide anyone who dared
to suggest otherwise.

*

It had become his night-time ritual – sneaking into the
study half an hour after his mother went to bed; long
enough to be sure she had fallen asleep and wouldn't
bother him. He didn't know why, but Geoffrey assumed
old people went to bed early. Not his mother. She was a
blur of activity in the evenings: wrote letters, baked bread,
cleared out cupboards. Perhaps keeping busy was her way
of dealing with bereavement.

Geoffrey watched the clock, impatient to have some
quality time with his laptop. He would have preferred to
indulge his guilty secret in the privacy of his bedroom but
couldn't get any Wi-Fi on that side of the house. And anyway, he hadn't managed a single orgasm in that bedroom.
It was as if it was cursed.

Cybersex seemed a reasonable solution to the problem
of the cursed bedroom and absent wife. There were two

sites he favoured. The girls were pretty and natural, a selection of blondes, brunettes and redheads. He liked the way they looked coyly at the camera, the way they undressed slowly, shyly. Since that first time, when he'd sneaked out of bed leaving Olivia sleeping soundly, he had ended every day with a visit to those websites. He missed his wife, his home, the life he had before it all went to shit. He wasn't hurting anyone. It wasn't infidelity if there was no third party. At least that was what he told himself when his conscience reared its sanctimonious head.

His mother found him in the snug watching a BBC drama about a murderer on the run.

'I'm going up then,' she said.

Ten thirty on the dot.

'I won't be far behind,' said Geoffrey.

Fifteen tedious minutes later, after a wholly predictable ending – the murderer didn't do it after all but managed to track down the man who did – Geoffrey went to the kitchen for a glass of water and was suddenly plunged into darkness. It took a few seconds to feel his way along the wall to the light switch but no matter how many times he flicked it, the light wouldn't come on. His mother called from upstairs.

'Don't worry,' he called back. 'I'm going to check the fuses.'

Using the light from his iPhone he found the fuse box – tucked unhelpfully in the darkest recess of the understairs cupboard – and saw that none of the fuses had tripped. It could be a power cut, or more likely the decades-old wiring. He made his way upstairs and checked on his mother.

She was sitting on the end of her bed in an ancient dressing gown. Her hair, pinned in a librarian-style bun for as long as he could remember, hung long and straggly over her shoulders. It altered her completely – made her seem elderly. Part of him was repulsed, as though he had glimpsed her naked. Another part buckled with compassion to see his self-possessed mother so vulnerable and undone.

'Would you like some candles, Mum?'

She shook her head. 'Fire risk. I was about to turn in anyway.'

He bent forward and kissed her cheek. It was cold, papery, dry.

For reasons he couldn't articulate, the whole scene unnerved him. Rowena Parry was respected and composed, not this shrunken old lady with parchment skin and bag-lady hair. It was as if her mortality had only then become apparent to him. He had just lost his father and at some point in the not too distant future, he would more than likely lose his mother as well. In the dim light from his phone, her expression was hard to read.

'Are you sure you're OK?' he asked.

She replied with a half-smile he could just make out but which, for a fraction of a second, reminded him of Edward.

Across the landing was his own bedroom, unwelcoming and austere. He slumped on the hideous velour chair and buried his head in his hands. A long time passed before he got undressed and into bed. He lay awake, eyes fixed on the ugly lampshade directly above him, surprised at how incomplete he felt without his fix of porn. Perhaps he should limit himself to every other night, just in case.

He didn't want to become addicted, although there were worse things to be addicted to: crack cocaine, alcohol, gambling, cigarettes. No, it didn't help to list them.

Begrudgingly resigned to a night without relief, he willed himself towards sleep. Ruth Rutherford floated into his consciousness – unexpected but more than welcome. Well-rounded breasts; haughty smile. Geoffrey took a long, deep breath and allowed his hand to drift towards his groin. She was in the cricket pavilion now, skirt up around her waist, her palm pressed firmly against a muscular chest. Geoffrey's chest. She was on top, riding him hard, head thrown back, moaning with pleasure. He stifled a cry when he came, breathless and ecstatically relieved. How wonderfully perverse. Ruth Rutherford, of all people, had broken the bedroom curse.

Five

An ominous note poked out of Olivia's pigeonhole. A4 paper folded into quarters; no envelope. She waited a moment before she opened it. Martin Rutherford requesting a meeting, his office, three o'clock tomorrow. Oh God. This would be about Ruth. Olivia felt physically sick – a horrible swirling sensation that she could taste – but then realised she couldn't make the meeting anyway. Peter Havant had asked her to accompany him on a geography trip to Cheddar Gorge. They would be out most of the day, exploring giant caves, clambering up steep footpaths, feasting on cheese. That was how he had sold it to her, although he didn't need to. She loved taking Edward and his friends to Cheddar Gorge. It had featured as a day trip in almost every school holiday. Happy memories, she reminded herself as an antidote to the unhappiness that had begun to close in on her.

When she had first arrived at St Bede's, learning the job, getting to know the girls, the staff and the school regime had absorbed her. She hadn't had much time to dwell on losing Downings or Manor Farm, or how Geoffrey could have allowed that to happen. He had introduced her to a standard of living far beyond anything she knew or expected, and once she had allowed herself to relax and enjoy it, he took it all away.

Now that she had settled in, although she was still busy (very much so), that overwhelming sense of newness had worn off, allowing more time to dwell on everything she missed. And while she longed for the comfort of Manor Farm, it wasn't material loss that predominated, it was leisurely dog walks with Lorna, getting tipsy at book club, a long soak in the bath with a glass of wine. Hardest of all was being virtually incommunicado.

Olivia was a talker. Before her parents had left for Sydney, she spoke to her mum every night and her dad and Sam at least once a week. She and Lorna were used to sharing thoughts and occurrences at various points throughout the day and Olivia called a handful of old schoolfriends once or twice a month. She chatted to everyone she bumped into in the village, was on first-name terms with the postman, the receptionists at the doctor's surgery, the dentist and the vet. Now, when she managed to log on to Facebook and saw that her friends' lives carried on quite happily without her, Olivia felt even more aggrieved than when the Wi-Fi was down and she couldn't log on at all.

Keeping things bottled up was completely alien to her. She believed the reason she had struggled after Edward was born wasn't because of postnatal depression – helpfully diagnosed by Rowena and confided in hushed tones to anyone who asked after her – but because the harsh winter had stopped her getting out and about. Impossible to push a buggy through a foot of snow. Lorna popping round out of the blue that first afternoon had saved her. Olivia missed her terribly. Snatched phone calls from the quad weren't the same as their long, impromptu ramblings about everything and nothing. Nor did they help remove the splinter embedded in the skin of their friendship; Olivia sworn to keep Johnny's secret, Lorna frustrated by their dogged insistence nothing was wrong when instinct told her that there was.

And then Olivia had left for St Bede's. Talking was the oxygen of their friendship; necessary at all times. The network dead zone had starved them of oxygen.

'Something interesting?'

Lisa Pearce peered over Olivia's shoulder at the contents of the note, prompting Olivia to fold it up again and put it her bag.

'Something about the Christmas newsletter,' she said, unsure how much Lisa had seen.

The bell rang, giving Olivia an excuse to rush off.

Silly that she felt so nervous about seeing Martin. She was a grown woman, for goodness' sake, and hadn't done anything wrong. But when she thought about the lies Ruth could have fabricated, her heart quickened to the point of pain. And how could Olivia defend herself without telling him the truth? Ruth certainly didn't deserve her silence but Olivia wanted no part in destroying the Rutherfords' marriage; their family. What would that do to the girls? No, irrespective of the consequences for herself, Olivia couldn't tell Martin what had really happened in the cricket pavilion.

Claire Heather passed her in the corridor, laden down with school brochures. She had been a regular visitor at the Rectory over the years, particularly in the weeks following Ronald's death. Claire's husband, Arthur, died of a heart attack too, a year before he had been due to retire from Downings. Geoffrey had never taken to him. He thought him 'shifty' – not the most inspiring quality in a book-keeper – but with his wife being one of his mother's closest friends, and Arthur having worked at the factory for over twenty years, there wasn't much he could do about it. When they compared notes, both Geoffrey and Olivia agreed that the Heathers didn't like them. Arthur let it be known he thought Geoffrey was an 'upstart' and Olivia felt disapproved of by Claire, although without any hard supporting evidence. Olivia's suspicion resided in the appraising way Claire looked at her, in the impression of stilted tolerance. Olivia often wondered what Rowena said about her over tea and scones at the Rectory, but then remembered her mother's wise words. *If you worried what people thought of you, you'd never leave the house.*

'Is the headmaster in?' asked Olivia.

'Do you have an appointment?'

'Tomorrow, but I'm on a field trip with Mr Havant, so I need to rearrange.'

'Right. Well, if you wouldn't mind waiting, I just need to drop these off.'

Olivia went along to the anteroom which led to Martin's office, aware that she was due to listen to the first-formers read in twenty minutes so couldn't hang around. She was about to write a note, explaining, when Martin's door opened.

'Olivia?' he said, looking around. 'No Mrs Heather?'

'She popped out with some brochures.'

'Is there something I can help you with?'

'I need to reschedule our meeting. Mr Havant has asked me to go on a field trip to Cheddar Gorge.'

'Oh yes. Alice and Maisie are going.' He checked his wristwatch; old-fashioned with a flat gold-rimmed face and worn leather strap. 'I'm free now if you are?'

The knot in her stomach twisted a little tighter. 'I'm supposed to be hearing the first-formers read.'

Claire Heather bustled in, dismayed to see an arrangement being made without her intervention.

Martin addressed her directly. 'Would you make Olivia's excuses to—?' He looked to Olivia to fill in the name.

'Mrs Roache.'

'Mrs Roache,' continued Martin. 'And hold my calls, please, if you would.'

He stood to one side and gestured for Olivia to enter his office.

'Please sit,' he said, pointing to the chair on the other side of his desk.

A gilt-framed photograph of Ruth and the girls took pride of place. Olivia crossed her legs and tidied her hands in her lap. Her heart felt too big for her chest as she waited for Martin to speak.

'This is rather difficult,' he said.

He put his forefinger to his lip, his thumb on his chin, and frowned. 'It's been brought to my attention that you and Mr Dubois had,' he paused, squirmed a little in his chair – 'a liaison in the cricket pavilion.'

So she had been right about Ruth's tactics. How dare she put her in this position. Olivia feared Martin would interpret the rising colour on her face and neck as guilt, when really it was anger.

'Would you care to comment?' he said.

'It was completely innocent. We did go to the cricket pavilion, to talk about Edward. Mr Dubois and I bumped into each other outside while trying to get some signal on our phones, and I took the opportunity to explore options about Edward's French. He's fallen a bit behind this term.'

Martin nodded, his forehead creased.

'I see. And did you?'

'Did we what?'

'Explore options about Edward's French.'

Olivia uncrossed her legs and then crossed them in the other direction. 'No.'

'Why not?'

She looked at the photograph again – carefree girls, smiling parents, something green and very English about the background – to underscore the reason she couldn't tell the truth.

'Mr Dubois remembered an appointment,' she said, hearing how feeble it sounded.

Martin leaned forward and rested his clasped hands on the desk. 'It has also been reported to me that a man's voice was heard coming from your quarters. You do realise it's strictly against school rules to entertain men, don't you?'

Men? What did he take her for? And who had done the reporting? Did Ruth have someone watching her, spying on her? Only when she exhaled did she realise she had been holding her breath.

'It was Geoffrey. He arrived early for Edward's match and there was a matter we needed to discuss. A private matter.'

Martin nodded. 'Ah, yes, I remember seeing him. We spoke briefly in the quad.'

Thank goodness. Even so, she had broken the rules so apologised, insisting it was an isolated incident and wouldn't happen again. Martin took off his glasses, produced a folded handkerchief from his pocket and gave each lens a good wipe. When he spoke, his tone was rather less formal than before.

'Look, Olivia, I'm very pleased with how you've settled in and I know that as well as all your good work with the boarders, you muck in and help out whenever you can.' He put his glasses back on and folded the handkerchief into a neat square. 'So on this occasion I'm willing to overlook any *indiscretion* on your part.'

Olivia opened her mouth to protest but Martin raised a hand to stop her.

'As long as I have your absolute assurance there will be no further cause for concern. We are, first and foremost, a Christian school, governed and guided by the Christian ethos.'

He paused again in a way that made it clear the meeting was about to come to a close. No. Olivia could not – *would not* – leave that room with Martin believing she had behaved in some sleazy, un-Christian way.

'Headmaster.' Her tone was calm but firm and she looked him in the eye. 'I accept I may have made an error of judgement going to the cricket pavilion with Mr Dubois, and another when I spoke with Geoffrey in my flat, but I can absolutely assure you, I am not guilty of any *indiscretion.*'

For the avoidance of doubt, she had copied Martin's very deliberate inflection.

'So your relationship with Mr Dubois is purely professional?'

'In so much as I *have* a relationship with Mr Dubois, yes, it is purely professional. We've only spoken on a handful of occasions.'

This seemed to satisfy him.

'Good.' He stood up and took a few long strides to the door.

'Listen,' he said, his hand on the doorknob. 'Ruth is having an Alpha meeting at the house this afternoon – her first; a bit nervous I daresay. I know she'd feel a lot better if you could go along.'

Olivia intended to avoid Ruth at all costs, not sit meekly while she offered instruction on Christianity and the Bible. Such staggering hypocrisy. Olivia was barely able to contain her contempt for the woman. Was Martin really that much of a dolt? Did he not know his wife at all? Olivia needed to breathe some fresh, clean air.

'I'll see what I can do,' she said.

It was his parting shot that left her speechless. 'She really is very fond of you, you know.'

*

Olivia relived the whole humiliating episode with Geoffrey that night as she shivered in the quad. She wasn't supposed to leave her post, even when the boarders were tucked up in bed, but Matron said she'd keep an eye on them for ten minutes.

Olivia tried to explain how being gossiped about had induced a horrible sense of injustice and isolation.

She didn't know who she could trust. The staff would believe the headmaster's wife and even if they didn't, they wouldn't be foolish enough to say so. Ditto with the mothers. Lisa Pearce told her the Alpha meeting had been well attended – *a chance to curry favour with the headmaster's wife.*

They were a tight-knit group, the St Bede's mothers – a coterie, Geoffrey called them – and Ruth's status put her at its centre. Olivia's status was less clear-cut. She was a St Bede's mother herself, of course, but now she was a house-parent too – an employee. That was a game changer; another one of Geoffrey's expressions. It was common knowledge they had lost their business and their home. A few of the mothers referred to their change of fortunes directly, but most commiserations took the form of a brave smile, a well-meaning squeeze of the arm, and, on one notable and humiliating occasion, a pledge to offer up prayer.

When Edward had started at St Bede's – pre-prep, four years old, adorable in his uniform – the other mothers mistook Olivia for an au pair. It made her feel very proud to tell them Edward was her son. The surprise on their faces spoke volumes. She could almost see them calculating how old she must have been when she had him. A teenager? Actually she had been twenty-one, at least a decade younger than the average St Bede's mother. Many of them had gone to university, had careers, become established before they started families. That Olivia had done none of these things rather set her apart. It didn't help that she was petite and pretty with abundant straw-coloured hair that tumbled down her back in soft, lustrous waves. St Bede's was not a yummy-mummy type of school. It was small and rural and devoutly Christian.

In an effort to fit in, Olivia had joined the weekly Alpha classes run by Teddy Clarke-Bowen's wife, Caroline. Olivia's parents weren't religious and she had only become a church-goer when she moved to Compton Cross. Ronald had delivered wonderful sermons, full of love and hope. He didn't dwell on the darkness in people, the demons that drove them to sin. Ronald believed more in forgiveness than judgement: in God's mercy, not his wrath. How sad that his determination to see only the good in people had caused so much suffering. When Olivia thought about what had happened to Johnny, it made her sick to her stomach. She had begged him to tell Lorna, or to let her tell Lorna, but he was adamant no one must ever know.

It was hard for Olivia to go to church after that. She had never been sure she believed in God, but she did believe in being decent, helping others, telling the truth, or a version of the truth that did the least damage. That her personal values were also Christian values was a happy coincidence. It placed her firmly within the ethos of St Bede's, irrespective of her theological beliefs. At Alpha she had learned about Jesus and the Bible, and over Sunday lunch at the Rectory, she and Ronald had enjoyed many a spirited discussion. He was patient with her questions, explained the things she didn't understand. She wished he were here now. He would have known what she should do, other than *keep your head down* – Geoffrey's only piece of advice.

It was a terrible line, crackly and distant, as though they were in a tunnel or underwater.

'What do you think your father would have said?' asked Olivia.

'Turn the other cheek?' said Geoffrey uncertainly.

No help at all. She looked up when a light went on in the dorm.

'Sorry – I have to go.'

She let herself in, locked the main door behind her and ran up the stairs, two at a time. Matron was squatting by Alice Rutherford's bedside, talking to her quietly. Olivia slipped off her coat and went over to relieve her.

'Sorry,' she whispered, touching Matron on the shoulder.

She stood up. 'Maisie came to get me. Alice was crying.'

'Thanks,' said Olivia. 'I'll stay with her.'

Alice had her thumb in her mouth. Edward had abandoned thumb-sucking a few months before his third birthday. Alice was nine.

'What's wrong, sweetheart?'

Her eyelids were heavy with crying and sleep. She didn't reply. Olivia thought it best to leave her alone to drift off again. She pulled the duvet over her shoulder and said goodnight. The poor child needed so much more than a houseparent could give her.

*

It wasn't just Alice Rutherford who had a bad night. Each time Olivia felt herself falling towards sleep, some flashback from her meeting with Martin leapt into her head and she was wide awake again, her heart tangoing in her chest. Obsessively checking the time only made it worse. Nothing ensured a bad night's sleep like fretting about a bad night's sleep. At six o'clock she admitted defeat, got up and started the day.

During her second cup of staffroom coffee – instant, black, two sugars for energy – Hugo Dubois walked in. Did she *imagine* a momentary lull in conversation, glances in her general direction? She sipped her coffee and flicked through the new school brochure: smiling children playing musical instruments, running round sports fields, relaxed and happy in their dorms.

'Madame Parry.'

Hugo approached her, nursing his own cup of coffee. He clearly hadn't been briefed about appropriate styles of address. In her peripheral vision, Olivia noticed Lisa Pearce watching them.

'Morning,' she said, not quite hitting the casual note she was aiming for.

That was when it occurred to her that Martin would want to see Hugo too. She had to warn him, make sure his account of events matched hers. Not here, though, not in front of prying eyes.

'Have you seen the new school brochure?' she said cheerily and a little too loudly.

Hugo made no effort to disguise his complete lack of interest.

She lowered her voice. 'Are you free for five minutes at morning break? There's something we need to talk about.'

He took a sip of coffee and grimaced. Presumably he was used to something rather better than Nescafé.

'Of course.'

Lisa Pearce had sidled into earshot. Where to meet posed a dilemma for Olivia. If she suggested somewhere discreet, it would give the impression of being furtive, of having something to hide. But meeting openly would only further fuel the gossip and make it difficult to discuss the delicate topic of Ruth Rutherford. Olivia was wrestling with this when Hugo suggested the French room, which made perfect sense. She still needed to sort out some holiday work for Edward.

'Break time,' she said. 'Oh, and it's Olivia when there are no pupils present.'

With a quick smile at Lisa Pearce, Olivia took her coffee and left.

*

The French room was just a classroom with pictures of France on the walls. Hugo sat marking a pile of exercise books, but stood when Olivia walked in. He sported a pair of Harry Potter style spectacles. She wouldn't have thought it possible, but they actually made him look more attractive. His cologne scented the air: floral and musky at the same time. She sat down on one of the child-sized chairs and crossed her legs.

'Thank you for meeting me,' she said. 'I thought you should know that the headmaster spoke to me yesterday. There are rumours about you and me.' She hated the way she blushed. 'I think his wife is trying to get me sacked.'

'Sacked?'

'Lose my job.'

He frowned. 'But you do nothing wrong.'

Olivia shrugged to confirm the point. She needed to remember that she was the innocent party here. The injured party, in fact.

'Anyway,' she continued. 'I told him we bumped into each other and went to the cricket pavilion to discuss Edward's French.'

'It's true.'

'Yes, but I didn't tell him what we saw in the cricket pavilion.'

This time it was Hugo who shrugged.

'It would be very damaging for his marriage, his family,' explained Olivia. 'And for the school,' she added, suddenly envisaging a plethora of salacious tabloid head-lines if word got out. The gutter press had had no com-punction about trying to destroy the school's reputation when Freddie Burton's prank went so disastrously wrong. It might not survive another scandal.

'I hear these rumours too,' said Hugo.

Olivia shifted her weight. Pressed against the hard wooden seat, her buttocks had started to go numb.

'You have? When?'

'Rugby. The other boys tease Edward.' He waved the comment away. 'It was nothing.'

'Nothing? You think that was nothing? Oh God, poor Edward. I have to speak to him. I can't believe it's gone this far.'

She cupped her hands over her mouth.

'Madame Parry,' said Hugo softly, clearly concerned he had upset her. 'Olivia,' he corrected. 'In France these things are de rigueur.'

Olivia stared at him, perplexed. He looked heavenwards, eyebrows knitted together, trying to pluck the correct word from his limited vocabulary.

'Acceptable,' he said.

He just didn't get it. Despite his apparent sophistication, he was obviously too young to understand the gravity of the situation. She needed to impress upon him exactly what was at stake.

'But we're not in France. We're in Somerset, and a married houseparent having an affair with an exchange student is most certainly not de rigueur. Nor is the headmaster's wife and her toy boy.'

The bell rang for end of break. Hugo clearly didn't understand the 'toy boy' reference, but in a few minutes children would file in for their lesson, Olivia would head off to Cheddar Gorge and she really didn't have time to explain. She needed to talk to Edward too, but there was no time for that either.

'Thank you, Madame Parry,' he said.

For what? The whole thing was a horrible mess.

*

Olivia cringed as she knocked on Matron's door. She didn't want her to think she was taking advantage, but she had to see Edward. The girls were in their pyjamas, glued to *Finding Nemo*, and she promised she wouldn't be long.

'Getting to be something of a habit,' Matron said, half joking, half not.

'I know. I wouldn't ask if it wasn't important.'

'You look tired, Olivia. Is everything all right?'

'Long day.'

'It's not just the girls you have to take care of, it's yourself too.'

The unexpected sense of being mothered caught Olivia totally off guard. It was her job to mother others; her job to be strong. Through nothing but good intentions, Matron had reminded Olivia that her mum was on the other side of the world. Falling apart felt like a very real possibility, and then where would she be? She turned to walk away.

'Oh, and Olivia.'

'Yes?'

'It's Harriet.'

*

Only thirty minutes until lights out. Olivia made her way over to the boys' dorm in the other wing, the corridors deserted and dimly lit. Pain throbbed behind her eyes. As if she hadn't been stressed enough, the field trip had been a nightmare. Alice Rutherford had clung to her, marsupial-like, her thumb in her mouth. Olivia should really air her concerns with Martin and Ruth but couldn't face seeing them together. Bad enough seeing one or the other, but both at the same time was a sickening thought.

Alice had been utterly terrified when the tour guide explained that the cave they were standing in was home to the British cave spider – one of the largest spiders in the British Isles – and a colony of rare lesser horseshoe bats. *If you look carefully, you can see the bats flitting around.* Alice grabbed on to Olivia and screamed, convinced she could feel spiders crawling on her legs. She kept swatting at them, her little hands flailing desperately in the gloom. Alice set off Helena Hardy-Leach, who sobbed that she didn't like bats and made a run for the exit. Peter Havant caught her but by this time mass hysteria threatened to take hold, so they cut the tour short and herded the children outside.

It took Olivia and Peter the best part of an hour to calm them all down. The weight of responsibility was daunting. One of the boys got an asthma attack as they climbed the steep path to the rim of the gorge. Peter waited with him, leaving Olivia to take the rest of the children – usually so well behaved, now hyper and unruly – to the top. She counted heads obsessively, fearful a child would wander off and get lost. Her requests to walk in single file on the descent were largely ignored. The boys thought it great sport to charge ahead and see how far they could get before they tumbled over. One of them cut his knees and tore the side of blazer. Olivia had never been so relieved to get back to school. She couldn't wait to shower and collapse into bed, but first of all she had to see Edward: her own child, her first responsibility. So what if the other boys made a fuss – this was more important than a bit of harmless teasing.

The boarders were sprawled on beanbags and sofas, watching some sort of wildlife programme. When Leo Sheridan spotted her he came out into the corridor.

'I'm glad you've dropped by. I was going to ask for a quick word about Edward.'

'He's all right, isn't he?'

Leo glanced into the dorm before he pulled the door shut.

Olivia had resisted the idea of Edward boarding at first (selfishly, she wanted to spare herself the pain of missing him), but Geoffrey said day boys were disadvantaged as seniors – never made head boy or prefects or sports captains. Those roles always went to boarders; that's why their numbers swelled in the final years of prep school. It prepared them for public school as well: fostered independence, self-confidence. All these points had some merit but it was Geoffrey's final point that had settled it. *And anyway, he wants to board.* Edward had confided this bombshell to his father so as not to upset his mother. How could she argue?

But before Olivia relinquished term-time care of her only child, she wanted to know more about the man who would be responsible for him. As well as being the school's senior houseparent, reluctant rugby coach – a task happily delegated to Hugo Dubois – and head of music and drama, it was rumoured that Leo had harboured ambitions to become a concert pianist but was too crippled by stage fright to pursue his dream. At school he always seemed so unflappable. Out of curiosity Olivia had googled him. Leo Bryce Sheridan, born March 1978, studied music at the Guildhall and the Birmingham Conservatoire. There was a picture of him before he lost all the hair from the crown of his head. How handsome he looked in his dinner suit and bow tie. She wondered how he felt accompanying the St Bede's choir rather than playing to an admiring audience at the Festival Hall. If he was crushed with disappointment, he hid it well.

'Nothing to be concerned about,' said Leo quietly. 'It's just some of the other boys have been giving Edward a bit of a hard time.'

Olivia felt her scalp tighten, sharpening the pain in her head.

'Apparently he took exception to a comment Freddie Burton made after rugby training. Some nonsense about you and Hugo Dubois. Just thought I should let you know.'

Freddie Burton? He could only have heard the rumour about her and Hugo (*overheard* it – surely she wouldn't discuss it with him directly?) from his mother, Alicia. Olivia didn't know her well, even though Edward and Freddie had been at school together since pre-prep. Alicia Burton always appeared suspiciously strategic in her friendships, and Olivia, it seemed, wasn't important enough to warrant favour. Geoffrey had a different theory. He said the reason Alicia was cool towards her was because Olivia was younger and prettier and Toby Burton had a roving eye. Maybe Geoffrey was right and that was part of it too.

But then Olivia had rescued Freddie from his changing-room stunt and Alicia appeared after chapel one morning with a beautiful hand-tied bouquet, and asked if there was somewhere they could talk. She looked as though she hadn't slept for a month. Over staffroom coffee she confided that Freddie had taken it badly when his father left and doing stupid things to get attention was his way of acting out. 'If you hadn't found him—' She brought her hand to her mouth, unable to finish the sentence. Olivia's heart went out to her and she felt sure a bond had been forged, that from now on, she and Alicia would be friends.

Not so. Olivia hadn't seen or heard anything of her since that morning, although according to Lisa Pearce, she could always be found 'sucking up' to Ruth Rutherford whenever the opportunity arose. Alicia brought cakes and flowers to the Alpha meeting Olivia hadn't gone to, and stayed afterwards to help Ruth clear up. And now Freddie was baiting Edward with comments about her and Hugo. It appeared that Olivia had been right about Alicia Burton all along.

'I appreciate it,' said Olivia. 'That's why I wanted to see him – make sure he's OK.'

'He's been a bit quiet this evening,' said Leo. 'I'm sure it will all be forgotten tomorrow.'

'Can I see him?'

'Of course. Wait here and I'll get him for you.'

Despite the trouble it had caused, Olivia felt proud that Edward had leaped to her defence. He certainly hadn't learned by example. Thirteen years of marriage and Olivia was still waiting for Geoffrey to do the same. His excuse was that Rowena attacked by stealth, never open confrontation, making defence difficult to pull off. They had hashed over the same argument so many times Olivia accepted that in this regard, her husband was destined to disappoint.

'Mum?'

Edward wore his old grey tracksuit, the one he mooched around the house in when he was under the weather. It looked a bit too small. She went to hug him but he took a step back.

'Mum,' he said again, a whine of disapproval now in his voice.

No public displays of affection. Got it.

'Sorry,' she said, putting her hands by her sides. 'I forgot. Look, I know you had a bit of an upset today and I just wanted to make sure you were all right.'

He looked her in the eye, unblinking. It was a moment before he nodded.

'Good,' she said, pushing her hands into her trouser pockets so she wouldn't weaken and try to hug him. 'I'm sorry you're having a hard time.'

A peal of laughter rang out from the dorm.

'I should go,' said Edward. He made a move towards the door.

'Of course. Night, darling. Sleep well.'

He hesitated for a second before he came back and squeezed his arms round her. A surge of love erupted in Olivia's chest and she had to turn away quickly so he wouldn't see the hot rush of tears.

Six

Geoffrey's long brisk strides ate up the path to Crook Peak, his breath white smoke in the frigid air. He had wrapped up warm but was too warm now. Rollo and Dice panted alongside, their coats slick and wet from playing in the stream. Geoffrey reached the brow of the hill and stopped, heart pounding, chest heaving. In the distance was the sprawl of the industrial estate. Closer was the village, a neat patchwork of fields and houses clustered round the church. On the outskirts lay Manor Farm.

The SOLD sign had floored him, made it all true. Even as their possessions were being loaded on to the removal lorry, he had told himself this was just a big mistake and once it was sorted out, they would be back home where they belonged. A sharp wind made his eyes water. He rubbed them hard with clenched fists. Word in the pub was that Manor Farm was now the second home of a city banker. Fucking bastard banker. Geoffrey couldn't hold it all inside: the rage, the regret, the lacerating sense of failure. He threw back his head and roared.

*

Today was his mother's day for hospital visiting, which meant Geoffrey would have the Rectory to himself. Daytime television beckoned: polished and preened presenters going on about fashion, holidays and reality shows. His favourite bit was when they interviewed ordinary people who, by dint

of good luck or bad, were catapulted into their fifteen minutes of fame. Yesterday they had talked to a woman whose
husband took his own life after being out of work for two
years. She cried and hung her head, long greasy hair falling
forwards over her face, as she described what a wonderful
husband he had been; what a wonderful father. When she
spoke of the hundreds of job applications that had yielded
nothing but rejection, Geoffrey found himself nodding in
agreement. That, he could relate to.

Geoffrey had lost count of the number of jobs he'd
applied for; the number of hours he had spent trying to
make his experience fit the vacancy; the number of times
he had explained, in not more than five hundred words,
why he was the best person to fill this position and what
qualities he would bring to the role. Those companies that
bothered to reply at all – *if you haven't heard from us within
four weeks, it means your application has been unsuccessful* –
were vague about why he was unsuitable. Was he over-
qualified, under-qualified, too young, too old? Apparently
those used to running their own businesses made terrible
employees – difficult to manage, a threat to their peers.
And manufacturing had been decimated by the economic
downturn: redundancies and cutbacks, factories like
Downings shutting up shop after years of hard work and
sacrifice. A horrible truth had begun to dawn. At thirty-
five years of age, Geoffrey had been tossed on to the scrap-
heap of broke and broken umemployables.

This morning's sobbing TV interviewee was a mother
of four whose husband was addicted to online pornography. The presenters nodded sympathetically and invited

the expert on the opposite sofa to explain exactly how this growing problem ruined lives. Geoffrey didn't want to hear it. He turned off the television and went to the kitchen to make a sandwich.

The electrical problem that had plunged them into the darkness cost three hundred and fifty pounds to fix and came with a warning that it would happen again if the whole house wasn't soon rewired. Geoffrey hadn't argued. It was obvious to everyone but his mother that the Rectory needed bringing into the twenty-first century. He had never questioned his parents' life of genteel poverty – asset rich, cash poor – but no longer had that luxury.

A discreet call from the estate agent who had sold Manor Farm – rugby teammate, Lamb and Lion regular – revealed it had gone for fifty thousand less than Geoffrey paid in 2008, when the market was at its peak. The bubble had burst two years later and prices had fallen ever since. The agent said Geoffrey was lucky to get as much as he did, then must have remembered it was the bank that had sold Manor Farm because he mumbled an apology and made an excuse to hang up. There would be nothing left once the loan was settled. Nothing to show for all the years Geoffrey had put work before family. He cringed, thinking how he used to swagger around the village like some captain of industry. Big fish, small pond. No wonder he was ostracised.

It angered Geoffrey to admit it, but whoever had been responsible for dripfeeding snippets of dirt to the newspapers – he had a long list of suspects – hadn't been too wide of the mark. The stories painted him in the worst possible light, but they all contained a hard kernel of truth. Yes, after Bob Downing's death, Geoffrey hadn't always sought or taken heed of advice. And yes, he had been aware that some of the equipment – essential to the core of the business – was coming to the end of its useful life. And no, he hadn't put sufficient funds aside to replace it, but chose instead to take out a whacking great mortgage to buy Manor Farm. He suspected he had overstretched himself but carried on regardless, head in the sand, hoping it would all get better.

It got worse. Downings lost a big client to an Asian competitor, then another, then another. Geoffrey couldn't compete with their prices. British manufacturing may have been amongst the best in the world, but thanks to high labour costs and a strong pound, it was also among the most expensive. He cut overheads to the bone, shaved profits to a sliver, but still they undercut him. An optimist by nature, and despite all evidence to the contrary, even then he believed that things would turn around. New orders, some government initiative to help small- to medium-sized enterprises, a low-interest loan from the bank.

Truth was, Geoffrey had never really had a head for the money side of the business. Bob had looked after the finances and once he had gone, Geoffrey was complacent enough to muddle along, convinced that he could manage. How difficult could it be? So when Arthur Heather had first alerted him to the growing pile of unpaid bills, Geoffrey almost accused him of fiddling the books. The man was a gambler – everyone knew that. But so, it transpired, was Geoffrey. Through a combination of ineptitude and poor judgement, he had unwittingly gambled with Downings' future and lost.

Two shaven-headed bailiffs, one with an earring, the other with a snake tattoo on his neck, had turned up at the factory on May Day. Geoffrey had needed to do a few hours' work first thing, before joining the village celebrations. Truthfully, celebrating was the last thing he had felt like, but there was the small matter of keeping up appearances.

A steady stream of final demands and solicitors' letters had languished in a file on his desk. Naive and hopelessly out of his depth, he hadn't realised the clock was ticking, that each debt was time-limited and there was no more time left. Nor did he realise that not all debts were equal. The debt that had brought these dark-suited thugs to Downings on a bank holiday Monday was non-payment of business rates. So it was the local authority that had been quickest off the mark – who would have thought? They plucked out the playing card that brought the rest of the deck crashing down around him.

Inexperienced in such matters, Geoffrey had been horrified to discover the extent of the bailiffs' powers. In a few hours they had made an inventory of everything – machinery, desks, chairs, computers – that could be packed up, taken away and sold. When he asked how he could stop that happening, snake man said it was simple: clear the debt in full. Not simple at all. The overdraft was at its limit and there was a dearth of new orders. He wasn't even sure he could meet that month's payroll. 'See you in seven days,' called earring man as they let themselves out.

*

Ironic that May Day was International Workers' Day. Celebrated as a medieval fertility festival, replete with maypole, morris dancers, beer tents and skittles, it had actually been co-opted in the nineteenth century by socialists fighting for an eight-hour day. This incarnation flourished with the rise of trade unionism and May Day became a bank holiday in 1978, when the Labour government decided to formally mark the working-class struggle against capitalism.

Bob Downing had explained all of this during one of their last Friday night sessions in the Lamb and Lion, just before Geoffrey took over Downings. *Aren't we the big bad capitalists?* he had asked, supping on his third pint of Wild Hare. He remembered Bob's reply because it was the first time Geoffrey had viewed himself through the lens of a responsible employer. *We're capitalists all right, but not big and not bad. We care about our workers and their families. It's not just about profit; it's about providing a livelihood, being at the heart of a community.*

The memory stung. On that May Day Geoffrey had stood in the empty factory, the bailiffs' cheap aftershave lingering and sour, and choked back tears of shame. Never had he missed his friend so keenly. Bob would have known what to do, but then Bob wouldn't have got them into this mess in the first place.

Out of habit Geoffrey had locked up, then realised it didn't matter if the place got robbed or burned to the ground – at least then he'd get the insurance money. For a second he even considered it. It took a vision of himself behind bars to bring him to his senses.

When he parked at the Rectory – closer to the May Day action than Manor Farm – and walked towards the green, he spotted Olivia chatting happily to Lorna and Johnny. Bob had been right; it was about so much more than profit. A lesson Geoffrey had learned too late. After twenty-five years at Downings – apprentice to skilled welder – Johnny was about to lose his job. Nearly half the village were about to lose their jobs.

Geoffrey had smiled, chatted, shook hands, pecked cheeks, all the time keeping this grenade of a secret to himself. Each time he saw one of his workers enjoying a day out with their family, he thought how they trusted him, relied on him to provide for that family. When he was called upon to present prizes – the raffle, best home-made jam, winner of the dog agility contest – it was in his capacity as a successful businessman. Soon they would all see him for what he was, and it wasn't that.

In reading hour at school, Geoffrey had amused himself with the witticisms of Oscar Wilde. It was as near to literary as he cared to tread, but as he doled out raffle prizes he remembered something about 'the curse of self-awareness'. He hadn't understood it then, of course – what fourteen-year-old boy would? – but on May Day he had discerned a dissonance between the affable, beer-drinking, rugby-playing friend to all, and the fool who hadn't thought about the collateral damage his commercial incompetence would inflict.

But as he had stood on the makeshift wooden podium – friends, employees and villagers looking up at him – the enormity of his conceit had become clear. It wasn't just his own life he had gambled with; it was these people's lives too.

*

He changed his mind about the sandwich and decided to go to the pub instead. A quick rifle through his pockets produced a ten-pound note and some change – enough for a few pints and a packet of crisps.

As he walked across the village green he thought again about how the Rectory, shabby and unmodernised though it was, represented prime real estate. Large rooms, high ceilings, original fireplaces and ornate plasterwork, country kitchen with an Aga, boot room, even an old-style pantry. The house stood alongside the green – which doubled as a cricket pitch in the summer – its acre of garden bordered by a drystone wall and five-bar gate. If he could persuade his mother to sell up and buy somewhere smaller and more manageable, his money problems would be solved.

Johnny Reed was at the bar with a pint, flicking through the jobs section of the *Western Daily Press*. Geoffrey wasn't sure how he would be received, but approached him anyway. Lorna had told Olivia they didn't blame Geoffrey for the factory going bust, but that was before the newspapers turned Parry-baiting into a blood sport.

It had started in the local papers – lots of human-interest stories about people like Johnny who had spent his whole working life at Downings. At least Johnny hadn't given an interview. Others did, and were quick to report how things had gone downhill after Bob Downing's death. They talked about him in glowing terms – a modest man who cared deeply about the welfare of his workers and their families. When asked about Geoffrey, it was his public-school education, his big house and flash car they spoke of. 'It'll soon be yesterday's chip paper,' Olivia's dad had said. He had a point. Geoffrey reasoned that if he kept quiet and took it on the chin, the papers would soon lose interest, turn their sights on some other poor bastard. But he hadn't bargained on the national press.

The *Guardian* wanted to run a series of articles aimed at localising the global recession – 'make the macro more micro'. They needed people who were deemed to have run small but vital businesses into the ground – even they had tired of writing about unaccountable bankers and hedge-fund billionaires – someone they claimed symbolised the greed and selfishness of the age. Geoffrey was one of the lucky winners. In a grossly unfair, one-sided polemic, he was pilloried for driving a new Mercedes (a picture of him at the wheel, captioned 'All Right For Some') and denounced for having a personalised number plate. Only ostentatious show-offs had personalised number plates, claimed the *Guardian* from the pulpit of self-righteousness. Braggarts desperate for attention. Olivia had warned him it was crass but he hadn't listened. When had he ever?

'Any luck?' he asked.

Johnny turned the page. 'Nope.'

Bert appeared from out the back, carrying a box of assorted crisps.

'Usual?' he asked Geoffrey.

'Please, Bert. Johnny?'

Johnny took a swig from the near empty glass in his hand. 'Go on then,' he said.

Geoffrey put the ten-pound note on the bar and asked Bert for a pack of salt and vinegar.

'Hope Edward didn't outstay his welcome,' said Geoffrey.

'Huh?'

'Half-term. He seemed to spend more time at your house than at home.'

Bert put two pints and the crisps on the bar, then gave him change from the ten-pound note.

'Didn't notice,' said Johnny. 'Wasn't home much myself.'

'Oh?'

Johnny took a few gulps of beer. He didn't say why he hadn't been home much. Geoffrey couldn't stand this – the stilted sentences, the lack of conversation.

'I saw you drop him off,' he said. 'Edward. You dropped him at the Rectory and drove away.'

Johnny's gaze stayed fixed on his pint.

'Why didn't you come in – say hi, have a drink?'

Johnny made an 'I dunno' face. 'Can't remember. Lorna probably had dinner ready.'

'Look, I'd really like to get past this. I don't know about you, but I could use a friend right now.'

Johnny still hadn't looked him in the eye. 'I saw Manor Farm got sold,' he said.

Geoffrey took a long hit of beer. 'Yeah.'

'Sorry, mate.'

Geoffrey wanted to sink the rest of his beer but didn't have the money for another round.

'At least that's not something you and Lorna need to worry about.'

Their thatched cottage – originally a tied cottage, but purchased before Johnny was born – had been in his family for generations. The whole row of five had been built by the lord of Manor Farm to house those who worked on the land. The irony wasn't lost on Geoffrey.

Johnny's phone beeped. He fished it out of his jeans pocket, read the message on the screen and slipped the phone back. 'Have to go,' he said, finishing his pint in one gulp.

Shame. For the first time in a long time, Geoffrey had felt maybe, just maybe, they could salvage something of their friendship.

'Thanks for the drink.' Johnny patted him on the back and left with a wave to Bert.

Geoffrey counted out the change – enough for one more pint. He downed what was left of his first one, thirsty rugby-player style, and set the empty glass on the bar.

'Put another one in there, would you, Bert.'

Johnny had forgotten his newspaper. Geoffrey glanced at the vacancies section and saw that two had been circled: both casual labouring jobs.

As a boy Geoffrey had hero-worshipped Johnny Reed. Five years older, cool and sporty, he had exactly the type of BMX dirt bike Geoffrey pleaded for each Christmas. Geoffrey was barely on Johnny's radar until a young curate came to live at the Rectory and started up a branch of the Boys' Brigade. Geoffrey was eight or nine so in the Junior section; Johnny and his friends in the Company section. For the most part

Geoffrey was bored – between home and school, he got all the 'Christian development' he needed – but when the curate brought them together for joint activities, Geoffrey couldn't have been happier. It meant he could watch Johnny at close quarters, study the way he spoke, walked, moved – all the better to copy him. Johnny must have noticed because he'd do this martial art thing, complete with Bruce Lee sound effects, pretending to kick-box him in the solar plexus. Geoffrey knew he was doing it to show off to the other Company boys but was euphoric just to be noticed.

Johnny was the curate's favourite, always singled out by him for praise and attention. It was the first time Geoffrey understood the sin of envy – a wriggling snake inside of him that wouldn't go away. On a camping trip to Exmoor, they sat in a circle round a campfire, toasted marshmallows and crumpets, and sang while the curate played the guitar. It had been the best night of Geoffrey's young life. Cut loose from the reserved atmosphere at home and the rules and regulations at school, he could run free. But when the curate told them where to sleep and chose Johnny and another of the older boys to share his tent, Geoffrey could have wept with disappointment.

Olivia said it was a boy crush but it wasn't. Geoffrey clowned around to get noticed, make himself popular, hide the loneliness of being an only child to older parents. They loved him but it felt formal, contained. Johnny was the big brother he prayed for. He knew it was impossible but that didn't stop him yearning.

The young curate left soon after the camping trip, Geoffrey's father disbanded the Boys' Brigade and Johnny stopped coming to the Rectory. A great chasm of loss ripped Geoffrey's world apart. It was as if the fake solar plexus kicks had never happened, as if Exmoor had never happened. Johnny ignored him when their paths crossed in the village. It wasn't until Olivia and Lorna bonded over babies and book club that he and Johnny picked up again. Adults now, equals, Geoffrey's star in the ascendancy. Public school, university, management material at Downings. Johnny was a welder and lived in a tiny cottage with twins. Not that any of that mattered. What mattered was that they were friends.

That was the problem with having nothing to do. It gave him too much time to dwell on things – wallow in nostalgia. Geoffrey had always been more of a doer than a thinker, but recently he found himself brooding for hours on end, reliving whole chapters of his life over and over in his head. What he should have done that he didn't. What he had done that he shouldn't. A spiral of fucked-up thinking if ever there was one.

The internet girls had provided a welcome distraction, but their appeal was starting to wane. How quickly he had become desensitised to their on-screen charms: too one-dimensional, their moves repetitive and predictable. He ached for a flesh-and-blood woman – one he could touch and taste and smell. And it had begun to disturb him that Olivia no longer played any part in his fantasies.

At night, as he lay in bed conjuring up his repertoire of arousing vignettes, Olivia was conspicuous by her absence. On an objective level he understood her sex appeal – the lean, toned body of a teenager, small firm breasts, trim bottom, a tumble of long blonde hair – but on a subjective level, familiarity hadn't bred contempt, exactly, but it had dulled desire. He no longer cast her in his erotic daydreams – those roles went to the bank teller with the tight blouse, the girl in the baker's whose sultry smile he felt sure offered more than a croissant or a French stick, the perky-bottomed weather girl who followed the BBC news. Or they had, until he found a new leading lady in Ruth Rutherford.

When he thought of her, he thought of wild sex in dangerous places, of discipline and threesomes. When he thought of Olivia, he thought of all the mistakes he had made. Through no fault of her own, Olivia had become the antidote to lust. In his fantasies at least, he wanted someone not as decent, not as sweet as his wife – someone a little bit nasty, a little bit dirty, and he was thoroughly ashamed of himself.

His phone rang. Olivia. He almost didn't answer but changed his mind just before it went to voicemail.

'Can't talk long,' she said, chirpy and breathless. 'Late for a staff meeting.'

'Are you running?'

'Walking briskly. Listen, a lot's been happening here – I'll explain later – but in the meantime, how would you feel about coaching rugby?'

'What?'

'Being rugby coach, here at St Bede's. Part-time of course, and hopeless pay, but it might be fun – get you out of the house.'

He didn't need to be asked twice. 'When do I start?'

Seven

The Compton Cross book club met on the first Friday of the month. Olivia had missed October and tonight she would miss November too. She read the book just in case something changed at the last minute and she could make it after all. She knew she was kidding herself, but having another part of her life snatched away stirred an unhealthy bitterness towards Geoffrey and she needed to keep that under control.

What she wanted to know was this. Was Olympia Biddeford – heroine of *Fortune's Rocks* – a good person who did a bad thing, or a bad person who did a good thing? This was exactly why Olivia hated to miss book club. It wasn't just sitting around with her friends, drinking wine and chatting – although that was wonderful – it was the chance to get to the heart of a book, unpick the plot, the sub-plot, the characters and all their flaws.

Lorna and Ellie wouldn't like it – too dense with flowery prose and period detail, a precocious young woman seduced by a married man, their illegitimate child spirited away, innocent lives ruined. Leslie and Jo, on the other hand, relished the drama of forbidden love, families ripped asunder by scandal, a newborn snatched from his unwed mother, only to be reunited years later.

It started Olivia thinking about her own unplanned pregnancy, although in more enlightened times, thank goodness. Her mum had cried a bit when she and Geoffrey broke the news. *Did you hear that, Dave? We're going to be grandparents.* Her dad had asked Olivia if she was sure. He didn't say what about, exactly – that she was pregnant, keeping it, Geoffrey – but she said she was.

Olivia had only ever seen Geoffrey in his university tracksuit or a T-shirt and jeans, but for that occasion he had worn a white shirt with a button-down collar, dark trousers and a leather belt. He looked like a waiter. A very nervous waiter. Olivia's dad gave him a beer and put a reassuring hand on his shoulder. *Looking forward to getting to know you better, son.*

So was Olivia.

She had first noticed him at the beginning of the summer term, hovering round the administration office, looking for excuses to come in and talk to her: checking exam dates, confirming coursework deadlines – information easily found online. Her co-workers teased her, said she had an admirer. He was tall and sturdy, legs thick with muscle. His hair – mid-brown, wavy – needed a good cut, and he really should shave more often. What drew her to him were his lips: full and fleshy, almost feminine. She imagined how they would feel against her own. Kissing was her favourite part of the dating ritual. Intercourse she found brief and perfunctory, but kissing she savoured.

Their first date was in a city-centre pub, crammed with students celebrating the end of exams. He drank beer; she drank wine. Conversation was difficult – 'pardon' and 'sorry, I didn't catch that' featured heavily. When she called him Geoff he corrected her, said it was Geoffrey.

'What's the difference?' she had asked, prompting him to explain that his mother said Cabinet ministers were called Geoffrey, plumbers were called Geoff. 'My dad's a plumber,' said Olivia. 'My mum's a snob,' said Geoffrey.

She asked if he had any plans for the summer and he told her about backpacking through South America, about the mountains, the beaches, the beautiful women. He stroked the side of her face, his meaty hand surprisingly gentle, and said she was beautiful too. The kiss was light as air but she breathed it in and wanted more. 'Let's get out of here,' she said, and he guided her through the crowd like a bodyguard.

The sultry June night had fizzed with energy. He pulled her close and kissed her again. It felt just like she'd imagined it would.

His room was a tip, the floor littered with clothes, empty pizza boxes, lads' mags, CDs and computer games. A grungy duvet hung halfway off the bed. He saw her expression and said, 'Sorry, it's a bit of a mess.' His idea of clearing up was to pile all the clothes in one corner, stack the pizza boxes in another, give the duvet a quick shake and throw it across the bed. The magazines, CD and games, he pushed underneath. He took two cans of beer from an otherwise empty fridge, and offered her one. She shook her head. His chunky index finger barely fitted into the ring-pull. He guzzled like he was quenching a thirst.

There was nowhere to sit but the bed. She kicked off her sandals, lay back and listened: the drone of traffic, a woman shouting, distant music, a car door slamming. 'Can you hear it?' she asked him.

'Hear what?' He put down his beer, lay next to her, propped himself up on an elbow.

'The city,' she said.

He thought about it for a moment before telling her she was funny.

His mouth was soft and tender. She could have lost herself in those kisses but he was impatient to hurry things along. He pulled his T-shirt over his head, revealing muscle and chest hair and the oniony smell of fresh sweat.

Olivia's boyfriends had all been of a type: well groomed and well dressed, the sort that wore aftershave and hair gel. Geoffrey's manliness crashed over her like a tidal wave of testosterone. He undressed her quickly, as though she were a present and he couldn't wait to see what he'd got. Definitely what he wanted, if the instant hard-on was anything to go by.

Jeans and boxers he discarded where he stood and then he lowered himself on top of her, weight on his elbows, hair flopping over his face. When he pushed himself inside her she gasped. 'Slow down,' she whispered, suffocating under the sticky heat of his flesh. He stopped, took a very deliberate breath and closed his eyes. When he opened them he looked at her differently, like it wasn't just her body he saw, but everything else too. He kissed her deeply. He kissed her the whole time. They came at the same moment, their bodies fused in carnal pleasure. She wanted to laugh and cry with the joy of it. It was the first time she had come with a man inside her. Usually she didn't come at all.

Geoffrey had peeled himself off her and rolled on to his back. They stayed like that while they caught their breath, then turned to face each other. He asked if he could see her again. 'Silly question,' she said, smiling. Of course he would see her again. This wasn't a one-night thing – of that she was certain.

Weeks later, when the shock wasn't so raw, she told him she suspected she had conceived that night, that she had felt different. Not in a way she could explain, but she wasn't totally surprised when the test was positive. Geoffrey, on the other hand, had been dumbstruck. He went on about false positives and made her take another test. 'Are you sure you want to keep it?' His way of saying that he didn't.

They had been in his room, cleaned and tidied by Olivia, the general fugginess vastly improved by scented candles and a few of those plug-in things. Geoffrey paced, shaking his head in disbelief. 'We didn't use a condom that first night,' she reminded him.

'I thought you were on the pill,' he said.

Moot point. It had happened – now they had to deal with it. She sat him down, kneeled in front of him, explained that she didn't expect anything. Her parents would look after her like they had always done. She made a joke about her dad and a shotgun wedding, but Geoffrey didn't smile. 'I'm saying I don't expect you to marry me, so you can wipe that look of terror off your face.'

Geoffrey had stood up and paced again. 'You don't understand,' he said. 'My dad's a vicar and my mother – don't get me started. A child born out of wedlock? Shock horror.' He turned away and mumbled something that sounded like 'shock fucking horror'.

Usually Olivia would have objected when he lit a cigarette but she made an exception under the circumstances. 'That's a bit old-fashioned, isn't it? And anyway, you're an adult – surely it's not up to them?'

He pulled on the cigarette as though it was his last, like in those films where the deserter is about to be executed but is granted a final wish. 'My trust fund doesn't pay out until I'm thirty, and only if I'm living my life according to *Christian values*. Big carrot, bigger stick.'

Olivia chose to ignore the emphasis on *Christian values* and made a suggestion. 'So don't tell them.'

He dropped his cigarette into an empty Coke can and tossed it in the wastepaper bin – another acquisition of Olivia's. She tried to hug him but the smell of smoke made her gag. 'That wouldn't work,' he said.

She looked around for a can of air freshener. 'Why not?'

He shrugged, as if resigned to his fate. 'Dunno. It just wouldn't. I'm a terrible liar. Even worse at keeping secrets.'

Good news for Olivia. Secretive liars weren't exactly boyfriend material. 'We'll tell my parents first and take it from there,' she said.

All five of them had had lunch together: Olivia, her parents, her brother, Sam, and Geoffrey. Sam seemed a bit smitten by the handsome rugby player in their midst. The few boyfriends he'd brought home had been big and brawny, just like Geoffrey. Olivia was going to tease him but thought better of it. Geoffrey looked uncomfortable enough already, although he seemed to relax once he saw how well her parents had taken the news that she was pregnant.

Despite Olivia's assurances to the contrary, Geoffrey had expected her dad to grill him about his intentions, a notion Olivia found laughable. *Your parents might say stuff like that but mine don't.* So when Geoffrey announced that he was ready to face up to his responsibilities, it was entirely of his own volition. Olivia didn't like to think of herself as a responsibility to be faced up to. If Geoffrey intended to stick around it should be because he wanted to, not because he felt he had to. When he reached into his pocket Olivia thought it was for cigarettes, but instead he produced a small velvet box. His hand trembled slightly as he opened it, revealing a miniscule diamond set high on a white-gold band.

Olivia's mum covered her mouth, eyes shining, and right there, in front of her family, Geoffrey proposed. If astonishment hadn't rendered Olivia speechless, she would have asked if this was some sort of noble but misguided gesture. She needed to know he was motivated by love, not duty. Her mum inhaled sharply and a state of suspended animation descended on the room.

'Do you love me?' Olivia had asked finally.

'I will,' he said. 'And I'll love our child.'

Until then Olivia had thought of it as *her* child. Geoffrey's involvement seemed once removed – almost theoretical. His pledge to love it moved her deeply. 'I'm willing to believe in our future together,' he said. 'Are you?' She nodded because the words were stuck in her throat. When he slipped the ring on her finger, the joy in the room was palpable.

Quite a different story the following weekend, when they drove to Compton Cross to share their good news with Geoffrey's parents. Olivia rarely ventured into the countryside and had never heard of Compton Cross. All her life she'd lived in the three-bedroom semi her parents had moved into when they married. The Morans were the first people in the cul-de-sac to buy their council house. Over the years they'd added a conservatory and a garage, triple-glazing and a downstairs loo. As they sped along the M4, Olivia had asked Geoffrey about his house but he didn't exactly paint her a picture. 'Old and draughty' was all she could get out of him.

Two hours after they had set out from Reading, they arrived at the Rectory. The front door had a pair of windows on either side and another five above. Ivy impinged on the honey-coloured stone, spreading up and out in tangled fronds. 'This is where you live?'

He cut the engine. 'It's where my parents live.' Her own parents' house could fit in it several times over.

Geoffrey had got out of the car and opened the door for her, his expression grim. She'd tried to hold his hand but he shoved it in his pocket. The front door had opened just before they reached it. Olivia assumed the woman with the steel-grey hair pinned into a bun was his grandmother, but he pecked her cheek and said, 'Hello, Mum.' Her attention turned to Olivia. 'You didn't say you were bringing a friend.' Friend?

'This is Olivia,' he said, moving aside so the two women could size each other up.

His mother extended a hand. 'Rowena Parry.' So formal.

'Olivia Moran,' she said, offering as firm a handshake as was polite. Rowena glanced at Olivia's engagement ring but made no comment.

They followed her into the house. 'You're father's in his study – he'll join us shortly.' A Jack Russell terrier ran towards them, skidding on the smooth flagstones. Geoffrey's face lit up. 'Alf.' He dropped to his knees and enveloped the dog in his arms. Olivia imagined him doing the same with their son. She was sure she was carrying a boy.

Rowena suggested they make themselves comfortable in the drawing room while she checked on lunch. The room was chilly, even though it was a hot August day. French doors overlooked the garden: a great expanse of emerald lawn, flower beds, a cluster of fruit trees. Alf jumped on to the sofa and squeezed himself between Olivia and Geoffrey, his chin resting on Geoffrey's thigh. The furniture looked old and a bit tatty, the sort that gets handed down from dead relatives. A threadbare rug covered much of the floor.

Rowena came in and announced Ronald was putting the finishing touches on tomorrow's sermon. She sat down on a worn leather chair and embarked on an oh-so-polite interrogation.

Olivia felt like she was being interviewed for a job she had no hope of getting. Her father was a plumber, her mother a receptionist, her brother a hairdresser. These facts appeared to make Rowena mildly curious as to why she was entertaining such an ordinary individual in her drawing room, although she did brighten at the news Olivia and Geoffrey had met at university. 'What did you read?' she asked. Olivia glanced at Geoffrey, willing him to steam in and tell the sweet story about how he used to find excuses to come into the office, but no. He let Olivia explain she was an admin assistant in the engineering department, that she'd got the job straight out of sixth-form college and didn't actually have a degree. Olivia felt she had admitted to something scandalous, like being a sex worker or a socialist, but before Rowena could comment, Ronald blustered in, profusely apologetic, and greeted Olivia warmly. With silver hair and half-moon glasses, he had the air of a kindly professor: a man of wise words and philosophical insights. She hoped she wouldn't have to go through her family history again, but Ronald was keen to catch up with his son. They chatted about rugby, his part-time jobs, how the village cricket team was faring this season.

Was Olivia the only one who noticed Geoffrey's foot tapping anxiously on the rug, or that he kept wiping his palms on the sides of his trousers? When Ronald asked if he'd managed to save much for South America, Geoffrey mumbled something about a change of plan. 'Oh?' said Rowena, her eyebrows raised. She had good posture for a woman of her age – spine straight, shoulders back. A soap-and-water kind of woman.

Geoffrey cleared his throat. 'Olivia and I are expecting a baby.' She loved him for the 'and I'. He could have put it all on her.

The dog must have seen something in the garden because he suddenly leaped off the sofa and launched himself at the French doors. Geoffrey leaped up too, evidently glad of the distraction. It loosened the silence that had tightened around them. He let Alf out and watched him tear across the lawn. Olivia wondered if Geoffrey might make a run for it too.

'Can I assume there will be a wedding?' said Ronald tentatively.

Geoffrey remained on his feet. 'I've asked Olivia to marry me and she said yes.'

With this, Ronald got to his feet too and took Geoffrey's hands in his. 'Congratulations,' he said. 'That's wonderful news.' He let go of Geoffrey and kissed Olivia on both cheeks. 'And what do your parents think, dear?' he asked.

'Oh, they're delighted,' she said.

Rowena made the smallest sound, an astringent smile on her face. 'It's wonderful news, isn't it, darling?' said Ronald with a little less conviction than before. In lieu of a response, Rowena had turned her head towards the garden where a terrified kitten cowered halfway up a tree, Alf at the bottom, teeth bared and snarling, daring it to come down.

*

The injustice of being trapped here at school, while the book club had fun without her, gnawed away at Olivia. If she had anything to barter with she could have asked Harriet to take over her duties for the evening, then she would drive to Ellie's, forgo the wine and be back again before eleven. But she had nothing to barter with and she couldn't ask Harriet to cover for her again. It was so unfair, being punished for decisions Geoffrey had made without bothering to consult her. She'd trusted him and he'd let her down.

Even the staffroom aroma of coffee and cake did little to elevate her mood. She spotted Leo Sheridan on his own, sipping from a mug and reading the newspaper. He looked engrossed, but she wanted to ask how Edward was doing – reassurance that the teasing had settled down. She made herself a coffee and was heading in Leo's direction when Martin came in. He clapped his hands to get everyone's attention.

'Sorry to interrupt your lunch break,' he said. 'If I could have a minute of your time?'

He waited for the hum of conversation to die down and announced that Mr Dubois had left St Bede's a month or so earlier than planned. Lisa Pearce and Peter Havant looked over at Olivia. Maddening that she blushed.

'How long before a replacement is found?' asked Rudd Lender. 'And who's going to cover for him in the meantime?'

Martin nodded a good deal to show that he understood Rudd's concern.

'My wife, Ruth, will take French for the remainder of this term. She has an A-level in the subject from Roedean and spent a year in Languedoc before going up to Cambridge. With regard to rugby, I know Mr Sheridan has a full workload, particularly with the Christmas concert coming up, but I do have one or two ideas. I'll let you know more in due course.'

He shot a grateful smile at Leo.

'Can I ask why Mr Dubois left so suddenly?' piped up Lisa Pearce.

Martin hesitated, as if unsure whether to share this information. 'His fiancée has been involved in a car accident – nothing serious, I understand, but naturally he wanted to return home.'

It seemed a bit too convenient to Olivia, but she kept her opinion to herself.

Martin clapped his hands again. 'Now, I've taken up enough of your time. Thank you, everybody.' With that he moved towards the door, touching Olivia lightly on the shoulder as he did so. She followed him into the empty corridor.

'There was something I wanted to ask you. Do you think your husband might consider coaching rugby until a replacement is found?'

That was unexpected. It could be exactly the boost Geoffrey needed. He hated hanging around the Rectory all day, applying for jobs he never got, waiting for the bank to make its next move, Rowena hovering in the background.

'What a terrific idea,' she said. Geoffrey in a tracksuit, running round the rugby field, just like when they had met. 'I'm sure he'd love to.' For the first time in a long while Olivia felt excited, but it didn't last.

'There is something I feel you should know,' said Martin. 'I wasn't sure whether to mention it but I think it's best that I do.'

'Oh?'

'It was Ruth who told me about you and Mr Dubois. She saw you disappear into the pavilion and jumped to the wrong conclusion. It was quite right of her to draw it to my attention, of course.'

How loyal of Martin to defend her. How little she deserved it.

'She really is terribly embarrassed.'

Ruth, embarrassed? Olivia seriously doubted that.

'Anyway, we'd like you to come to dinner tonight, if it's not too short notice. You and your husband. Put the whole misunderstanding behind us.'

Wonderful. Instead of a lively evening with her village friends, she was condemned to another evening of torment with the Rutherfords. Olivia had never hated anyone but what she felt for Ruth came pretty close. How could she sit across the table from her and make polite conversation? An image of her naked breasts kept repeating, rather like a greasy burger. And the look on young Tom's face made her cringe every time she thought of it, which was alarmingly often. Martin took her hesitation the wrong way.

'I'm sorry,' he said. 'I assumed your husband knew about our little misunderstanding.'

Olivia wished he would stop calling it that. The only person who had misunderstood was him. Everyone else – Ruth, Hugo, Tom, Geoffrey – knew exactly what had gone on.

'He does,' said Olivia. 'That was the matter we discussed in my quarters.'

Martin nodded. 'Ah, yes. Well, as I say, best to put it all behind us. So, this evening, around seven?'

She did her best to smile. 'Seven.'

*

Geoffrey met her in the car park at six forty-five, a bottle of Pinot Noir in one hand, a bunch of garage-bought flowers in the other. Under her coat Olivia wore a black woollen dress and the little ankle boots Geoffrey said made her legs look sexy. Her hair was pulled back into a loose knot and a pair of silver earrings sparkled around her jaw line.

He had gone a bit overboard in a suit and tie, but it turned out he'd had a creditors' meeting in Bristol and hadn't gone home to change. His manner was subdued as he brushed his lips against hers. Olivia asked how it went as they headed along the path to the Rutherfords' house, but he said he'd rather not talk about it. Typical. He routinely excluded her from anything to do with business or money, adopting either an infuriating 'I know best' attitude, or more recently, an 'it's my problem, I'll deal with it' stance. Yet he failed to grasp the blindingly obvious: they were in this together. Decisions Geoffrey made impacted on them both, as evidenced by the fact he was living at the Rectory and she was living at St Bede's. She squeezed and relaxed her hands a few times to offset the urge to say this out loud. An evening with Ruth was as much as Olivia could endure without the added friction of falling out with Geoffrey. As if he had been reading her mind, he asked if Martin still had no idea about his wife and the toy boy.

'None whatsoever. I feel sorry for him and the girls. Well, Alice more than Maisie. She got that "rabbit in the headlights" look when I mentioned Harriet would be looking after them tonight.'

'Harriet?'

'Matron.'

'And Alice doesn't like her?'

'No, it's not that. Alice doesn't cope well with change. The slightest deviation from her routine throws her completely. You should have seen her when I said I was having dinner at Mummy and Daddy's house. She pleaded with me to take her too.'

He responded with 'Poor kid', but Olivia could tell he wasn't interested. She struggled to keep up with his pace. He jogged up the steps to the front door and pressed the bell. What to expect? Would Ruth be drunk, hostile? Was contrite too much to hope for?

The door swung open and Martin ushered them in out of the cold. He and Geoffrey shook hands and Martin enthused about the wine, even though it was nothing special. He relieved Olivia of the lacklustre mix of carnations, freesia and gypsophila, wrapped in a sheath of cellophane, and put them on the sideboard so he could hang up their coats.

'I'll take these to Ruth in the kitchen,' he said, gathering up the wine and flowers. 'Why don't you make yourselves comfortable in the sitting room.'

Olivia dreaded coming face to face with Ruth. She was about to confide this to Geoffrey when Ruth breezed in, jeans tucked into leather riding boots, blouse snug over her bust, a jaunty silk scarf tied at her throat. Her poker-straight fringe had been cut into a sharp line just above her eyebrows, giving her face a strong, geometric look. Martin followed behind with a bottle of Prosecco – Geoffrey's least favourite drink.

'Darling,' said Martin, pouring the Prosecco into flutes. 'You remember Geoffrey Parry.'

'Of course,' she said, air-kissing him. 'Lovely to see you again.'

Olivia had underestimated how hard being pleasant and smiley would be, now that she knew what a loathsome individual Ruth was. Not a trace of remorse or regret. Quite the opposite – she set about quizzing Geoffrey, her questions polite but probing: *Where are you living now? What are your plans? How are you managing on your own?*

When Martin suggested they make their way to the dining table Geoffrey led, even though he'd never been to the house before. 'Left,' called Martin when Geoffrey stopped in the hallway. They walked in single file, Olivia warily bringing up the rear.

The table was set more formally than the last time she had eaten here: starched white tablecloth, place mats depicting hunting scenes, silver cutlery and linen napkins. That had been supper with the children – this, apparently, was a dinner party.

Olivia's parents didn't have dinner parties. If friends came over to eat it was usually a take-away – Chinese, Indian, pizza if Olivia and Sam had their way – or some sort of buffet arrangement with everyone helping themselves. Seating was informal – plates on laps the preferred option. Bottled beer and supermarket wine fuelled lively conversation. If her dad started on about politics her mother would cut him off – *that's enough of that, Dave –* and top up everyone's drink.

Nothing in Olivia's simple, no-nonsense background had prepared her for the complex rituals of the formal dinner party: effusive greetings, wine, exaggerated interest in the life and opinions of others, wine, endless discussion of school fees and house prices, wine, thinly veiled competition as to who has had the most exotic holiday, wine, inappropriate comments about a mutual acquaintance, wine, a glimpse of marital discord between at least one couple, wine, indiscriminate flirting, wine, escalation of marital discord, wine, coffee offered and declined, yet more wine, disproportionate gratitude towards the hosts, amid slurred and emotional farewells. Such evenings left Olivia with a hangover and a voyeuristic sense of having seen and heard too much.

The first course was avocado – smoky, creamy, perfectly ripe – and prawns. Olivia disliked seafood but washed it down with wine. Martin made a fuss of thanking Geoffrey for stepping in as rugby coach, saying how lucky they were to have the makings of an excellent team, not to mention first-rate facilities.

'Those groundsmen do sterling work,' he said, popping a prawn into his mouth.

Nobody moved or spoke. Olivia couldn't look at Geoffrey, his ribald sense of humour a clear and present danger, but nor could she look at Jezebel Ruth, or clueless, cuckolded Martin. She picked up her glass and drained it. Thank God for wine.

The chicken languished in some sort of curry sauce, served with brown rice and a platter of roasted root vegetables. It was actually rather good but Olivia had no appetite. Watching Ruth play wife, hostess and friend had literally sickened her.

Geoffrey had no such qualms, it seemed. He tucked into his food with gusto, complimenting Ruth on her culinary skills. She responded with compliments of her own: on his smart suit, his reputation as a sportsman, his man-sized appetite. If she had stuck her tongue down his throat she couldn't have been more obvious. Was she flirting with Geoffrey because she found him attractive, or was it to annoy Olivia or humiliate Martin? All three, perhaps. Martin chose to ignore it.

'How are the girls?' he asked Olivia, topping up her glass with a splash more Pinot Noir.

She anticipated tomorrow's headache but drank anyway. 'Maisie's settled in well. She has friends, gets stuck into things. She seems happy.'

'Good, good,' said Martin. 'One always wonders about boarding them so young.'

Olivia wondered about boarding them at all given that their mother didn't work and their house was at the end of the driveway. She suspected it had been Ruth's idea and any objections Martin may have had were swiftly overruled.

'And Alice?' asked Martin.

Ruth turned away from Geoffrey and looked directly at Olivia. 'What about Alice?' she said, pushing her hair behind her ears.

Olivia feared she had been unprofessional, that this was a discussion she should have had privately with the Rutherfords. Ruth kept her gaze level, waiting for an answer.

'Alice is more timid than her sister,' said Olivia.

'Go on,' said Martin.

'She gets rather homesick, especially at bedtime.'

Martin looked concerned, parallel creases appearing between his eyebrows. He was about to speak when Ruth jumped in.

'Alice needs to toughen up a bit,' she said, jutting her chin forward in the same way Maisie did when she made a point.

Olivia lowered her eyes, sad to hear a child's unhappiness so thoughtlessly dismissed, and by her own mother of all people.

'Desert?' said Ruth coolly, standing to clear away plates.

More food Olivia didn't want. Geoffrey squeezed her knee under the table and threw her one of his 'chin up' smiles. She was surprised when Ruth opened another bottle of wine. She was already tipsy – flushed cheeks, heavy eyelids, speech a little less clipped than usual – and Geoffrey had to drive back to Compton Cross. Those narrow country lanes were lethal.

'Cheesecake,' said Ruth, plonking a serving plate in the centre of the table. The cake was heaped with berries and thin curls of chocolate.

'Wow,' said Geoffrey. 'That looks amazing.'

'Doesn't it?' said Ruth. 'Sadly, I can't take the credit.'

She placed a thick slab on a plate and handed it to Geoffrey. Olivia watched his eyes widen in anticipation. The next plate she handed to Olivia.

'Alicia Burton's work,' explained Martin. 'Just a small one for me, darling.'

Ruth rolled her eyes and cut him a slab. Everyone waited for Ruth to start.

'Mmm,' she said, her mouth full. She wiped some chocolate from the corner of her lips. 'Alicia was here all afternoon. Just found out that Toby, her ex, is getting married again. Utterly heartbroken.'

Olivia pictured Toby Burton: dark-haired, stocky, a bit full of himself.

'He keeps her terribly short of money,' said Ruth.

'Darling,' said Martin gently. 'I don't think we should—'

Ruth took a slug of wine before she cut him off. 'So she's starting up her own little cottage industry, making cakes. We're her guinea pigs. What do you think?'

'Delicious,' said Geoffrey, scraping the last bits of berry and chocolate from his plate.

'And as if he hasn't hurt her enough,' continued Ruth, 'Toby has asked Freddie to live with him and his new wife. Can you believe it?'

Divorce was rotten, doubly so when children were involved. Olivia was no fan of Alicia Burton, but to lose her husband and her son? She couldn't imagine the pain. 'Maybe he won't want to go,' said Olivia. 'And even if he does, once the novelty wears off I'm sure he'll want to come home.'

'Let's see, shall we,' said Ruth with a derisory snort, as if Olivia had said the most stupid thing in the world.

*

Spits of icy rain accompanied their walk back to the car.

'That was horrible,' said Olivia, wrapping her scarf around her neck.

'It wasn't too bad,' said Geoffrey. 'Food was first rate.'

God, he was infuriating, bouncing along on the surface of things, oblivious to the tangled undercurrents that swirled beneath, content to be fed and watered and patted on the back. It took a hefty dose of willpower not to say so, but Olivia didn't have the energy for an argument until Geoffrey followed up with, 'Martin's a bit of an old woman,' at which point she had to protest.

'Martin isn't the one shagging a junior – *very* junior – member of staff. Martin isn't the one putting his family in jeopardy. Martin isn't the one using me as a scapegoat. But hey, you're only my husband – no reason to expect your support.'

She huffed off down the path, leaving Geoffrey standing there, palms open in a 'what the hell was that?' stance. He jogged after her and grabbed her shoulder.

'Olivia?'

She stopped but wouldn't look at him.

'Have I done something wrong?' he asked.

Seriously? His feigned innocence was enough to detonate the row that had been brewing all evening. 'Yes, you've done something wrong. You're the reason I have to live here and not Manor Farm. You're the reason I have to miss book club again. You're the reason I have to put up with that vile woman.'

Geoffrey opened his mouth to say something but Olivia wasn't finished.

'How can you be so pally with her? She lied to Martin about me to cover up her own sleazy behaviour and instead of apologising, or thanking me for keeping her sordid secret, she acts all imperious and spends the entire evening coming on to you. How do you think that makes me feel?'

Geoffrey looked genuinely surprised by her tirade. 'I'm sorry,' he said, gripping her shoulders. 'I thought you wanted to build bridges, smooth things over. You were worried about losing your job and then I got a job of sorts, and I just thought –'

Did every argument have to be like this? Olivia launching into justifiably hurt mode – *why don't you ever defend me?* – Geoffrey acting all hard done by and turning it round on her.

She dislodged his hands with a quick flick of her shoulders and strutted off down the path, but her resolve weakened to nothing. Perhaps he thought befriending Ruth was the best way to support her. When he caught up she allowed him to fold her into a bear hug, her cheek resting against his chest. She remembered the first time she saw his chest, his Herculean body, naked and eager to devour her.

'Sorry,' she said. 'Tough couple of weeks.'

'Tell me about it,' he said.

The spell of discontent had been broken. Geoffrey kissed her, his mouth warm and winey. Spits of rain became sheets of rain. They pulled apart and hurried towards the car.

'Are you sure you're OK to drive?' she asked.

All manner of anxieties churned inside her – the Mercedes spinning into a ditch, Geoffrey bleeding to death from a head wound. She never used to think like that – a side effect of losing control over so much of her life.

'Are you offering a bed for the night?' he said, his tone faux seductive.

He kissed her again – not a goodnight kiss but a passionate 'I want you now' kiss. His hand found its way inside her coat and kneaded her bottom. Her own hand, he pressed against his erection. It had been so long since she'd had him inside of her and she wanted him badly, but not here, not like this.

'Get in the car,' he said.

She looked around.

'There's no one here,' he said, his hand now cupping her breast. 'Come on, it'll be good.'

She was tempted, she really was, but the whole evening had made her feel tainted by association. And there was something desperate about Geoffrey's overture, as if he needed to put right all the recent failures of their shrivelled sex life.

'I can't,' she said. 'I'm sorry.'

She waited for him to say something but he let go of her and took a step back.

'I'm sorry,' she said again, wondering if maybe she should have put her own reticence aside and done it for him.

He shook his head, as if it was nothing. 'Better make a move then,' he said, turning his back on her and opening the car door.

She stood in the slanting rain and watched him drive away. Loneliness swelled inside her, dense, heavy and cold.

Eight

Well, that was a bucket of iced water in the face. Ruth coming on to him all night had made him horny as hell, and it wasn't as if he and Olivia couldn't have done with a bit of spur-of-the-moment sex. Anything to put some heat back into their relationship. Would it have killed her to have a quickie in the car? The way Ruth had revved him up, it would have been very quick indeed.

He overshot his turning and realised how fast he was driving. If he wasn't actually over the limit, he must have been close. Every time he had taken a drink of wine, Ruth had topped up his glass. Her own too. Having her flirt with him right in front of Olivia and Martin thrilled Geoffrey more than he could have imagined. It smacked of exhibitionism, only fully clothed. Ruth had shown no trace of embarrassment – not about flirting, not about the whole lurid groundsman thing. On the contrary. She breezed around, shoulders back, chin up. If anything, she seemed proud of herself.

It was the first time Geoffrey had come face to face with Ruth since he had begun fantasising about her. He didn't much care for her haircut – too severe – but there was something strict about it that aroused him. She wasn't pretty in the conventional sense. Sparse eyebrows that faded into her skin tone. A strong, patrician nose was her best feature. Her mouth was something of a disappointment. A voluptuous pout would have made all the difference, but Ruth's lips had little flesh or shape – no more than a straight pink slash. Her smile revealed smallish teeth and a tad too much gum. And maybe it was the blunt bobbed hair, but her jaw seemed wide and angular, almost masculine. Individually, none of her features stood out as attractive, but the combined effect was very attractive indeed. It defied explanation, but there it was. The eye of the beholder, perhaps? Maybe confidence was what made her sexy, and she had that in spades.

Her breasts strained against the sheer fabric of her blouse. A D-cup he'd guess, with dark, cigar-stub nipples. Her stomach looked reasonably flat considering she'd had two children. Jeans allowed a good view of her bottom. Not as pert as Olivia's but nicely rounded. The odd thing was, Ruth wasn't his type: older than him, more promiscuous than him, cleverer than him. None of these things appealed, yet *she* appealed.

University had taught Geoffrey to be wary of clever women. Engineers were practical rather than intellectual – doers rather than thinkers.

In his first year he had had a brief relationship with a dusky-skinned English literature student called Anna. To say she was well read was an understatement. The occasional reference to Oscar Wilde aside, never had Geoffrey's ignorance of great literary works been more obvious. She talked about Chaucer, Shakespeare, Austen and Dickens as if they were personal friends of hers. It was Geoffrey's first taste of regular sex so he was willing to put up with a lot. He feigned interest in her mind to gain access to her body. After they'd had sex, all he wanted was to drift into blissful oblivion, but Anna would pull a book from one of the many piles that littered her room, and read to him. He could have coped with that – memories of being lulled off to sleep with a bedtime story – but she expected him to contribute, to comment, even analyse, for Christ's sake. It was beyond him. He thought Chaucer and Shakespeare impenetrable, Austen irrelevant and Dickens a purveyor of human misery. When he and Anna parted company after two months together, she detailed his shortcomings in a handwritten ten-page letter. He stopped reading after four and tossed it in the bin.

A mathematician named Lucy took Anna's place in his bed. Born of an English mother and Japanese father, she had been schooled in the Kumon method from the age of three. Geoffrey regretted admitting he had never heard of the Kumon method because it prompted a long and comprehensive explanation. He made a mental note of key phrases to give the impression he had listened: *self-learning programme, independent study skills, resolve complex problems.* It sounded dire but she was pretty in an elfin sort of way, with straight black hair and a china-doll face. When they had sex she made a bewildering array of noises – squeals, yelps, moans, cries. At first he found them distracting but if he stopped doing what he was doing, she urged him to carry on. The soundtrack to her orgasm was a long, high-pitched whine. Geoffrey suspected that everyone in the halls of residence knew when Lucy was coming. On one occasion he thought he heard a distant round of applause. That wasn't why he finished with her, though – it was her complete lack of humour. Geoffrey liked few things more than a bloody good laugh and he didn't know if it was a by-product of her ethnic heritage, her extreme braininess, or some irreversible developmental damage inflicted by the mysterious Kumon method, but outside of the bedroom, the girl just didn't know how to have fun.

These first-year relationships set a precedent for the rest of Geoffrey's time at Reading. He spent three months being analysed by a psychology student – everything he did or didn't say, everything he did or didn't do. If she hadn't been so adventurous in bed he would have finished with her sooner, but in the end even the inventiveness of their sex life wasn't enough to endure endless probing about his dreams, his motivations, his early masturbatory experiences.

An economist named Janey pursued him during his second year – had a thing about rugby players, apparently. She was earnest, intense and ambitious; the exact opposite of Geoffrey. Yet again, it was sex that kept him interested. Janey liked to be picked up and thrown around a bit, carried to bed over his shoulder, put across his knee and spanked. That didn't stop him dumping her after a long and tedious polemic about inherited wealth. All the ills and excesses of capitalism could be laid at the door of people like him. News to Geoffrey. Turned out she was a communist with Maoist leanings, but Geoffrey chose to remember her simply as a good lay.

By his final year he had learned his lesson. He substituted one-night stands for relationships until a dose of chlamydia made him stop and think. It was during this period of enforced celibacy that he spotted Olivia putting mail into the student pigeonholes and struggling to reach the top two rows. She was on tiptoes, calf muscles taut, bottom clenched with the effort of stretching her arm as far as it would go. He walked up behind her and plucked the mail from her hand. 'Let me,' he said. For a second she just stared at him, surprised, and he wondered if she was like those strident feminists on campus, mortally offended by the assumption she needed the help of a man. Not Olivia. She smiled coyly. 'Thank you.' He hadn't expected this petite, ponytailed girl with the tiny waist and angelic face to have the huskiest, most seductive voice he had ever heard. It delivered a shot of excitement straight to his groin. Turned out it was the tail end of laryngitis but dear God, it was sexy. He watched her walk towards the admin office, bottom like a ripe peach, ponytail swishing from side to side.

It wasn't just about Olivia's physical appeal. After three years dating clever undergraduates, he was ready for someone easy-going, uncomplicated, less likely to make demands. OK, that hadn't worked out quite as he had imagined, but he'd had his fill of academic women – of that, he was sure. Until Ruth Rutherford. She mentioned in passing she had read history at Cambridge, but was more interested in hearing tales from the village, the rugby club, his annual skiing trips. 'Go on,' she teased, nudging him with her elbow, 'tell me what you boys get up to.' Her interest appeared risqué and genuine, and he was ridiculously flattered. It had been a while since a woman had shown any real interest in him. Not even his own wife.

*

The next morning he slept in, his thick head the after-effect of too much red wine. Perhaps he shouldn't have driven after all. Still, he got back in one piece and it wasn't as though he made a habit of it.

By the time he padded down to the kitchen to make a cup of tea, his mother had already walked the dogs. They lay curled in their beds, quiet and obedient, not bothering to get up and greet him.

'Late night?' she asked, vigorously kneading a lump of dough.

Geoffrey filled the kettle. 'I'm out of practice,' he said.

Radio Four was on, a sombre, slightly nasal woman droning on about the enduring nature of misogyny.

'Cup of tea?' he asked, reaching for a mug.

'Please,' said his mother.

She slapped the dough into a bowl to prove and covered it with a damp cloth. Geoffrey heaped a couple of spoons of English Breakfast into the teapot and poured the boiling water. It seemed as good a time as any to broach the subject he had been dreading.

'Manor Farm has been sold,' he said. 'Got a call from the agent last week.'

His mother sat down and gave the tea a quick stir. That she didn't say anything suggested this wasn't news to her.

'It got me thinking,' he said.

'Oh?' she said, pouring the tea.

Geoffrey fetched some milk from the fridge, turned down the radio and took a seat opposite her. 'It got me thinking about this house,' he said, casting his gaze around:

bottle-green paint peeling from the walls, brown Bakelite switches, marked and chipped quarry tiles.

'What about it?' she said, following his gaze.

'I wondered if maybe it was time to think about getting somewhere a bit more manageable?'

There – he'd said it. His mother pulled her chin into her neck.

'Why would I do that?'

It was important that he cut through the fogginess in his head and dealt with this sensitively. He put a splash more milk in his tea to cool it down, then took a few gulps.

'It's such a large house – a complete money pit.'

'What do you mean, a money pit?'

'So much needs doing. The wiring is a liability – you remember the power cut a few weeks ago? – and the windows need replacing. Not to mention the kitchen.'

'It's a perfectly good kitchen.' Her tone was defensive, warning Geoffrey to proceed with caution.

'It's so expensive to heat too. Oil costs a fortune, Mum. And you don't even use half the rooms.'

She pursed her lips. 'What about the school holidays when Edward and Olivia are here?'

Geoffrey put the milk back in the fridge. Maybe he needed to come at it from a different angle.

'Mum, you've been wonderful, offering us a home in our hour of need.' He reached over and patted her hand. 'And you know how much I, *we*, appreciate it, but it won't be forever. I just wonder if this might be a good time to think about downsizing?'

She turned her face towards the window, milky with condensation. 'Downsizing? How can you even suggest something like that when you know how much I'm missing your father?'

So was Geoffrey. A heart attack in someone with no history of heart disease, a healthy non-smoker, meant that the most likely cause, surely the only cause, was stress. And what did his father have to be stressed about? Very little, until Geoffrey's showy avarice and poor business judgement robbed many of his parishioners of their livelihoods. When the press named and shamed Geoffrey, they made much of the fact he was a vicar's son, insinuating he should have known better, thereby dragging his kind, fair-minded father into it. Death by disappointment.

His mother emptied her tea into the Butler sink, scrubbed the mug with a shrivelled Brillo pad, grabbed a tea towel and applied so much elbow grease you would have thought she was trying to erase the pattern. It was like watching a malevolent mime. When she had finished she remained facing the window, her back to him.

'It's been a comfort having you here, Geoffrey, but I'm shocked that you would ask me to sell my home. Your home too. You grew up here. All my memories of your father are here.' Her voice trembled with recrimination. She turned towards him, eyes wet and rheumy.

'I'm sorry. I didn't mean to upset you. Forget I said anything.'

She nodded and dabbed away a few tears. Geoffrey wondered if making his mother cry – a widow in mourning – was a new low for him?

He had planned to make a bacon sandwich – grease to soak up what remained of last night's alcohol – but couldn't stomach it now.

*

The one good thing on the horizon, the only thing he had to look forward to, was coaching rugby. Edward said he wouldn't believe it until he turned up on the pitch. Well, here he was.

His first session was with the top-formers: Edward and his friends. Geoffrey introduced himself even though most of them knew him anyway, and told them a bit about when he had played rugby at St Bede's. He was quite enjoying the indulgence of a trip down memory lane, but wrapped it up when he saw Edward roll his eyes. Geoffrey began to put the boys through their paces: tackling, passing, kicking, rucking. Despite some individual talent – most notably, Edward and Freddie Burton – as a team they were shambolic. Geoffrey wasn't sure they were playing in the correct positions so set about reassigning them. Freddie Burton wasn't happy to be moved from fly half to the wing and wasn't shy in saying so. Geoffrey got Edward to take his place and moved short, thickset Finn Harding from the wing to front row. He took the taller, faster Ben Scott-Lessing from the scrum and put him on the wing, where speed was of the essence.

Their biggest problem was a lack of tactical skills, but those could be taught. What impressed Geoffrey was their commitment, how hard they tried. Edward was fearless, charging into every situation even if he ended up in a heap on the ground. In the scrum, Finn Harding used his bull-like strength to steamroller his opponents. And once Freddie Burton had sulked a bit about his move to the wing, he showed off his speed and agility. Geoffrey didn't like it when he heard the other boys call Edward 'Goldilocks', although Edward himself didn't seem too bothered. As a nickname it seemed a bit effeminate. Geoffrey had tried to persuade Edward to have a haircut during half-term but he always found some excuse or other. None of the other boys had a mop of blonde curls. Over the Christmas holiday, Geoffrey would insist on a visit to the barber.

The steel-hued sky had dumped a week's worth of rain and waterlogged the pitch, but the boys were undeterred. If anything, they revelled in the chance to roll around in the mud. When their ninety minutes was over, Geoffrey was all fired up to deliver a rousing pep talk before sending them off for their showers, but they were soaked and filthy and he didn't want them to catch cold.

He had half an hour before his next session with the under nines, enough time for a coffee in the staffroom. Olivia had warned him about the staffroom coffee but as long as it was hot and strong, he didn't care. He was slightly embarrassed about having tried to persuade her to have sex in the car, but then why should he be? They were man and wife, and it wouldn't have been the first time they had done it in a car.

They bumped into each other outside the main hall. It was odd seeing her at school but not at home. She did a double-take, like it was odd for her too. Neither of them mentioned the previous night.

'You're soaked,' she said. 'How did it go?'

'Good. Very good actually.'

He instinctively leaned in to kiss her but she pulled away and looked around.

'You can't do that here,' she said in one of her loud whispers.

'Sorry,' he said, mimicking her.

'Where are you heading?'

'Boys' changing room, then staffroom.'

'I'll see you in there,' she said with a flirty little wave.

He knew it was a cliché, but everything about the changing room actually did seem smaller. Geoffrey remembered having to stand on the slatted wooden bench to hang his games bag on his hook – he couldn't have been more than seven or eight. The familiar fug of wet clothes, socks and stale sweat brought it back with a rush. His nostalgia was interrupted by raised voices, one of them Edward's.

Geoffrey followed the commotion to the shower area where Edward and Freddie Burton, towels around their waists, were squaring up to each other. Before they saw him there, Edward lunged forward, pushed Freddie hard and shouted at him to shut the fuck up. Geoffrey had never heard his son use that word. In the split second before he reacted to whatever the hell was happening, he registered a pang of loss. His kind, sweet boy was growing up: less kind, less sweet. Inevitable though that was, Geoffrey wished he hadn't witnessed such irrefutable evidence.

Freddie reached a hand to the wall and steadied himself.

'What's going on?' said Geoffrey.

He was here to congratulate them on their hard work, not break up a fight. Edward's face was tight with rage, his fists clenched, chest heaving. Freddie goaded him with a sneer.

'Will someone please tell me—'

Before Geoffrey could finish, Edward threw a punch. As Freddie staggered back, his towel came undone and dropped on the wet floor.

'Stupid fag,' he yelled, scooping up the towel and quickly covering himself.

He wiped his bloodied nose and took a counter-swipe at Edward. Geoffrey grabbed his arm before he made contact.

'Get off me,' said Freddie.

'What on earth—?'

Geoffrey let go of Freddie's arm and turned to see a shocked Leo Sheridan. Before Geoffrey could attempt an explanation, Leo took control of the situation.

'Freddie, get dressed and ask Matron to look at your face. Edward, sort yourself out and wait for me at the headmaster's office. The rest of you have classes to get to.'

He looked at Geoffrey. 'If I could see you outside, Mr Parry.'

Geoffrey felt like a naughty schoolboy again. He wanted to go to Edward; chastise him, comfort him, be his dad, not his rugby coach. Instead he followed Leo.

They stayed in the corridor just outside the changing room so they could hear if anything started up again.

'What the hell was that about?' asked Leo.

'I've no idea. It started before I got there.'

'And what happened to Freddie's face?'

It went against every paternal instinct, but what choice did he have? 'Edward hit him.'

The first of the boys traipsed out, animated with the excitement of having witnessed a fight. They shut up when they saw Geoffrey and Leo, only to carry on when they thought they were out of earshot.

'I didn't realise it had escalated,' said Leo.

'What had escalated?'

'Didn't Olivia tell you?'

'Tell me what?'

'Edward and Freddie had a bit of a set-to.'

'When? What about?'

'It's been brewing for a week or so. Freddie implied something inappropriate between Olivia and Hugo Dubois. Edward jumped in to defend her.'

Olivia hadn't mentioned it, but then apart from dinner at the Rutherfords', they had hardly spoken. So, Edward had gone into battle for her, certainly not something he'd learned from him. When had he ever defended Olivia against his mother's subtle attempts to undermine her? Yet without a moment's hesitation, his twelve-year-old son had stood up for her. Geoffrey felt proud and ashamed at the same time.

'There was a bit of friction between them during training,' he said. 'Nothing really.'

Leo sighed, exasperated. 'Well, whatever it was, it's gone too far.'

Edward came out of the changing room, his expression sullen but defiant. They walked in silence to Martin's office, where Geoffrey was momentarily taken aback to see Arthur Heather's wife; his widow. He had forgotten she worked as school secretary.

'Mr Parry,' she said. 'This is a surprise.'

He was in no mood for social pleasantries. 'Mrs Heather,' was all he said, no 'how are you', or 'nice to see you'.

'Is the headmaster free?' asked Leo.

'One moment,' she said, picking up the phone.

Ten seconds later they were in Martin's office, Leo recounting what he witnessed in the changing room, Geoffrey doing the same. Edward said nothing until asked a direct question.

'Why did you hit Freddie Burton?' said Martin.

Edward's shoulders rose and dropped. 'I'm sorry, sir.'

'I don't doubt it,' said Martin, 'but that doesn't answer my question.'

Geoffrey wanted to encourage him to own up to whatever it was, but before he could, Edward spoke.

'We had an argument, sir.'

Martin didn't hide his impatience. 'Clearly. What was it about?'

'Rugby, sir.'

'Rugby?'

'Yes, sir. Freddie was angry that Dad – Mr Parry – made us change positions.'

'Is that correct, Mr Parry?'

Geoffrey nodded. He wanted to justify himself, say how much better they had played in their new positions, but what was the point? His son was in trouble and it was his fault.

'Well, I shall be speaking to Freddie Burton once Matron has finished with him, but I want you to understand that your behaviour was totally and completely unacceptable.'

'Yes, sir.'

'As Christians we abhor violence,' continued Martin sternly. 'And frankly, Edward, I expect better of you.'

'Yes, sir.'

'I want you to think about the example you have set, and in the meantime, I will think about how you should be punished.'

'Yes, sir. Sorry, sir.'

Once they had been dismissed, the three of them stood in the corridor beyond Claire Heather's desk, each waiting for the other to speak. Leo appeared to have nothing to add to Martin's comments, so excused himself, leaving father and son alone.

Geoffrey was at a loss. Aggression and surliness were so out of character for Edward. A stark reminder that he was changing – getting to the age when hormones did strange things to a boy. There was a question that had been preying on Geoffrey's mind and he needed to ask it, even though he was wary of the answer.

'What is it with you and Freddie Burton?'

Edward looked at him from under his hank of damp curls and replied with an exaggerated shrug. He seemed to have slipped into the moody teenager phase without Geoffrey having noticed.

Geoffrey wished Edward would talk to him, tell him what was going on. And why hadn't Olivia mentioned this bad blood between Edward and Freddie – given him the heads up before he steamed in and started changing the team around?

'I have to get to class,' said Edward.

That didn't answer Geoffrey's question. He watched Edward walk away, his shoulders hunched. They had always been so close – had so much in common. Weekends they would go hiking or fishing, maybe watch Bath play rugby at the Rec. And Geoffrey never missed Edward's own rugby matches, home or away.

Geoffrey thought about trying to find Olivia for her take on it, but he had another coaching session to get to. His heart wasn't in it now. As he trudged back over to the pitch, he wished he hadn't taken the bloody job.

*

His mother gave him the silent treatment that evening, but Geoffrey wasn't in the mood for chit-chat so her aloofness was something of a blessing. He had his dinner on a tray in front of the television and went to bed early, having polished off the last of his father's Scotch.

Olivia sent a text saying she'd heard about Edward and Freddie and would try to phone tomorrow. Geoffrey had so looked forward to coaching the team, spending time at his old school. Spending time with his only son. Could nothing ever go right for him? His relationship with Edward was one of the few elements of his life that had survived intact when everything else was falling apart, and yet he felt something had shifted.

Freddie had called Edward 'Goldilocks', a stupid fag. Was it just a bit of name-calling or was it recognition? Children can be very intuitive. They have an uncanny knack of sniffing out the merest hint of difference in their peers. Did the other boys see something in Edward that Geoffrey didn't?

Nine

Adversity doesn't build character; it reveals it. Something Olivia had heard or read – she couldn't remember where. Not important anyway. What was important was the truth of it.

Last week she had learned that her sweet, gentle boy had punched another boy with enough force to blacken both his eyes.

Freddie had been in a throng of top-formers – Edward conspicuous by his absence – that filed into assembly a few yards ahead of her. One of the boys said something that made Freddie turn his head, and Olivia's stomach curdled. His left eye was puffy but the vicious purple swelling around the right had almost closed it. She covered her mouth.

When Geoffrey had explained what happened, she heard the words but couldn't relate them to their son. Edward wouldn't hurt anyone – he wasn't capable. Then she had seen Freddie's face.

Edward was banned from rugby for two weeks. He also had to write an essay on why violence was never the answer, and read it out at school assembly. His voice had begun to deepen. The faintest sheen of oil highlighted his nose and forehead. He spoke of shame and regret, things a boy his age should know nothing about. Olivia had listened, her heart a jagged stone in her chest.

A few days later Martin told her he was satisfied with the way Edward had accepted his punishment and once the rugby ban was spent, best if they put it all behind them. Fine in principle but how could they when it was written, quite literally, all over Freddie's face?

It was difficult for Geoffrey too. He had to train the team without Edward, who spent those sessions confined to the library. Freddie had been made captain and Edward would have to win back his place when he rejoined the team. Geoffrey said Freddie treated him with contempt – had no respect whatsoever. Olivia reminded him of the Burtons' domestic troubles and how difficult it must be for Freddie, caught between his warring parents. Geoffrey had little sympathy, adamant that Edward would only have acted under extreme provocation. Burton is a nasty little shit, was how Geoffrey put it.

When Olivia wasn't worrying about her own child, she was worrying about other people's. She had hoped that once Alice Rutherford got used to the boarding regime she would grow in confidence. Instead, she became more timid and withdrawn, inseparable from her one-eyed teddy bear. Alice spoke only when spoken to – never chatted or initiated conversation like the other girls did. Olivia mentioned it to Harriet but she didn't seem unduly concerned. *They're not all bubbly little things, you know.*

Maisie was the polar opposite: gregarious, always showing off, only happy when she was the centre of attention. That was wearing enough, but she had started picking on the quieter girls, taking pleasure in their distress. Alice was beside herself when Teddy mysteriously vanished.

She ran round the dorm, eyes wide with unspoken terror, pulling back every duvet, searching under every bed, until after a demented ten minutes Maisie 'found' him behind a bookshelf.

A similar thing happened with Helena Hardy-Leach. She had spent hours completing a project on 'The Meaning of Christmas', painstakingly cutting out nativity scenes from old Christmas cards and sticking them in her folder, when it suddenly went missing from her bedside locker. Another search ensued, only this time when the folder was found (stuffed under Helena's trunk), it had been ruined with what looked like orange squash. Helena sobbed for the best part of an hour, unable to understand how such a thing could have happened. She only calmed down when Olivia offered to help her make a new one and as they hunched over the table, cutting out figures of baby Jesus and the Virgin Mary, Maisie and her little gang sniggered in their sofa huddle, clearly delighted with themselves.

Olivia regretted having raised her concerns over dinner at the Rutherfords'. Ruth's dismissive remarks had made her feelings on the subject abundantly clear. And anyway, given Edward's recent behaviour, Olivia no longer felt in a position to comment. Easy to share your thoughts on parenthood when your own child was a paragon of goodness. Less so when they patently were not.

The person she longed to talk to was Lorna, to compare notes, find out if Josh had had any angry outbursts, shown any signs of aggression. She wanted Lorna to reassure her it was normal, a phase, something and nothing.

The half-term afternoon they spent together in Bath, Lorna had bemoaned Lily's mood swings, the week of hell before her period arrived, her sudden interest in make-up and padded bras. Josh hardly got a mention. Olivia remembered Lorna's throwaway comment about boys being so much easier. Naturally she had agreed.

She walked round the quad, eyes fixed on her phone, searching for that elusive signal. A diamond frost glinted under the pale mid-morning sun, rendering everything pristine and brittle. Five minutes until break, until she was surrounded by a swarm of noisy children. She squinted against the light, her perseverance rewarded with three whole bars. When Lorna answered it was in a hushed voice.

'Can I call you back?'

Four minutes until break. 'Not really. Is it a difficult time?'

'I'm working – not supposed to take calls.'

'Working? Where?'

Silence. Olivia checked the magic bars again – two now – and waited for Lorna's reply.

'Axbridge.'

'Really? Doing what?'

Another silence.

'Lorna?'

'Cleaning.'

Lorna had taken a cleaning job? Clever, witty, acerbic Lorna, with an English degree and encyclopedic knowledge of the war poets. She had run the library in Cheddar until it closed down last year.

'I didn't realise things were that bad.'

Olivia couldn't be sure, but she thought she heard an intake of breath. When Lorna spoke, her voice had an edge. 'Sorry, Olivia, I have to go.'

*

When she was eight, Olivia fell off a garden swing. A sharp pain shot from her wrist to her elbow but she was frightened of hospitals, so nursed the pain in stoic silence, determined not to go to the Royal where her grandmother had shrivelled away in a bed with metal sides. At teatime, when Olivia couldn't cut up her fish fingers and chips, her mum saw the swelling on her thin little wrist, ignored her tears and protests and took her straight to A & E. An X-ray revealed a greenstick fracture. 'It's a funny name, isn't it?' the doctor said to Olivia. To her mother he said, 'It means the fracture is incomplete.'

That's what Olivia thought about when she thought about Lorna and just like when she had fallen off the swing, she could pinpoint the exact moment the damage had been done.

A Friday afternoon in late July, the air syrupy and still. Geoffrey had taken Edward fly-fishing at Chew Valley Lake and Olivia had dropped by the Rectory to return a book Ronald had lent her. When she let herself in the back door she heard his voice and was already outside his study when she heard another voice, familiar yet unfamiliar and spitting with condemnation. *You let him get away with it.* Through the partially open door she recognised Johnny's broad back. They hadn't noticed her. If she had slipped away, she wouldn't have heard that a young curate Ronald had taken under his wing had recently been exposed as a paedophile, that he had preyed on Johnny, that Ronald could keep his fucking apology because it was twenty-seven years too late.

She wished she had slipped away. When Johnny spun round and saw her, the pain and fury on his face turned into something else. Shame? Humiliation? Ronald's face was the colour of bone. Johnny stormed out, slamming the front door so hard it made the whole house shake. Olivia left without a word, still clutching the book.

For over half an hour she had sat in the Land Rover, parked just along the lane from Johnny and Lorna's cottage, unable to decide if she was doing the right thing. Johnny probably wouldn't want to see her and certainly wouldn't want to talk, but she couldn't pretend she hadn't heard.

He was in the kitchen, smears of blood in a fist-sized dent in the wall, a scatter of plaster on the floor. She had no idea what to say to him. He ran his grazed knuckles under the cold tap and let Olivia dab them with a few sheets of kitchen roll.

That was how Lorna had found them. They hadn't heard her come in, a bulging Tesco bag in each hand. *What's going on?* Johnny embarked upon some improbable tale about losing it for a mad five minutes – frustration at being out of work – and how Olivia happened to have dropped by and caught the worst of his meltdown. Lorna looked at Olivia, whose simple nod of the head corroborated his story.

The greenstick fracture of their friendship.

Geoffrey thought it was the chill between him and Johnny that had cooled things, but Olivia and Lorna had been fine until that moment in the cottage. Lorna filled the kettle and began to unpack the shopping. Olivia didn't stay for tea.

Later that evening Johnny had called. He was taking Benji for a walk and could Olivia meet him on the track to Crooke Peak? She roused Rollo and Dice from their beds and told Geoffrey she wouldn't be long. The air was a riot of flying insects: in her face, her hair, her mouth. Johnny was already there, the knuckles of his right hand scabby and raw. The second the dogs were off their leads they went their separate ways – sniffing tree trunks and patches of grass, marking their territory with indiscriminate pools of pee.

Johnny hadn't looked at Olivia when he swore her to secrecy, but focused on some random point in the distance. At first she had misunderstood and was hurt by his inference. 'I won't breathe a word. How could you think that I would?'

Then he had been more explicit. 'Not to Geoffrey, not to Lorna, not to anyone. Ever.' Olivia had assumed – hoped – he'd told Lorna the truth that afternoon. Surely a man couldn't keep something like that from his wife? But Johnny said he'd kept it from her for sixteen years and they'd been just fine.

'She's my best friend. I can't lie to her.'

He had stopped walking and taken Olivia by the shoulders, a sharp urgency in his voice. 'You have to forget about this afternoon. It didn't happen, understand?'

She had shaken her head. 'No, I don't. I mean, I know it's awful, but Lorna –'

An older couple had appeared with a pair of whippets and Johnny let go of her. They'd waited for the couple to pass before Johnny told her he would rather die than have anyone know what had happened to him. Subject closed.

The change in Olivia and Lorna's relationship was subtle and incremental. Brief lulls in conversation were no longer companionable silences, but cracks that needed to be filled. Husbands had been an inexhaustible source of discussion but the topic vanished from their repertoire. Olivia knew something Lorna didn't and it fatally skewed the order of things. No matter how natural and cheery they tried to be, it was clear that nothing sucked the lifeblood out of friendship like the imposition of taboos.

Still, optimism was Olivia's default position. She never left the house without a pair of sunglasses, however inclement the weather, because there was always a chance the sun might battle its way through the gloom. And when she had fretted about the move to St Bede's she told herself that with time and distance, her friendship with Lorna would reboot itself, like when you turn off a misbehaving computer and then turn it back on again. And it did for a bit. During half-term she convinced herself that the incomplete fracture was nicely on the mend. She really believed that.

And then she didn't.

*

The first snow of winter fell, shyly to begin with, in light, almost ghostly flurries, then thicker, until the ground was rendered white and flawless. Great excitement gripped the school. The children stared longingly out of their class-room windows, fidgeting and eager for break time.

Olivia too. She pulled on her coat and took a walk round the grounds. The air was fresh and frigid, the sky a pale dove-grey. How lovely it would be to have Rollo and Dice there, tearing around in the snow, delirious with happiness.

With the approaching end of term loomed the endurance test of Christmas. The first without Ronald. It was hard to think about him without thinking about Johnny. Ronald had refused to talk about it too – a high wall of impenetrable silence. Olivia assumed that after more than forty-five years of marriage, he must surely have confided in Rowena. Olivia knew she should make a special effort with her this year, but it was hard not to dwell on memories of Christmas past and feel the familiar squirm of animosity towards her.

When Olivia and Geoffrey had hosted their first Christmas as a married couple (at her insistence – Geoffrey said she was mad), she'd worked tirelessly, determined everything would be perfect. She'd genuinely believed that once Rowena got to know her better, once she saw how hard Olivia tried, they would get on famously. Olivia had such high hopes for their relationship. No one had ever taken against her the way Rowena had, and Olivia had no strategy to deal with it. She was intuitive, not tactical. It was inconceivable that her mother-in-law derived satisfaction from undermining her, but the evidence was compelling.

That first Christmas, heavily pregnant with Edward, Olivia had cooked roast turkey with all the trimmings, only to have Rowena describe, in remarkable detail, the wonderful recipe she had found for goose. Determined to do better, Olivia cooked goose the following year. Rowena pushed the meat around her plate, declared it a little rich and expressed a preference for good old-fashioned turkey.

A young wife in need of reassurance – would it have killed Rowena to offer it? Those memories still smarted. What a pity something as beautiful as virgin snow stirred up the pain of being judged and found wanting. Rowena had never really forgiven Olivia for falling pregnant, diluting the pure Parry bloodline with less auspicious stock. And Olivia had never really forgiven Rowena for thinking that. They had learned to tolerate one another, to rub along with the minimum of friction, but there was no warmth or affection between them. And even though Olivia felt genuine compassion for Rowena at having lost Ronald, that didn't mean she forgave her.

It started to snow again – a flurry of flakes like celestial confetti. From the main entrance, Martin beckoned. Olivia jogged over to him, leaving dainty footprints in her wake.

'We need to talk,' he said.

His tone alarmed her.

'There's been a development,' he continued.

'Oh?'

'Are you free now?'

Her mind was blank. She gave her head a little shake to liven it up. 'Reading,' she said. 'Pre-prep.'

Martin put his index finger to his lips. 'I see. Well, come to my office after that, would you? I've asked Mrs Heather to call Geoffrey and see if he can join us.'

Olivia's skin prickled. 'Geoffrey. Why?'

Martin's raised hands said 'stop'. 'We'll talk about it in my office.'

Reading hour dragged interminably. Olivia could think about nothing but 'the development'. What was so serious that Geoffrey had to be summoned? Dread accumulated in the pit of her stomach. When the bell rang for end of class, she braced herself for whatever lay ahead, half anxious to know, half not wanting to know.

Geoffrey was already there, in conversation with Claire Heather. Olivia threw him an unconvincing smile and he arched an eyebrow, as if to ask what was going on? She shrugged. Martin opened his door and invited them to step inside. Claire Heather's quizzical glance said it all. *What now?*

Martin looked grave as he gestured for them to take a seat.

'I'm afraid I have some bad news,' he said. 'The Burtons have involved the police.'

Olivia turned from Martin to Geoffrey. 'I don't understand.'

'They want Edward charged with assault.'

Olivia hadn't cried when Geoffrey told her about the bailiffs, nor when their belongings were driven away in a lorry. She sulked when Edward was around and rowed with Geoffrey when he wasn't, but she vented without recourse to tears. Even the night he'd left her at St Bede's, she had only allowed herself a few token tears of self-pity before she pulled herself together and resolved to make the best of it. But this – this was too much. Martin offered her a tissue from a box on his desk.

'Please, take a moment to compose yourself,' he said. 'I'll ask Mrs Heather to organise some tea.'

Martin could have picked up the phone but tactfully stepped outside, leaving Olivia and Geoffrey alone. He put his arm round her.

'What's happening to us, to our family?' she said. 'Why is everything going wrong?'

Geoffrey had no words of comfort. As a rule she disliked bland platitudes – it'll be OK, everything will be all right, etcetera – but would have made an exception on this occasion.

Martin returned with a tray of tea and biscuits, the English answer to everything. Olivia blew her nose and mumbled an apology, which Martin dismissed with a sympathetic smile.

'Can the Burtons be dissuaded?' asked Geoffrey, taking a cup and saucer from the tray.

'They've already made a complaint,' said Martin. 'Toby Burton called yesterday and told me himself. I tried to reason with him but he seemed determined.'

Olivia could feel herself unravelling again and reached for another tissue. 'I know it was wrong of Edward to hit Freddie,' she said. 'But surely it's not a police matter – just boys being boys.'

Martin sipped his tea and considered this. 'It seems unlikely they will press charges,' he said. 'As you say, it was essentially a quarrel that got out of hand. However, Freddie was injured.'

'What if I speak to Toby Burton?' said Geoffrey. 'Or maybe you could ask Ruth to talk to the mother – Alicia, is it?'

'I will certainly ask Ruth if she would intervene on Edward's behalf,' said Martin, 'but I think it's Mr Burton who's the problem. Just between ourselves, I got the impression he was angry that Freddie had come off worse.'

Male pride – really? Edward might end up in juvenile court because Toby Burton couldn't bear to think of his son losing a fight. She remembered him on sports day, bellowing for Freddie to win every race.

'I'll talk to him,' she said. Martin and Geoffrey stared at her. 'Toby Burton – appeal to his vanity, his better nature; throw myself on his mercy if I have to. I'll remind him I saved Freddie's life.'

'Well, that's up to you, of course,' said Martin. 'But if you remember how adamantly he blamed the school for Freddie's *accident*, for want of a better word, I do wonder if bringing it up again would be wise?'

Olivia thought about this for a moment. Alicia Burton had come to St Bede's to thank her in person. Not a single word from Toby Burton.

'But in the meantime,' said Martin, 'I would ask that you speak with Edward. I think it should come from you. He ought to be waiting in his dorm.'

'Thank you,' said Olivia, more composed now, but she pulled a handful of tissues from the box on Martin's desk, just in case.

*

Edward looked so lost sitting all alone on his bed, his beloved Manchester United duvet crumpled beneath him. His hands lay restless in his lap, thumbs twiddling round and round. Olivia and Geoffrey sat down on the next bed, each waiting for the other to speak. Geoffrey went first.

'I don't know how much the headmaster has told you,' he began gently, 'but Freddie Burton's parents have made a formal complaint.'

'I know,' said Edward, gazing at his hands.

His nails were bitten. When did Edward start biting his nails? He picked at a ragged cuticle and winced.

'Freddie told me,' he said. 'Am I in a lot of trouble?'

He addressed his question to Olivia, who didn't trust herself to speak. She turned her head to Geoffrey.

'We're hoping it won't come to anything,' he said.

Edward chewed at the raw skin around his thumbnail. Olivia couldn't help herself – she reached over and gently moved his hand from his mouth like she used to when he was a toddler.

'What happens now?' he asked.

Olivia kept hold of his hand and gave it a reassuring squeeze. 'Mrs Rutherford is going to speak to Mrs Burton and I'm going to speak to Mr Burton,' she said in the soothing, nursery voice she used with Alice Rutherford.

'Don't,' he said, alarmed.

'Why not?'

Edward lowered his eyes and mumbled. 'He called you a MILF.'

Had she heard correctly? She looked at Geoffrey.

'Is that what you were fighting about?' asked Geoffrey, his face flushing crimson.

A mute Edward picked at the cuticle again, this time drawing a speck of blood. Olivia wasn't sure which shocked her more: to be referred to in that way by a St Bede's parent, or that Edward knew what it meant. And yes, it was crass and even a little creepy that Toby Burton would make such an inappropriate comment to his twelve-year-old son, but it did explain why Edward had behaved the way he had. Imagine hearing that his mother was a MILF – such a vile acronym. And knowing Freddie, he would have enjoyed spelling it out. Olivia could just imagine him taunting Edward. Now she was even more determined to confront Toby Burton and shame him into dropping the complaint. Edward had stood up for her and she would stand up for him.

*

The café's windows dripped with condensation, marring the view of Axbridge's historic town centre. Olivia and Lorna used to bring the children here in the school holidays. Olivia tried calling her but when she didn't pick up, left a message: *I'm meeting someone in Axbridge but maybe we can get together afterwards. It'd be good to see you.*

She put her phone on silent and ordered a cappuccino from the dewy-faced waitress, her prettiness spoiled by a tattoo that seemed to have colonised one side of her neck. A giant cobweb? Some sort of mesh? Olivia didn't understand the appeal. She envisaged future generations of grandmothers still branded with what they'd considered to be cool thirty or forty years before.

A small bell on the café door announced Toby Burton's arrival. He scanned the room, stuffy under heavy beams and a low ceiling, before locking eyes with Olivia. No smile, just a quick nod of acknowledgement. He wore the uniform of the hunting, shooting, fishing set and bore a remarkable resemblance to Freddie: same prominent eyebrows and dark, deep-set eyes. He slipped off his jacket and discarded it over the back of the chair. When the waitress offered him a menu he declined and asked for a double espresso. He watched her walk away, appraising her legs and bottom. Only when she was out of sight did he turn back to Olivia.

'So,' he said, evidently expecting Olivia to kick things off. Fair enough. This had been her idea. 'Thank you for meeting me,' she said.

The speech she had prepared didn't seem right now they were face to face; too formal and evidential. She changed tack. 'First, let me say how terribly sorry I am about what Edward did. There was no excuse for it.'

The waitress brought Burton's coffee and this time it was her milk-white cleavage that caught his attention. Olivia waited for her to leave.

'And I understand your anger. I would feel the same in your position.'

At this he took a hit of coffee, frowned and reached for a couple of packs of sugar.

'However,' she continued, 'Edward has expressed genuine remorse and has been punished. I can't see what's to be gained by involving the police.'

Burton finished stirring and put down his spoon. 'What he did constitutes assault. Do you think he should get away with it?'

Olivia needed a moment to get the words right in her head so ran her fingers through her hair, pulling a handful of blonde waves casually over her shoulder. That got his attention.

'He was provoked,' she said.

Burton sat back in his chair and crossed his legs. She wanted to be wrong, but got the impression he was enjoying this.

'How so?'

Bastard. He was going to make her say it. She forced herself to look him in the eye. 'You told Freddie I was a MILF, something he felt compelled to share with the entire changing room. I'd say that was provocation, wouldn't you?'

Burton's lips curled into a repellent smirk. 'Is that what he told you?'

Was Burton trying to confuse her? Originally Geoffrey had said the argument was something to do with rugby – aggression on the pitch spilling over into the changing room. But then Edward owned up to the whole MILF thing. He wouldn't lie, would he?

Burton uncrossed his legs and leaned towards her, so close she could smell the coffee on his breath.

'Mrs Parry,' he said smugly. 'Olivia, if I may. It was your son dishing out the provocation, your son who ripped off my son's towel, your son who pummelled my son's face.'

His voice was quiet and controlled, but with an unmistakable edge of threat. What towel – what was he talking about? And pummelled? It was one punch. She had expected the MILF revelation to afford her the moral high ground, but maybe Edward had lied to her. Toby Burton obviously knew something she didn't.

The waitress asked if she could get them anything else. Burton ordered another espresso and smiled at an elderly couple on the next table, who, in lieu of conversation of their own, appeared engrossed in theirs. In Burton's version of events Edward sounded like a common thug. This wasn't going well at all and Olivia was about to play her trump card – remind Burton who it was that had found Freddie hanging from a coat hook and saved his life – when his mood inexplicably lightened.

'Relax,' he said. 'You were right about the police. An overreaction on my part.'

Had he just given her what she wanted?

The elderly couple got up to leave; a slow and laborious process assisted by Toby Burton. Olivia watched in mild amazement as he helped them move their chairs and put on their coats, then held the door open for them. Sleazy guy to nice guy in under sixty seconds. He slipped back into his seat.

'Well,' said Olivia, confused but determined not to show it. She should quit while she was ahead. 'Thank you for understanding.'

Burton's leering smile made her long for piping hot water and lots of soap. She checked her watch with feigned resignation.

'I have to get back to school.'

When she reached into her bag and pulled out her purse, he laid his hand on hers: a dense, clammy weight. 'Allow me,' he said.

She slipped her hand from underneath his, smoothly, so as not to offend. He walked her to the door, just as he had the elderly couple. With his chapped lips almost touching her ear, he said, 'In the spirit of full disclosure, I should point out that it was Freddie, not me, who called you a MILF.' He straightened himself up. 'The boy has taste.'

*

Olivia didn't know how long she had sat there, watching sleet spill from a blank sky. Wet flakes tried and failed to settle on the windscreen, forming tiny tributaries that made her think of tears. She ached to go home but no longer had a home.

When Geoffrey phoned he said she sounded strange. *Did that bastard Toby Burton upset you?* She didn't want to talk about it. *Mission accomplished*, she told Geoffrey, trying to sound a whole lot better than she felt.

Dusk blotted out the dull excuse for daylight. A traffic warden walked towards her car – ten minutes left on the ticket. She was waiting for Lorna to call back but gave up and called her again.

'Did you get my message?' asked Olivia when Lorna answered.

'What message?'

'I'm in Axbridge – wondered if you had time for a coffee?'

'I can't. Josh and Lily just got home.'

'Isn't Johnny there?'

'Johnny's leaving.'

Ten

'Were you going to tell me?'

Geoffrey had barely walked in the front door before his mother ambushed him. Ever since the ill-advised conversation about selling the Rectory she had been noticeably frosty.

'Tell you what?'

'That Edward was in some sort of trouble.'

She looked at him and waited. When Geoffrey didn't immediately respond – busy checking his pockets, taking off his jacket, finding a place for it on the coat stand – his mother ploughed on.

'Fighting?' she said. 'Like some sort of delinquent. What on earth has got into him?'

Geoffrey was trying hard not to think about what might have got into him. He dropped his keys on the heavy walnut sideboard. Family heirloom – ugly thing.

'Claire Heather, I assume. So much for confidentiality.'

He had no idea if school secretaries were bound by a code of confidentiality but felt they should be. His mother sniffed defensively.

'I called her about the village newsletter and she mentioned you and Olivia had been in to see the headmaster.'

'It's all been sorted out,' said Geoffrey.

No thanks to him. That Olivia had dealt with it was particularly emasculating. Geoffrey should have been the one squaring up to Freddie Burton's bully-boy father, man to man.

In the quiet solitude of the study, Geoffrey brooded. The question of how to dig himself out of the shit had consumed him for months and he always came up with the same answer – money. But it was starting to dawn on him that it wasn't that simple. Even a huge lottery win wouldn't magically heal his damaged reputation, his friendships, his relationship with Olivia. It wouldn't bring his father back.

Geoffrey had finally begun to realise that material concerns and emotional concerns were qualitatively different. With money he could pay his debts, get another house and end the physical separation from Olivia. But what about their emotional separation? They hardly spoke – although that wasn't usually through choice – and hadn't made love in three months. Would money mend their marriage? And if it did, what did that say about their marriage?

A black and white photograph of his parents on their wedding day hung on the opposite wall. It was hard to imagine them young and in love. He barely recognised them. His mother was thirty-seven when she gave birth; his father two years older. On his first day at school, Geoffrey came running out with a drawing he'd done and scanned the group of waiting mothers for his own. He distinctly remembered thinking she looked old and rather stern, and wondering what it would be like to go home with one of the young, smiley mothers instead.

The days when his father collected him were a rare and wonderful treat. His father wasn't young either but he was smiley. Geoffrey would gabble on about what lessons he'd had, what he'd eaten for lunch, who he'd played with at break, his father supremely interested in the minutiae of his day. As a boy, the way Geoffrey loved his father was so real and immediate it felt big inside him, like when he stuffed himself with ice cream and fizzy pop. Even at a very young age, Geoffrey sensed his mother's presence enforced a subtle form of restraint: don't laugh too loud, don't run too fast, don't love too much. With his father, there was no restraint. Sometimes missing him felt like being underwater: the weight, the silence, the lack of air.

Not everything could be solved with money.

*

A swirl of snow had fallen on ice, rendering the lanes glassy and lethal. The car skidded twice before Geoffrey adjusted his speed to match the conditions. What was the hurry anyway? He wished he had never agreed to coach the rugby team, now captained by the perfidious Freddie Burton while Edward was exiled to the library.

Geoffrey managed to swallow his feelings, though, and other than a bad tackle by Finn Harding, who remonstrated aggressively when Geoffrey threatened to take him off, the training session was uneventful. Geoffrey spent the last five minutes talking them through their positions for Saturday's match against Colstons, then dismissed them. It was as they made their way towards the school building that he overheard Ben Scott-Lessing ask Freddie how he would feel next week when Goldilocks was back in the team. Geoffrey didn't catch Freddie's reply but it made the other boys howl with laughter. An incensed Geoffrey was about to tear into them when he spotted Olivia heading in their direction. It took a lot of restraint for him to walk straight past the ingrates laughing at his son, and the anger must have shown in his face because Olivia mouthed 'What's wrong?' as she approached.

'Freddie fucking Burton.'

'Geoffrey,' she hissed. 'You can't use that language here. Suppose someone heard you?'

He took a lungful of air, held it for a few seconds, then exhaled. 'Sorry,' he said. 'He's just the most insufferable little cunt.'

'Geoffrey!'

'Sorry, sorry. You're right.'

'You can't say that, especially about a child.'

He nodded. 'I know. I'm sorry. He winds me up.'

Olivia took his arm. 'Tell me over coffee,' she said, turning back towards the school.

It wasn't a conversation he wanted to have in the staffroom, so he told her as they walked.

'You know they call Edward "Goldilocks",' he said.

Olivia huffed. 'Leo promised he had put a stop to this bullying.'

'Well, it's not bullying, is it? And anyway, Edward can look after himself. Burton should remember that.'

The cold began to creep into Geoffrey's bones. He blew on his hands to try and warm them up a bit.

'What do you mean?' said Olivia. 'You don't want them to get into another fight?'

'No, of course not.'

'I'm going to speak to Leo.'

'For God's sake, Olivia. It's a bit of name-calling – don't make a fuss.'

She stopped walking and stared at him, genuinely aggrieved. 'You were the one making a fuss.'

'I don't like them calling Edward "Goldilocks", that's all.'

'Well, compared to what you just called Freddie Burton –'

'It's not the same.'

'No, what you called Freddie was much worse.'

The sky had darkened to the colour of steel. Geoffrey's toes were starting to go numb and he stamped on the frozen ground to get the circulation moving.

'He called him a "fag" as well, you know, when Edward pushed him in the showers and Freddie's towel fell off.'

'Oh, his father said something about a towel. I didn't know what he was talking about.' She shook her head, frowning. 'Those Burton men are real charmers. I'm a MILF – Edward's a fag.'

Hearing Olivia say it made it sound worse, as if it were a statement of fact rather than just an insult hurled on the spur of the moment.

'That Freddie should watch what he's saying – going round implying Edward's gay or something.'

Olivia took a step back and stared up at him. 'Is that why you're angry?'

Her tone was accusatory, as if he wasn't allowed to be upset. In Geoffrey's day it was the weak boys, the crybabies, the boys who weren't boyish enough, who were called fags. Not boys like Edward.

Olivia was on a different trajectory; more concerned with the 'bullying that wasn't.' 'Well, I don't care what you think,' she said. 'I'm going to talk to Leo.'

'Christ, will you stop mollycoddling him. The last thing he needs is his mummy telling on the other boys for calling him names.'

Olivia's eyes widened in disbelief. 'Mollycoddling?'

She looked like she had been slapped and opened her mouth to speak, but huffed loudly and shook her head. Geoffrey hadn't meant to blame her but now that he thought about it, yes, she did mollycoddle Edward. Look how over-protective she was when he played rugby. Boys needed a bit of rough and tumble. What they didn't need was their mothers fretting about them all the time. That was one of the reasons Geoffrey had quietly encouraged Edward to board. If Olivia had her way, he would be a proper little mummy's boy.

'So it's my fault,' she said, close to tears. 'Edward's being bullied because of me.'

Geoffrey knew he should have toned it down, back-tracked, said he didn't mean it, but he did. 'Oh, for God's sake, Olivia – he's not being bullied. Just leave him alone to sort it out.'

Sleet had seeped into Geoffrey's tracksuit and it clung to him. He couldn't feel his fingers or toes at all. 'Are you coming?' he said, turning towards the school.

He needed to warm up, but Olivia didn't move – just fixed him with a wounded stare.

'Please yourself,' he said, and left her there.

*

Three days of sulking, introspection and self-justification followed. It was unlike Geoffrey, who usually dealt with problems by going to the pub, having four or five pints, engaging in a bit of superficial banter about sport, cars or work, then walking home unburdened and refreshed.

He had meant to tell Olivia that Johnny was going to London but was too busy berating her about Edward. When his mobile had rung and Johnny's name flashed on to the screen, Geoffrey's reaction had been one of blind optimism. Johnny wanted to meet for a pint – an oasis in Geoffrey's arid social life. He could casually ask how Lily and Josh were doing, if Lorna fussed over Josh like Olivia did Edward? He might mention the name-calling but only to point out that Edward had stood up for himself; given the other boy a bloody good hiding, in fact.

It turned out Johnny had wanted a reference, not a pint. He had been offered a welding job on the Crossrail project. 'How does Lorna feel about it?' Geoffrey had asked. 'Not thrilled,' was the answer, 'but there's nothing round here and we need the money.' That told him.

*

First thing Saturday, Geoffrey relented and called Olivia. Mornings were when he missed her the most – those amnesic seconds between sleeping and waking before all the bad stuff came rushing at him. He would punch her pillow a few times so it looked as though she had slept there. Stupid really. The call went to voicemail. He would have left a message but couldn't think what to say.

His mother had cooked bacon, eggs, black pudding and mushrooms. The smell lured him downstairs even though he didn't have much of an appetite. He hadn't shaved for a few days, his skin itchy under rough dense bristle.

'You look tired,' she said, concerned, indicating that her frostiness towards him had finally thawed.

He padded over to the sink, scratching his chin.

'Kettle's full,' she said. 'And I've walked the dogs.'

He checked his watch. Eight fifteen. 'You have been busy. What time were you up?'

She put on her rubber gloves and started the washing up. No fancy dishwashers at the Rectory. Complete waste of money when you had a perfectly good pair of hands.

'Seven,' she said. 'Same as always.'

Geoffrey used to rise at six thirty and be at his desk an hour later. These days there wasn't much to get up for. Not much to go to bed for either. No warm body to cuddle up to. No sex. Even self-gratification seemed beyond him now, his dick limp in his ineffectual hand. Porn, it turned out, had been a temporary pleasure, like everything else in his life. He ate his breakfast in silence, his mother at the sink, Radio Four in the background, just like when he was a child. All that was missing was his father.

*

The Colstons team piled off the minibus looking fit, keen and confident. Their coach shook hands with Geoffrey and they wished each other good luck. So far so civilised. He showed them to their spot in the changing room and then gave his team what would have been a rousing pep talk if his heart had been in it. Without Edward, there seemed little to get excited about. He had been their friend, their captain, and now he was the butt of their jokes. With a bit of luck Colstons would kick their sorry arses.

It was a good turnout, as many Colstons parents as there were St Bede's. In between bellowing instructions to his players, Geoffrey scanned the crowd for Olivia, but there was no sign of her. No sign of Edward either, even though he was banned from practice sessions, not from watching matches. Toby Burton was there, though, shouting louder than Geoffrey, a tall, inappropriately dressed blonde by his side. Who wore high heels and fur to a rugby match? Big, blingy sunglasses too, despite the absence of sun. Burton probably thought he'd traded up, but the second Mrs Burton looked like a Russian hooker.

Colstons were winning twelve–three when the referee blew the whistle for half-time. That was when Geoffrey spotted Edward on the far side of the pitch, slightly apart from everyone else. Geoffrey beckoned to him, but he hung back. While the players scoffed oranges and Lucozade, Geoffrey jogged over to him.

'All right, son?'

Edward's nod was non-committal and he had the look of a sullen teenager again. Geoffrey was keen to have a father–son chat, but not here.

'Have you seen Mum?' he asked.

Geoffrey had hoped she would come along to the match. It was difficult to move past an argument when they hardly ever saw each other. But then he thought back to half-term, when they saw each other for ten days straight, and that hadn't been an advert for marital bliss.

Edward shrugged. 'Not today.'

The Colstons coach was on the pitch, talking to his players – lots of hand and arm gestures, the odd slow-motion kick. Geoffrey's lot stood around looking lost.

'I'd better go,' he said to Edward, and jogged back over to try to rally his players.

He had three pieces of advice: remember everything we've done in training; remember you're a team, which means working together; and remember we have the home advantage, so use it.

The second half was no better. A marked improvement in St Bede's quality of play didn't translate into points. The final score was fifteen–three. Geoffrey told them 'good effort', before dismissing them to get showered. He intended to head back himself but was intercepted by Toby Burton.

'That was a bit of a shambles,' said Burton.

He pulled a cigarette from a packet, put it between his lips and lit up. Christ, Geoffrey missed smoking. It was as much as he could do not to ask Burton if he could cadge one.

'Colstons are a good team,' said Geoffrey, savouring an intoxicating whiff of tobacco.

'Freddie's not suited to the wing,' said Burton, taking a long, luxurious drag.

Geoffrey was in no mood to defend his team selection. He looked around for Edward.

'It's almost as if you wanted him to play badly,' said Burton. 'Maybe even wanted them to lose.'

'Why would I want them to lose?' asked Geoffrey.

'To make your boy look better when he's back on the team. I saw him skulking around.'

'He wasn't skulking,' said Geoffrey, not quite managing to hide his irritation.

Olivia's voice was in his head, irritation present and correct, telling him *not* to upset the sleazeball who had agreed to drop criminal charges. She was right, of course, but that didn't stop Geoffrey wanting to tell him to go fuck himself. The blonde tottered towards them, spiky heels sinking into the sodden grass, fur coat pulled around her spindly frame. How absurd did she look?

'Darling,' she said, slipping her arm into Burton's. Not Russian after all.

'When can we leave?' Estuary vowels – flat and nasal.

Burton dropped his half-smoked cigarette and let it smoulder at his feet. 'Quick cup of tea and we're out of here,' he said, still glaring at Geoffrey.

The blonde pouted. More of a champagne and canapés girl than a tea and sandwiches girl, presumably. They set off across the pitch, the blonde hanging on to Burton's arm for balance, and for the first time that day – many days, actually – Geoffrey laughed.

*

Ruth Rutherford was playing tea lady again, the atmosphere lively considering the trouncing St Bede's had received. Geoffrey joined the queue and accepted good-natured commiserations, which were probably more than he deserved. When he reached the front, Ruth cocked her head to one side.

'Scotch, is it?'

He played along. 'Double.'

She handed him a cup of tea and told him it would have to do.

'Olivia not here?'

'Netball over at Millfield.'

Geoffrey's memories of playing against Millfield centred on the conviction that it was never a fair fight. First-rate facilities and a huge number of players to choose from – many selected and offered bursaries on the basis of their sporting ability – meant opponents were rarely victorious. Geoffrey didn't imagine the St Bede's netball team would prove to be the exception.

'Yes. Sorry. Forgot.'

The next person in the queue moved forward and Geoffrey stepped aside. He scanned the room for someone interesting to talk to but Toby Burton collared him again, the blonde still hanging on his arm. Her coat had been discarded, revealing expensive clothes and improbably generous breasts. Had he seen her on an internet porn site? Those girls had all started to look the same.

'Didn't finish our conversation,' said Burton.

'Thought we had,' said Geoffrey.

Finn Harding's father patted him on the back. 'Tough match,' he said. 'Colstons were bloody good.'

'Certainly were,' said Geoffrey.

Harding disappeared into the throng.

'Our conversation,' said Burton.

Geoffrey had had enough of this. He hadn't asked for the job as coach: a poisoned chalice if ever there was one.

'What is it you want?' he said.

Burton dispatched the blonde to fetch her coat.

'I want you to be grateful I'm not pressing charges. I want Freddie to stay as captain and play in the position of his choice.' Burton lowered his voice. 'And I want your son to keep his filthy hands off my son. Is that clear enough for you?'

His rugby days aside, Geoffrey considered himself a placid sort of chap. Not a pushover, but someone who didn't court confrontation; who preferred to sort things out reasonably over a pint and a chat, rather than go steaming in with his fists. Until now. A hot plume of anger rose up from his gut.

'Outside,' he said.

Burton's expression changed instantly he registered the threat. 'Like father like son,' he said, smirking.

Geoffrey moved towards the door, jaw clenched, face burning. He had taken only a few steps when someone gripped his arm.

'Can I borrow you for a moment?' said Ruth.

'What?'

'Problem with the tea urn. Need a strong pair of hands.'

He stared at her, baffled. 'We're in the middle of something here.'

Ruth put her mouth to his ear. 'I know,' she said quietly, her grip on his arm tightening. She turned to Burton. 'Excuse us, would you,' she said, and led Geoffrey away.

The kitchen was empty. A faint but familiar odour hung in the air: boiled greens, floor polish, mince. His anger had dissipated enough to realise he had been about to make a huge mistake.

196

'Why am I here?' he asked.

Ruth leaned back against the stainless-steel counter, a hand resting on either side, white blouse straining over her breasts. 'I could see something was going on with that prick Toby Burton. Word of advice – never play poker.'

'Was it that obvious?'

She raised her eyebrows. 'I thought you were going to combust. What did he say to get you so fired up?'

Geoffrey rubbed his forehead. 'Doesn't matter.'

It was her turn to speak but she fixed him with her pale grey eyes and allowed a sensuous silence to settle on them. She was sizing him up – trying to decide what to do with him. Hunter and prey. He could hear himself breathe.

Using her forefinger and thumb, Ruth deftly undid the top three buttons of her blouse. They sprang apart, as if grateful to be released. Geoffrey didn't move. He flashed back to the dinner party, to how outrageously she had flirted with him, how aroused he had been, how desperately he had wanted sex, how Olivia had turned him down.

Ruth waited for a reaction. Geoffrey took in the gaping blouse, the small red bow on her bra, the stuck-up expression of supreme confidence. In the space between them – six, maybe seven feet – lay their lives: marriages, families, futures. He went to her, trampling all of it underfoot.

In his uncensored imagination he had fucked her countless times. Reality was different, enhanced by all five senses. Risk too. In some still lucid recess of his brain, not addled by muscle-burning lust, he knew they could be caught at any moment, but that only intensified the experience.

He unzipped her jeans and yanked them down with a single tug. Her flimsy knickers had a red bow that matched the one on her bra. She slid her hand into his sweatpants, took hold of his dick and applied expert pressure and rhythm. He could have come there and then but was loath to waste the opportunity that had so unexpectedly presented itself. The way Ruth smiled inferred triumph, victory, dominance: *look what I can do; look what I can make you do.* Fuck that. Geoffrey wasn't some toy-boy conquest. He spun her round so her back was to him, and lowered her face on to the cold metal surface, his hand on her head. She complied without protest and for the first time since she had led him away from a punch-up with Toby Burton, Geoffrey was in control.

When he entered her she cried out and he pressed his palm over her open mouth, a gesture that seemed to excite her more. She gripped the edge of the counter and pushed hard against his groin, bringing him deeper inside her. It was all over in a dozen thrusts, but still a most satisfying fuck. He fell forward, dizzy and breathless, until the sound of a woman singing brought him bolt upright. The sound came closer – a hymn Geoffrey vaguely remembered from his school days. Ruth dressed and tidied her hair with impressive speed, while Geoffrey went to the sink for a glass of water.

'There you are.' Ruth's helper – Linda, Lisa? – bustled in holding an empty milk jug. 'I wondered where you'd got to.'

Ruth smiled casually, her air of control effortlessly re-established. Geoffrey had to admire her cool. His heart was pounding like a jackhammer.

'Mr Parry said he'd take a look at that wretched tap,' she said.

Geoffrey turned the tap on and off, which seemed to satisfy the helper's curiosity.

'It's thinning out now,' she said. 'Colstons' lot are leaving.'

'Excellent,' said Ruth. 'I'll be there in a minute.'

The helper replenished the milk jug and left, humming the hymn.

Geoffrey had no prior experience to guide him through this situation. What was the etiquette when one has just fucked the headmaster's wife? Surely she was the expert in this regard. Right on cue, she spoke.

'A promising start, Mr Parry, but next time I'll expect rather less haste.'

Eleven

With the exception of Alice Rutherford, the girls were in high spirits on the minibus back from Millfield School. They sang pop songs, some with startlingly inappropriate lyrics. Olivia didn't intervene, reasoning it was the catchy tunes that appealed and they wouldn't know what a *ménage a trois* was anyway. Olivia certainly hadn't at their age. At thirty-three, her understanding was still purely theoretical.

'Who's that song by?'

She threw the question open. No great surprise that Maisie Rutherford jumped in with the answer. 'Katy Perry, miss.'

Ah yes, the girl who kissed a girl and liked it. Had Edward kissed a boy and liked it? Maybe he had punched the boy instead, or maybe Geoffrey had got himself all fired up over nothing.

Three days, two missed calls, no messages.

Olivia couldn't believe he had blamed her for the other boys picking on Edward. Yes, she had gone over to his dorm to say goodnight, but just the once. OK, twice. It wasn't as if she made a habit of it.

Geoffrey's reaction to Freddie's name-calling was completely over the top and it had clearly hit a nerve. If she didn't know better she would think him homophobic, but he had always been so fond of her brother, Sam; made harmless jokes about his camp manner, the hours he spent on his appearance, the well-muscled boyfriends he mooned over. Edward reminded her a bit of Sam – the way they were both kind and sensitive. Olivia thought of Edward's bedroom at Manor Farm, the walls bright with posters, games and gadgets everywhere, bunk beds for when he had sleepovers. Not once had he complained or said how much he missed it in case he made her and Geoffrey feel even worse than they already did.

Still, Olivia had taken Geoffrey's advice – if it could be called advice when it was delivered as a bad-tempered tirade – and not said anything to Leo. She and Geoffrey may have different ideas as to what constitutes bullying, but perhaps he had been right and it was best to let Edward fight his own battles.

If she and Geoffrey had gone home together after they had argued, Olivia would have seen the regretful droop of his shoulders, heard his weary sighs, and known that he was sorry. Her doleful eyes, her hand brushing his, would have said that she was sorry too. A glass of wine, a kiss, an embrace – the wrong righted.

But they hadn't gone home together – hadn't even spoken – and the wrong most certainly had not been righted.

When Olivia accepted the job at St Bede's, a determination to avoid living with Rowena had been her primary consideration. She hadn't understood how detrimental it would be to live apart from Geoffrey; how it would tip and tilt their marriage – unbalance its natural equilibrium.

That was why she had asked Lorna to meet her at Millfield – so she could explain that living apart was an unnatural state for a married couple. If Lorna knew what to expect, maybe she and Johnny would think twice about it; or at least handle it better than she and Geoffrey had.

Lorna had got there nearly an hour later than arranged. Olivia had begun to wonder if she would come at all. They hadn't spoken since the brief phone call after Olivia's meeting with Toby Burton in Axbridge. Johnny's leaving; that's all Lorna had said. Olivia had visions of him throwing his things in a holdall, a mystified and heartbroken Lorna begging him to tell her what was wrong – why he was being like this.

Not ideal talking by the side of a netball pitch, trussed up against the cold, but better than not talking at all. It was the first real chance Olivia had got to see Lorna and find out what had happened. Turned out Johnny hadn't been driven away by the intolerable burden of shame, but had left for a job in London. Lorna seemed perturbed by Olivia's efforts to put a positive spin on it. 'It's good that he's working – earning again,' she had said sunnily. Lorna looked gaunt, her long legs thinner than Olivia had ever seen them. You have to lose a lot of weight for it to show in your legs. 'So I don't have to clean other people's houses, you mean.' No, that wasn't what she meant. It didn't matter anyway. Lorna had her own theory about what was going on with her and Johnny. 'I think he's seeing someone. He hasn't touched me in months.'

What sort of person allowed their dearest friend to believe her husband didn't want her any more, that he found what he wanted in another woman's bed? Olivia had been sorely tempted to tell her the truth and to hell with Johnny's oath of silence, but the referee blew her whistle and the moment passed. All she could do was try to make Lorna feel better, or at least, not quite so bad. 'It's hard for men like Geoffrey and Johnny to have nothing to do all day. And the bedroom thing? – Geoffrey hasn't been exactly Don Juan lately, I can assure you.' She arched an eyebrow for emphasis. 'On the outside they're all brawn and bravado but on the inside, well, they're the weaker sex in my opinion. Men brood, women talk. It's a Mars, Venus thing.' Lorna had stared blankly into the middle distance. 'Maybe.'

Olivia had wanted to talk for longer but duty called. She had to commiserate with the St Bede's girls, congratulate the Millfield girls, help usher them towards the changing rooms and muck in with match tea. She noticed Maisie and her little gang sniggering at a girl with a pink plastic patch over one eye. Maisie whispered something in the girl's ear that made her turn and stomp away.

'You'd better go,' Lorna said. 'I should get back too.' Olivia had watched her head towards the car park, her walk less brisk and bouncy than usual, as though weighed down by an invisible force.

*

All the way back to school, Olivia fretted about Lorna and the rights and wrongs of keeping Johnny's secret. She had the power to put Lorna out of her misery, explain what was really going on, but was it her place? Wasn't Johnny entitled to his privacy? Surely it was his secret to tell? But then shouldn't Olivia's loyalties rest with Lorna, irrespective of what she had promised?

'Alice is feeling sick, Mrs Parry.'

Helena had walked the length of the minibus to report this. Olivia suspected Alice just wanted some attention but dutifully went to her. She looked like a waif huddled in the far corner, her skin's fragile translucence magnifying the greyish sweep beneath her eyes, the faint blue vein down the centre of her forehead.

At match tea Maisie had pushed her hard and deliberately. Alice slammed to the floor, arms splayed, orange squash spilling everywhere. Olivia rushed over and helped her to her feet, Alice's bottom lip trembling with the effort of being brave. Maisie had watched, unmoved. This wasn't high spirits or a prank gone awry – this was bullying. It made Olivia think again about her argument with Geoffrey and see that he was right. There was a big difference between Freddie Burton calling Edward a fag and Maisie Rutherford deliberately hurting her sister. Sticks and stones . . .

When Olivia had chastised Maisie, told her in her sternest voice it was wrong to push people, she shrugged in that little-madam way she had and said Mummy did it to Daddy.

'Helena told me you weren't feeling well,' Olivia said to Alice.

She opened the minibus window an inch, allowing a blast of cold air to rush in. Six thirty but dark as midnight. She sat down in the empty seat next to Alice. There always seemed to be an empty seat next to Alice.

'We're almost there.'

This didn't cheer her up. The school gates came into view, a car waiting to pull out on to the road. The minibus slowed down to let it pass: GP 007. Geoffrey's Mercedes. So he hadn't waited for her to get back.

*

Olivia counted the girls off the bus – she had started to count heads in her sleep. Alice got off last and bolted towards her mother, who was talking on her mobile by the main entrance. She ended the call and visibly braced as Alice launched herself at her, wrapping her arms tightly round her waist. Maisie skipped past with a cheery 'Hello, Mummy'. Olivia ushered the stragglers into the building before she asked Ruth if they could have a quick word.

'Can I come home with you?' pleaded Alice.

Ruth patted her daughter's hair. 'Don't be silly,' she said, and then to Olivia, 'I'll pop up now if you like.'

Ruth untangled herself from a whimpering Alice and led the way.

'Hope the netball team fared better than the rugby team,' said Ruth. 'They lost to Colstons. Geoffrey wasn't happy about it but I think I managed to cheer him up.'

Olivia flashed back to supper, to the uncomfortable spectacle of the two of them flirting, and then her silly argument with Geoffrey on the way back to the car. She regretted not having had sex like he wanted. She regretted the argument about Edward too. Was that why he hadn't waited for her to get back from Millfield: to avoid the possibility of another argument? It wasn't as if he had anything to rush home for, other than an evening with his mother – captive audience to her reminiscences and opinions.

Olivia wished she hadn't suggested talking to Ruth. She wasn't in the mood for it, but couldn't really back out now. In half an hour or so the boarders would have finished supper and be on their way up to the dorm. Olivia could really have done with the time to herself: a mug of hot chocolate and a sit down – maybe try to Skype her mum, although it was six in the morning in Sydney so that might not have been too welcome.

She unlocked the door to her flat, took off her coat and put it in the bedroom. When she came back Ruth was on the sofa, scrutinising her phone.

'I can never get a signal up here,' said Olivia.

'Orange,' said Ruth.

'Pardon?'

'Orange. It's the only network with coverage.'

'Good to know. Can I take your coat?'

Ruth dropped her bag on the table. 'No, you can't. It's bloody freezing.'

'Sorry. The boiler has a mind of its own.'

Ruth looked around in the manner of a prospective purchaser viewing a wholly unsuitable property. 'So what did you want to talk about?'

Olivia sat on the chair opposite. 'I'm concerned about Alice.'

'We've discussed this already.'

'Yes, I know, but things have cranked up a gear, I'm afraid. This afternoon, Maisie deliberately pushed her to the ground. Alice was very upset.'

Olivia could have been describing some mundane domestic matter for all the concern Ruth showed.

'I see. Well, it sounds like normal sibling stuff. Alice has always been more clingy, but if she doesn't learn to stand up for herself people will walk all over her.'

Olivia couldn't fault Ruth's logic. If an animal sensed fear, it knew it had the upper hand. Alice exuded fear. She cast herself in the role of victim and Maisie responded accordingly.

'I agree Alice is too timid. I wonder if perhaps she's not quite ready for boarding?'

The dismissive shrug of Ruth's shoulders was pure Maisie. Olivia remembered a book that posed the nature versus nurture debate. It had been Lorna's turn to host book club, generous pourings of wine fuelling a variety of family anecdotes, revealed in the spirit of the confessional. Leslie Winter, the quietest, newest member of the group, disclosed that her parents had lived separate lives under the same roof and that mealtimes were conducted in a cold and choking silence. Anorexia was the inevitable corollary – not because of size-zero models or the prevailing cult of thinness, but because as far back as she could remember, it was hard to swallow food past a tight, tense knot of incomprehension. When the two people you loved most in the world were the two people who hated each other most in the world, it was difficult to make sense of the world. No one knew what to say. Lorna had opened another bottle of wine and moved the subject on to Josh and Lily, how in some ways they were so alike and in others, so very different.

Maisie and Alice were different too and that was fine, but there was an unhealthy imbalance at the core of their relationship: an emerging malice that went far beyond the good-natured, short-lived disagreements Josh and Lily had.

'If a lack of confidence is the problem,' said Ruth, 'I would have thought boarding was the perfect solution. They just have to muck in and get on with it, don't they? Exactly what Alice needs. When she's at home she follows me round all day – wants my undivided attention. Maisie is much less demanding.'

Again, Olivia found it difficult to argue. She regretted broaching this without Martin. His natural empathy might have counterbalanced Ruth's insistence that nothing was amiss.

A photograph on the sideboard caught Ruth's attention – Geoffrey and Edward running out of the sea at Lyme Regis. Easter holidays, just a month before the factory closed down. Olivia had dared them to swim but the water was so cold they only made it in a few yards before racing back to the shore. Olivia could barely keep the camera still, she was laughing so much.

Ruth went over to have a closer look. 'You think I'm a bad mother, don't you?' Her tone was matter-of-fact rather than accusatory, but the directness of the question shocked Olivia.

'That's not what I'm saying.'

'It's implied.'

Ruth picked up the photograph and examined it. 'Tell me, does Edward lashing out at Freddie Burton make *you* a bad mother?' If Ruth's intention was to offend, she had succeeded.

'That was an isolated incident.'

Ruth put down the photograph and picked up another – a headshot of Geoffrey.

'And wife?'

'Pardon?'

'Are you critical of me as a wife?'

Olivia had promised never to speak of the incident with young Tom and didn't understand Ruth's motives for bringing it up.

'I'm not prepared to discuss—'

'I'm a terrible wife,' interrupted Ruth. 'But you already know that. Just out of interest, why didn't you tell Martin what really happened in the pavilion? Certainly would have made your life easier with all those nasty rumours flying around.'

Olivia took a slow breath to try to flatten the sharp spike of rancour. She thought of Rowena, opposite in terms of approach: Ruth searingly direct, Rowena artfully oblique – but with remarkably similar intent. Olivia often reflected on what it was about her that piqued dislike in a certain type of woman. Jealousy, her mother always said, although it was difficult to imagine that was the case with Ruth. Her towering confidence, her 'couldn't give a toss' arrogance suggested jealousy was an alien emotion. How satisfying it would be to tell Ruth exactly what she thought of her. *You're a selfish slut who doesn't deserve Martin or the girls.* The words tasted bitter on Olivia's tongue. It took heroic willpower not to spit them like venom in Ruth's smug face. Olivia took another slow breath and reminded herself she needed this job.

'I didn't want to destroy your family.'

Ruth made a 'huh' sound, as if mildly amused. 'How noble.'

'Not entirely. I didn't want to fall foul of that whole shoot-the-messenger thing either.'

Ruth seemed to have lost interest in the topic anyway. She studied the photograph of Geoffrey a few moments more before placing it back on the sideboard. 'It's not all it seems, is it? Marriage. Family.'

Olivia assumed the question was rhetorical.

'And what about you, Olivia? Are you a good wife? It can't be easy for you and Geoffrey, being apart for weeks on end. All that enforced celibacy.'

Boundary issues. That was Ruth's problem – she had no respect for boundaries. The only person Olivia discussed her marriage with was Lorna. She would certainly never discuss it with Ruth Rutherford.

'That's none of your business,' said Olivia curtly.

Ruth raised an eyebrow, a hint of a smirk suggesting she enjoyed getting a rise out of Olivia.

'The girls will be back soon,' Olivia said, getting to her feet. 'I should really—'

Ruth pulled a tissue from her coat pocket and blew her nose. 'Can I use your loo?'

Olivia wanted her gone but could hardly refuse. She pointed at the bedroom door. 'Through there.'

A hissing sound signalled the boiler had sprung into action. Olivia needed a long, hot shower and for this day to end. Another sound – a phone ringing – emanated from Ruth's open bag. Her mobile lay on top, its screen lit up.

GP 007. It took a few rings before Olivia made the connection. Geoffrey?

Ruth swept in, buttoning up her coat. 'Was that my phone?'

She glanced at it without comment and threw her bag over her shoulder.

'I'll have a word with Maisie, tell her to be kinder to her sister. Don't want to raise a little tyrant now, do I?'

With that she breezed out, leaving Olivia to try and fathom why Geoffrey's number was saved in Ruth's phone, and why he was calling her.

Harriet popped her head round the door. 'I saw Mrs Rutherford go. Everything all right?'

Olivia wasn't sure how to answer that.

*

Pinned to the corkboard over the fridge was a copy of Olivia's job description: two pages of duties and responsibilities under the headings 'Nurturing and Educating Students (60%)', 'House Management (20%)', 'Programme and Professional Development (20%)'.

When Martin had first gone through it with her, he had noted her bewildered expression and played it down. *Don't look so worried, Olivia. It's much less onerous than it seems.*

Not true. Most evenings she stayed up late sorting the girls' laundry and mending their uniforms. There were reports and Christmas cards to write for the end of term; travel arrangements to be made for those girls whose parents couldn't collect them. This evening she was too tired for any of it. She climbed into bed shortly after ten and opened the book that had sat, neglected, on her bedside table all week. Dense historical tomes weren't her favourite reading but she needed something to take her mind off Geoffrey.

She had braved the elements in the quad to phone him after Ruth left, but got his voicemail. He would have been back at the Rectory by then so why hadn't he taken her call? Was it some sort of payback for her not having taken his? He knew what her timetable was like and how difficult she found it to get any service on her mobile. She had been tempted to phone him on the landline, but Rowena might have answered and Olivia wasn't in the mood for strained small talk. Rain had found its way inside her collar and she shivered. Again she had tried Geoffrey's mobile and again it went to voicemail. That time she left a message. *Thought you might have waited for me after rugby – would have been nice to see you. Actually, I did see you, driving away.* She shut her eyes and counted to three. *Why did you call Ruth Rutherford?*

*

Some of the Alpha group had volunteered to meet at the Rutherfords' house and help sew costumes for the Nativity play. Naturally Olivia had been roped in too. General dogsbody, unable to say 'No, I'd rather not if you don't mind', because she had to make up for Edward's fall from grace, for Geoffrey's poor performance with the rugby team, for Maisie Rutherford bullying Alice Rutherford, and for anything else that might possibly go wrong despite none of it being her fault in the first place.

She admired the confidence with which Lisa Pearce had declined the invitation to participate. 'I said I was too busy with actual school work to do favours for the headmaster's wife.' Olivia had been slumped on a sagging armchair in the staffroom, Lisa next to her, perched on a matching chair, working her way through a four-finger KitKat. 'And speaking of favours,' she broke one of the fingers in half, 'it was good of your hubbie to step in as handyman the other day.'

Olivia had stopped brooding about being put upon for a minute. 'Oh?' she said.

Lisa popped the KitKat finger in her mouth and made an *mmm* sound. 'Saturday, after rugby. Found him in the kitchen with Mrs Rutherford, mending a tap, I think. Something like that.'

This information had been disturbing on several levels. First, Geoffrey had no aptitude for any kind of DIY, so the likelihood of him mending a tap was remote. Second, the school had a handyman on call seven days a week for such eventualities. And, third, Olivia had spoken to Ruth in her flat that Saturday evening and she had mentioned nothing. In fact, that was when Geoffrey had called Ruth's mobile.

It was at times like that Olivia missed Lorna the most. She would have been straight on the phone to her, outlined the facts as she knew them and then worked through every conceivable scenario in great detail before deciding what action, if any, to take. Lisa's casual revelation had baffled and unnerved her, and there was no one she could talk to.

This was what Olivia was ruminating about as she hurried between the school and the Rutherfords' house in the rain. That, and the fact that five days had passed since she and Geoffrey had spoken. First she hadn't taken his calls and now he wasn't taking hers. Silence fed the distance between them.

The front door was on the latch and Olivia could hear voices inside. She let herself in and found Ruth and Alicia Burton in the kitchen, doing battle with a set of angel wings. The last time Alicia had spoken to Olivia, it was to thank her for having saved Freddie. They hadn't spoken about the boys' fight, or about involving the police only to un-involve them after Olivia had met with Alicia's ex. Olivia had enough on her mind without worrying how she might be received by Alicia Burton but as she hung back, reluctant to interrupt, her heart raced.

'They're enormous,' shrieked Ruth, grappling with the angel wings.

Alicia took them from her and wheezed with laughter. Olivia was tempted to leave before they saw her but felt a tap on her shoulder.

'Olivia – haven't seen you for ages.'

Wendy Harding – Finn's mother. A brief career in the theatre had spawned a bohemian flamboyance: elaborately draped scarves, long floaty skirts, brightly coloured beads.

'Cavalry's arrived,' said Ruth, raising a glass.

Alicia and Wendy air-kissed, each telling the other how wonderful they looked. The kitchen smelled of alcohol, cloves and baking.

'Mulled wine?' said Ruth, reaching into a cupboard for more glasses. 'Mince pies to follow. Alicia's recipe – liberally laced with Cointreau and brandy.'

'Sounds yummy,' piped up Wendy, slipping off her oversized woollen coat to reveal a red dress with a bold, ethnic-style print. A diamanté Christmas tree dangled from each earlobe.

Ruth ladled warm wine from a copper saucepan on the stove, and handed a glass each to Olivia and Wendy. Olivia disliked mulled wine even more than mince pies. What she wanted was a nice cup of tea but that wasn't on offer.

'Cheers,' said Ruth, raising her glass. 'Merry Christmas.'

Merry indeed. Ruth's cheeks shone with an uncharacteristic blush and Alicia's hiccups were a source of great hilarity. Neither woman looked capable of threading a needle. Wendy blew on her wine and asked Alicia how Freddie was doing. An innocent enough question, general in tone – no mention of black eyes or strangulation – but it rippled through the air, disturbing the smooth fit of atoms and molecules. Alicia didn't look at Olivia when she said he was doing well and thanked her for asking.

The sense of being unpopular was not something Olivia would ever get used to, despite all her years of practice with Rowena. It jarred and diminished her: the outsider, the interloper. Alicia was positively animated when she chatted to Ruth and Wendy, but with Olivia she was cool. If it hadn't been for the hour spent in her ex-husband's company, Olivia would have written Alicia off as a self-serving sycophant, but you never knew what people endured in the name of marriage, what injustices were subsumed beneath its solemn vows and promises. Olivia had read an Iris Murdoch novel – dense, brilliant, horribly depressing – that was dissected and discussed over a good deal of wine at Manor Farm. It wasn't the four hundred pages of literary slog that had captured the imagination of the Compton Cross book group. It was the quote at the beginning: *Marriage is a very secret place.* Everyone had an opinion on that.

Alicia opened the oven door and checked on the mince pies.

'I'm doing catering now and you lucky ladies are my focus group.' Her face and neck suddenly glowed crimson. Sweat gleamed on her forehead and upper lip. She grabbed a Christmas card from Ruth's display and fanned herself, making small puffing sounds.

'So,' she said, once the hot flush had passed, 'I've used three different types of pastry and I need you to tell me which you like best. Shortcrust, puff or filo.'

Celia Scott-Lessing turned up with her mother-in-law who was visiting from Toronto – an elegant silver-haired lady in a brown suede suit and flat, fur-lined boots. She must have been hard of hearing because Celia did the introductions in a slow, loud voice. When it was Olivia's turn – *This is Olivia Parry, she's a houseparent here at the school, her son Edward is a friend of Ben's* – Mrs Scott-Lessing appraised her as if she were a work of art.

'You don't look old enough, dear. Does your husband work at the school too?'

'He coaches the rugby team,' said Olivia.

'Alicia's son, Freddie, is captain,' chimed in Ruth.

Did Ruth imagine that the dowager Scott-Lessing was interested in the temporary captaincy of the rugby team? Hardly. That snippet was imparted purely for Olivia's benefit.

A pinging sound signalled that the mince pies were ready. Alicia produced them from the oven with a flourish and set the baking tray down on the granite worktop. They did smell good: rich and aromatic. Once they had cooled, Alicia arranged them on a plate and offered them round. She reminded everyone to say which type they preferred, but Olivia disliked them all. The intensity of the liqueur overwhelmed the fruit, reminding her of when she had sneaked a sip of dark amber liquid from her grandad's glass and its sour heat made her choke.

'Filo,' announced Wendy, wiping crumbs from the corner of her mouth. 'With puff a close second.'

A murmur of agreement hummed round the kitchen.

'I hope your husband appreciates your cooking,' Mrs Scott-Lessing said to Alicia. 'It was one of the things I missed most when my husband passed away. Hardly worth going to all that trouble for oneself.'

Celia looked down as if to apologise for not having briefed her mother-in-law on Alicia's marital status.

'One of the few things he did appreciate,' said Alicia wryly.

Ruth patted her arm.

'Divorce,' she said, offering Mrs Scott-Lessing another mince pie. 'He had the temerity to bring his girlfriend to rugby on Saturday.'

'Which meant I couldn't go,' said Alicia, 'even though Freddie was captain.'

Mrs Scott-Lessing titled her head in sympathy. 'Men can be so insensitive.'

'That's one word for it,' said Ruth. 'He and Geoffrey almost came to blows after the match. I had to step in and prise them apart.'

They looked at Olivia, waiting for an explanation she didn't have – meat to flesh out the bones of the story.

'Oh, it was nothing,' she said, checking her watch by way of diversion. 'Rugby stuff. Actually, I have to be back in an hour.'

Ruth rolled her eyes. 'I suppose we'd better get on then.'

She breezed out of the kitchen and returned a few minutes later with a large cardboard box that brimmed with half-made costumes, more angel wings, gold turbans, white feather halos, a roll of red velvet trim. Olivia needed a few minutes to herself to process what Ruth had said about Geoffrey and Toby Burton, and piece that together with what Lisa had told her earlier about Geoffrey and Ruth and a kitchen tap.

She went upstairs to the bathroom and swilled Listermint around her mouth to get rid of the taste of mulled wine and mince pie. Whatever had happened after Saturday's match, it was clear Geoffrey didn't want to share it with her. That in itself was suspect. She put down the toilet seat and sat, legs crossed, trying to decide if (a) Geoffrey had something to hide, or (b) he was still brooding over their argument about Edward.

Laughter floated up from the kitchen, Ruth's louder than the rest. An uncharacteristic darkness tugged at Olivia, ominously reminiscent of the isolation she had felt after Edward was born. Different cause; same effect. Lorna and her mother had saved her then, but now Olivia was on her own.

She had held steadfast to the belief that although she was living a lesser version of her life, her real life – the one in which Geoffrey owned Downings, Manor Farm was home, Edward was a happy child, Lorna and Johnny were their best friends, and she and Geoffrey slept in the same bed – still existed in a parallel universe, waiting for her return. She didn't believe that any more.

As she let herself out of the bathroom another wave of laughter smacked her in the face. For all she knew they were laughing at her. She couldn't go back down there; not yet.

When she noticed a bedroom door ajar, she didn't see the harm in taking a few moments to regroup. Only when she was inside did she realise it was the master bedroom – Martin and Ruth's room. She knew she should leave, that there was something voyeuristic about being in the place where a couple were at their most intimate, but she was curious.

Curtains and matching bedding: beige, bland, boring. Cream wallpaper with a darker beige stripe; fitted wardrobes across the entire length of one wall. In the opposite corner was a chair with a white bathrobe thrown over it. Tucked neatly under the window stood one of those faux French dressing tables, the sort with names like 'Louis' or 'Versailles'. On it, nestled between a box of tissues and a bottle of perfume, was a mobile phone. Martin always carried his with him so this one must belong to Ruth. Olivia knew it was wrong, an inexcusable invasion of privacy, but picked it up anyway. No code to crack, just a factory settings screensaver.

There was one message from GP 007. *Can't wait.* That was it. Olivia stared, waiting for a logical explanation to reveal itself. No reply, no previous messages. The rest of the conversation must have been deleted. Voicemail was empty too. In Recent Calls, GP 007 was listed five, six, seven times. Olivia let the phone drop back on to the dressing table, an incongruous mix of heaviness and panic spreading outward from her chest.

'Everything all right?'

She turned round. Wendy Harding stood in the door-way, looking puzzled and a little tipsy. The fringed silk scarf around her neck was twice as long on one side as the other.

'I can't hear a phone ring without rushing to answer it,' said Olivia, forcing a jolly St Bede's smile. 'Terrible habit.'

'All slaves to technology these days,' said Wendy.

Olivia took this as her cue and exited stage left. 'Bath-room's just there,' she said, pointing along the landing.

Olivia walked downstairs, shaken by the certainty that something significant had happened. She didn't know the specifics – the how, what or when – but she did know she couldn't be around Ruth Rutherford right now.

'Her husband lost his business and their house along with it. That's why she lives here at the school.' Ruth's voice carried into the hall. It took gumption for Olivia to walk into the kitchen, politely but firmly make her excuses, grab her coat and leave.

Twelve

'We're going to burn in hell.'

Geoffrey took a long drag on his cigarette and inhaled deeply, impatient for the acrid sharpness to hit the back of his throat. He savoured the light-headed sensation that was his reward for all those years of enforced abstinence. A nicotine virgin reborn. He exhaled small, white puffs of smoke that floated up like Polo Mint clouds. Ruth took the cigarette from between his lips and put it between her own.

'Don't be so dramatic,' she said.

Geoffrey stared at her rounded mouth, her parted lips, the cotton-wool billows she so expertly formed. He wanted to fuck her again. The crisp white sheet barely covered her breasts. She handed him the cigarette to finish and sat up, the sheet pooling around her hips. He thought of a school trip to the Tate – not the folly of exposing a group of sniggering, adolescent boys to paintings of naked women – but the voluptuous beauties depicted by Rubens. The swell of Ruth's belly, the weight of her breasts, held an unexpected and novel appeal. Olivia's body was tight and toned: all lean, athletic lines. Ruth's was soft and curvaceous, its flesh warm and yielding.

She reached for the room-service menu. 'I'm starving,' she said.

He tried to kiss her nipple but she swatted him away with a playful slap.

'Food first.'

Odd that her bossiness turned him on. He disliked bossy women as a rule – something Freudian to do with his mother, no doubt – but with Ruth it fuelled a dominatrix fantasy. He pictured her in a black leather corset, high-heeled boots, a riding crop in her hand. She noted the beginnings of his erection with a disapproving look and repeated herself, more sternly this time.

'Food first,' she said, handing him the menu.

He glanced over the options and told her he'd have a burger. Ruth picked up the phone, ordered two burgers and a bottle of house red.

'How long will that be?' she asked.

Geoffrey slowly peeled the sheet away from her hips, revealing a fine horizontal scar and sparse wisps of the palest hair.

She put down the phone and turned to him. 'Ten minutes,' she said, sliding down the bed.

*

The way she ate surprised him, and very slightly disgusted him. Forget table manners. She relished every mouthful: greedily licked the mayonnaise from her fingertips, the salt from her lips. He couldn't help but compare Ruth's gluttony with the dainty way Olivia nibbled at her food.

Ruth's appetites were varied and voracious. Three days ago he'd fucked her at St Bede's and he had eagerly fucked her every day since. When he wasn't with her time was a burden to be endured, marked off, minute by empty minute. Cliché or not, he only felt alive when he was with her. There, he'd said it. Not out loud of course – she'd laugh at him, tell him to get a grip. She wanted nothing from him except what he was willing to give. That he was naked in a hotel room, breaking his marriage vows as often as his body's powers of recovery allowed, suggested he was willing to give a lot.

Around her neck she wore a small gold crucifix. He took it between his thumb and forefinger and examined it closely. No tortured, dying Jesus, just a plain, unadorned cross.

'Religious symbol or jewellery?'

She poured them both a large glass of wine. 'Self-flagellation.'

Had her extraordinary powers of sexual perception picked up on the dominatrix thing? 'I'm up for it if you are.'

She took a long drink and lit another cigarette. 'What?'

OK, maybe he had got that wrong.

She rolled the crucifix between her fingers. 'A gift.'

'From Martin?'

Her sardonic snort suggested, no, it wasn't from Martin. She picked up the phone and ordered another bottle of wine, even though they hadn't finished the first. A full stomach and post-lunch lethargy meant that sex wouldn't be on the agenda for a while. Geoffrey settled back against a pile of pillows and passed the time by trying to tease information from Ruth. She was something of an enigma: a well-brought-up, well-educated Christian wife and mother, yet serially unfaithful and with scant regard for social mores. He opened by asking how old she was when she lost her virginity. She gave him a narrow-eyed look that said 'mind your own business', and lit a cigarette.

'OK, I'll go first. Seventeen, summer holidays, Weston-super-Mare, Susan Richie, back of my father's Vauxhall Cavalier. I should point out that my father wasn't in the car at the time.'

Ruth looked mildly amused. Encouraged, Geoffrey said, 'Your turn.'

She took a drag of her cigarette and released a long slow ribbon of smoke. 'Nineteen, freshers' week, Rupert Westingham, my room at Magdalene College.'

'Nineteen? That's late. I imagined you'd have got rid as soon as it was legal, if not before.'

The cigarette had almost burnt down to the brown filter. She mashed the butt into the ashtray and drained her glass of wine. 'Chance would have been a fine thing. Hyper-religious, hyper-vigilant parents. Going up to Cambridge was my first real taste of freedom.'

'Me too – not the Cambridge thing, obviously, but the hyper-religious thing. My father was a vicar.'

Geoffrey took a cigarette from the pack and lit it. The instant he said it, he regretted mentioning his father. Lying naked in a hotel room with another man's wife was an atrocious betrayal of the values with which he had been raised. He needed to say something good to offset the sense of being very, very bad.

'Lovely man, my father.'

'Lucky you,' said Ruth. 'Mine was both distant and controlling. Not easy to pull off but he managed it.'

Room service arriving with the second bottle of wine was a blessed relief. Why the hell were they talking about their fathers? Geoffrey had never been eager to talk about

224

feelings or relationships, and had certainly never intended to do so with Ruth. He perceived her as functioning on a physical level – I'm hungry so I eat, I'm horny so I fuck – rather like he did, and that suited him just fine. Geoffrey signed for the wine, a towel around his waist, and scrambled together some change for a tip. He filled their glasses and got back into bed, hoping for a shift in tempo: less talk, more sex. Ruth had different ideas.

'So, you and Olivia. Childhood sweethearts? Love at first sight?'

Geoffrey couldn't do what he was doing if he thought about Olivia. Ruth mistook his lack of response as an invitation to carry on.

'She can do no wrong in Martin's book. Even when I told him she had sneaked off to the pavilion with that gorgeous French chap, Martin refused to believe there was anything going on between them.'

'There wasn't. And that was a rotten thing to do, by the way.'

Ruth didn't so much shrug, as move one shoulder up and forward as if to dismiss his opinion as irrelevant. 'Not the point. Martin thinks she's beyond reproach. So' – she struggled for the correct adjective – 'nice. Always so eager to please. So annoyingly *fair*.'

Geoffrey didn't need to be reminded of his wife's many virtues, nor of the magnitude of his betrayal. Ruth had tried to fuck things up for Olivia and here he was, fucking Ruth. The very least he could do was defend his wife, albeit half-heartedly. 'She's a good person.' He noted the wine bottles, the full ashtray, the discarded clothing and naked adulterers. 'Better than I deserve, I think it's true to say.'

All this talk of Olivia had drowned Geoffrey's libido in guilt and highlighted Ruth's many character flaws. Time to steer her in a different direction. 'How did you and Martin meet?'

Ruth poured two glasses of wine and lit a cigarette for them to share. She took the first drag. 'He nearly ran me over on the towpath along the Cam. Bicycle clips on his suit trousers – can you imagine?'

'Actually, yes. Bicycle clips seem very Martin. And what's with the zany socks? Is he trying to make some sort of weird fashion statement?'

She sipped some wine and fixed Geoffrey with a cool stare. 'If I can't speak ill of your wife, you can't speak ill of my husband. Agreed?'

Loyalty. He didn't see that coming. 'Agreed.'

Geoffrey took a few puffs of the cigarette and handed it to Ruth. He would have to drive back to the Rectory later so shouldn't really drink any more, but being in Ruth's company made him irresponsible and reckless. He poured another glass of wine.

'There is something I'm curious about.'

'Oh?'

'Does Martin know about your' – he trod carefully, not wanting to draw attention to her promiscuity – 'dalliances?'

She shifted so that she was lying on her side across the foot of the bed, propped up on one elbow, scrutinising him. It seemed like she was trying to decide whether or not to answer the question.

'He looks the other way,' she said.

Geoffrey had doubts about pursuing this line of questioning but was intrigued as to what possessed a man to turn a blind eye to his wife fucking other men. 'I couldn't do it.'

'No, I don't suppose you could. I daresay you'd beat the living daylights out of any man who sniffed round your precious Olivia.'

'I daresay I would. Is that what you want Martin to do?'

Ruth smiled, but in a mocking way. 'How perceptive.'

She rolled on to her back, hands clasped behind her head. Her breasts lolled to either side, nipples rose-pink and hard. From that angle he could see stretch marks, as though a snail had slithered over her belly, leaving a thin trail of silvery slime. He would have found it off-putting if all this talk of sex and beatings hadn't got his blood pumping again. He felt himself stir beneath the crumpled sheet, but Ruth hadn't finished answering his question.

'The first time was a sort of test to see if he had any backbone. He's always so passive – on his best behaviour. I wanted him to be angry. Enraged.'

'And was he?'

A sigh of disappointment. 'No. He's too docile, too Christian.' She sat up and took a sip of wine. 'I do my best to provoke him but he will insist on forgiving me.'

'And speaking of which,' said Geoffrey, sipping from his wine glass too, 'I'm dreading seeing Olivia at rugby training tomorrow. She knows I called you – left a message on my mobile asking why. I haven't worked out what I'm going to tell her yet.'

Ruth had no opinion on the subject. She got up and went to the bathroom. Wonderful posture. Shoulders back, breasts lifted and pushed forward. Her hips had a subtle but definite swing and her hair, fine though it was, looked attractively tousled and messy.

It was years since he had been so infatuated with a woman. The way she talked about Martin always being on his best behaviour really struck a chord. That was how Geoffrey felt. His whole life had been about meeting other people's expectations, trying to do the right thing, even if he failed or if it wasn't the right thing for him. And where had it got him? His affair with Ruth was the first time in his entire life he had ever deliberately been bad. He had crossed a line that couldn't be uncrossed and was in no doubt his day of reckoning would come, but until that day, it felt fucking amazing.

*

Freddie Burton hit the ground hard and rolled. He held his shoulder, his face contorted with pain. Edward was still on his feet, the ball in his possession. They had collided at pace but Freddie, being the smaller of the two, had come off worse. Geoffrey blew the whistle to stop play and jogged over to them. Freddie's moans were interspersed with a rich variety of swear words. He muttered them under his breath, but just loud enough for Geoffrey to hear. 'Fuck' appeared to be his profanity of choice, with 'bloody bastard' a close second. Geoffrey was sure he hadn't used that sort of language at Freddie's age – certainly not in the company of adults. How times had changed.

He offered his hand but Freddie turned away and pushed himself up on his good arm. Edward's tackle had been on the aggressive side but it was rugby, for God's sake – get over it. After two weeks off the team, Edward was fired up and fierce. Geoffrey blew the whistle for them to play on. Freddie hissed something in his direction and hobbled to the centre of the pitch.

In Geoffrey's peripheral vision a groundsman was raking leaves. He wore one of those oversized woollen hats that looked like a tea cosy. Difficult to be sure from that distance but Geoffrey supposed it must be young Tom. He looked so menial, the sort of lad you see collecting rubbish in the park or digging holes in the road. It tarnished Geoffrey's view of Ruth as a free spirit – brought her flaws and faults into sharp focus. What the hell had she been thinking? She was pushing forty, for Christ sakes. A mother of two. Yes, he was aware of the double standard – older man, younger woman, perfectly acceptable – but still. Seeing the scruffy teenager forced Geoffrey to confront the shocking extent of Ruth's carnality.

His heart leaped into his throat. A leaflet the university doctor had given him along with the news he had chlamydia, all of a sudden was frighteningly relevant. 'Be Sure To Be Safe – Be Sure To Wear A Condom.' A couple kissing on top of a pyramid and below them, all their previous sexual partners.

Geoffrey hadn't thought to wear a condom. Christ, what diseases could the grungy youth have passed on to Ruth, and Ruth to Geoffrey? He would have to get himself tested, although not with the family GP. Geoffrey tried for a deep breath but his heart took up all the space in his chest and throat. A vision of sitting in one of those awful STD clinics flashed across his mind. He'd seen them on Channel 5, populated by perverts and prostitutes. Had it stung when he peed this morning? No – he would have remembered if it had stung.

Angry shouts brought his attention back to the pitch. He hadn't seen the tackle that put Edward on the ground and a self-satisfied smirk to Freddie Burton's face. Edward's face had a muddy bootprint on one side. Geoffrey didn't have the patience for this. Deaf to protests that they still had ten minutes to go, he sent the whole lot of them off to the showers and walked with them in case Edward and Freddie started something.

In an effort to try to banish thoughts of clinics and diseases he struck up a conversation with Edward – told him how good it was to have him back on the team and to take no notice of Freddie Burton. Geoffrey was tempted to bring up the subject of name-calling, casually of course. He wanted Edward to reassure him that there was nothing more to it, no specific incident that had prompted it, but school broke up at the end of next week – he'd take him fishing or on one of their day-long hikes in the Brecons and they'd talk properly then.

As they rounded the corner he spotted Olivia coming towards him. He felt sure the minor explosion in his chest was a heart attack. Or guilt. He had a prepared script but now she was in front of him, looking tired but achingly pretty, it vanished from his head. Why did he always forget how pretty she was? The pictures on his phone didn't capture the smoothness of her skin, the flecks of green and gold in her eyes. Each time he saw her it hit him all over again. His heart lurched with love and fear. If she found out about Ruth, he would lose her.

Olivia managed a smile, but he knew it was more for the boys' benefit than his. When she asked Edward what had happened to his face he told her not to make a fuss. The boys carried on into the building, leaving Geoffrey and Olivia alone.

'So you're alive then?' she said.

'Yes, sorry. I called a few times but could never get hold of you.'

He didn't mention that he'd timed his calls knowing she wouldn't answer: early morning when she was busy with the boarders; after lunch, when she'd be listening to the little ones read; early evening when she was busy with the boarders again.

'We can't talk here,' she said, looking around. 'The staff-room should be empty, more or less.'

He walked alongside her, his heart a machine gun in his chest, about to discover how good a liar he was.

The staffroom had a comfy, shabby homeliness that reminded him of the snug at the Rectory. Olivia made coffee in silence and handed him a mug. They sat down in a far corner where they wouldn't be disturbed.

'Why have you been avoiding me?'

No preamble – straight to the point. He half expected her to see his infidelity, visible and obvious, like a stain on his skin.

'I haven't.'

Her gaze was steady and searching. However hard he tried not to, he had to look away.

'We haven't spoken in a week. A week, Geoffrey. What the hell is that about?'

He shifted in his chair. 'We had that row about Edward.' He shrugged. 'I was cross, upset, I don't know.'

'Why did you call Ruth Rutherford?'

'What?'

'You called her on Saturday evening. GP 007 flashed up on her phone. I assume that was you.'

He affected an air of vague recollection. 'Oh, that. Yeah, I fixed a tap in the kitchen and thought I left my wallet there.'

'And you swapped phone numbers?'

'Uh huh.'

'Why?'

'Umm, she said there might be some more odd jobs – she'd let me know.'

'Odd jobs? You? The school has a caretaker for odd jobs.'

Geoffrey rearranged his expression to one of bemusement. 'Maybe he's busy. It's not a big deal. I was just trying to help out.'

'And the text?'

'What text?'

'The one I found in Ruth's phone. *Can't wait*. What was it you couldn't wait for?'

Fuck. How did she know about that? Think, think. 'Training.'

'Pardon?'

'Edward's first time back on the team since his ban. Ruth asked if I was looking forward to it – to training. *Can't wait* was how I replied.'

Olivia did that long, intense stare thing again. Wait a minute – could he get the upper hand here? 'What were you doing with Ruth's phone?'

Olivia blinked a few times in quick succession. 'Doesn't matter. What does matter is all those calls between the two of you. I counted seven.'

Jesus. He'd told Ruth to delete everything, and that was before he realised Olivia would go all Miss Marple on him. Then a brainwave. 'Look, I've been worried about Edward. At this rate there's no way he'll get a scholarship and we don't have the money for school fees. I've been talking to Ruth about it, you know, if there's anything we can do to improve his chances.'

Geoffrey thought he sounded pretty convincing but Olivia's expression was one of deep scepticism.

'And is there?'

'Maybe. She's going to talk to Martin.'

The muscles in her face relaxed – not much, but just enough for Geoffrey to hope that the worst of the interrogation was over. Would it be pushing things to feign indignation, maybe demand an apology? Perhaps. He reached for her hand but she pulled it away.

'I have another question,' she said, although her tone was less probing than before. 'A long time ago you told me you were a terrible liar and hopeless at keeping secrets. Do you remember?'

In his bedsit, reeling from the news she was pregnant. She'd asked why he had to tell his parents if he didn't want to. 'I remember.'

She studied him for an uncomfortably long time. 'Is it still true?'

That she needed to pose the question suggested she already suspected the answer. A brave man would have owned up, asked for forgiveness and taken his punishment. Geoffrey wasn't that man.

The door swung open and the plump dark-haired woman from match tea blustered in, humming 'Oh Come All Ye Faithful'. When she saw them she came to an abrupt stop and made a 'what's going on here?' face. The same face she had made when she had walked in on him and Ruth.

'Olivia. Mr Parry. How nice to see you both. Usually it's one or the other.'

'Hello, Lisa,' said Olivia, her voice flat.

Right then. Inquisition over as far as Geoffrey was concerned. He stood up and said he needed to check on the boys; make sure they were behaving themselves in the changing room. Olivia walked him to the door, Geoffrey unsure whether she believed his version of events or not. Her demeanour was non-committal, as though she hadn't made up her mind. What if she didn't believe him – if she saw him for the dirty liar that he was? Maybe she could forgive a one-off affair – an isolated blemish on an otherwise blameless track record of fidelity – but not an affair with Ruth Rutherford. Olivia, who hated no one, hated Ruth. Perhaps hate was too strong but dislike wasn't strong enough. And not without reason. Ruth had been a total bitch to Olivia over the whole Hugo, young Tom thing. Geoffrey was sleeping with the enemy. The possibility of losing Olivia was terrifyingly real. He wanted to hold her but Lisa was watching and it didn't feel right. He told Olivia he would call her later, a promise greeted with a resigned nod – no smile. Geoffrey strode along the corridor with a new-found sense of purpose. The spell cast by Ruth had been broken and he knew exactly what he had to do.

*

That haunting 'Snowman' song played on the car radio. In happier times it had made Geoffrey feel all warm and nostalgic: memories of Edward ripping the wrapping paper off his haul of Christmas presents, long dog walks over snowy fields, evenings in front of a roaring fire, Olivia snuggled next to him. Now the song made him unbearably sad. He listened anyway – punishment for his steadily accruing sins. Catholics could own up in the anonymity of the confessional and have their sins absolved. Geoffrey had to carry his sins around, a dead weight of guilt and gutlessness.

The more he thought about it, the more he was convinced Olivia knew he was lying and had been offering him a way out. Confession, penance, absolution.

He closed his eyes and listened to the song. The boy's voice was beautiful. Unbroken. Sadness pressed against Geoffrey's chest; a dense, dull pressure. He let his head fall back against the cream leather headrest and waited for it to pass.

A newsreader reminded him there were other problems in the world – war, famine, parents murdering their children – that were infinitely worse than his own. Geoffrey stared out into the darkness and waited.

Ruth was late. She'd said there was no point paying for a hotel room when they only had an hour. The spot she'd suggested was roughly equidistant and reassuringly remote: a track off a lane off a road. Her directions were too precise for her not to have been there before. And this was what Geoffrey had risked his marriage for.

It was no excuse, of course, but Ruth's interest had flattered him: made him feel manly and potent and the way he used to be before it all went to shit. He had never set out to be unfaithful – creating false profiles on internet dating sites or hanging out in bars looking for women. Ruth had seduced him and he was easy prey. Three months without sex can do that to a man.

The glare of headlights filled the car. Ruth parked her old BMW and tottered over the icy ground.

'Fucking freezing out there,' she said, getting in next to him.

She wore a grey tea-cosy hat similar to that of the groundsman, except hers had a large, crocheted flower on one side. The tip of her nose was red and shiny with the cold, her lips a bluish purpley-pink. Once she had pulled off her mittens – a grown woman wearing mittens? – she fiddled with the radio until she found something 'a bit more cheery'. It wasn't until she had undone her coat and unwrapped her scarf that she noticed he wasn't exactly chipper.

'Everything all right?'

Her tone was clipped and a tad irritated. It would have felt good to unburden himself, tell her all the reasons why everything was most certainly not all right, but she wouldn't have been interested. She ran her hand along his leg, moving slowly from knee to groin. He took a long breath.

'I saw Olivia today.'

Ruth's hand continued its trajectory, kneading his quads as it went.

'She knows something's going on.'

Ruth had reached his balls and gave them a playful squeeze.

'I didn't admit to anything but—'

'Do be quiet, Geoffrey.'

She unzipped his fly and pulled out his dick. Her mouth was on him before he had time to object. Object? Who was he kidding? Half-heartedly he had told himself he wouldn't do this. Such was his conviction he had bought a packet of condoms and slipped them into his pocket, where they were likely to stay. He hadn't used a condom in years and was fuzzy about the etiquette: the point at which you interrupted proceedings, tore open the packet (teeth – he remembered he always used his teeth), and rolled the thing on.

In a blur of activity Ruth's knickers and tights were around her ankles and she was astride him. Oh well, he had probably already caught anything he was going to catch. She moved her hips as though cantering a horse, and out of nowhere, slapped his face.

'What the fuck?' said Geoffrey, bringing a hand to his stinging cheek. When she slapped him again, this time on the other cheek, he grabbed her wrist roughly, an action that induced a slow, triumphant smile. Whatever game she was playing, he was unwittingly playing along. In his ear she whispered, 'Harder, harder,' before her teeth drew blood from its lobe. He grabbed the other wrist and pinned her arms behind her back, all the time pumping her fast, just like she wanted him to. It was over quickly, the car windows steamed up, that awful Slade Christmas song playing in the background. Not Geoffrey's finest hour.

As Ruth climbed off him she caught the soft flesh of her inner thigh on his belt buckle.

'That fucking hurt,' she said, as though it were his fault.

She flopped back into the passenger seat and examined the angry weal on her milk-white skin.

'I thought you liked a bit of pain.'

'Not like that,' she said, wrestling with her knickers and tights.

Geoffrey zipped his fly, disgusted with how rapidly sexy had become seedy. Ruth swore under her breath as she buttoned her coat and fished around for the ugly hat and mittens. There was no air, only the cloying odour of semen and damp wool.

'That was the last time,' he said.

She didn't even look at him. 'Of course it was.'

'I mean it, Ruth. I hated lying to Olivia this afternoon. I can't do this to her.'

'You're not doing anything to her – you're doing it to me.'

Cliff Richard was on the radio now, crooning about mistletoe and wine.

'I'm not saying it hasn't been good, because it has. But when I saw Olivia this afternoon—'

'Oh dear God, stop going on about your bloody wife. If you don't want to do this any more, then fine, but please, spare me the whole guilty husband routine. I'm simply not interested.'

Her couldn't-give-a-fuck attitude made it easier for him to end it. They'd had some fun and now it was over. With Ruth's track record, he'd probably be replaced by the end of the week anyway.

'No hard feelings?' he said.

'No feelings at all.'

He couldn't figure out if it was bravado; an act. When she had talked about testing Martin, trying to rouse him into a jealous frenzy, Geoffrey got the impression she needed visceral evidence of his love, that his doting, beseeching manner wasn't enough for her. And yet he must love her very much because he forgave her every time. The question of why Ruth stayed with him was more puzzling. Given that she was the centre of her own universe, that she unfailingly put herself first – a snippet from daytime television about narcissistic personality disorder flashed into Geoffrey's head – he assumed she wanted to have her cake and eat it. Adoring husband and children, a home, status and security, and very little asked of her in return. And Geoffrey had bought into the whole selfish charade.

The DJ said the next song was for all you lovers out there. Coldplay's 'Christmas Lights', Johnny's favourite band – he had all their albums, knew all their songs. The four of them had gone to London for a weekend and seen them in concert at the O2. It had been Lorna's present for Johnny's fortieth birthday. When they performed this song, everyone held up their mobiles and swayed from side to side. Geoffrey was too self-conscious at first but then joined in with the rest of them.

Olivia had played it last Christmas morning, Edward complaining it was too soppy and please could she put something else on? She told him Daddy waved his mobile like a candle to this song. Edward had looked at him, appalled. Olivia said he should ask Josh and Lily if he didn't believe her; that their dad did it too. They played up to Edward's mock revulsion by slow-dancing and singing along. He mimed his fingers down his throat and said next year he was asking Santa for new parents.

A gust of wind sliced through the car as Ruth opened the door. She turned to Geoffrey and for the briefest moment, he glimpsed something other than carefully crafted nonchalance. The tenderness of her kiss took him by surprise. Usually she was all tongue and teeth, as though eager to devour him. No intimacy or affection, just a quick prelude to the animal pleasures that followed. This kiss was altogether different – soft and lingering. Not a prelude but an ending.

Thirteen

A soft tapping on the door roused Olivia from a fitful sleep, full of unsettling, half-formed dreams. Searching for something lost was a consistent theme. Much of the night she had lain awake trying to decide if there was anything going on between Geoffrey and Ruth Rutherford. She kept replaying her conversation with him in the staffroom, analysing his answers, his explanations, why he couldn't look at her for more than a second or two before he looked away. And why had that tiny muscle in his jaw twitched and flexed?

She got out of bed and pulled on her dressing gown. Six twenty: still dark for at least another hour. Which one of the girls needed her this time? Last week it was Fleur Jameson announcing she had just started her first period and please, miss, what should she do? The week before it was a tearfully homesick Helena Hardy-Leach.

Olivia opened the door to find Martin standing on the other side. It wasn't only his presence that surprised her; it was his dishevelled appearance. Iron-filings stubble, creased shirt and those brown suede moccasins she thought were slippers. He wasn't wearing socks or a jacket. His ankles were stick-thin and anaemic. Olivia stared at him open-mouthed, waiting for an explanation as to why he was there, but he just stood shivering in the doorway.

'Martin? Is everything all right?'

He seemed confused, unsure how to respond. Olivia waited, and after a few moments he cleared his throat.

'May I?'

She stood aside. 'Yes, of course, please come in.'

He sat on the sofa and stared straight ahead, still shivering. The heating wasn't on yet and Olivia didn't know how to override the timer on the boiler. She slipped into the bedroom and grabbed a throw, but when she came back and tried to hand it to him, he continued to stare straight past her. She draped the throw around his shoulders and filled the kettle. While she waited for it to boil she pulled a chair near to Martin and sat, not sure that he had fully registered her presence. His fixed stare had a disturbing trance-like quality.

'Martin – what's wrong? Has something happened?'

He looked at her now, his eyes filled with the worst kind of pain.

'Ruth's dead.'

Olivia clamped a hand over her mouth. The whistle from the kettle startled her and she jumped up. Was it possible that she wasn't quite awake and this was part of a weird dream in which she *wanted* Ruth dead? That seemed unlikely. If it was a dream she wouldn't feel the cold and she wouldn't need to pee. She went to the bathroom before she made Martin a mug of strong tea with three heaped spoons of sugar. He took a sip, a slight tremor in his hand.

'She lost control of the car. Black ice, the police think. They left a short while ago.'

It was too much to take in. Olivia had spent half the night despising Ruth; imagining her and Geoffrey together, believing it one minute, not believing it the next. And now she was dead.

'I'm so sorry, Martin. If there's anything at all I can do –'

'The girls.'

He swallowed hard. Alice and Maisie were still asleep, their worlds still intact. Yesterday she had helped them make Christmas cards for Mummy and Daddy. Alice drew a picture of the four of them in Santa hats. Maisie's featured a baubled tree and the kitten she so desperately wanted.

He started to say 'Would you—' but his voice faltered. Grief poured out of him in muffled sobs, hands covering his face, his body rigid with the effort of trying to hold the shock and pain inside. Olivia sat in respectful silence and waited for it to pass.

When, at last, Martin shook his head and attempted an apology, Olivia gently touched his arm and said there was nothing to apologise for. She was aware of time slipping towards seven, when she would have to wake the boarders.

'I'm sorry, Martin, but it's almost time for the girls to get up. Would you like me to ask Matron to take care of it?'

He nodded.

'And what about Alice and Maisie?'

At this he breathed deeply through his nose and made a visible effort to gather himself. He stood up and straightened his back.

'May I use your bathroom?'

Olivia pointed to the bedroom door. When Martin returned a few minutes later he looked tidier, more composed. He wasn't only a bereaved husband; he was father to two bereaved children.

'If you could bear it, I'd like you there when I break the news to the girls.'

'Of course.'

'Perhaps you could brief Matron and bring Alice and Maisie to the house. Ruth's parents are on their way. My mother isn't well enough to deal with this. Alzheimer's. She's in a nursing home near Bath. I'm not sure she would understand.' He shook his head. 'It would be too distressing.'

Olivia said she was sorry, that she didn't realise. She thought of her own parents having the adventure of a lifetime on the other side of the world; how lucky they were. How lucky she was. Martin made no mention of his father so she assumed he had passed away. And now he had lost his wife too.

He stopped at the door and turned towards Olivia. 'Thank you,' he said. 'You've been very kind.'

She offered a sympathetic smile and steeled herself for what lay ahead.

*

Alice and Maisie skipped along the driveway ahead of Olivia, overjoyed at the unexpected treat of going home instead of to class.

'Will Mummy and Daddy be there?' asked Alice excitedly.

Olivia pretended she hadn't heard.

When she had woken them and said they didn't need to wear school uniform today, they had been thrown into a frenzy of indecision. Maisie had tried on a knitted skirt and jumper, then a red dress, quickly discarded in favour of pink cords and matching cardigan before going back to the original skirt and jumper. Alice had worn jeans and her favourite *Sleeping Beauty* sweatshirt, but when Maisie said it was stupid, she'd replaced it with a blouse patterned with small pink bows.

The other boarders hadn't helped: complaints about why they had to wear uniform, why they couldn't have a day off, that it wasn't fair, just because their dad was the headmaster. No, it certainly wasn't fair. Harriet stepped in and took control. Olivia confided that there had been an accident and Martin wanted the girls at home. When she asked for details Olivia shook her head. *I can't say any more right now. I'm sorry.*

Ice lay thick and treacherous, impervious to the pallid December sun. Olivia told Alice and Maisie to stick to the gravel path and be careful not to slip. She had never seen them hold hands before. It made her both happy and sad. She was torn between hurrying them along and wanting them to enjoy every single second before their world was blown apart.

They neared the house where a car Olivia didn't recognise – an old-fashioned but meticulously maintained blue Jaguar – was parked in the driveway.

'Grandma and Grandpa are here,' shouted Maisie, running ahead and dragging Alice with her.

They were ecstatic at the prospect of a day with their family, Olivia complicit in the deceit. She felt she should have prepared them in some way, but how? It was too late anyway. They were on tiptoes, ringing the doorbell. Olivia reached them just as Martin answered. He looked more like himself: clean-shaven, tidy, fresh shirt. His socks were a sober dark blue. The girls jumped on the spot with antici-pation. *Is Mummy here? Where's Grandma? I want to tell her about my kitten.* Olivia's expression said 'sorry'. Martin took each child by the hand and led them into the house. Olivia helped with their coats and scarves and then took off her own. On the row of hooks behind the door hung a jacket of Ruth's and her Cambridge University sweatshirt.

Olivia followed Martin into the sitting room where Ruth's parents were waiting: elderly, well-dressed, stricken. The physical similarities between Ruth's father and Martin were striking. He could have been Martin's own father. There were other similarities too: both of them reserved, formal, reticent. Had Ruth fallen for the cliché of marrying a man who reminded her of her father? Olivia didn't know enough about psychology to ponder what that meant, but it was irrelevant now anyway.

Martin made the introductions without ceremony and gestured to Olivia to sit. A tray of tea and biscuits was laid out on the low table in front of the sofa, two cups already poured. Martin pointed to the tray but Olivia shook her head. In the corner was a Christmas tree, its lights not switched on, and to one side, a Nativity scene complete with angels, wise men, and baby Jesus in a manger. Alice went over to the tree but Martin asked her to come and sit next to him on the sofa.

How do you tell young children their mother has died? Martin wrapped it in religious metaphor, talk of Mummy sleeping in heaven, being cared for by beautiful angels, how she was watching over them from above. First came stunned silence, then Maisie told Martin it was naughty to tell lies. Alice ran all over the house, calling for Ruth. Olivia offered to go to her but Martin shook his head. They waited for her to come back, each futile plea for Mummy a sharp stab to the heart. When she did come back, her tear-stained face had a look of terror.

'I can't find her.' Her voice was small and thin. 'I can't find Mummy.'

Ruth's mother pulled a hanky from her sleeve, removed her spectacles and dabbed at her eyes. Alice curled up next to Martin, her thumb in her mouth. They all sat mute as the truth of it burrowed inside them.

The silence was too much for Maisie. She jumped up, went over to the Nativity scene and kicked it hard, sending the plaster figures flying in all directions. An angel landed at Martin's feet. Maisie ran up and stamped on it, again and again and again, until Martin gathered her in his arms and held her while she yelled.

Despite Martin having asked her to come, Olivia felt she had no place there. The stoic grandparents, the brave father, the angry little girl and her stunned sister, all united in disbelief that a life so crucial to their own could be snatched away without warning. Ruth's life – a woman Olivia neither liked nor respected.

At last Maisie quietened down. Her rigid little body went limp and collapsed on to Martin's lap. She breathed in big, shuddery gulps.

'There, there.' That was all he said. He repeated it like a mantra.

Olivia felt she was intruding on their grief. She picked up the tray and said she would make some fresh tea. Martin got up and held the door for her.

'Would you mind if I called Geoffrey?' she asked in a respectful whisper. 'I left my mobile at school.'

'No, please. Use the phone in the bedroom – second on the right.'

Olivia put the tray in the kitchen, rinsed the cups and then went upstairs. She paused outside the door to Martin and Ruth's room, ashamed to think she had been in there without their permission. This time the bed was unmade, the curtains closed. The organic scent of sleep and skin lingered in the air. Olivia picked up the receiver and dialled Geoffrey's mobile. Two rings and he answered.

'I wasn't expecting to hear from you.'

She froze.

'Ruth?' he said.

So he had Ruth's home number programmed into his phone. Olivia wasn't sure of the significance of that revelation but she was sure it was significant. She hung up. For a moment she stood motionless, looking at the phone as if it might explain itself, but then flinched when it suddenly rang again. Slowly she lifted the receiver.

'Hello?'

'Ruth? Why did you call and then put the phone down?'

'It's Olivia.'

Silence. She counted to three. 'Geoffrey?'

'What are you doing at Ruth and Martin's place?'

'There's been an accident. Ruth's dead.'

She hadn't meant to blurt it out like that. She heard a sharp intake of breath.

'Are you serious?'

'Her car skidded out of control. That's as much as I know. Martin wanted me here when he broke the news to the girls. Her parents are here too.'

This time she counted to five. 'Geoffrey?'

'Sorry. It's hard to take in.'

Olivia was tempted to examine and obsess: did she detect guilt in his voice, was he more or less upset than expected, were his silences a symptom of shock or a sign he didn't want to incriminate himself? She shook those thoughts from her head. Downstairs was a family in mourning. They should be her priority right now, irrespective of her low opinion of Ruth.

'I have to go,' she said. 'We'll talk later.'

*

The day had a surreal quality to it. Tea was made and drunk, food offered and declined. Absent was the sort of small talk that reassured everyone of the ordinariness of life. Time dragged.

Ruth's father was due in hospital the next day for a minor procedure and Martin wouldn't hear of him cancelling. They left in the early afternoon, Ruth's mother quietly tearful, her father straight-backed and solemn. Olivia suggested the girls go play in their bedroom for a while and they skipped upstairs, perhaps forgetting for a moment why they were so privileged on a school day.

Martin asked Olivia to join him in the sitting room. There was much he had to attend to and would be grateful if she could take responsibility for the girls. The nature of Ruth's death meant a post-mortem would have to be carried out, then there would be a funeral to arrange, people to notify. Staff and pupils should be told as soon as possible. Leo Sheridan had called a special assembly for later that afternoon. Olivia reassured Martin he could rely on her to help in any way possible.

Martin stood up and walked over to the window. It overlooked a small walled garden, laid to lawn, a wooden swing set at the far end. He stared for a long time, lost in thought, before turning back to Olivia.

'I don't know where she had been.'

'Pardon?'

'The police asked me where she had been. I had to tell them I didn't know. Ruth came and went as she pleased, you see.'

He gave Olivia a moment to respond and when she didn't, he carried on. 'It wasn't a happy marriage, but I daresay you knew that. I expected to lose her one day, but not like this.'

'I'm so sorry, Martin. I know you loved her.'

He turned back to the window. 'I did love her. Very much.'

*

The pet store heaved with Christmas shoppers. Olivia had persuaded Martin to get a pair of kittens for the girls – a bit of joy among the devastation – and found a litter for sale a few miles outside of Compton Cross. She was glad to have an errand to run, to shrug off the claustrophobic cloak of grief for a few hours. Harriet had taken over Olivia's school duties so she could stay in the Rutherfords' guest room and be on hand whenever she was needed.

Martin put on a brave face for Alice and Maisie, but to Olivia he looked haggard. In the two days since Ruth's death he hadn't eaten a proper meal. At night Olivia could hear him moving around downstairs. He couldn't sleep, he said, and was too tormented to lie there staring into the darkness. The sheets and pillows smelled of Ruth. He thought he heard her breathing beside him. A few snatched hours on the sofa was the best he could manage.

The girls woke at night too. Olivia read to them, sang to them, sat patiently until they drifted off again. It had been a long time since she was up all hours with a crying child. She remembered those early months with Edward, so exhausted she could barely function.

During the day she kept the girls occupied, making cupcakes, watching films, reading, drawing. And she insisted on at least an hour of fresh air, either playing in the garden or going for a walk. As a strategy it worked well most of the time.

They grieved in ways that reflected their personalities. Alice tended to withdraw into herself, curl up with her teddy, thumb in her mouth. She regressed to being an infant, a time when her mother took care of her every need. Sometimes she wept quietly, but mostly she suffered in unnatural silence.

Maisie, on the other hand, lashed out indiscriminately. She snatched a Lladro ornament from the mantelpiece and threw it against the wall. Ruth's make-up bag was ransacked, the bathroom mirror covered in pink lipstick.

Maisie's excuse was that Mummy wouldn't need make-up in heaven. One minute she was animated with fury; the next, paralysed with despair. There was nothing to do but try to soothe her. She was entitled to feel angry; to rail and roar. Her mother had left her and she wasn't coming back.

'If you think it will help,' was Martin's verdict on the kittens. First Olivia had to buy one of those carriers to transport them in, a litter tray, food and water bowls, a few toys for them to play with.

She couldn't drive so close to Lorna's and not drop in. No car, but Johnny had probably taken it to London. Olivia parked and spotted Lorna looking out from the upstairs window. She waved and came down to open the door. An old jumper of Johnny's swamped her slender frame. The silver spangly hairband must surely belong to Lily. Olivia hadn't seen Lorna since that afternoon at Millfield. They had spoken only once, and that was for less than five minutes.

Instead of tea Lorna offered her a glass of wine from an open bottle on the kitchen table. Since when did Lorna drink in the afternoon? Olivia hated that she had the power but not the courage to put Lorna out of her misery. It felt as though too much time had passed, and secrets grew bigger with time.

Olivia did have a small glass of wine, not because she wanted one but because she didn't want Lorna to have to drink alone. They went into the sitting room; warmer than the kitchen. The wood burner radiated a gentle heat, Benji contentedly curled on the shaggy rug in front of it.

Olivia told Lorna about the Rutherfords.

'God, that's terrible. It's the sort of thing that makes you count your blessings, no matter how bad things seem.'

Olivia couldn't ignore the prompt. 'How are things with you and Johnny?'

'I wear this old jumper because it smells of him. Does that answer your question?'

'Do you talk?'

She curled herself up against the armrest. 'Yes, but not about anything that matters. Just everyday stuff: the kids, his job, my job, village news, that sort of thing.' She drank some wine – a rough, tannic red. 'I think I've lost him.'

Lorna wasn't one of those women for whom tears came easily or often, but with this she began to cry. It made Olivia want to cry too.

'You haven't lost him. He's sort of lost himself.'

Lorna blew her nose. 'What do you mean?'

'Nothing. I just think it might be more about him than you.'

The mood in the room shifted. They had been on the same side and now they weren't. Lorna's stare drilled into the place where Olivia had hidden Johnny's secret.

'You know something.'

One thing to lie by omission; quite another to lie outright. Olivia couldn't do it.

'That afternoon you came home and I was here with Johnny. He said he was upset about not being able to get a job.'

'Yes?'

'I'd overheard him and Ronald talking at the Rectory. Arguing.'

Lorna uncurled her legs and sat forward. 'About what?'

'He made me promise not to tell anyone.'

'I'm not anyone, I'm his wife. Tell me.'

Olivia thought the Rutherfords had exhausted her emotional reserves but a whole new set of anxieties twisted inside her.

'It was years ago. Ronald had a young curate at the Rectory and suspected he had an unhealthy interest in boys.'

'Boys? You don't mean Johnny?'

Olivia nodded.

'Oh God.' Lorna gripped her stomach and doubled over. It took her a few moments to straighten up and ask, 'But why was he talking to Ronald about it all these years later?'

'It was in the news. The curate was arrested but killed himself before the trial. He'd been abusing boys his whole career. I think Ronald wanted Johnny to understand how sorry he was.'

Lorna got up and paced, too agitated to sit any longer.

'And you knew all this?' Her incredulity confirmed that Olivia had been wrong to keep it from her.

'I wanted to tell you.'

'So why didn't you? I've been going crazy, trying to figure out what's wrong with him; with us. We don't have sex. He doesn't touch me, won't let me see him naked. I thought he didn't love me any more, that he had another woman. I drove myself insane trying to work out who it was! Do I know her, is it someone from the village, one of the mothers from school, how long has it been going on, does he love her? I search for evidence, look through his phone, empty his pockets. And all the time you knew.'

Her hands were on her head, her eyes wide and wild.

'Lorna, sit down, please. You're scaring me. Let's talk about this.'

'The time for talking was months ago. I've been going through hell. My marriage is at breaking point and I had no idea why.' She was shouting now. 'But *you* knew.' She pointed at Olivia, her index finger stabbing the air. 'You knew and you said nothing. You watched me suffer and you said nothing.'

'Oh God, Lorna, I'm so sorry. I thought Johnny would tell you before it got to this. I've hardly seen you. I was going to tell you at Millfield –'

Olivia rummaged through her bag for a tissue. She had cried more in the last few days than she had in the last few years. Benji woke up, looked sheepishly from one to the other, then crept out of the room, his tail between his legs.

'I thought I was doing the right thing.'

Lorna looked at her, askance. 'How could it be the right thing? How?'

Olivia swallowed hard and attempted to marshal her thoughts into a coherent defence. She needed Lorna to understand that her motives were pure. 'If you'd seen how he was that day. He couldn't face people finding out – knowing that about him.'

Lorna's chest rose and fell with the effort of trying to calm herself. 'That's why he left, isn't it? That's why he took a job on the other side of the country. He can't bear to be touched, to be loved. He's ashamed. He hates himself.'

She began to cry again but when Olivia reached out to her, Lorna pulled away.

'Please, Lorna.'

Lorna shook her head and held her hands up in a 'stop' gesture. 'I trusted you. You were my best friend. I told you everything. I knew something was going on between the two of you. I knew it. But you denied it and I thought, Olivia wouldn't lie to me. If she says there's nothing, then there's nothing. What an idiot I am. What a stupid idiot.'

'You're not.' Olivia was shouting too, trying to get through to her. 'I'm the idiot for getting it wrong. I'm so sorry.'

The front door opened – Josh and Lily home from school. The thud of rucksacks hitting the floor, then they were in the sitting room.

'What's happened?' asked Josh.

Lorna wiped her face with the sleeve of Johnny's jumper. 'Nothing.'

'Mum?' said Lily. 'Has something happened to Dad?'

Lorna shot Olivia a warning look.

'No, it's me,' said Olivia. 'Well, a woman at St Bede's. She was killed in a car accident. I'm looking after her little girls. It's very sad. I got a bit upset, that's all.'

'Why don't you two go and change out of your uniforms,' said Lorna. Their reluctance suggested Olivia's explanation had failed to convince, but Lorna followed up with the promise of take-away pizza and that did the trick.

'I'm sorry about your friend,' said Lily as she left.

Olivia didn't point out that Ruth had never been a friend.

'I should go too,' said Olivia. 'People to see, kittens to buy.'

A failed shot at humour. Lorna crossed her arms to discourage any attempts at a hug. She looked on in silence as Olivia put on her coat and took her keys out of her bag.

There was nothing she could say to fix this. Lorna didn't see her out.

*

A police car was parked outside the house. Olivia let herself in with the key Martin had given her. She could hear the girls playing upstairs and voices from the sitting room.

The policewoman was young and overweight, her male colleague older, his face deeply lined. They stopped talking when Olivia entered. Since that morning in her flat, Martin had borne his grief with dignity and reserve, which made his stark, hollowed-out look all the more alarming. Olivia was reluctant to interrupt but it was too cold to leave the kittens in the car and she needed to know what to do. Martin looked confused for a moment but the girls ran in, pleading to watch *Despicable Me* (the sitting room had the only television), and he told Olivia they could have their present now, but please take them upstairs.

'Have what?' asked Maisie.

It was clear Martin wanted the girls out of the way, shielded from whatever was being said in that room.

'Your surprise – it's in my car.'

She ushered them outside and took the carrier from the Land Rover to apoplectic squeals of delight.

'An early Christmas present,' said Olivia. 'Now let's get them in the warm.'

The next hour was almost enough to dull the pain of what she had done to Lorna. Almost. Skittish and nervous in their new surroundings, the kittens darted under the girls' beds and had to be coaxed out with titbits and a furry mouse on a string. At the first meow, Alice scooped up the ginger kitten and kissed it on the nose. The striped one purred and stretched as Maisie stroked its soft fur. The girls were utterly captivated, but even their joy wasn't enough to lift Olivia's spirits and stop her dwelling on the damage she had caused by keeping a secret she shouldn't have kept.

Lorna had been so sure of Johnny's infidelity; the go-to explanation when a man loses sexual interest in his wife. How easy to misread the signs. Olivia wondered if that was what she had done with Geoffrey. It was hard to see clearly from deep within the no-man's-land of doubt. The evidence against him was circumstantial, not conclusive: text messages and phone calls he claimed he could explain. Was Olivia wrong to doubt him? Had she assigned blame where none existed; jumped to the most obvious conclusion without considering the alternatives? He had never given her reason to think he was anything other than faithful, but that was before Ruth Rutherford had him in her sights.

The sound of the front door closing brought her downstairs. She told the girls to stay put, but they were too captivated with their new furry playmates to even register the request. Martin was in the kitchen, filling a glass from the tap.

'The girls adore the kittens. Would you like to see them?'

He took a long drink of water. 'Could you close the door, please?'

Olivia did as he asked. 'What's happened, Martin?'

He finished the water and put the glass in the sink. His answer was addressed to the blank space ahead of him. 'The police think it's possible Ruth may have been raped.'

Olivia heard the words but was unable to comprehend them. 'What?'

'The post-mortem: she had bruises on her wrists and thigh. There was blood too – just a speck on the cuff of her blouse – but the police say it wasn't Ruth's.' He lowered his voice. 'And they found semen.'

Olivia looked at him, loath to ask the obvious question, but Martin spoke and she didn't have to.

'They asked if Ruth and I had been intimate the day of the accident.' He shook his head. 'Intimate. She barely let me touch her.'

He gripped the side of the worktop and folded forward, arms outstretched. Olivia pulled out a chair and guided him to it. She sat opposite.

'I can't take it in,' she said. 'It's too awful.' Incongruous laughter filtered through the ceiling. 'But the police aren't sure she was raped?'

Martin stared at her. 'What are you suggesting?'

'Nothing. I—' She hung her head, unable to finish the sentence or meet Martin's quizzical stare.

'They're not sure of anything,' he said after a short but uncomfortable silence. 'They'll run the DNA through a database but other than that, it's guesswork. The policeman said they may consider asking staff to give DNA samples in order to rule them out, but I hate the idea of everyone knowing. It seems such a violation.'

The girls burst into the kitchen, each one cradling a kitten.

'Daddy, look,' said Alice, lifting hers up for him to admire. Her cheeks had a healthy blush. 'Her name is Miss Kitty. Would you like to hold her?'

'Maybe later.'

'Mine's called Tiger because she's got stripes,' said Maisie. She laid the kitten in Martin's lap. 'If you cuddle her you won't feel so sad about Mummy.'

He rubbed his eyes, murmured something about being allergic, handed the kitten back to Maisie and excused himself. Olivia thought it best to leave him alone. She wondered if his faith would bring relief, or if he'd blame God for taking the wife he loved so blindly, for robbing his young daughters of their mother. Ronald used to say faith tested was faith strengthened. Time would tell.

'Why don't you take Tiger and Miss Kitty back up to your room,' said Olivia, 'while I make us some supper?'

The girls skipped out, their cheerfulness the only light in a dark and disturbing day.

*

Olivia found a modicum of consolation in the simplest of tasks: taking a shower, doing the laundry, preparing a meal. They reassured her that some things remain unchanged, even in times of sepulchral change. The world may be in chaos but you still have to wash, dress, eat, especially when there were children to consider.

The day of her grandmother's funeral, Olivia's mum had busied herself making dozens of sandwiches: carefully trimming the crusts, cutting the bread into perfect triangles, arranging them in uniform rows according to their filling. Olivia's dad had tried to get her to sit down, but she kept making more and more sandwiches.

As Olivia stood in front of the open fridge, thinking about what to cook for supper, she understood her mother's compulsion. So much was out of our control. There was comfort in routine, in even the most mundane of chores.

Spaghetti bolognese: Alice and Maisie's favourite. In the cupboard Olivia found tinned tomatoes and a pack of dried pasta. Penne, not spaghetti, but close enough. She already had a bulb of garlic and half an onion from the chiller at the bottom of the fridge. There was a courgette and some broccoli too – she would sneak those into the sauce. The mince was left over from Olivia's home-made beefburgers, which the girls said weren't as nice as the ones they had on the beach at Weston-super-Mare. Martin let it go. He had more important things on his mind than pulling up Alice and Maisie on their manners.

He had made spaghetti bolognese the first time Olivia came to supper. Ruth had been so wantonly unhappy and didn't care who knew it. Drunk, dismissive of Martin, indifferent to the girls. Was it that unhappiness which had driven her to young Tom?

Olivia didn't believe Ruth had been raped. More likely she had met young Tom or some other lover and the bruises were an unfortunate coincidence. Martin said the police had nothing to go on and Olivia had information that may well be relevant. On a rational level she knew she should go to the police, tell them what she had witnessed in the cricket pavilion, but when she thought of the hurt that would cause Martin, her resolve weakened to the point of atrophy.

She plunged the pasta into a saucepan and watched the maelstrom that ensued. Boiling water erupted into a fury of bubbles and steam. The penne shuddered to life, rising stridently to the surface as if trying to escape its fate. Olivia looked on, mesmerised, her mind a maelstrom too. Keeping Johnny's secret had been a mistake. Was keeping Ruth's secret another mistake? When Olivia's parents had taught her right from wrong, they hadn't covered such moral ambiguities. The starchy water boiled over on to the stove, making a horrible mess on the stainless-steel hob. Another mess Olivia would have to deal with.

It was only later, when supper had been eaten and cleared away, the girls bathed, their hair washed, the kittens fed and Martin retired to his study, that Olivia conceded this wasn't a decision she could make alone. The responsibility was too great, the stakes too high. She needed to talk to Geoffrey.

Fourteen

Geoffrey slumped back against the wall. He tried to take a deep breath but his chest muscles were a tourniquet and he couldn't fill his lungs.

Ruth was dead. How was that possible? He had been with her just last night. No, Olivia must have got it wrong. He lowered himself into a squatting position, his back still supported by the wall. Melting ice soaked into his socks. His feet ached with the cold but it seemed right that he felt pain. God knows he deserved it.

And why did he have to hear about Ruth from Olivia, of all people? Maybe it was some sort of cruel payback, a way of tricking him into a confession. Could Ruth have told her about the affair as an act of revenge for him having ended it? And if so, could Olivia have made up the car crash as a sick way of punishing him? It didn't seem like the sort of thing she would do, but then having an affair didn't seem like the sort of thing he would do.

He had been in such a state of shock he couldn't remember what he said when Olivia called. Nothing to incriminate himself he hoped, although she now knew it wasn't just Ruth's mobile number he had saved in his phone, but her home number as well. Still, all it proved was that he and Ruth talked, and he had already explained that: Edward's scholarship.

He put his hands over his eyes, as if hiding from his own towering selfishness. A woman had died and his greatest concern was whether he'd covered his tracks, got his story straight.

'Geoffrey? Are you all right?'

His mother was at the back door. She didn't venture out but craned her head to have a good look at him, curious and concerned. He stood up.

'Just needed some air.'

'Are you sickening for something?'

Guilt, remorse, an abject sense of failure. He shook his head.

'You're not wearing shoes. You'll catch your death.'

Death. He thought he might throw up. As he walked past his mother into the kitchen he fabricated an appointment in Bristol. He needed time and space to try to understand what the hell was happening, and there was no chance of that if he stayed there. His mother had taken to regaling him with reminiscences about his father: protracted tales of their courtship; how he had proposed on one knee with his grandmother's engagement ring; the summer they went to Venice and ate gelato in St Mark's Square. Often she told the same story two or three times.

'Will you be long?' she asked. 'Only I was thinking of doing fish pie for lunch.'

Geoffrey said he didn't know how long he would be. She asked again if he was all right because he did look a bit peaky, and he should really change those wet socks. He knew she meant well but living under the same roof had plunged them back in time. It was as if all his years of living an independent, adult life had vanished into the ether.

The phone ringing was Geoffrey's chance to bring the conversation to a close. It would be for his mother; no one ever called him on the landline.

When he came downstairs ten minutes later, his mother was waiting for him.

'I've just had the most upsetting call from Claire Heather.' She put her hand to her chest to signify just how upsetting. 'Mr Rutherford's wife was killed in a car accident last night.'

Geoffrey had been clinging to the 'Olivia getting her own back' theory. It hit him all over again – Ruth was dead. And if it hadn't been for their sordid sex session she would still be alive. Had he smelled alcohol on her breath? He couldn't remember. When he tried to scan back through the details, they were all blurred and jumbled, and he was terrified something might lead back to him. If Olivia found out that would be it. Thirteen years of marriage over.

'Are you sure you're all right, Geoffrey? You look very pale.'

'I'm fine.'

His mother followed him to the coat stand and watched him put on his Barbour. 'Isn't Olivia houseparent to the Rutherfords' daughters?'

Geoffrey never thought of Ruth as a mother and certainly never thought about her children. Yet another layer of selfishness and treachery. While he had been fucking Ruth, Olivia had been looking after her little girls. He didn't even know their names.

*

An hour driving aimlessly on icy country lanes and one near collision with a tractor made Geoffrey wonder if he had some sort of death wish – an unconscious desire to die like Ruth by way of atonement. He found himself at the spot where they had met the previous night. How different it looked. Dappled light filtered through the gnarl of bare branches. Frost glittered like finely crushed glass.

He reached into the glove box for his stash of cigarettes. No smoking in the car. Some rules shouldn't be broken, however extenuating the circumstances. He got out and lit up.

Ruth had claimed not to care when he told her it was over. It was just sex, after all: base and animalistic. Not so much a meeting of minds as a clashing of bodies. The equivalent of feasting on foie gras and rare steak – wonderfully decadent until you felt sick to your stomach. Had he treated her badly? Fucked, dumped and died. Of course he had treated her badly.

He took a long drag on his cigarette, remembering how Ruth had snorted with derision when he told her Olivia made him give up when she was expecting Edward. 'Life's too short' had been Ruth's retort, delivered as she blew smoke rings in Geoffrey's face.

If he believed in such spookery, he might think she had enticed him back to this place from the afterlife. He shook his head to dislodge that thought and flicked the smouldering butt to the ground. As he stamped it out something in the undergrowth caught his eye. He walked over and picked it up: Ruth's mitten. He gasped and spun round, half expecting to see her. A beady-eyed squirrel darted in front of him and he jumped back, stupefied. He dropped the mitten, walked briskly to the car and got the hell out of there.

*

Despite never having met Ruth, his mother seemed genuinely upset by what had happened. It started her talking in a fatalistic way about death in general, about his father, about loss and how hard it was to be the one left behind. She didn't require any input from Geoffrey, merely that he should listen and agree. These weren't conversations so much as monologues, and they smothered him in guilt.

When his mother tried to supplement the limited details gleaned from Claire Heather by asking if Olivia had said anything about how Ruth's family were coping, Geoffrey was non-committal. He didn't want to own up to not having spoken to Olivia since she had called to break the news, scared he might inadvertently give himself away. He had started to fear that he was transparent, that his betrayal of Olivia and his role in Ruth's death could easily be identified by anyone who cared to look hard enough. And the tragic irony that Olivia was probably helping Martin care for Ruth's bereft daughters felt too perverse to even contemplate.

In the bleak days that followed, Geoffrey tried to stay out of the house as much as possible but apart from lonely walks with Rollo and Dice, he didn't have anywhere to go. The pub should have been his refuge of choice but there was only so long he could string out a pint and he felt like Billy No-Mates sitting there on his own.

A visit to his father's grave rendered him overcome with shame and he had to walk away. When he got back to the Rectory his mother asked him to run an errand for her at the village shop. Geoffrey had avoided it in the aftermath of the factory closing. An incident in which the wife of one of his former sheet-metal workers had to put back items from her wire basket because she was a few pounds short was emblazoned on his memory. He had tried to make up the shortfall, offering the woman some money, but she refused to take it. Pride, probably, or maybe she resented taking it from him.

'Just a couple of things,' his mother said, handing him a yellow Post-it note.

When she opened her purse he shook his head. 'I've got it,' he said, because his mother giving him money like that was a humiliation too far.

Each time he walked into the shop, Geoffrey did a quick scan to see who was there. He didn't want to bump into a disgruntled ex-employee or anyone else for that matter. His head was full of Ruth and Olivia and the dire consequences if the truth got out. When he spotted Lorna Reed out of the corner of his eye, he instinctively felt a surge of relief – friend not foe – but then remembered that Johnny had gone to the other side of the country to earn a living and Lorna may well blame Geoffrey for that. He wanted to speak to her but wasn't sure what sort of reception he'd get. He paid for the bin liners, bleach and Brillo pads – his mother got through a lot of bleach and Brillo pads – and looked at Lorna again. This time she noticed him too. She didn't smile, which cleared up the question of what sort of reception he'd get, but did abandon her wire basket and come over.

'Can we talk?' she said quietly.

She looked tired – washed out. Her eyes had lost their 'I don't suffer fools gladly' sparkle; the promise of sharp wit and playful put-downs. She seemed troubled, as though her suffering was no longer limited to the company of fools.

'Yeah – of course.'

She glanced round the shop and then back at Geoffrey. 'Not here. What about the Rectory?'

'My mother's there.'

'Mine then.'

They didn't say much on the five-minute car journey; small talk about the weather mostly. Still, he was pleased she wanted to talk at all, although wary of the subject matter. Certainly nothing light, if her grim expression was anything to go by.

When they reached the cottage, the familiar smell of old wood and yesterday's embers triggered a dozen years of memories. Great memories. Geoffrey wanted to say so, but Lorna might not want to be reminded how good things used to be; how much fun they all used to have.

The sitting room was too cold to take off his Barbour. Lorna turned the thermostat up a couple of notches, then threw some logs and a firelighter into the wood burner. She looked around for a box of matches and Geoffrey said, 'Let me.' He produced a box from his pocket, lit one, touched it to the firelighter and watched the flames take hold.

There was something primeval and satisfying about creating fire. One of his favourite memories from those

boyhood camping trips – collecting wood, twigs for kind-
ling, piling it all up and coaxing it to life. Nothing tasted
as good as warm, squidgy marshmallows toasted by a
roaring blaze. Geoffrey had a terrible singing voice but it
didn't matter round the campfire – the pleasure was in the
camaraderie. Rousing choruses of 'ging gang gooli gooli
gooli gooli watcha'; surely the most ridiculous lyrics ever
written. No one had a clue what they meant.

Lately he had longed to go to bed at night and wake up
a child again. Not that his childhood had been the stuff of
Enid Blyton adventures, but it was safe and uncomplicated.
What he wouldn't give now for uncomplicated.

'I saw Olivia yesterday,' said Lorna.

What? He had walked straight into a trap. Olivia must
have told Lorna her suspicions about him and Ruth. That's
why Lorna wanted to talk to him, why she looked so
wrecked. She had been tasked with extracting a confession.
It made perfect sense. Who would Olivia turn to if not her
best friend? All he could do was play innocent and deny.

'Where did you see Olivia?'

'Here – we had an argument. A fight really. I was very
upset.'

'You and Olivia had a fight?'

Lorna pulled the sleeves of her jumper over her hands
and hugged her waist.

'She kept something from me, something she shouldn't
have. Something about Johnny.'

Johnny? So this wasn't about Geoffrey at all?

'Did you know?' asked Lorna.

'Know what?'

Her gaze was unrelenting. 'About what that curate did to Johnny? Did he do it to you too?'

'I'm sorry, Lorna. I have no idea what you're talking about.'

'The curate who lived at the Rectory when you were a boy. He was a paedophile.'

'A paedophile? How—'

'Your father suspected he had abused Johnny and moved the problem on. When he finally got caught, he killed himself.'

No, Lorna had this wrong. His father would never have protected a paedophile. Geoffrey rewound to Boys' Brigade; camping on Exmoor, envious because Johnny and another boy got to sleep in the curate's tent. The curate had left soon afterwards – the end of Boys' Brigade; the end of his child-hood friendship with Johnny. Geoffrey swallowed hard to staunch the upward swell of bile.

'You didn't know?' said Lorna.

He shook his head. 'How did Olivia know?'

'She overheard Johnny and your father arguing.'

'What? When?'

'She didn't say but I googled it. He hanged himself in July. And when I think back, that was when Johnny changed: became distant, morose, angry. I thought it was because he couldn't find a job.'

That was when his father had changed too. Geoffrey had assumed it was all the shit going round about the factory; all those out-of-work parishioners. So did this mean that his father's heart attack might not have been Geoffrey's fault? And Johnny cutting him out – that wasn't his fault

271

either? How could Olivia not have told him? She knew he blamed himself for all of it.

'I can't take this in,' he said. 'Have you spoken to Johnny?'

'It's not the sort of thing you discuss on the phone. He's coming home this weekend. I've asked my sister to have the twins.'

A heavy sigh hinted at how much she was dreading it.

'I don't know what to say, Lorna.'

'And you're sure Olivia never told you?'

'Never said a word.'

'She told me Johnny made her promise not to, but I'm so angry with her. I've been going through hell – even convinced myself Johnny had another woman.'

Geoffrey shook his head. 'He wouldn't do that to you.' *Because he's not an unfaithful bastard like me.*

Geoffrey was still getting his head around Ruth's death and now he had to try to make sense of this too. Olivia, his father, Johnny – they had all lied by omission.

Lorna checked her watch. 'I'm sorry, I have to get to work.'

'I didn't realise you had a job.'

'Didn't Olivia tell you that either? I clean for a woman in Axbridge.'

Lorna was a cleaner? An image of her scrubbing floors made his gut twist. Christ, is this what she had been reduced to? The four of them were golden, and now look.

'Olivia and I haven't talked very much,' he said.

Such a statement would usually have propelled Lorna into full-blown marriage guidance mode – pick up the bloody phone then, send her flowers, sneak her out to lunch – but she had nothing to say on the subject.

'Will you forgive her?' he asked.

Lorna thought about it for a moment before she shrugged. 'Will you?'

Too complicated a question to even try to answer. Knowing what had gone on with the curate would have made Geoffrey feel less culpable, and in keeping it to herself Olivia had compounded his misery. A lesser betrayal than his own, but a betrayal all the same.

*

He dropped off Lorna in Axbridge and had just parked at the Rectory when Olivia called. She sounded flat and exhausted when she asked if he could meet her in the café at the out-of-town Tesco. She needed to do a food shop. *Thirty minutes. See you there.*

Even at eleven in the morning, he had to drive round the car park twice to find a space. It was mayhem – flustered mothers unloading bulging carrier bags from unwieldy shopping trolleys; strapping uncooperative toddlers into their child seats. All of this in the name of Christmas.

Olivia was already there, sitting alone at a table in the corner. His heart kicked at the sight of her. The tumble of blonde hair loose around her shoulders, the perfect symmetry of her face, made him think of purity and innocence and how far he had strayed. As he walked towards her, bristling with adrenalin, the compulsion to unburden himself gripped him like a fist. He would tell her it had meant nothing, that it was already over and he was the one who had ended it. That wouldn't cancel out the infidelity – not even death could do that – but it would make Olivia see he was sorry, that it was her he loved.

Geoffrey was already at the table before she looked up. No smile, just a cursory nod of acknowledgement. He would have leaned across and kissed her but there was a cool stillness about her that deterred him. Instead, he pulled out a chair and sat down.

'You look worn out,' he said.

Olivia sighed. 'I am.' She cupped her hands around the coffee mug, as if to comfort herself. 'I said I'd get some food in, although Martin is barely eating.' Small talk. Safe territory.

'Things have got much worse,' she said, her voice so quiet he had to lean forward to hear.

A woman on the next table shouted at her little boy, who objected to the indignity of being strapped into a high chair. Everyone turned and stared, the collective opprobrium enough to silence the mother but not the boy.

'In what way?' said Geoffrey, wishing the small talk could have lasted a bit longer and trying to screen out the toddler's noisy tantrum.

Olivia looked at him from under the long sweep of her eyelashes. 'The police are considering the possibility that Ruth had been raped.'

Geoffrey tried and failed to swallow.

'Are you all right?' asked Olivia. 'You don't look well.'

He managed a breath, and another. His throat hurt, like he was trying to choke down something too big and too dry. 'Raped?'

The toddler had suddenly and inexplicably gone quiet, so everyone heard him say it. Geoffrey's turn for collective opprobrium.

Olivia shushed him and leaned closer, lowering her voice to little more than a whisper. 'None of this information has been released yet, but the police told Martin Ruth had bruises and they found a few specks of blood that apparently weren't hers.' Olivia did little more than mouth the next part. 'And she'd had sex, but not with Martin.'

Geoffrey felt the muscles in his face loosen, his jaw quite literally drop. Olivia studied him, her eyebrows knitted together in either confusion or concern – it was difficult to tell. Did she think he was overreacting? He wiped his brow with the back of his hand and offered an explanation, albeit a lame one. 'I think I'm coming down with something.'

'Do you want to go?'

No, he wanted to know more about this spurious rape allegation. Geoffrey shook his head. 'What were you saying about Ruth?'

'I'm not sure if I should tell the police about young Tom. They said they might take DNA from male members of staff so if it was him, then I suppose they'll find out anyway, but am I concealing evidence if I don't say anything? He could well be the person Ruth had sex with.' Olivia ran her fingers through her hair and gathered it behind her head, bunching it untidily in her hands. She looked achingly young and vulnerable. 'I don't know what to do.'

Geoffrey knew he should put her first, reassure her everything would be OK, but he was in the grip of panic so that wasn't going to happen. Blood coursed through his body at a ferocious pace. He could feel it, hear it, taste it. A few moments passed before he recovered his voice.

'The police are going to take DNA from all the male members of staff?'

'Possibly. It was mentioned.'

Oh God. Geoffrey was going to be arrested and charged with rape. He retched into his hand and grabbed the paper serviette next to Olivia's mug. People were staring now, even the little monster in the high chair. Olivia jumped up and rubbed Geoffrey's back, just like she did to Edward when he felt sick.

'Are you OK?'

Geoffrey just managed to get outside before he vomited. Shoppers looked on in disgust, making sure to give him a wide berth. Olivia took a wodge of tissues from her bag and handed them to him. He wiped his mouth and tried to gather himself.

'You should have told me you were ill,' she said, her sympathy a punch to his aching gut. 'I wouldn't have dragged you out here.'

How sympathetic would she be if she knew why he was in this state?

'Sorry,' he said. 'I need to go home.'

'Of course. I'll call Martin. The girls will be fine for a few hours.'

'No, don't.'

Geoffrey must have been too sharp because she looked hurt. He straightened himself up and took a few gulps of cold air. 'Sorry,' he said again. 'I'll feel better after a lie down.'

He left her standing there alone and walked blindly across the car park in the general direction of his car.

*

Amazing what Scotch could do. The tumultuous panic he had succumbed to in front of Olivia had settled into a pleasantly numbing paralysis. He lay on his bed, fully clothed, the room swimming and spinning, half a bottle of Scotch on the floor beside him. Olivia had called twice to see how he was feeling. He only answered the first time and kept it short. 'Better. I need to get some sleep.' He did get some sleep too, if the alcohol-induced stupor counted. At the first sign of sobriety he drank more. His plan was to drink himself to death.

A single knock and his mother let herself in. 'Olivia said you were sick.'

He rolled over to face her. 'Olivia's here?'

'No, she telephoned. I told her that you'd looked peaky for a couple of days now.'

His mother took a few steps towards him and sniffed the air like a bloodhound. 'Are you drunk?'

'Yes, Mother, I'm drunk. And I intend to stay that way.'

She walked round the bed and picked up the bottle. Geoffrey closed his eyes so he wouldn't have to see her disapproval.

'Have you had an argument with Olivia? Has she upset you?'

Of course. His blameless wife was always to blame. 'No, Mother, but you're upsetting me so please leave.'

'I wish I knew what was going on with you,' she said, her tone tight with frustration. 'If your father was here –'

'Speaking of which, did you know about the paedophile curate?' Geoffrey struggled with 'paedophile curate'. Not easy to say when you're pissed.

'The what?'

Did he really have to repeat it? He did so slowly, enunciating each syllable. 'Pae-do-phile cur-ate.'

When he opened his eyes and saw two of her, both versions were slack-jawed with astonishment.

'You know, the curate who sexually abused Johnny Reed.'

'Sexually abused' was difficult to get his tongue round too. If he failed in his quest to drink himself to death he might write a dictionary: *Words You Can't Say When You're Shit-Faced*.

'Geoffrey.' Her stern voice now, only deployed in extreme circumstances. 'I don't know what possessed you to get blind drunk in the middle of the afternoon, but I suggest you sleep it off.'

With this she turned towards the door, the bottle in her hand. She hesitated for a few moments before she looked back at him over her shoulder. The censure had gone from her voice, which trembled a little now. 'And whatever problems you have, just remember there are two little girls who have lost their mother, and a husband who has lost his wife. Do you imagine he's drowning his sorrows? No. According to Olivia, he's bearing up with dignity. Perhaps you'd like to think about that.'

She shut the door behind her. No, Geoffrey would most emphatically not like to think about that. He rolled into a foetal position and, for the first time since his father's death, he cried.

*

278

Two reasons not to down half a bottle of Scotch on an empty stomach. First was the brutal hangover. Nausea, headache, tremors, the works. With that came the second reason – a gradual return of memory. Had he really said those things to his mother and then cried himself to sleep? He sat mortified on the bathroom floor, his arm resting on the toilet seat, waiting for the next bout of vomiting.

A knock on the door and his mother's voice. 'Are you all right?'

No, he wasn't. His head throbbed with the effort of standing. He splashed cold water on his face, avoiding his mirrored reflection, and unlocked the door. His mother was in her dressing grown and slippers.

'I'm sorry about earlier,' he said sheepishly.

'You look awful. Can I get you anything?'

He shook his head. The last thing he wanted was to be fussed over.

'Well, if you're sure, but I do need to use the bathroom.'

'Of course,' he said. 'And sorry. Really.'

Downstairs he made himself a cup of tea, took it to the snug and turned on the television. The local news was on, a solemn young presenter reporting that police were investigating the circumstances of a fatal car accident involving Ruth Rutherford, the wife of Martin Rutherford, headmaster of St Bede's Preparatory School. Ruth smiled at him from the screen. Geoffrey's insides seemed to liquefy as he wondered how long it would be before it was his face on that screen. He couldn't prove he hadn't raped her, that the sex was consensual and she liked it rough. Would

a jury of his peers believe him or condemn him? He imagined himself being led from the dock, his distraught wife
and mother watching wet-eyed from the public gallery.
Five years? Ten? What did rapists get these days?

The bitter taste of bile filled his mouth. He needed to
throw up again and just made it to the kitchen sink. A lot
of painful retching yielded nothing but hot sour liquid. He
got a glass of water, his hands shaking. Sweat pricked his
forehead, his palms, the back of his neck. How could he
stand up in court and recount the debauched details of his
sex sessions with Ruth? He couldn't.

And then it came to him – his only option. Run. What
did he have to stay for? Olivia would never forgive him, so
no marriage. He had no money, no job, and was about to
be made bankrupt. His mother would be alone again but
if he went to prison she would be alone again anyway. But
then there was Edward. Was it better to have an absent
father or a disgraced, possibly imprisoned father? Surely
the former. He would explain it all in a letter once things
had settled down. Not the affair, but how he couldn't
take it any more – his money problems, the shame he felt
over losing Downings and Manor Farm. If he dwelled on
Edward he wouldn't be able to go, so he pushed him to the
back of his fuzzy, panic-stricken mind.

Geoffrey looked for the Scotch, figuring hair of the dog
might help, but found the empty bottle in the bin. This
must be how alcoholics feel every day, poor bastards. Pull
it together, he told himself crossly. He washed down three
aspirin with another glass of water and tried to marshal his
thoughts into some sort of order.

The plan was to disappear for a while but with so little money, his options were limited. For a mad five minutes he considered South America, and finally having the gap year he missed out on after university. A quick Google search produced a list of last-minute flights to Rio de Janeiro but the cheapest was over six hundred pounds, and what would he live off when he got there?

He wished the aspirin would hurry up and work. Pain hammered in his head and he had to squint against the brightness of the screen. He needed to find somewhere closer and cheaper. As he trawled through bucket-shop flights from Bristol he spotted Toulouse – only a couple of hours' drive from Alex's vineyard. Geoffrey could crash there for a while and earn his keep helping out around the place. When he called Alex and got no answer he didn't leave a message – his brain still wasn't up to forming coherent sentences – but fired off an email instead. They had been friends for twenty-five years. It was the perfect solution.

Printing the e-ticket, holding it in his hand, made running away frighteningly real. Geoffrey had to remind himself he was doing it to protect his family – that his motives were honourable. As long as Ruth had deleted all trace of him from her mobile, no one would ever find out about their affair. And he wouldn't be a rape suspect. No DNA, no evidence.

A scatter of disparate thoughts intruded as he searched for his passport. Imagine being defined by the worst thing you had ever done; all those years of good behaviour wiped out by one terrible mistake. It was so fucking unfair. He wasn't a bad person; he had simply made some bad decisions. These last months had been a shitstorm of bad decisions. No, time away would do him good, if he could only find his bloody passport.

He turned out drawers, searched cupboards, emptied his briefcase, all in vain. He ransacked the bedroom in case Olivia had 'tidied it up'. When he sat on the bed, livid with frustration, it dawned on him it might have been packed away and put in storage. Fuck. He kneaded his forehead with his fingertips. After an exhausting amount of pacing, he talked himself down. It was a setback, not a catastrophe. He'd go to the storage unit first thing and in the meantime, he'd try to get some sleep.

Surprisingly, he did manage a couple of hours. By the morning the worst of the hangover had passed and he tucked into poached eggs on toast with his mother. He wished he could tell her this was their last breakfast together for a while, that he was sorry to leave her alone but it was something he had to do.

When he finished eating he put his plate in the sink, kissed his mother's cheek and told her that he loved her. She looked up at him with a puzzled smile, wondering, no doubt, what had prompted such an unexpected declaration. It would have been nice if she had said it back.

*

Boxes were stacked on boxes behind other boxes. God knows how he would ever find his passport among that lot. He ignored the labels, figuring it could have been tossed into any of them. The first box had a stack of photographs on top: family holidays, snaps of Edward at various ages, a candid shot of Olivia in a bathrobe.

Underneath was their wedding album and the locket he gave to Olivia on their three-month anniversary, when she was already three months pregnant with Edward. Given its sentimental value, Geoffrey was surprised to find it there. Olivia used to wear it all the time. Things change, he thought sadly, as he thumbed through the photographs. He selected one of Edward, one of Olivia, one of all three of them together, and put them aside along with the locket.

The next box had kitchen paraphernalia, and the next. Panic bubbled up as he searched yet another box. Suppose his passport wasn't here at all, that it had been lost or inadvertently thrown away. Stacks of paperwork they had no reason to keep: household bills, home insurance documents, old Christmas and birthday cards, and then eureka – his passport. He hugged it to his chest, eyes shut tight, and thanked a God he wasn't sure he believed in.

Now he could get back and throw a few things into a rucksack. He'd pack light: shirts, jeans, pants, his laptop. Six hours until his flight but he wanted to leave early, hang around at the airport. Once he was through security it would be too late to change his mind. He'd have a few beers, steady his nerves.

It was his mother's day for hospital visiting so he wouldn't have to explain the rucksack. He would leave his Mercedes at the airport and email the leasing company telling them where to find it. Apart from a brief moment of bewilderment when he realised Rollo and Dice were the only ones he could say goodbye to, packing up and walking out proved deceptively simple.

Should he leave his house keys or would that arouse suspicion? He considered writing a note but what could he say? His mother would worry when he didn't come home. He'd call her from the airport, say he needed to get away for a couple of days, and figure the rest out from there. Best not to think too far ahead. Best not to think. For weeks he had oscillated between anxiety, despair and, when he was with Ruth, an unhealthy conflation of excitement and disgust. But faced with the moment of truth, Geoffrey felt nothing much at all. Numb. Self-preservation perhaps. If he allowed himself to feel, he wouldn't have the courage to leave.

Fifteen

The endless festive cheer was hard to stomach but impossible to escape. Bright and jolly Christmas cards dropped on to the matt alongside condolence cards. Martin had abandoned the one-hour television limit for the girls and every advert – there were an awful lot of adverts – showed happy families cooing over an epicurean feast, hanging sparkly baubles on a tree, opening presents to paroxysms of joy. At the centre of all this merriment was a loving mother, misty-eyed with wonder at her own good fortune. The girls hugged their kittens and watched.

Martin had begun to make arrangements for Ruth's funeral and disappeared into his study for hours on end. The last funeral Olivia had been to was Ronald's. The small parish church wasn't able to accommodate all the mourners and they had spilled out into the graveyard. A couple of speakers had been set up outside so they could follow the service. Edward did a Bible reading from the pulpit, Olivia more nervous for him than he was for himself. She shed many tears that day, some of them tears of pride. She wondered how many people would turn up to pay their respects to Ruth.

Martin's quiet resolve to put on a brave face was weakening by the day. In time he could have accepted Ruth's passing as God's will, he said, but the thought of a man forcing himself on her was too abhorrent. And yet he chose to believe it. The police had mooted rape as a possibility but for Martin it had become fact. When he raised the subject with Olivia over a late-night tot of brandy, a version of events in which the sex was consensual was never mentioned. If she thought it would alleviate his pain, Olivia would have told him about Tom and her suspicion that Ruth may not have been raped at all, but she sensed it would do the opposite. Rape, despicable though it was, allowed the marriage to remain intact. They had loved and honoured and forsaken all others until parted by death. Olivia understood that when someone you love dies, it's only natural to focus on the good and gloss over the bad, which made her decision about going to the police all the more difficult.

Geoffrey had been no help, but then he was sick so it wasn't really his fault. In all the years she had known him – through the raucous rugby tours and marathon drinking sessions – not once had she seen him throw up in public. Olivia had been desperate to confide the harrowing sadness of the Rutherford household, to explain about Ronald and Johnny and the secret that may well have ruined her friendship with Lorna, but how could she when he looked so unwell? There was something else stopping her too: a tangible sense of detachment. It had been brewing for months, reinforced by a lack of conversation, of intimacy, of sex, and sitting opposite him (in Tesco's of all places) brought it into sharp focus. Confiding in Geoffrey would have felt wrong, like undressing in front of strangers.

The girls rushed downstairs to answer the doorbell – Alicia Burton with a casserole dish and a bouquet of white lilies. Olivia greeted her politely, took her coat and hunted around for a vase. The one she found wasn't tall enough for lilies, so she cut the stems and arranged them in a spray.

'Tea or coffee?'

'Coffee,' said Alicia, looking round the kitchen. 'The last time I was here, Ruth and I got tipsy on mulled wine.' She smiled. 'Drunk, actually.'

Olivia didn't need to be reminded. That was the day she had gone through Ruth's phone and found all those calls from Geoffrey. However many times she went over his explanations, she still couldn't decide if she believed him.

'She was so full of life,' said Alicia. 'It's impossible to imagine she's gone.'

When the girls ran in to show Alicia their kittens, she hastily wiped her eyes and made a big fuss of the furry creatures being placed in her lap. Five minutes later Maisie asked if they could watch television and Olivia said yes, but not too loudly.

'They seem to be coping,' said Alicia once they had skipped out.

Olivia handed her a coffee. 'Ups and downs. The kittens help.'

'Your idea?'

Olivia nodded. She put a milk jug and sugar bowl on the table.

'Look,' said Alicia, 'I know you and I haven't been the best of friends, but I do admire what you're doing for Martin and the girls. And I think Ruth would be grateful to have someone looking after them.'

Was Alicia's overture genuine or was it influenced by a perceived rise in Olivia's stock? She did, after all, have the trust and confidence of the headmaster, and a central role within the Rutherford household. Cynicism didn't come naturally to Olivia, though, and neither did second-guessing people's motives. Frankly, she was too emotionally drained to care and gave Alicia the benefit of the doubt.

'It's kind of you to say so,' said Olivia.

'How long are you planning to stay?'

'As long as Martin needs me, I suppose.'

'How is he?'

Before Olivia could answer Martin appeared in the doorway. 'Alicia,' he said, 'I'm glad you're here. I've just had a call from Leo Sheridan – Edward and Freddie have had another scrap, I'm afraid.'

The women looked at each other, exasperated. 'Those boys of ours,' said Alicia, rolling her eyes.

'It seems Edward has been hurt. I don't know the details, except that Leo has called an ambulance.'

Olivia's heart punched hard against her chest. 'An ambulance? Why? What's happened?'

She was on her feet now, a jumble of worst-case scenarios bursting in her head. Alicia put down her cup and stood up too, taking Olivia's arm in an attempt to calm her – *I'm sure it's nothing: a precaution* – but Olivia wouldn't be calmed.

'Is it serious?' she asked Martin.

'I'm afraid I don't know any more than—'

Olivia was out of the front door before he finished the sentence.

*

Later, when Olivia tried to piece it together, her recollection was masked by an amnesic blur that Leo said was shock. She had a vague sense of sprinting along the drive, of the school becoming bigger as she got closer, of it being spectacularly cold but not feeling cold, even though she had run out of the house without her coat.

Lisa Pearce was waiting at the main entrance and led her by the arm to the boys' changing room. Leo was there, and Harriet, both of them kneeling over a still and silent Edward. Olivia remembered asking what had happened and crying too hard to make sense of the answer. Leo gave her a handkerchief and explained Edward had hit his head against the corner of the sink. That was when she saw the blood. Her legs seemed to liquefy but Leo grabbed her before they buckled.

Bizarrely, a picture of a fainting couch came to mind, together with threadbare flashbacks to a book-club discussion about why Victorian women were of such frail and nervous disposition they required a specially designed piece of furniture on which to pass out. None of the book-club women had ever passed out. Yet here was Olivia, dizzy, weak-legged and weeping, being guided not to a fainting couch, but to a hard wooden bench. And all she could do was look on helplessly as Harriet shone a light in Edward's unseeing eyes.

Leo noticed Olivia was shivering and put his jacket around her shoulders. When Alicia arrived a minute or two behind Olivia, she wanted to know where Freddie was, but then looked down and saw Edward. Her audible gasp didn't bolster Olivia's confidence that everything would be all right, which was what Harriet and Leo kept insisting. Leo stepped in and said Freddie had been sent to Peter Havant, who was standing in for Martin. Alicia seemed unsure whether or not to stay, but then sat down next to Olivia and told her how sorry she was. Olivia distinctly remembered saying it was as if the place was cursed. *I knew something bad would happen. First Freddie and now Edward.*

When she kneeled down by Edward and rested her cheek on his chest, Leo gently moved her away and said Harriet needed to monitor him. 'Why don't you phone Geoffrey,' Leo said, probably thinking it would be better if she had something to do. She couldn't get a signal, so Alicia offered her phone along with a small pack of Kleenex from her bag. Olivia blew her nose and made an effort to compose herself as she dialled Geoffrey's number. Voicemail. Edward was awfully still, his face bled of colour. So much for composure. The message she left was a sobbing plea to call her. A patch of Edward's golden hair wasn't golden any more.

Two paramedics arrived, both of them worryingly young. Leo held Olivia back so she wouldn't get in the way. Edward was strapped on to a stretcher, an oxygen mask placed over his mouth. Alicia led her to the ambulance because she was blinded by a sluice of tears. The shrill scream of sirens confirmed it was urgent, an emergency, a matter of life and death. They could ignore speed limits and red lights. Olivia held on as they bumped and swerved, imploring her beautiful boy not to die.

*

The family room consisted of functional Ikea-style furniture, framed botanical prints, a window on to the corridor, a slatted wooden blind. In the far corner a water cooler gurgled. Lifestyle magazines lay in small piles on a low table.

This was where people waited to be told if the people they loved would live, die, or linger somewhere between the two. 'Life-changing injuries' was an expression newsreaders had begun to use. It conjured up terrible scenarios – tapped into the most fundamental of fears: blindness, paralysis, amputation, scarring. You would give anything for your loved one to be spared – make all sorts of bargains with God. Olivia now understood why people prayed. Not because they believed they had a direct line to the Almighty, or that they could telepathically commune with an omniscient being. They prayed because it was meditative, repetitive, an antidote to the horror film exploding in your head. And it felt as though you were at least doing something.

The woman said her name was Trish and she was the family liaison person. *Is there anyone you'd like me to call?* Right on cue Geoffrey rushed in, breathless and panic-stricken. He threw his arms round Olivia, their marital problems overshadowed and irrelevant. She needed him and he was there. When she pressed her face against his shoulder, she didn't understand why he smelled of cigarettes.

Trish explained what had happened in the manner of an adult speaking to a child. Edward was being assessed by the medical staff and a doctor would be along shortly to let them know what was happening. The only question they asked was the one she couldn't answer: will he be OK? She left them alone, promising she would be back as soon as she had news.

It was an hour and eleven minutes before she came back. Olivia watched the hands of the wall clock move. A doctor was with her, still in his scrubs. The blow to Edward's head had caused a deep cut, a hairline fracture of the skull and some swelling to the brain. An operation to relieve the pressure caused by that swelling had gone well. The cut needed eight stiches. He was in intensive care but they could sit with him. Don't be alarmed by the tubes and machines. He was sedated and being monitored – standard procedure with an injury of this kind. All being well they would wake him tomorrow.

'And then?' said Geoffrey.

'And then we'll know more,' said the doctor.

The intensive care unit was brightly lit and eerily quiet except for the steady bleep of machines. Edward had a bandage on his head, a breathing tube in his mouth, a drip in his arm, a little clamp on the index finger of his right hand. Olivia held his left hand and talked to him in a soft, soothing tone. 'Mummy and Daddy are here. There's nothing to be frightened about. You're going to be fine. Get some rest now, darling.'

Rowena arrived and was moved to tears by the sight of Edward hooked up to all the medical paraphernalia. It was her hospital visiting day and she had been in another wing when Geoffrey called her. The nurse told them she was sorry but only two visitors were allowed. Olivia needed to pee so said Geoffrey and Rowena could sit with him while she took a quick break. Her head was throbbing and she scooped up Geoffrey's Barbour in case she stepped outside for some air.

The toilets were reassuringly spotless. You heard such dreadful stories about hygiene in hospitals. She was walking through the maze of corridors when she saw Alicia coming towards her.

'I brought these for you,' she said, holding Olivia's full-length shearling and shoulder bag. 'How is he?' Alicia had screwed up her face as though it was a question she was almost too frightened to ask.

'He's had surgery. The doctor said it went well.'

Alicia made a 'phew' sound and said again how sorry she was; how sorry Freddie was. He assured her he had never meant to hurt Edward like that. It was a push, nothing more, and he was horrified when Edward hit his head. Olivia nodded. She couldn't imagine that Freddie had deliberately put Edward in hospital.

'I don't really want to lug that around,' she said, nodding towards the heavy coat Alicia was still holding. 'I'll dump it in the car. Why don't you walk with me?'

'Thank you for understanding,' said Alicia as they walked. 'And when Edward's better, I suggest we sit our sons down and have a serious talk. This animosity between them has to stop.'

'Agreed,' said Olivia, remembering the shock of being told the Burtons had reported Edward to the police. 'Did you know I met with your ex-husband?'

Alicia nodded. 'The police were his idea, not mine.'

Olivia believed her.

'Can I tell you something?' said Alicia. They passed through a set of automatic doors that led into the car park, the sudden drop in temperature prompting Olivia to drape Geoffrey's Barbour around her shoulders. Alicia carried on talking without waiting for an answer to her question. 'My ex-husband used to bang on about fancying you. It amused him to make me jealous. He actually called you a MILF right in front of me.'

So Geoffrey had been right all along. It sickened Olivia to think how Toby Burton had leered at her. 'I assure you it wasn't reciprocated.'

Alicia smiled. 'Good to know. Fresh start?'

Olivia spotted Geoffrey's Mercedes and fished his keys out of the pocket of his Barbour. 'Fresh start.'

Before Alicia walked off to her own car, she reached out and hugged Olivia. The gesture was unexpected but welcome. Something to work on when this latest crisis was behind her.

It was as Olivia laid her coat across the back seat that she noticed a rucksack in the footwell – a tatty old thing

Geoffrey used for his sports kit. What was that doing there? Curious, she undid the zip to find a packet of cigarettes and some clothes: boxer shorts, shirts and a hoodie, jeans. More puzzled now than curious, she unzipped the front pocket and found Geoffrey's passport and a ticket to Toulouse. She stared at the ticket, read it and reread it, stared at it some more. The flight was at five thirty this evening, one way, Geoffrey the only passenger. It made no sense whatsoever. Why on earth would Geoffrey have a ticket to Toulouse? The explanation was both obvious and impossible. She thought her heart might burst.

A fierce gust of glacial wind slapped her in the face. She shut her eyes and took a quick sharp breath, determined not to cry. *One catastrophe at a time* – another of Olivia's mum's overused expressions. Whatever the hell was going on with Geoffrey would have to wait. Edward needed her full and undivided attention. Once he was out of danger she would deal with Geoffrey and in the meantime, he wasn't going anywhere. She put the ticket and passport in her shoulder bag, zipped up the rucksack and locked the car.

*

Rowena and Geoffrey sat in silence on either side of Edward's bed. The nurse saw Olivia walking towards them and mouthed 'two visitors'. Olivia gave a quick nod that said, yes, I know, and stared at the back of Geoffrey's head. Despite her resolve, she wasn't sure she could trust herself to be around him. Part of her was too shocked to take it in. Another part – the crushed, betrayed, deceived part – despised him with a vengeance.

He saw her and stood up, offering his seat, but then Rowena stood up too and said they should be with Edward; she would come back in the morning. Did Rowena know what Geoffrey planned to do? There was no sign that she did. Olivia put his Barbour over the back of the chair and sat down, avoiding eye contact. Best he didn't suspect what she was feeling at that moment. One catastrophe at a time.

Nurses came and went with quiet efficiency, checked Edward's vital signs, made notes on his chart, smiled in a sympathetic, 'I know how worried you must be' way. Olivia and Geoffrey watched and waited, hoping for the slightest sign that Edward would be all right: a twitching finger, an attempt to speak or open his eyes.

Their vigil lasted through the night, neither of them daring to sleep. Geoffrey made periodic trips to the drinks machine for coffee but Olivia declined and sipped a bottle of water. He brought back a cellophane-wrapped cheese and tomato sandwich, offering half to Olivia. She shook her head, unable to stomach food even though she hadn't eaten anything since breakfast with Alice and Maisie. When Geoffrey tried to engage her in conversation she pretended to doze until he lost interest. It was a long night.

The doctor's arrival at eight the following morning filled Olivia with equal measures of hope and dread. She was desperate for good news, but suppose the news was bad? She wasn't sure she could cope with more bad news. The doctor spoke quietly to the nurse and read Edward's chart before reporting that since he was stable, they would reduce his sedation and wake him up.

'What if he doesn't wake up?' said Geoffrey.

'Well, let's see, shall we?' said the doctor, with only the merest hint of impatience.

Olivia and Geoffrey were asked to leave the room. They waited on the other side of the paper-thin wall and Olivia paced backwards and forwards so Geoffrey wouldn't try to hold her. He probably thought her refusal to be comforted was a reaction to all the stress, but then she didn't really care what he thought.

It seemed an age before the nurse beckoned for them to come back. Olivia braced herself, reluctant to face what she might have to see or hear. Her characteristic optimism had taken such a battering of late it was becoming impossible to sustain.

'Olivia?' said Geoffrey.

She took a deep breath and swept past him, her gaze fixed on the nurse, whose expression gave nothing away.

The sight of a groggy Edward, eyelids heavy, a weak but beatific smile on his face, brought on a hot surge of mother love. Did Geoffrey not feel that same immutable love? Olivia had never doubted it, but if he did love Edward as much as she did, how could he even think of leaving?

The doctor said he expected Edward to make a complete recovery, that he needed to stay in hospital for a few days but then they could take him home. Geoffrey made a long 'phew' sound and reached for her hand, but

Olivia brushed him off and went to Edward. He was what mattered. He was all that mattered.

She longed to call her mum but couldn't trust herself to hold it together. If her mum had the slightest inkling of what Olivia was going through, she would be straight on a plane back home. Instead, Olivia sent a short text: *Edward's fine. I'll call you later x*

'Why don't you get us some coffee?' said Geoffrey, now sitting in the chair by Edward's bed.

Edward was doing his best to keep his eyes open, reminding Olivia of those endless nights when he was a baby, worn out from crying but still stubbornly refusing to sleep. She tried now what she used to try then, and gently blew on his face. 'So it does work,' she whispered, smiling, as he finally gave in and slept.

With her bag slung over her shoulder, Olivia headed towards the coffee machine but stopped when she saw a sign for the chapel. Ronald had often spoken of the power of prayer and how it could bring comfort in even the most testing of times. Olivia could really do with some comfort.

The chapel was small, quiet and simply adorned with half a dozen rows of wooden seats and a plain gold cross on the altar. Olivia closed her eyes and tried to recite the Lord's Prayer, but the words held no meaning for her. She might as well have been reciting a nursery rhyme. Perhaps it was expecting too much to find solace without first finding answers.

If it hadn't been for Edward, Geoffrey would be in France now. Passport, ticket, bag: pretty conclusive evidence. What she didn't know was why. True, their marriage wasn't in great shape but you talk about it, try to work things out. If you can't work things out you might separate, see how it goes for a while; maybe further down the line you divorce. What you don't do is buy a one-way ticket to another country and disappear without a word. How did she know he wouldn't book another flight once Edward was on the mend? And even if he didn't abandon them, Olivia knew he had intended to, a realisation that ignited the slow burn of resentment that had simmered for months.

*

Olivia kept up the charade of blissful ignorance until Rowena arrived, at which point she suggested they take a quick break.

'You two go,' said Rowena, shooing them and taking up vigil beside her dozing grandson.

For what Olivia had in mind they needed privacy so she led the way to the family room, ignoring Geoffrey's complaints about being hungry and wanting to go to Costa Coffee for breakfast. 'This won't take long,' she said, trying to shut him up.

The family room was empty, just as she had hoped, but a horrible reminder that only twenty-four hours before she had sat sobbing and shaking and not knowing if Edward would live or die.

'Thank God he's on the mend,' said Geoffrey, filling a paper cup with water.

So casually deceitful. Olivia began to tremble with the effort of not screaming at him.

299

'Hey,' he said, reaching for her. 'It's OK. He's going to be fine.'

She pulled her arm away. 'Are you leaving me?'

It took a moment for him to arrange his features in a way that conveyed the appropriate amount of confusion. You would think she had asked him to recite the capital cities of every country beginning with the letter 'A'.

'What?'

'It's a simple, "yes–no" question. Are you leaving me?'

'What are you talking about?' His attempt to smile, suggesting this was some kind of joke, was ill-advised. It produced a rictus grin that served only to further stoke her simmering rage.

She clenched her hands into fists. He was going to lie to her. To her face. It was difficult to keep her voice steady but critically important that she did. 'I'll ask you again – are you leaving me? And I would warn you, I already know the answer.'

He knew he was cornered. She could tell by the way he was breathing – quick and shallow, like an animal faced with danger. His eyes narrowed slightly, as if assessing both her and his options. Lie and hope she was bluffing? Tell the truth and hope she would understand? Come on, Geoffrey – make your move.

'Look, I don't know what's going on here, but—'

So this was how he wanted to play it. Right. Slowly she unzipped her bag, pulled out his passport and the e-ticket. Exhibits A and B. She laid them on a copy of *Hello* magazine, obscuring the beaming smiles of William and Kate. Geoffrey's expression was sheepish and shifty and scared all in one. A triumvirate of disappointments. She had seen that expression before, in the drawing room, when faced with telling his parents she was pregnant. The French doors had been open on to the garden and she thought he might make a run for it. This time she was standing between him and the door.

She waited for a response.

'So you've been going through my things?'

That was it? Feigned chagrin was his defence? The intensity with which she hated him at that moment was quite terrifying. She wanted to injure him, grievously assault him, to see his smug, lying face smashed into the wall.

'Leave if you want but for fuck sake have the balls to tell me. Thirteen years of marriage, and you plan to sneak off without so much as a word?' She was shouting now but why wouldn't she? 'Was I supposed to report you missing? Believe you were dead? Lie awake night after night, not knowing what happened to you, worrying myself sick. And what about Edward?'

Geoffrey spoke in a deliberately quiet voice, hoping, no doubt, it would encourage her to do the same. 'I had no choice. I did something bad and I had to get away. Trust me – it was for the best.'

'For the best? What did you do – kill someone?'

He squirmed, his creased forehead shiny with sweat. 'I can't—'

'Don't you dare say you can't tell me. If you've done something so bad you have to disappear, I need to know what it is.'

A minute ago she had wanted to see him in pain and hey presto, wish granted. His expression was one of pure agony. 'I had an affair with Ruth.'

Olivia felt as though she had been Tasered. She reeled back, momentarily stunned. Even though she had suspected, his explanations had seemed plausible, her misgivings unreasonable. She had weighed everything up and given him the benefit of the doubt. What had swung it in Geoffrey's favour was that she simply couldn't believe he would cheat on her with Ruth – the hypocritical liar who had treated her with utter contempt. The adulteress who had spread malicious lies about her. Ruth Rutherford – the enemy.

It was only pride that stopped Olivia crumbling into a snivelling heap of hurt. She took a breath. 'And you don't think foreign exile is overreacting, just a tad? The woman is dead, after all.' She knew it was cruel but she felt cruel. Geoffrey looked destroyed. Christ, had he been in love with her? Was he so devastated that he had to run away and lick his wounds?

He rubbed his forehead as though trying to erase a stain. 'I was with her the night she died.'

Another zap of the Taser, then a slowly dawning horror. 'It was you.' She reeled back, her legs suddenly weak. 'It was you.'

He turned away, unable to look at her. Oh no you don't. She grabbed his arms and turned him roughly so that he was facing her again. His tears threw her, but only for a second.

'The bruises – did you hurt her?'

He was crying properly now, his breath ragged. 'Of course not.'

'Then how . . . ?'

'She liked it.'

'Liked what? What did she like? Tell me.'

'Rough.' He was mumbling and sobbing. She could barely hear him.

'What?' She still had hold of his arm and gave it a hard shake to say, come on, spit it out, Geoffrey.

'Rough. She liked it rough.'

Olivia pulled her hand away. An image of the pair of them fucking like caged animals branded itself on her brain, never to be expunged. Then another image – Martin, Alice, Maisie, Ruth's parents. A grieving family.

Such was the force with which Olivia's open hand made contact with Geoffrey's face, she cried out in pain. Her palm burned. An electric jolt shot up her arm and came to a shuddering stop in her shoulder. He staggered back, his mouth gaping. Olivia glared at him with un-diluted hatred, her breathing laboured, her heart galloping at a dangerous pace.

'Rough enough for you?' she screamed.

She fled the room in a haze of tears, her whole body alight with fury.

*

It seemed impossible that life carried on as if nothing had happened. People parked their cars between white painted lines, piled on and off buses, came and went without a

303

second glance at the woman who had been sucked into a cesspit of depraved revelations.

Olivia lowered herself on to a cold metal bench, too dazed to move. Every scintilla of energy had been drained in that room and her limbs and head felt too heavy to carry. A woman with a pushchair hurried past her and dropped coins into a collection box. Christmas carols piped out from somewhere inside the hospital. Santa Claus in full regalia made his way through the revolving doors.

Slowly Olivia realised that this wasn't just about her pain, her suffering. The shock waves would spread like a tsunami, swamping not just the Parrys but the Rutherfords and St Bede's.

The possibility of rape had devastated Martin, but would the truth be any less devastating? That his wife had an affair with a man he trusted, a man he invited into his home. And if the police took DNA from male staff members, Geoffrey's would be a match. Would they believe the sex was consensual? What if they didn't? There would be a trial, a media frenzy, journalists camped out at the school, Martin and Olivia hounded, their children stigmatised. Edward would have to leave St Bede's, life as he knew it irretrievably lost. Panic tightened around her until she could barely breathe. She stood up, her bottom and thighs numb from the freezing bench, and tried to calm herself. Damage limitation – that was the way forward. A strategy, a plan. One of them needed to show courage and it sure as hell wouldn't be Geoffrey.

Back inside the hospital she peeked into Edward's room. Rowena had her back to her, a magazine open on her lap. Edward was asleep and there was no sign of Geoffrey. Olivia sneaked away without disturbing them, determined to track him down. She marched along the starkly lit corridors, past the drinks machine and Costa Coffee, expecting to see him skulking in a corner, feeling sorry for himself. He was a known flight risk but Olivia had the car keys so he must be around somewhere. The last place she looked was the chapel and there he was, kneeling, his head bowed low as if in prayer. Again she thought of Ronald and how disgusted he would be with his only son.

Olivia sat down at the end of Geoffrey's pew and looked straight ahead at the cross. 'We have to go to the police,' she said. A command, not a suggestion. Geoffrey didn't respond. 'I'll tell them about young Tom, about the sort of woman Ruth really was. It'll make your version of events more plausible.'

He turned towards her but she couldn't look at him, preferring to stare steadily at the cross. 'You'd do that for me?' he said.

She almost laughed. 'God, no. As far as I'm concerned you can rot. I'd do it for Martin and for Edward – try to minimise the possibility of scandal and make this degenerate mess go away.'

He nodded. 'I don't know what to say, except I'm more sorry than you will ever know.'

'Running away doesn't say sorry. Running away says spineless.'

'I deserved that.'

'Oh, you deserve much more, but let's not get ahead of ourselves.'

If she didn't do it now, she might lose her nerve. It felt wrong to leave Edward, but Rowena was with him and he seemed to be sleeping most of the time. They would drop by the ward and explain that they needed to get a change of clothes.

As Olivia stood and turned to the door, Geoffrey got off his knees and followed at a respectful distance.

*

It could have been worse, considering. Olivia was interviewed by the policeman and woman who had been at Martin's the afternoon she arrived home with the kittens. They listened as she recounted the scene in the cricket pavilion, Geoffrey's confession of an affair, her hope of avoiding a damaging scandal. It was difficult to say if they believed her. How many loyal wives had they caught out lying for their cheating husbands? Without committing themselves either way, they showed Olivia to a waiting room but couldn't say how long she would have to be there. She called the hospital and the nurse said Edward was comfortable and resting. Olivia promised she would be back soon and could the nurse please tell Edward that if he asked where she was.

It seemed like an age before the policewoman came back and said that her colleague had spoken with the groundsman and he had corroborated Olivia's story. Geoffrey had been interviewed separately and wouldn't face any charges.

'It was brave of you to come forward,' she said. 'Not many wives would do that for their husband.'

'I didn't do it for him.'

The policewoman gave her a knowing look.

'What about Martin Rutherford?' asked Olivia.

'We'll update him.'

Olivia felt sick at the thought of it. If he must hear the whole sordid truth, then he should hear it from her and Geoffrey. 'I think my husband and I should speak to him too.'

The policewoman raised her eyebrows. 'Are you sure?'

'No, not really, but this is personal – intensely personal. It involves all three of us and we need to be brave and own up to our part.'

'What about your husband? Will he agree?'

Olivia couldn't help her wry smile. 'Bravery isn't his strong suit, but yes, he'll agree.'

Geoffrey was outside smoking a cigarette. In the scale of things it was pretty irrelevant, but that didn't stop Olivia registering yet another way in which he had lied and gone behind her back.

In the car on the way back to the hospital, Geoffrey attempted bumbled gratitude but Olivia ignored him and stared out of the window. They didn't speak until he had parked, when she told him that first thing tomorrow they would go and see Martin. She expected him to object, make excuses, let his inner coward list all the reasons why that really wasn't such a good idea. Instead he acquiesced, a distinct element of defeat in his voice.

'Whatever you think best.'

They walked into the hospital like strangers. Edward had been moved from the intensive care unit to a side ward. When Olivia saw his empty bed she panicked, but the nurse calmed her down, said he was much better and didn't need to be in intensive care any more. For a minute or two the sight of him sitting up drinking chocolate milk made everything else fade into the shadows. One more day of observation and then they could take him home, the nurse said brightly.

But where was home? Not the Rectory – not any more. Her parents' house was empty so she and Edward could go there, but how would she explain that to him? She didn't want to do anything that might upset him. A thudding heaviness settled in her chest as another vile truth revealed itself. For the moment at least, Olivia was trapped.

Sixteen

The nurse on night duty – a timid young man with wire-rimmed specs and an earnest expression – brought a folded camp bed, a pillow and a couple of those hospital blankets with little square holes in them – Edward had a smaller version when he was a baby, except in pale blue. Seeing him lying there, his curls hidden under a thick white bandage, it was inconceivable to Geoffrey that he could have walked out of his life. What the fuck had he been thinking? That he could start again – make a new life in France and forget all about his family? Even if he had boarded the plane, he would probably have been back within a week. Anyway, it didn't matter now that the police knew the truth. If he had gone to them in the first place he wouldn't have needed to run. Olivia often told him to 'man up'. She used her jokey voice but they both knew it held a hard little pellet of censure.

Geoffrey insisted Olivia take the camp bed and he would have the chair. She refused to look at him or speak to him but when he stole the odd furtive glance, he saw that she was wrecked: deathly pale, parallel worry lines between her eyebrows, her mouth set in a tight frown. And all because of him – because of what he had put her through. He hoped she was asleep under the blanket and not just pretending. Edward must be in a deep sleep because he barely stirred. The nurse said it was normal, that he would still have some sedative in his system and why didn't Geoffrey try to get some sleep as well? Not a chance. His long day of reckoning was still whirring around his head, each snapshot memory deepening his savage sense of shame.

The policewoman had done all the talking while the policeman sat next to her, silently studying him. She had eased into the interview benignly enough: where had he and Ruth met on the night in question, what time had Ruth got there, what time did she leave? Geoffrey badly needed a cigarette. The policewoman jotted his answers in a note-book – her writing slanted and incongruously childlike – and then put down her pen. For an uncomfortably long time she stared at him without speaking. Was she waiting for him to fill the silence or trying to unnerve him? He was already unnerved so that was redundant. The police-man's inscrutable expression didn't help. If they were playing 'good cop, bad cop', Geoffrey hadn't figured out which was which.

Tell me, Mr Parry, did you rape Ruth Rutherford?

OK, she was bad cop. It was crucial he appeared credible, a victim of circumstance, a good man caught out in a bad situation. He realised he was drumming his fingers on the desk and shoved his hands in his lap.

No, I did not.

She didn't write that down. The subject turned to sex – intercourse, she called it.

So you're saying Mrs Rutherford consented to intercourse?
Yes.
And you had intercourse in the car?

Yes.

Whereabouts in the car?

The front seat.

Did you undress?

No.

What position were you in when you had intercourse?

Ruth, sorry, Mrs Rutherford sat astride me.

Did she undress?

No. Yes, sorry. She pulled down her underwear.

Did you restrain Mrs Rutherford?

No. Well, sort of, I mean, she wanted me to.

She asked you to restrain her?

No. She slapped me and I grabbed her wrist, so she slapped me again with her free hand and I grabbed that one too. I could see it excited her so I put her hands behind her back and held them there.

Held them with enough force to cause bruising?

I didn't know I was causing . . . I didn't mean to cause bruising. It was in the heat of the moment.

Mrs Rutherford had traces of blood on the sleeve of her blouse. Can you tell me anything about that?

He pointed to the scab on his earlobe. She bit me.

Mrs Rutherford bit you during intercourse?

Yes.

So, Mrs Rutherford bit you and slapped you and you restrained her while you had intercourse.

I know how it must seem but—

Did you rape Mrs Rutherford?

No, I did not.

311

Mrs Rutherford had bruising and scratches on her inner thigh. Can you tell me anything about that?

She caught it on my belt.

Your belt?

Yes, when she climbed off me.

Mr Parry, I'm going to ask you again. Did you rape Ruth Rutherford?

No, I did not.

Geoffrey had sweated guilt from every pore, squirmed in his seat, picked at the dry skin around his fingernails. Relating the intimate details of a sexual encounter – that sexual encounter – to a young woman, was degrading. Indecent. He heard how it sounded; how it made him sound. She glared at him, unflinching.

Someone knocked on the door and handed a note to the policeman. He read it, showed it to the policewoman and said the interview was concluded for now, but Geoffrey should wait there – would he like some tea?

A minute ago he was being asked if he was a rapist and now was being asked if he'd like some tea. The policeman's demeanour offered no clue as to whether or not he believed him. After one last scorching stare, Geoffrey's interrogator closed her notebook with a decisive snap.

Geoffrey had been raised to place an inordinate amount of store in the opinion of others, to be acutely concerned with what people thought. And here he was, a rape suspect.

Two hours of solitary self-loathing later, the policeman returned with the news that he wouldn't be charged. Geoffrey had buried his face in his hands, overcome with relief. It didn't last long. Despite the policeman's neutral tone, Geoffrey felt the sharp sting of judgement. He knew what sort of man Geoffrey was. Olivia knew what sort of man he was and tomorrow, Martin Rutherford would know too.

'Dad?' Edward stirred, a welcome diversion from the disgust and humiliation that clung to Geoffrey like a bad smell.

'I'm here, son.'

'Can I have a drink?'

Geoffrey filled a plastic cup from the water jug and held it while Edward took a few sips. He hoped to God that Edward would never know what sort of man he was, but irrespective of her own feelings, Geoffrey couldn't imagine Olivia would say anything that might hurt Edward.

Geoffrey wished she would talk to him: shout, scream if she must. The scene in the family room had been terrible, but this glacial silence was almost worse. If she gave him the chance he would explain that he had told Ruth it was over, that he was determined to be a better husband. He realised it was futile, that Olivia would probably never believe another word he said. And maybe she was right. There was no way to dress this up and make it look pretty. He had fucked another woman and now she was dead.

Without any expectation of sleep, Geoffrey shifted this way and that in the chair, and closed his eyes. Exhaustion must have got the better of him because he woke with a start at six thirty, aching and disorientated. As he squinted against the light, it crashed over him all at once: hospital, Olivia, Ruth, the police.

Edward was already awake, the nurse who had brought the fold-up bed taking his pulse and temperature and asking what he wanted for breakfast. The fold-up bed was empty, the blanket neatly folded.

'Sleep all right, son?'

Edward scratched his head and said the bandage was itchy. When he asked if he could watch television the nurse said that was a sure sign he was getting better.

Olivia came in, a plastic carrier bag in her hand and wearing a T-shirt that she hadn't been wearing yesterday. She must have bought it in the hospital shop. Her hair was tied back and a faint smell of toothpaste and talc wafted into the room with her. She walked past Geoffrey as though he were invisible. When she cupped Edward's face in her hands, her eyes shone with love.

'How are you feeling?' she asked.

Edward fiddled with the remote and said he was OK – did this TV have *Nickelodeon*?

Geoffrey picked up his Barbour. He had clean clothes and toiletries in the car and as Olivia had dictated they would see Martin Rutherford this morning, it seemed important to smarten up a bit. Not that Martin would give a fuck what Geoffrey looked like once he heard what he had to say. As he walked across the car park, sky still dark, air cold and damp, Geoffrey felt like a condemned man.

His second day of reckoning.

*

The traffic crawled, stopped altogether, crawled some more. Olivia had told Martin they would be there by nine but it was nearly that already. She called him from the car, said they might be a bit late, and then stared resolutely out of the window. Her silence, her determination not to look at him, were reminiscent of Geoffrey's mother. But if Rowena had noticed an atmosphere between him and Olivia, she was being uncharacteristically tactful and pretending that she hadn't. She was at the hospital now, reading *Moby Dick* to Edward. Geoffrey had concocted some unlikely story about him and Olivia having an appointment at the solicitor's to sign important papers – he had forgotten all about it and it was too late to rearrange. His mother had seemed unconvinced but didn't question him, which was just as well because despite all his recent practice, Geoffrey wasn't a very competent liar.

His whole sense of purpose had been focused on facing Martin. That's what he had mentally prepared for, braced himself for, so when the girls ran out to greet them, it threw him completely. How could he not have factored them in? The younger one had Ruth's defiant eyes, her strong jaw. The older one didn't so much look like Martin as have his diffident air. They were tactile with Olivia but called her Mrs Parry. She didn't introduce him.

Martin had lost weight he could ill afford to lose. His shirt and trousers hung off his tall, bony frame, but it was his face that shocked Geoffrey. His eyes had sunk into dark craters, his cheekbones sharp above two hollows. He shook Geoffrey's hand, thanked him for coming. Thanked him. Jesus, Martin thought this was a social call, two friends supporting him in his darkest hour. The girls produced a pair of kittens and said they were called Tiger and Miss Kitty. *Mrs Parry got them for us so we wouldn't miss Mummy so much.* It sliced right through Geoffrey's breastbone and pierced his treacherous heart.

Olivia had her back to him, which was fortunate because he might not be able to do what he had to do if he looked into her eyes and saw stone-cold loathing reflected back.

Martin made up a tray of tea and mince pies. He enquired after Edward and thanked Olivia for keeping him informed. 'Everyone was so relieved at school,' he said. 'We prayed for him.'

Geoffrey felt a whoosh of blood surge to his head and wondered if he might have a stroke. He rubbed his temple at the point where pain pressed against it. Martin asked if he was all right, was there anything he could get him? His kind concern was too much for Olivia, who sent the girls to play upstairs. The three of them went to the sitting room and Olivia closed the door. When Martin handed him a cup and saucer, Geoffrey disguised the tremor in his hand by drawing attention to the Christmas tree. Martin said he kept it there for the girls, to make everything as normal as possible under the circumstances.

Geoffrey's cue to confess. He could smell his own sweat, feel the dampness down his back, in his armpits. When he opened with an apology, Martin thought he was offering his condolences and thanked him again. Olivia shot him a look. *Just get on with it.*

Right.

He said he and Ruth had had a brief relationship and that they had been together the night of the accident. He was profoundly sorry both for the affair and for Martin's loss. He had never intended to cause hurt, but understood that was no excuse. He didn't expect and so wouldn't ask for forgiveness.

Martin listened in what appeared to be a state of catatonic shock. His face became more sallow, his jaw more slack. His eyes darkened, as if they had sunk even further into their sockets. Upstairs the girls sang Christmas carols. The lights on the tree twinkled on and off, on and off.

Martin's wide-eyed horror shifted from Geoffrey to Olivia.

'I found out yesterday,' she said. 'I thought Geoffrey should tell you himself, before you hear it from the police.'

Martin covered his mouth with his hand the way people do when they've been told something truly awful. The girls skipped in, took a mince pie each from the tray and announced it was snowing and they were going to play in the garden. Olivia reminded them to put on their coats and boots.

'Yes, Mrs Parry,' said the younger one cheekily.

They listened to them in the hallway, chatting as they dressed in their outdoor clothes, then the sound of the back door opening and closing with a slam.

Martin sat forward, his gaze fixed on Geoffrey. 'You were having an affair with Ruth?'

Geoffrey nodded. A mercy lie seemed in order. 'Briefly. She ended it that night. The night of the accident.'

Martin's shoulders rose and fell. 'But the police – they suspected rape.'

Geoffrey lowered his eyes in contrition. 'They made a mistake.'

'A mistake?' Martin's eyebrows knitted together as he tried to understand what exactly Geoffrey was telling him. An audible gasp punctuated the moment of realisation. 'The bruises, the semen. That was you?'

Martin lunged at him, knocking the tray to the floor. Tea, milk, sugar spilled over the beige carpet. Geoffrey jumped to his feet, fists raised, ready to defend himself. He didn't mean to; it was instinctive. Truthfully, a punch from Martin might have made him feel better – proof he wasn't the only one who couldn't control himself – but then Olivia was on her feet too, prising them apart.

'Please,' she said. 'Martin, please.'

It seemed to bring him to his senses. His breathing was heavy and loud: big gulps in and short gasps out. He stepped on and crushed a teacup before collapsing back into his chair. The three of them sat in dumb horror, no words adequate enough to express what they were feeling. Olivia got down on her knees, collected up the china and put it back on the tray. She was crying quietly and trying to hide it. How ironic that this was exactly what Ruth had wanted all along – Martin jealous and enraged: a red-blooded man prepared to fight for her. She would have been so proud of him.

That the truth was neither black nor white was a cliché too banal to quote, so Geoffrey didn't. His confession deliberately omitted the mitigation that Ruth had led and he had followed. It was Ruth who seduced him, Ruth who pursued him, Ruth who liked to be fucked so hard it hurt, and Ruth who cared nothing for the consequences. Geoffrey had been a willing participant, undeniably so, but without her there to own her share of the blame, it was all heaped on his shoulders. Ruth was dead, the ultimate victim; Geoffrey alive, the callous aggressor. What he said next was solely for Martin's benefit, a shred of comfort plucked from the dirty grey chasm between truth and lies.

'She loved you and regretted what we did. I regret it too and would give anything to undo it, to make different choices. Please believe me when I say how truly sorry I am.'

Geoffrey stood up to leave. There was nothing more he could add, no way to ameliorate Martin's pain.

As a pupil at St Bede's, Geoffrey had often been called in front of the headmaster to explain himself and his bad behaviour. Punishment would be handed down, apologies made, case closed. If only.

He let himself out and smoked three cigarettes while he waited in the snow for Olivia.

*

The doctor had said Edward was well enough to go home. He was already dressed in his school uniform, his head still heavily bandaged. Geoffrey's mother sat watching television with him – *Top Gear*, Edward's favourite. 'He has to take it easy,' she said. 'And come back in a few days to have those stiches looked at.'

Olivia hugged him for longer than he wanted. 'Mum,' he whined. 'Get off me.'

They hadn't talked about it, and Olivia certainly wouldn't be happy about it, but the only place they could take him was the Rectory. Geoffrey, Olivia and Edward went in the Mercedes, Geoffrey's mother following behind in her Mini. He had locked the rucksack in the boot but Olivia still had his passport. Maybe she didn't trust him not to abscond. It was perfectly possible she would never trust him again.

Olivia didn't look at Geoffrey as he held the front door open for her. She guided Edward inside and shooed the dogs away in case they jumped up at him. The heating was cranked up high, Edward's room aired and ready for him. Geoffrey's mother had made sandwiches and soup and there was a chicken slow-roasting in the Aga. Edward tucked into lunch but neither Geoffrey nor Olivia did any more than pick politely. When Olivia sent Edward upstairs to rest, he complied without objection. Olivia said she needed to get some rest too, and Geoffrey waited twenty minutes or so before taking her a cup of tea.

First he checked on Edward, sleeping soundly, the covers tucked under his chin. Geoffrey closed the door with barely a sound and tapped on his own bedroom door before opening it. The room was empty. He checked the bathroom but that was empty too. The bedroom across the landing hadn't been used for as long as he could remember, but that was where he found Olivia, curled on her side facing the wall, a sickly pink eiderdown draped over her legs and hips. The curtains were closed, the air thick and musty. He put the cup on the bedside table and hovered uncertainly. She didn't move or speak.

'Tea's there,' he said.

When she turned towards him, he saw that she had been crying. He perched on the end of the bed, encouraged that she let him.

'So she ended it?'

'What?'

'Ruth. You told Martin she ended it.'

Geoffrey clasped his hands together and pressed them against his mouth. 'I said that for Martin's benefit, but it wasn't true. I was the one who ended it that night – the night she was killed.'

Olivia wiped her face with her sleeve. 'I don't believe you.'

What could he say to convince her – to make that singular truth stand out from the sewer of lies? 'I don't blame you. I made a terrible mistake and panicked, but you have to understand – Ruth meant nothing to me.'

Olivia punched him hard on the thigh – an expression of her own hurt rather than a serious attempt to hurt him. 'Well, she meant something to me. A bitch, a whore, a rubbish wife, a rubbish mother. That's what you destroyed our family for.'

She was inconsolable now, her hands over her face as she sobbed, and it brought it home to him afresh. This was what he had done.

*

Geoffrey took the dogs for a long walk, unable to be around Olivia. Snow had settled underfoot and hardened in the plummeting cold. Rollo and Dice loped and chased, ate the snow and then shook it from their muzzles in a comedy of quick, erratic moves. Geoffrey kept seeing Martin lunge at him, the girls holding their kittens, the ruined carpet, his ruined marriage.

Not even four o'clock, but an insipid sun had already begun to dip low on the horizon. In the fading light he could make out Manor Farm, the village, the industrial estate with the derelict factory and the storage unit that held all their worldly goods. He knew every building, every field and contour – his entire world mapped out in front of him. Everything he had lost.

When he returned home Olivia and Edward were under a blanket in the snug, the television on quietly in the corner. His mother stood tight-lipped at the Aga, vigorously stirring gravy in a roasting tin. It was obvious something was wrong and out of duty and politeness, Geoffrey asked what it was. After the slew of inevitable denials – *nothing at all, I'm perfectly fine* – she got to the point. *Why go to all the effort of a roast when Olivia had already announced* – Olivia never said anything, only announced – *she didn't have much of an appetite and wasn't sure Edward was very hungry either.*

Geoffrey gave the dogs a biscuit each and told them to go to their beds. How little had changed since he had first brought Olivia home. Pregnancy and apprehension meant she hadn't eaten much then either. She was small, yet his mother continued to judge her for the small amount she ate. Food became the unlikely catalyst for so many of their proxy battles and, as always, he was caught in the crossfire.

Seventy-two hours ago he had walked away from this life, and yet here he was. It was like *Groundhog Day*, but without the laughs.

'What's wrong?' asked his mother, testy that he hadn't sworn immediate allegiance to her camp.

He shook his head. 'I wouldn't know where to begin.'

*

Geoffrey had a quick bath before supper, and a sneaky cigarette. Olivia and his mother were already round the table when he joined them. Olivia still wouldn't look at him but Edward launched into an account of the *Star Wars* film they'd just watched.

'I hope it wasn't violent,' said Geoffrey's mother. 'All these fights you've been getting into at school – I wonder if it's too much violence on the television.'

'It wasn't violent,' said Olivia.

'It has "wars" in the title,' said Geoffrey's mother.

Edward looked down at his plate, reluctant to be in the middle of it, but his grandmother pressed on regardless.

'What *were* you fighting about at school, Edward? It must have been quite serious.'

Geoffrey wouldn't mind hearing the answer to that question either. With so much else going on they hadn't talked about why Edward and Freddie Burton were scrapping again.

'Edward?' he said gently.

His eyes still on his plate, Edward mumbled that Freddie had said Mum was Mr Rutherford's girlfriend, that was why she was living with him. Olivia's cheeks flushed crimson. Irony heaped upon irony. She put her arm round Edward's shoulder. 'I know you mean well, darling, and I appreciate you standing up for me, but promise that in future you'll walk away. Freddie Burton is a silly boy who says silly things.'

Edward nodded and Geoffrey swiftly changed the subject before his mother interjected her opinion. The atmosphere was morose until she tried to lighten it with talk of Christmas, enlisting Geoffrey to help choose a tree. They could all decorate it together, wouldn't that be fun? A vision of the Rutherfords' tree with its twinkly lights and angel on top brought an icy shiver of remorse.

'Well, Geoffrey?' said his mother, clearly taken with the idea. 'Shall we get one tomorrow?'

The thought of a beautifully decorated Christmas tree seemed to parody the happy family they were before he tore it all to shreds. He went to the fridge and got a beer, wishing he could drink enough to make the pain go away.

After Edward declined apple crumble and custard, Rowena offered to get him settled for the night, as if he were an infant and not about to turn thirteen. He didn't complain, though; far too well-mannered for that. When he asked to borrow the laptop, Geoffrey panicked for a second. All those porn sites: girls with spread legs and naked breasts. 'I'll bring it up,' he said, slipping into the study to clear his history and any evidence of his sleazy pastime.

The sight of Edward tucked up in Geoffrey's own narrow childhood bed brought back memories of the teddy bear he'd loved, his father reading to him, a sense of being cocooned and safe. The bandage lent Edward an air of vulnerability – a stark reminder of how even the most precious things can be snatched away without warning. Geoffrey handed Edward the laptop and kissed the top of his head.

Geoffrey longed for his own bed after two nights sleeping (not sleeping) in a hospital chair, but went to the kitchen first to make some tea. When he saw Olivia washing dishes at the sink, he was about to retreat but then reasoned that as they were living in the same house, they were bound to end up in the same room occasionally. This was one of those occasions. He picked up the kettle and took it over to the sink to fill. Olivia moved aside without a word and when Geoffrey asked her if she wanted a cup, she offered a terse shake of her head in reply. He put the kettle on the Aga and stood waiting for it to boil, while she carried on with the dishes.

Despite the silence, Geoffrey decided to chalk this up as a minor victory. She didn't tell him to get out, or storm out herself. He was about to attempt conversation when his mother blustered in and made a fuss of tidying away the place mats and coasters. This turned out to be a prelude to her raising the thorny subject of sleeping arrangements. She had noticed Olivia's things in the spare room opposite Geoffrey's and wanted to know what was going on.

'Is there any truth in what this Freddie chap said to Edward?' The question – the accusation – was levelled at Olivia, whose vivid blush his mother appeared to interpret as guilt. 'Claire Heather mentioned that your name had been linked to a young French student who left rather abruptly.'

Olivia opened her mouth to say something but merely spluttered in disbelief. Her eyes blazed, first at his mother, then at Geoffrey. Time to man up.

'Don't speak to Olivia like that,' he said crossly. 'I'm the one who's been unfaithful. Me. I'm the adulterer, not Olivia.'

His mother put her hand to her cheek, as though she had been struck. 'Geoffrey,' she said.

He registered the crushing disappointment in her voice but didn't allow it to deter him. 'I think you owe Olivia an apology.'

His mother looked flustered now – backed into a tight and seedy corner. It took a few moments before she elevated her shoulders and chin, just enough to convey an element of duress. 'If I have spoken out of turn then yes, I apologise, but—'

'No buts. For years I've stood by and watched you undermine her, too weak to speak up.'

'I've done no such thing,' said his mother, clearly appalled at the suggestion.

'You know you have,' said Geoffrey. 'And it stops now.'

In a chest-beating swell of manhood, he watched her turn on her heel and leave. He had always made excuses for her, but this time she had gone too far. Olivia was speechless. Geoffrey took a beer from the fridge, downed it rugby-style and crushed the can in his fist. 'I'm sorry. I should have done that a long time ago.'

Maybe it was the light, or maybe wishful thinking, but he could have sworn he saw a fleeting smile pass across Olivia's face.

Seventeen

Olivia had gone to St Bede's to pack up Edward's things and bring them back to the Rectory. Leo met her in the dorm with everything Edward needed for his holiday homework, and kept banging on about Ruth: such a terrible loss, how senselessly tragic, etcetera. *She seemed such a wonderful person.* Olivia quelled the urge to demur. Few things impinge on the belief you're a good person like compulsively despising a dead person. She found herself obsessing about the showdown she had been denied, the questions she never got to ask, the answers she never got to hear.

It would have been cathartic to purge herself of all the reasons why Ruth was *not* a wonderful person, to tell Leo about the emotional carnage that woman had caused, but that wasn't an option. When he carried the trunk to the Land Rover and commented that she seemed a bit quiet, Olivia blamed the worry of Edward's head injury and the whole business between him and Freddie Burton. Leo didn't question it – why would he? – but swallowing the truth felt like choking on rocks.

At the top of the driveway Olivia had to pull over and wait for the fogged-up windscreen to clear. She jumped when she heard a tap on the window. Martin. They looked at each other through the cloudy glass with a mutual recognition of anguish.

'Come inside, Olivia.' He was in his shirtsleeves, the front door wide open. She didn't want to go back in there, to see the stain on the carpet, Ruth's jacket on the coat stand. 'I was going to call,' he said. 'There's something I need to ask you.'

How much more did he expect of her? She had tolerated his duplicitous wife, nurtured his damaged children, delivered up her unfaithful husband with a full and frank confession. Truly, she had had her fill of St Bede's and everyone to do with it. *Please*, mouthed Martin, pointing towards the open front door. Reluctantly Olivia turned off the engine and followed him into the house.

Alicia Burton had taken the girls out for the day – a pantomime in Bath and then tea at Jollys – so the house seemed unnaturally quiet. Martin made coffee while Olivia sat at the table in the alcove, neither of them inclined to speak. Her mind went back to the evening Ruth had flirted so outrageously with Geoffrey and to the evidence on Ruth's phone. Olivia was astonished at her own stupidity. Instead of meekly believing Geoffrey's lies and excuses, she should have connected the dots, seen red flashing lights, heard klaxons blaring.

Martin sat down and apologised for his violent outburst, but Olivia shrugged it off. Geoffrey had got what he deserved in her opinion.

'It was a shock,' said Martin.

Indeed. Bad enough that their spouses had had an affair, but to do so on their own doorstep, so to speak, was appallingly inconsiderate. 'You said there was something you wanted to ask,' said Olivia, hurrying him along.

Martin put his hands together, fingers pointing to the heavens. 'I realise I've already asked so much of you, and I'm not sure where yesterday's disclosures have left our friendship, but I wondered if you would consider coming to the funeral?'

Seriously? Olivia wanted to tell him how much she loathed Ruth and that going to her funeral would be an act of gross hypocrisy, but Martin's evident desperation stopped her. None of this was his fault.

'For the girls,' he said. 'It will be a very quiet affair.'

Olivia sighed wearily. How could she refuse? 'Of course.'

Martin nodded in gratitude and put Olivia's coffee in front of her. 'Did you have any idea?' he asked, stirring sugar into his own sludgy coffee. 'You know, about what was going on.'

Olivia told him of her suspicions – the phone calls, the texts – but that she had believed Geoffrey's explanations. 'Truthfully, Martin, I never thought he would do that to me.'

Martin pushed his cup away without having taken a sip. 'I can't say the same about Ruth, I'm afraid. Geoffrey wasn't the first.'

Feigning surprise would have been disingenuous.

'Do you think you will forgive him?'

Olivia shook her head. 'I'm too angry to even consider it.' She found it difficult to reconcile this quiet, dignified man with the man who had flown at Geoffrey with his fists.

'Angry with Ruth too, I daresay.'

Olivia didn't deny it.

*

Fine drizzle hung listlessly in the air, the sky an oppressive leaden canopy. The funeral was small and private, just immediate family and a handful of Ruth's friends. Martin chose the last day of term so it would be inconvenient for staff and parents to attend, all of them too busy with frantic and seemingly endless preparations for Christmas. He said he didn't want a fuss, that Ruth hated fuss.

Alice and Maisie wore matching navy-blue coats with red piping round the collars, white woollen tights and their T-bar shoes, polished to an impressive shine. They held their father's hands and watched their mother's coffin lowered into a deep gash in the earth. Neither of them cried. Olivia had reservations about allowing them at the graveside. If they didn't understand, it was pointless, and if they did, it was cruel. They knew Mummy was in heaven and they wouldn't see her again, but didn't equate either of those things with the solemn church service or the crowd that had gathered to say nice things about her.

Olivia remained in the background and when she was asked how she knew Ruth, she offered a sanitised version of the truth: friend of Martin's, houseparent at school, Alice and Maisie in her dorm.

Alicia Burton had put on a nice spread, as Olivia's mum would say. A rug had been placed over the stained carpet. Martin slipped into professional mode – greeted everyone personally, graciously accepted condolences, enquired after their health, their families, and thanked them warmly for coming.

When everyone had left, Olivia stayed behind to clear up and make sure the girls were all right. She felt they had coped remarkably well until Maisie gleefully pointed out how many more presents there were round the tree, at which point it became obvious they thought today was some kind of Christmas party, not their mother's funeral. When Olivia raised it with Martin, he confessed to feeling overwhelmed. A single father to two young daughters – how on earth would he cope? Olivia poured him a small brandy. He grimaced as he sipped, seemingly encouraged by its medicinal qualities rather than its taste.

'And what about you, Olivia?' he asked. 'What does the future hold?'

She shook her head. 'I have absolutely no idea. All I know is that I can't bear being under the same roof as Geoffrey, but unfortunately I don't have a choice.'

'Well, perhaps I can help – repay your many kindnesses.'

'I can't live here, Martin. It wouldn't be right.'

'Of course not. No, I was thinking about Gardner Cottage. It's been empty since the Clarke-Bowens' day. I think the deputy head lived there.'

'Sheila Fitzwilliam. Yes, she did.'

'I've asked Mr Hill to take a look at it, see to any repairs. It's rather on the small side but there are two good bedrooms, so if you were interested, you and Edward could use it out of term-time.'

It seemed wrong to feel a shot of happiness on such an unhappy day, but Olivia couldn't help herself. 'Are you serious, Martin?

'Perfectly. Think of it as your second home here at St Bede's.'

Olivia grabbed the lifeline Martin had thrown her. 'How soon can we move in?'

*

Christmas Eve confounded bookmakers by dumping two inches of unexpected snow across the West Country. Geoffrey liked a flutter on such things but Olivia didn't ask him if he had bet on a white Christmas. He might take it as a sign that she was starting to forgive him and she absolutely wasn't.

They had taken Edward to the hospital to have his wound checked and bandage removed the previous day. Olivia hadn't wanted Geoffrey to come with them but Edward was keen on the idea of a family outing – *we haven't done that in ages* – so she had relented. The wound on his head was scabbed and livid and bisected a saucer-sized bald patch above his left ear. Geoffrey had insisted on taking him for a haircut afterwards and Olivia watched his golden curls fall to the floor, thinking how nothing would ever be the same again. Even the shock of losing Downings and Manor Farm seemed minor compared to the discovery of Geoffrey's affair. She had held on to the hope that in time Geoffrey would start another business or maybe get a job, that they would find another house, be a family again and reflect with hindsight on their troubles: wiser, stronger, more mature. No hope of that now. There was no way back from this.

Edward wanted to go to Cribbs Causeway but Olivia said it would be mayhem so close to Christmas. He looked to Geoffrey for a second opinion and when he overruled her – *come on, it won't be that bad* – she hated him all over again.

An hour in traffic just waiting to get into the mall, and another forty-five minutes looking for a parking space. Cooped up together in such close proximity, Edward had sensed the tension and thought it was his fault for asking to go there in the first place. Despite their attempts to convince him otherwise, his earlier enthusiasm petered out and he became quiet and withdrawn. Geoffrey cheered him up with the promise of junk food and when they managed to get a table at McDonald's, Edward visibly brightened. He wolfed down his double cheeseburger and fries while Olivia picked apathetically at her chicken peri peri wrap.

'I need to buy some Christmas presents,' he said, standing up.

Olivia wanted to go home. Her head throbbed with the glaring light and incessant din.

'Half an hour,' Geoffrey said, checking the time on his phone. 'Meet us back here.'

After Edward had disappeared into the throng of shoppers, Olivia found a couple of aspirin in her bag and washed them down with a Diet Coke.

'Are you OK?' asked Geoffrey, playing the ill-fitting role of concerned husband.

Olivia replied with a contemptuous stare.

*

It had taken twice as long as it should have done to get back to the Rectory. Tiredness clawed at Olivia, the nervous energy that had kept her going throughout the day now dissipated, leaving her flat and depleted. She went to her room and flopped on the bed, never having felt less like celebrating Christmas. Her parents and brother were on the other side of the world, her marriage was over and the effort of hiding it all from Edward was gruelling.

She tried to imagine herself and Edward in Gardner Cottage but couldn't remember what it looked like. She had only been there once, years ago, when Sheila Fitzwilliam had hosted an Alpha meeting. It was small, that she did remember, but then Manor Farm had been far too big with all its unused rooms and colossal heating bills. Moving there had been Geoffrey's idea – a way of showing off to the world how clever and successful he was. Her reticence had mystified him, but Olivia had never wanted to play Lady of the Manor. She was better suited to the cosiness of her parents' house: huddled into the sitting room watching TV, squeezed round the kitchen table at mealtimes. Gardner Cottage would be cosy – she would make sure of it.

Was it wrong that she relished the idea of telling Geoffrey she was leaving? She wanted to hurt him, inflict pain. But what about Edward? Telling him the whole truth was out of the question, but Olivia was loath to have him think she had any part in destroying their family.

This was what had been going through her mind when she fell into an uneasy sleep, only to wake hours later, fully clothed, cold and hungry. At first she didn't think she could be bothered to eat or get undressed, that she might as well just pull the covers over her and try to last out until morning, but hunger had got the better of her.

She got up, wrapped the candlewick bedspread around herself and went quietly downstairs to the kitchen, feeling her way in the darkness rather than risk waking anyone by switching on a light. Rollo and Dice watched lazily from their beds as she heated a saucepan of milk and stirred in three heaped teaspoons of cocoa.

The door opened, startling her.

'I thought I heard someone get up.' There was an implicit innocence in Geoffrey's dishevelled hair, his middle-of-the-night confusion, his bare feet; a boyish quality that had attracted Olivia to him at the very beginning. 'Can't you sleep?' he said, rubbing his eyes.

She poured the milk into a mug without answering. It was a stupid question anyway. If she had been able to sleep she would be in bed, not the kitchen.

'You can have my room if you like,' he said, taking more milk from the fridge. 'It doesn't seem fair that you have the worst room.'

Suddenly he was concerned with fairness, being gentle-manly, doing the right thing? A bit late for that. She held the bedspread around herself with one hand, picked up her hot chocolate with the other and swept towards the door. It would have been more dramatic if she had been able to open the door. Geoffrey came up behind her and tenta-tively touched her shoulder. She shrugged him off.

'Don't.'

When he sighed she felt his breath on her neck and hated how it made her skin tingle. He reached over her and turned the handle. She didn't look back when he said her name.

*

Olivia kept checking her watch, waiting for midday when she would have a glass of wine. Much too early for a drink under normal circumstances but it was Christmas Eve, so normal rules didn't apply. Plus, alcohol deadened the insult of having to be around Geoffrey and his mother, although at least Rowena had been keeping out of Olivia's way. The bite of her accusations were too raw for forgiveness, despite her begrudging apology. She would never have spoken to her like that if Ronald had been alive. And to think Olivia had been going to make a special effort with her this Christmas. She huffed at the irony. Well, she would be moving into Gardner Cottage soon. Knowing her days at the Rectory were numbered was the one thing that kept her going.

Geoffrey came into the drawing room and found her putting Edward's presents round the tree. Ignoring him felt childish but she did it anyway.

'Mum's out,' he said, 'and Edward's playing computer games upstairs, so I wanted to give you this.'

Olivia looked up from what she was doing to see Geoffrey nervously proffering a small box.

'What's that?'

'Christmas present.'

Did he really think she would accept a gift from him? 'I don't want it.'

He stepped nearer to where she was kneeling, holding out the box for her to take. It was like one of those cheesy Christmas adverts that were all over the television.

'Please.'

She stood up, cross that he couldn't see how asinine he was being. 'I said I didn't want it.'

He pressed it into her hand. 'Just open it, please.'

She huffed, realising it was easier to open the damn thing than to argue about it. He stood over her, infuriatingly pleased with himself. She removed the lid and found the heart-shaped locket she had seen in his rucksack. Geoffrey was obviously waiting for her to say something and when she didn't, he jogged her memory.

'It was the first present I ever gave you.'

Yes, of course. She remembered prising it apart with her thumbnail, full of expectation, only to find nothing there. He hadn't known you were supposed to put a memento inside a locket. She had found his cluelessness charming back then, but what was he playing at, giving this to her now?

'Look inside,' he said.

Mildly curious, she did, and there, under the thin slither of glass, lay a tangle of hair. She stared at it, puzzled. Again he waited for her to speak and when she didn't he said, 'It's ours. Yours, mine and Edward's.'

The strands blended together perfectly but under the tree lights she could just make out the subtle differences in colour and texture. It took a moment for her to understand that he was trying to manipulate her with nostalgia, remind her that they had married because of Edward and the three of them were a family.

A hot flame of fury shot right through her and she flung the locket back at him. 'Well, that's a cheap shot, even for you.'

His look of hurt surprise infuriated her further still. 'What did you think would happen? That I'd forgive and forget?'

He picked up the locket from the floor. 'I wanted you to know how sorry I am.'

'Sorry you got caught.'

'No. I was going to tell you, I swear.'

'So why were you running away? Why were you fucking Ruth Rutherford? Don't you know what you've done? Are you really that stupid?'

Attempting to shush her was a big mistake. It only made her louder.

'The police said she had been raped. *Raped*. Do you have any idea –?'

Geoffrey covered his face with his hands. So now he didn't want to see her. Now he didn't want to hear what she had to say. Olivia was shaking, furious that he had made her relive the nightmare of discovery, the humiliation of going to the police, the shame of having to confess to Martin.

She hated feeling like this and yet Geoffrey stoked and stirred that feeling. Her chest heaved with the poison he had put there. She wanted rid of it – rid of him. She was about to storm out, leaving him with his meaningless trinket and appalling judgement, when the front door slammed hard. Geoffrey moved his hands away from his face, his eyes wide with fear. They didn't move or speak. They barely dared to breathe. It was as if all the air had been sucked from the room.

Eighteen

They separated and ran along the lane, Geoffrey towards the pub and Olivia towards the shop, but there was no sign of Edward. Olivia phoned Lorna who said she hadn't seen him but would call if he turned up. Geoffrey heard no reference to their terrible argument, which he assumed had been buried beneath this latest crisis. Lorna must have asked what was going on, why Edward had run off, because Geoffrey heard Olivia say that she couldn't talk about it now, she would explain later.

Geoffrey suggested he get the car and drive around looking for him. They went back to the Rectory and while Geoffrey fetched his keys, Olivia searched outside again and said Edward's bike was missing. She had planned to stay there in case he came back, but changed her mind and insisted she go with Geoffrey in the car.

'We should take the Land Rover,' she said. 'So we can throw the bike in the back when we find him.' The anger had vanished from her voice. She was shaking, her arms wrapped around her chest as though bound by a straitjacket.

Geoffrey had been so pleased with himself when he gave her the locket. He wanted to show how much thought he had put into it, getting little bits of their hair and fitting them all together underneath the glass. He hadn't expected her to forgive him there and then but he certainly hadn't expected the reaction he got.

Olivia scribbled a note telling Edward to call her mobile, just in case he came home. In big capitals she wrote 'SORRY'.

It was Olivia's car but Geoffrey drove. He started to apologise, explain that he hadn't meant to upset her, but she shook her head and he stopped talking. It could wait. They didn't know how much Edward had heard. Maybe he had heard Olivia shouting and left just because he hated it when they argued. It didn't mean he'd heard what she was shouting about, necessarily.

They drove all over the village, past Lorna and Johnny's and back towards the Rectory, but there was no sign of him. Geoffrey wondered how Edward was managing to cycle through the slushy snow and hoped he was wearing a helmet. A vision of him lying in the road made Geoffrey flinch, as if from a sudden shooting pain.

'Where is he?' said Olivia, more to herself than to Geoffrey.

'We'll find him,' he said.

As they drove past the path that led up to Crooke Peak, Geoffrey remembered that was the place he used to run off to when he was a boy. He pulled over on to the verge so as not to block the lane, and switched off the engine.

'What are you doing?' asked Olivia.

'He could have gone up here,' said Geoffrey, pointing to the path. 'I'll go and look.'

Olivia undid her seat belt. 'I'm coming with you.'

Fresh snow was falling: big dry flakes that quickly settled. An arctic wind had whipped up from nowhere, stinging

Geoffrey's eyes, numbing his exposed skin. Never mind the helmet – was Edward even wearing a jacket?

They picked their way along the steep path in silence. Once or twice when Olivia slipped, Geoffrey grabbed her arm to steady her, but as soon as she regained her balance she pulled it away again. In a moment of unwelcome clarity, he realised there was nothing he could do or say that would make her forgive him. The locket, defending her against his mother, apologising a thousand times – none of it could undo what he had done. A deep ache in his chest meant all he could manage were short, staccato breaths. He thought heartache was an expression, not a real thing, but his heart really did ache.

'Did you hear that?' said Olivia, coming to an abrupt stop. Her hair was damp with melted snowflakes, her lips tinged blue with the cold.

'Hear what?'

She shushed him and he listened hard, hearing only the whoosh and whine of the wind.

'That,' she said, suddenly sprinting up ahead.

He followed, not sure what she heard that he didn't, until the track flattened out and there, smashing his bike with a fallen branch, was Edward. The relief Geoffrey felt at finding him was quickly swallowed up. Edward saw them and stopped, but only for a moment before he raised the branch above his head and brought it down with enough force to buckle the front wheel.

Olivia ran over and tried to wrestle the branch from him, but he shook her off and headed for Geoffrey, taut with rage and purpose. 'Is it true what Mum said about you and Mrs Rutherford?'

So he had heard. Geoffrey stood still, sick with shame. He opened his mouth but before he could say anything, Edward hauled the branch over his shoulder and swung, catching Geoffrey's cheek with a glancing blow. He recoiled backwards, his hand instinctively going to the point of contact.

'Why didn't you move?' screamed Edward, dropping the branch on the ground. 'Why did you let me hit you?'

Tears scalded Geoffrey's eyes. 'Because I deserved it.'

'Did you rape Mrs Rutherford? Did you kill her?'

'No. God, no. How could you think—?'

'Mum said—'

'She died in a car accident, Edward,' cried Olivia. 'An accident. I never said he killed her. And the other thing—' She couldn't bear to say the word any more than Geoffrey could bear to hear it. 'The police made a mistake. That's all it was – a mistake.'

Edward was shaking. No jacket, just a thin T-shirt and jeans. His hair was wet, the scar shockingly vivid. Geoffrey took off his own jacket and tried to put it around Edward's shoulders.

'Get away from me!'

He lashed out with his fists and took a couple of steps back, tripping on a small rock that poked sharply through the snow. Geoffrey tried to catch him but they both fell on to the hard ground, sobbing. Edward's trainers were soaked through, his T-shirt stuck to his skin. This time Geoffrey insisted on the jacket and Edward didn't refuse.

Geoffrey crouched next to him and gave Edward his gloves too. Thick candles of clear snot hung from his nostrils. Olivia fished a tissue from her sleeve and wiped them away with maternal efficiency. The fight had gone out of him. He sat in the snow, spent and defeated.

No one spoke on the short ride home. The air was laced with a terrible truth and there was nothing Geoffrey could say to change that. Edward sat shivering: short, involuntary spasms like an electric current shooting through his body. When Geoffrey pulled into the Rectory, Edward ran inside and took the stairs three at a time. He couldn't get away fast enough. Olivia followed him upstairs, leaving Geoffrey alone. A new low in months of new lows. What would Edward think of him now?

Geoffrey went inside, relieved that his mother was still out on parish business. He poured two large glasses of wine and got a carton of apple juice from the pantry. It took a few minutes before he mustered the courage to face his wife and son.

The bathroom door was ajar, Olivia running a bath.

'Where is he?' asked Geoffrey.

'In his room,' answered Olivia, her jacket and scarf still on.

She swirled the water with her hand, mixing hot with cold. In the steamed-up mirror Geoffrey could make out the cut on his cheek, an inch or so long, jagged at one end and scabby with dried blood. He scooped a few handfuls of water from the bath and splashed it on his face. Olivia handed him a clean flannel, stiff from having been pegged out to dry in the winter wind.

'I didn't mean for him to hear,' she said.

Geoffrey lobbed the flannel in the laundry bin. 'I know.'

'Edward worships you. Whatever has happened between us, I would never spoil that for him.'

'I think I'm the one who's spoiled it.'

A fine frizz of damp blonde hair around her crown and temples gave the impression of a halo. She turned off the water and draped a couple of towels over the radiator. 'I'd better get him,' she said.

'Should we talk to him?'

'In a while. Give him time to calm down.'

She was right, of course. And beautiful. What the hell had he been thinking? Ruth Rutherford. Jesus.

'Is that for me?'

He had forgotten about the wine and handed a glass to Olivia. She drank as though she needed it. Geoffrey watched and waited, reluctant for the most civilised conversation they had had in ages to end. Edward came out of his bedroom, his wet clothes discarded in favour of the fleecy dressing gown they'd bought him last Christmas. He stopped when he saw them, his eyes red-raw.

'Let me look at you,' said Olivia. Her voice was gentle and cajoling as if she expected him to object, but he didn't. She inspected the scar and said it looked OK – did it hurt? Edward shook his head. He still hadn't looked Geoffrey in the eye.

How to begin? 'I'm sorry, son.'

Edward took the apple juice and drank from the carton: long, noisy gulps – juice dribbling down his chin. He wiped it with the back of his hand. A deliberate show of bad manners to express his disgust, no doubt. 'Were you going to leave us?' he asked, his voice cracking, already beginning to break.

Geoffrey wanted to tell him that of course he wasn't going to leave, that it was crazy talk, but how could he? The pleading look he shot Olivia, desperate for help to make the truth sound less callous, prompted no response. Down to Geoffrey then. 'I couldn't do it, son. I couldn't leave you.'

'Are you getting a divorce like Freddie Burton's parents?'

Again Geoffrey looked at Olivia and again she looked away. 'We haven't talked about it but—'

Wrong answer. She cut him off. 'Whatever happens, we will both be in your life, just like we are now. We love you very much. You're the most important person in all of this.'

Edward seemed to think about that for a moment before asking, 'Does Mr Rutherford know?'

Geoffrey lowered his eyes at the memory: Olivia on her knees, crying and picking up bits of broken china. He nodded.

'Does he hate me?'

'No.' Geoffrey and Olivia answered emphatically and in unison.

'No, darling, of course he doesn't,' said Olivia. 'This is nothing to do with you. None of it is your fault.'

'It's my fault,' said Geoffrey. 'No one else's. All mine.'

*

Being with Johnny and Lorna again was a sweet kind of torture. Rather than having a few drinks and a laugh, they were moving Olivia and Edward into Gardner Cottage.

Olivia broke the news on Boxing Day: Martin had offered her somewhere to live and she had accepted. Geoffrey couldn't help but wonder if this was Martin's way of getting his own back. Touché.

The cottage was unfurnished so she needed to collect some things from the storage unit. Johnny was helping with the lifting and shifting. Lorna was there for moral support.

She had turned up at the Rectory on Christmas Eve, not long after all the drama with Edward. The initial awkwardness between her and Olivia quickly fizzled out, resolved in hugs and tears and heartfelt apologies. Geoffrey excused himself, aware that Olivia would want to speak to Lorna alone. Part of him dared to hope Lorna would talk Olivia into giving him another chance. Maybe she had tried and failed or maybe she hadn't tried at all. Either way, Olivia was leaving.

She'd told him as they headed up Crook Peak to fetch Edward's bike. It was Olivia's idea to go together – give them a chance to talk. Stupidly, Geoffrey had taken it as a good sign. Not only could she tolerate his company, but she was ready to talk. His optimism had been wildly misplaced. What Olivia wanted to talk about was separating – how it would work, what they would tell Edward. Apparently they had moved past the hate phase of their relationship and were now in the practical phase. Geoffrey was too gutted to respond. He'd thought Edward's meltdown had brought them closer, that they were a team again, their common goal to make him feel safe and secure. What it had actually done was make Olivia see that they needed to formalise their estrangement so everyone knew exactly where they stood.

Edward's bike had been at the top of the hill in the spot where they had left it. Both wheels were buckled, paintwork chipped and scratched, the leather on one of the handlebars ripped. It lay there, destroyed, just like their marriage.

*

Johnny borrowed a friend's van and met them at the storage unit. Geoffrey saw him looking over at the factory, with its broken windows and graffiti, but neither of them said anything. Theirs had been a more subdued reunion – no embrace, certainly no tears – just a manly handshake and an unspoken acknowledgement to never mention the Boys' Brigade. Neither of them mentioned the affair either, although Geoffrey imagined that they soon would, maybe over a boozy session in the Lamb and Lion. Maybe Johnny would even understand.

They loaded furniture on to the van while Olivia and Lorna sorted out boxes of bedding and kitchen equipment and things to make the cottage look homely: rugs, cushions, books, photographs.

It was a strange morning. A few times Geoffrey and Johnny found themselves joking about how to fit everything in the van, then remembered why they were doing it and stopped talking for a while. Olivia and Lorna were more businesslike, ticking things off a list and stacking them neatly next to the van to be loaded around the furniture. They were done in a couple of hours and set off in convoy to St Bede's.

*

The cottage was round the back of the cricket pitch with a view across the manicured lawns. It was out of bounds when Geoffrey had been at school there but that hadn't stopped him sneaking up to peek in the windows as a dare.

All four of them were quieter now, putting things where Olivia told them but otherwise not saying much at all. Lorna unpacked the kettle and four mugs and made instant coffee to go with the Christmas cake she had brought from home.

The kitchen was clean and compact with fitted wooden units and a stainless-steel sink. Olivia said to leave the box with china and stuff on the work surface and she would unpack it later. The three-seater sofa dwarfed the sitting room, leaving just enough space for a coffee table and the flat-screen TV that had been in Edward's room at Manor Farm. None of it looked right here. It didn't belong.

Olivia began to arrange photographs on the coffee table but changed her mind and prioritised getting the bedrooms straight instead. There were two, both doubles, with a bathroom in between. At least it had a bath. Olivia's bed was from the guest room her parents used when they came to visit. Geoffrey and Olivia's grand four-poster would never have got through the door, let alone up the narrow staircase. Olivia probably wouldn't have wanted it anyway.

When the van was empty they all stood around, no one knowing quite what to say. Seeing Johnny put his arm round Lorna heightened Geoffrey's sense of loss and loneliness. They would go home together, share intimacies, hold each other in bed. He knew it wasn't the same – there had been no affair, no terrible accident – but Johnny had tried to run away from his problems and had withdrawn from Lorna rather than confiding in her, just like Geoffrey had done with Olivia. However glad he was that Johnny and Lorna had found a way back to each other, he couldn't help but feel a pang of envy because he and Olivia hadn't.

'Don't worry about Edward,' said Lorna, addressing herself to Olivia. 'He'll be fine with us until you get settled.'

Geoffrey had bought him a new bike in the Boxing Day sales. He wasn't sure Edward would take it from him but he did. He even mumbled a 'thank you'.

'Well, I'd better get this van back to its rightful owner,' said Johnny, producing a big bunch of keys from his jacket pocket. After an awkward pause, he and Geoffrey shook hands and Lorna hugged Olivia, whispering something in her ear. Olivia smiled the way she did when she was putting on a brave face.

Geoffrey and Olivia stood there in the watery sunshine and watched their best friends drive away. So much had been damaged and lost, but only now did it seem irrevocable.

'Can we talk?' he said.

Olivia looked wary.

'Please. I won't stay long.'

Reluctantly, she led the way into the cottage. It was hard to believe this would be her home, his family's home, but with no place for him. He followed her into the kitchen and remembered seeing Lorna put a bottle of wine in the fridge.

'Do you mind if I open this,' he said, getting the wine.

It had a screw cap so they didn't have to search around for a corkscrew. Olivia produced a couple of glasses and Geoffrey filled them almost to the brim.

The kitchen was a commotion of unpacked boxes so they took their wine into the sitting room and sat at opposite ends of the sofa. Geoffrey remembered christening it the afternoon it had been delivered. Olivia had insisted on putting a towel underneath them so as not to risk staining the fabric.

'I need to ask you a question,' he said.

Olivia inhaled sharply, clearly uncomfortable with the notion, but he asked anyway. 'If it had just been an affair, could you have forgiven me?'

She looked at him, aghast. '*Just* an affair?'

'Sorry. I meant—'

She shook her head. 'I know what you meant.' She took a long drink of wine and closed her eyes. 'Maybe,' she said, opening them. 'I don't know.' After another glug of wine she said, 'Now I have a question for you.'

Geoffrey braced himself. 'Fire away.'

She stared at him, perhaps preparing herself for an answer she didn't want to hear. 'Why did you do it?'

He drank deeply from his glass. 'I have no fucking idea.'

She stopped herself from smiling but he could tell she wanted to. 'No, really – why did you do it?'

How best to put this? 'She caught me at a low point and I was too weak to say no. And I realise it's no excuse, but she did all the chasing.'

'You're right. It's no excuse.' She took another drink, almost emptying her glass, and her shoulders dropped a bit, as if she was beginning to relax.

'I felt like a failure,' he said. 'I *am* a failure.'

'Self-pity? Really, Geoffrey?'

'Sorry. Did I mention I was pathetic too?'

'You didn't need to. I worked that out for myself.' She finished the last of her wine and poured another.

'Look,' she said, 'I have no desire to rake over all this again but for the sake of closure, you need to understand that if you had to fuck another woman, you could not have chosen anyone worse. Your disloyalty to me was beyond forgiveness.'

She had told him what he already knew, and of course she was right. But she was also right about closure. He had needed to hear her say it. 'I'm sorry,' he said, knowing how lame and inadequate it sounded but wanting to tell her anyway.

Olivia stared into her wine glass. 'What will you do?' she asked.

'My mother has decided to sell the Rectory and buy that cottage for sale up by the church. She can't bear the thought of me going bankrupt, so she's paying off my debts and giving me a loan to start another business. Something small, less ambitious than Downings. I'm going to talk to Johnny about it, see if he'd be interested in coming in with me.'

'He doesn't have any money.'

'I know, but he has other things: technical skills, experience. And he's a good friend. I can trust him. It's just a thought . . .'

They sat in silence for a while, taking in the room, the furniture, the confusing mix of familiar and unfamiliar things: a metaphor for their new reality.

Geoffrey had one last question. He hoped that he already knew the answer, but needed Olivia to confirm it. 'Before all of this' – he waved his hand around to encompass her move to the cottage and everything that had precipitated it – 'we had a good marriage, didn't we?'

The way she looked at him made Geoffrey think of the girl with the swishy ponytail who couldn't reach the pigeonholes. She leaned across and touched his hand.

'We had Edward.'

Acknowledgements

A novel is primarily the work of the author, but getting it into print requires much help and collaboration. This novel would not have been published if it hadn't been for the work, support and tenacity of my agent, Robert Kirby. Huge thanks to him, and to Wanda Whiteley, Manuscript Doctor extraordinaire. Thanks also to my editors, Joel Richardson and Claire Johnson-Creek, for their patience, kindness and skill.

I would like to thank my steadfast friend, Amanda Muir, for the morning hill-walks, the laughter and occasional tears. What's said on our walks stays on our walks.

Love and gratitude go to my wonderful children, Charlotte, Matthew and Nicholas. I hope I make them as proud as they make me. And finally, love and gratitude also in abundance to my handsome husband (he told me to say that). Thirty-six years and counting.

Enjoyed *An Unsuitable Marriage*?
Read on for an extract from Colette
Dartford's debut novel, *Learning to
Speak American.*

One

Lola remembered how only Darcy had enjoyed that foray into the Mendips, bounding along rutted paths, scampering through swampy fields, rolling joyously in cowpats. She should have told him off – bad boy Darcy, bad dog – but she was grateful to have him there, a welcome buffer between her and Duncan.

It had been almost a year since Clarissa's accident and Darcy would still lie outside her bedroom door and whimper, unable to understand why she wasn't there. Lola didn't understand either.

As Duncan had consulted an Ordnance Survey map, Lola felt it best not to mention that she and Clarissa used to hack over the myriad of bridleways that criss-crossed the Mendip hills, rendering the map somewhat redundant. If she had mentioned it, Duncan would have got that dark, brooding look she had become all too familiar with, followed by a punitive silence – the price she paid for saying their daughter's name out loud. But as they picked their way along the muddy tracks, memories of those precious times had flooded back; one so vivid Lola couldn't hold it inside.

'Polo spooked along here,' she blurted, pointing to a bend in the bridleway. 'A pair of terriers appeared out of nowhere, barking and getting under his hooves, then he took off.' Grief stabbed at her chest. So painful to talk about her little girl, but more painful not to. She swallowed hard. 'Clarissa didn't have time to gather up her reins, but she managed to grab a handful of mane and cling on until I could get past and pull him up.'

Lola relived the scene in her head, eyes closed, face tilted to the milky sky. Clarissa had let out a shrill cry when Polo bolted. Lola listened hard, trying to hear something, anything that might pull her further back into that moment, but the only sound was the wild October wind cavorting among the trees.

When she opened her eyes Duncan was gone. She called his name but he didn't answer. Darcy headed along the track at a jog and Lola followed. She spotted Duncan ahead, his back to her. He ignored her when she reached him.

'I didn't mean to upset you,' she said. 'It just reminded me …' Her voice trailed off when he quickened his pace. Darcy dropped a stick at his feet, tail wagging, but Duncan ignored him too. Lola resigned herself to the inevitable silence, but Duncan stopped abruptly and turned.

'I don't need to be reminded we had a daughter,' he said. 'Nor do I need to be reminded why we lost her – '

Was that what he had taken from her recollection? That she had saved Clarissa from danger and he hadn't? He turned his back to her again. She wanted to touch him but he looked rigid, unyielding. A string of riders appeared, galloping towards them. Duncan and Lola retreated to the edge of the path and when the riders had thundered past Duncan muttered something about rain and that they should probably head home.

*

How bizarre that memory should intrude here, now, in a smart San Francisco hotel room, a world away from the windswept Mendips. But how much had really changed? Any mention of Clarissa was still taboo and Duncan's strategy was still to distract her, keep her busy, not give her time to think. Moping, he called it. She called it missing Clarissa.

Duncan didn't say why he chose San Francisco for their anniversary and Lola didn't ask. She feigned delight, all the time thinking how exhausting it would be to have a whole two weeks of his undivided attention. At home they had mastered the art of avoidance – Duncan ensconced in his study, Lola busy with the horses – but such enforced proximity would quickly deplete their arsenal of small talk.

The hotel room was a shrine to French antiques. While Duncan dealt with the luggage, Lola wandered over to the tall arched windows. A glassy cyan ocean glistened beneath a blood-orange sun. Swirls of pink and peach washed through the dusk sky. Parallel to the water a long, wide street pulsed with traffic and pedestrians. Lola stared unblinking, mesmerised by the unfamiliar scene. She was used to sky that teetered between various shades of grey and narrow muddy lanes that convoluted through the English countryside, as if to go anywhere directly was to miss the point of the journey. The contrast surprised her, sparked a flicker of interest she hadn't expected.

'Do you like it?' asked Duncan.

'I do,' said Lola, and not just because that was what he wanted to hear.

Nothing shone a spotlight on unhappiness like the pressure of a happy occasion, but she knew how much trouble he had gone to and that it wasn't just about their anniversary. He was trying to make recompense for Clarissa, as if such a thing were possible. Lola didn't believe it was possible to get over the loss of a child, but Duncan was determined they should move on with their lives, put it all behind them. He never said as much – that would have meant talking about Clarissa – but he offered all sorts of diversions, his way of saying, see, life goes on, without actually having to say it. He planned weekend trips that Lola would cancel, or offered a litany of hobbies in which she had no interest: tennis, bridge, a little golf perhaps.

'I've planned a pretty full itinerary,' he said, unpacking his suitcase.

'Of course you have,' said Lola quietly.

He disappeared into the bathroom saying something about an exhibition that Lola didn't quite catch. She looked at her own suitcase but couldn't summon up the enthusiasm to unpack. Instead, she went back to the window and pressed her forehead against the cool glass. They had been married twenty years. Clarissa had been dead for two. Lola wondered quite what they had to celebrate.

Duncan was brisk and full of purpose the following morning, already showered and dressed before Lola had finished her first cup of tea. His shirt – cornflower blue with a faint white stripe – had sharp creases, as though just removed from its packaging. Only the very top button was undone.

'New shirt?' asked Lola.

He adjusted the starched collar and nodded. She noticed he was wearing cufflinks: square, gold and shiny. Distinguished – it described him perfectly. No hint of the paunch that afflicted most men in middle age, or the 'scourge of alopecia', as he called it. Duncan was mystified by the fashion among young men to shave their head, as if baldness was something to aspire to. His own hair was thick and dark but for liberal glints of gunmetal grey. Lola saw the way women looked at him and remembered that she used to look at him that way too.

'Come on,' he cajoled. 'Why don't you get up?'

'I didn't sleep very well,' she said. 'Jetlag, I suppose.'

He sat on the end of the bed and offered an indulgent smile.

'It's a beautiful day,' he said. 'A walk will do you good. You'll feel much better when you're up and about and doing something.'

Lola wasn't convinced, but she stifled a yawn and asked what he had in mind.

'There's an exhibition at MOMA I thought you might enjoy,' he said, on the move again. He fetched a colourful flyer from the desk and handed it to her. 'Matisse as Sculptor'.

His pleased-with-himself smile reminded her how hard he was trying and the least she could do was play along.

'Sounds great,' she said, draining her cup and pouring another tea.

*

The sun was warm and a cool breeze fluttered off the ocean. Lola looked at the ferries, the trams, the giant double-decker bridge, and thought how foreign it all seemed. The vibrancy of the city, its barefaced vitality, flooded her fragile senses, reminding her how insular her life had become. She tried to compare it to London, but San Francisco felt different – younger and more rebellious. And besides, Lola couldn't remember the last time she had visited London – nowadays she rarely ventured beyond the Somerset village they had moved to six months after they were married, let alone made the hundred-mile journey to the capital. Duncan encouraged her to meet him there, tempting her with museums, galleries, the theatre – all the things she once loved. Maybe next week, she would say.

Yet he'd got her to San Francisco, and it did seem to seep through the veil of sadness that shrouded her from the world. It unsettled her, though, this reminder that there was so much in life that she used to take pleasure in.

Their timing could not have been worse. They arrived at the museum just as a party of schoolgirls filed in, and suddenly all Lola could see was her daughter. Their blazers were like the one Clarissa used to wear, navy blue with a white crest on the right breast pocket. A couple of the girls had the same long glossy hair. Lola willed them to turn around so she could see their faces. Even now, part of her couldn't quite believe she would never see her child again. The girls' excited chatter echoed in the huge marble hall, and Lola watched how they moved, laughed, spoke, longing to see some mannerism or gesture that reminded her of Clarissa – something physical to flesh out her memories, give them shape and form, right there in front of her eyes. One of the glossy-haired girls turned and looked straight at her. She was nothing like Clarissa.

'Darling?' said Duncan.

He was holding two exhibition guides that she hadn't noticed him buy.

'Yes?'

'Where would you like to start? I thought we might go straight to the Matisse?'

Lola couldn't have cared less. She longed to say, look at what we've lost, but she saw the set of his mouth, the tightness in his jaw, and realised Duncan was thinking about Clarissa too. Lola took one of the guides.

'Yes,' she said. 'Let's start with the Matisse.'

She let Duncan take the lead, even though art was her field, not his. He asked what she thought, what she knew about Matisse, why he took up sculpting so late in his career, but her monosyllabic responses must have worn him down because he said that if she wasn't interested they could leave. She wanted to say yes, but that would have spoiled the whole day, and what then? They'd go back to the hotel, be polite to each other while avoiding eye contact and any mention of the one subject Lola wanted to talk about. No. She racked her brains to remember what she knew about Matisse, what fragments of knowledge she could piece together to reward Duncan for having thought of the exhibition in the first place.

'He sculpted throughout his career,' she said, 'but his sculptures were overshadowed by his paintings. It's his painting people recognise.'

Duncan looked at her, his head tilted slightly to one side. 'Really? I didn't know that.'

'Yes. He often sculpted and painted the same figures, like this one,' she said, pointing to *Large Seated Nude*.

'Is it me,' asked Duncan, studying the sculpture, 'or is it ugly?'

'He liked to challenge idealised notions of gender, represent women as thin and muscular at the same time, blend elements of masculine and feminine.'

Duncan nodded. 'Impressive,' he said.

'You like it?'

'Not particularly. I meant you – your knowledge of Matisse.'

Lola smiled, said she'd forgotten most of it.

'Maybe you should take a course, brush up on your art history.'

'Maybe,' said Lola, although she knew she wouldn't.

It was later, back at the hotel, when Duncan phoned room service and ordered a bottle of champagne, that Lola was on her guard. What better opportunity to resurrect their dormant sex-life than in a five-star hotel on their wedding anniversary? It wasn't that she didn't want him, more that they had lost the rhythm of being a couple – intimacy nurtured through small, everyday gestures of love and affection. Their intimacy had been so violently disrupted that it had never recovered. Lola no longer undressed in front of him. They didn't talk about that either.

'I'm going to have a bath,' she said, shutting the bathroom door behind her.

When Duncan knocked ten minutes later, she quickly arranged the foamy bubbles so that only her head and shoulders were visible.

'Yes?' she said.

He came in holding two flutes of champagne, perched on the side of the bath tub and handed her one of the flutes. She rarely drank champagne any more, but instantly recalled the sweet sherbet taste, the way the bubbles danced on her tongue.

'It's Schramsberg,' said Duncan, holding up his glass.

'Pardon?'

'The champagne – it's Schramsberg, produced in the Napa Valley. Official wine of the White House. We could do a tour of the caves if you like.'

'Could we?'

There it was again – that pleased-with-himself look. 'I didn't think you'd want to spend too long in the city so I found a hotel right in the heart of wine country.'

'Clever you,' said Lola, although she now realised she was coming to enjoy the novelty of the city.

He grazed her shoulder with his hand and offered to wash her back.

'Already done,' she said too brightly.

She willed him to leave but he sat there in his thick white robe, sweat beading on his face and neck. It was easier at home – so many rooms that avoiding each other hardly seemed like avoiding each other at all. Here there was nowhere to hide.

'I won't be long,' said Lola when the silence became unbearable. 'Why don't you see what's on TV?'

He never watched television, but got the message and left. She closed her eyes and slid under the water.

Duncan hired a sleek red convertible for the drive to the Napa Valley and insisted on having the roof down, even in the chilly morning air. Lola tilted her face to the sun and breathed deeply, detecting a faint tang of salt. She could see him out of the corner of her eye, watching her, monitoring her mood. It felt strange to be sitting next to him in an open-top car – not like them at all. Over breakfast he had mentioned something about pushing her out of her comfort zone, an expression Lola thought was very un-Duncan-like, one she'd expect him to dismiss as psychobabble.

'You worry about me too much,' she said.

He kept his eyes on the road.

'It's a while since you've been more than ten miles outside of Piliton,' he said. 'I don't want you to feel' – he seemed to struggle for the right word – 'overwhelmed.'

Lola was surprised. Had Duncan just alluded to the fragility he carefully tiptoed around without ever mentioning by name?

'I don't,' she said. 'Actually, I've rather enjoyed the strangeness of it – the fact that it's so different to home.'

The tightness in his jaw relaxed.

'I'm doing my best,' she said.

He patted her leg.

'I know you are.'

Duncan's uncanny ability to find his way around foreign cities had always impressed Lola. It reminded her of a time before Clarissa was born, when she sometimes accompanied him on business trips. He travelled to alien, exotic places and she was flattered he wanted her with him. She assumed men used these occasions for extra-marital sex, a sort of adultery amnesty, so far from home that it didn't count. During the day she'd busy herself sightseeing and at night Duncan would ravish her, aroused by some hotel-room fantasy she willingly fulfilled.

'Look,' Duncan said, jolting her back to the present. 'The Golden Gate Bridge.'

Lola pushed her sunglasses onto her head, wanting to see the bridge in all its glory, illuminated by the dazzling yellow sun. The way it spanned the ocean, disappearing into what remained of the Pacific fog, endowed it with an almost mystical quality. Its colour seemed to change from one moment to the next – reddish orange, then brown, then more of a brick red. The sailing boats bobbing below looked like toys. Everything sparkled: the bridge, the white sails, the infinite expanse of water. She was gripped with the same feeling she'd had when she looked out of the tall arched window – that momentary sense of awe.

When Duncan had announced they were going to California, Lola thought of vast arid landscapes and endless sandy beaches, yet just forty minutes out of San Francisco, they were in lush, verdant wine country. She liked how the breeze whipped through her hair, the way the air smelled sweet and clean. Duncan fiddled with the radio and found a station called Vine. He sang along to the Eagles like he didn't have a care in the world. Lola sat back and tried to imagine what that would be like.

Hotel Auberge clung to a hillside above the Silverado Trail that ran between Yountville and St Helena. It mimicked the style of a Tuscan villa, with terracotta walls and tall shuttered windows. Duncan pulled up outside and two young men in polo shirts and Bermuda shorts opened the car doors for them.

Honeysuckle, jasmine and sage: as the bellboy led them through the luxuriant gardens, Lola marvelled at how intense even familiar scents became with the kiss of warm air.

'Here we are.'

The bellboy stopped outside a whitewashed cabin framed with vivid pink bougainvillea.

'This is a cottage?' said Lola.

'Uh-huh,' he said. 'You have cottages in Britain, right?'

Lola thought how 'Britain' was something only a foreigner would say in that context.

Inside it was cool and surprisingly spacious. A huge bed stood in the centre of the room, an oak armoire and dressing table to one side, a chaise longue and coffee table to the other.

'The bathroom is through here,' said the bellboy, opening a door at the far end of the room. 'Is there anything else I can help you with?'

'No, thank you,' said Duncan, pressing a ten-dollar bill into his hand.

'Have a great day.'

'Such an effusive expression,' said Lola when the bellboy had left.

'It's their way of being polite.'

'I suppose.'

'Welcome to America,' he said.

Lola wasn't sure if it was because she had resolved to try harder, or if it was the intoxicating effect of the wines, but over dinner that evening she relaxed, found herself enjoying Duncan's company, even flirting a little. She wore a black silk dress and high heels, her hair arranged in an elegant chignon. Duncan kept refilling her glass and when she asked if he was trying to get her drunk, he said *absolutely*. She wanted to reward him for not giving up on her. The odds were against them – that's what it warned in one of the bereavement counsellor's booklets, although not in so many words. The loss of a child, an only child, was more than most couples could bear. But their marriage had survived – if that was what this was. Lola wasn't sure any more, but she was a little drunk and they hadn't made love in such a long time. He must have read her mind because he asked for the bill as the waitress cleared their dinner plates.

They made their way back through the garden, the high-pitched frenzy of a thousand crickets ringing in their ears, and when Duncan opened the door to the cottage and reached for the light switch, Lola put her hand over his.

'Leave it,' she said softly, removing the clip from her hair.

In the thin shard of moonlight that sliced through the shutters, he looked so grateful that Lola ached with regret for all the times she had rebuffed him, turned away when he had reached for her in the night. She cupped his face in her hands and tried to banish thoughts of Clarissa. Duncan unzipped her dress and let it fall to the floor. As she stood there in a puddle of black silk, she struggled to remember what it felt like before they were damaged, and wondered if it would ever feel like that again. She closed her eyes and willed herself back to those hot, passionate nights in far-flung hotels, when she yielded to his fantasies and thrilled him with her own. He moved her hair aside and kissed the soft, warm skin on her neck. Shivers of pleasure radiated from his touch, rousing some sensual memory, long forgotten. She undressed him quickly, fearful the memory would vanish into the darkness, and when he whispered – what's the hurry? – she didn't answer. Instead, she lay down on the bed and opened herself to him, knowing that if they lost this too, there might be nothing of their marriage left to save.

When Lola woke in the unfamiliar room, it took a few moments to remember where she was. Her head hurt and her mouth was parched. She needed water but there was none on the bedside table. Then she remembered: anniversary, wine, sex. She covered her face with her hands. What had seemed so natural last night felt faintly embarrassing now. They had got out of the habit of having sex, of being intimate. Duncan opened his eyes and stretched.

'Do we have any water?' she asked.

He got out of bed and fetched a bottle of Pellegrino and two tumblers from the coffee table. It seemed strange watching him walk across the room naked. At home he wore pyjamas in bed and as soon as he got up, he put on a dressing gown and slippers. He filled one of the tumblers and handed it to Lola.

'How are you feeling?' he asked.

'Hung over,' she said.

Duncan poured some water for himself and got back into bed. When she had finished drinking he took the tumbler and pulled her into an embrace. His body felt warm and strong – familiar yet unfamiliar at the same time. He ran his fingers along the length of her spine, kissing her neck and shoulder. Lola closed her eyes and tried to relax, but the pressure in her head and the sour taste in her mouth were too much.

'I need the bathroom,' she said, freeing herself from his long limbs. 'Do we have any aspirin?'

'In my toilet bag.'

Lola could hear the disappointment in his voice but sex was the last thing she wanted. After five minutes in a hot shower, the pain in her head subsided. Duncan came in as she was drying herself, lifted the toilet seat and peed. She unhooked a robe from the bathroom door and as she was putting it on, he suggested she come back to bed.

'I'm hungry,' she said, though she wasn't at all.

'I'll order room service,' he said.

A romantic breakfast in bed would make it more difficult to fend off his advances.

'Let's wander over to the restaurant,' she said.

He turned to face her.

'Last night was wonderful,' he said.

Lola unhooked the other robe and handed it to him. She knew his nakedness shouldn't bother her, but it implied an intimacy she didn't feel. He took the robe but didn't put it on.

'Did you hear what I said?' he asked.

She nodded. He put down the robe, opened Lola's and slid his hands around her waist. She rested her forehead on his shoulder and tried to find the right words. His skin was smooth and smelled of her.

'It was wonderful,' she said. 'But be patient with me, give me time.'

He said nothing at first, just held her. She worried that she'd spoiled things – said too much, or not enough.

'Does this mean I have to get you drunk every time we have sex?' he asked.

'Not every time,' she said and he laughed.

Wine tasting was top of Duncan's agenda, but Lola couldn't face alcohol and suggested they go for a walk around town instead, get to know the place a bit. She thought he might be disappointed but he seemed pleased that she was taking the initiative, not just going along with whatever he wanted because she didn't care one way or another.

'Good idea,' he said, picking up the car keys and handing them to her. 'Why don't you drive?'

Her heart quickened at the thought of it; driving on the right, on unfamiliar roads with unfamiliar rules. They had played out variations of this scenario many times since Clarissa died. Lola wanted to be left alone, surprised that he expected anything of her when simply getting through the day took all her strength. Yet he set her tasks and tests to prove she was fine – they both were fine.

'Come on, darling,' he said, opening the driver's door. 'It's easy.'

It would take more effort to protest than to drive a few miles, so even though her head still felt fuzzy, she got in, adjusted the seat and turned on the ignition. And he was right – it was easy.

'Brilliant,' he said as she negotiated a crossroads and turned onto St Helena's tree-lined Main Street. 'I knew you could do it.'

When she reversed smoothly into a parking space and positioned the convertible in perfect parallel to the kerb, Duncan beamed with satisfaction.

'That's my girl,' he said and Lola had to look away, remembering how he used to say exactly the same thing to Clarissa.

As they strolled along Main Street, Duncan took her hand. Focus on the positive – that was his philosophy. He would be thinking about the rare closeness of last night's lovemaking, not her unwillingness to repeat it this morning. He seemed relaxed, almost content. She wondered if he faked it like she did. It was hard to tell with Duncan.

'I'm glad you suggested this,' he said. 'It's a glorious afternoon.'

'Have you noticed how everyone here smiles at you?' asked Lola.

'Can you imagine in London if everyone you walked past offered a cheery smile? We'd think them insane; hardly dare to make eye contact. I must say, I find it rather odd, all this unfettered friendliness.'

'Maybe it's the sunshine.'

'Or the wine.'

Their easy rapport made it seem as though they had stepped back in time, reconnected with an earlier version of themselves. It was Duncan's idea to stop by the estate agents. In the window were photographs of everything from hundred-acre estates to small wooden houses squeezed onto tiny scraps of land.

'See anything you like?'

A young, fair-haired man stood behind them – styrofoam cup in one hand, mobile phone in the other. The logo on his T-shirt looked like a fish and his faded jeans had the beginnings of a tear over the knee. His smile revealed dazzlingly white teeth, straight and perfectly spaced. Perhaps it was the artist in Lola, but a face like his, defined by predictably symmetrical features, seemed to lack character. Imperfections and irregularities were what made faces interesting.

'Sorry,' he said as Duncan spun around. 'Didn't mean to startle you.' He slipped the phone into his pocket and held out his hand. 'Cain McCann. I work here.'

His air of casual confidence, the ease with which he inhabited the world, struck Lola as very American. Duncan wore his confidence on the inside, strong but private. This man's confidence was of a different vintage and calibre, displayed for all to see. Duncan shook his hand.

'Duncan Drummond. This is my wife, Lola.'

'Great to meet you,' said McCann. 'Where are you guys from?'

'England,' said Duncan. 'We're staying at the Auberge.'

'Good choice,' said McCann. He took a sip from the styrofoam cup. 'You thinking of investing in some property? A vacation home, maybe?'

All they had done was look in the window. To Lola he seemed pushy, although Duncan didn't appear to mind.

'It's all rather expensive,' he said.

'Yeah,' said McCann, 'St Helena is pretty pricey. Still, if you want to come in out of the heat, I'll see what I can tempt you with.' He opened the door and waited.

Lola stayed put, reluctant to be subjected to the inevitable sales pitch, but Duncan gave her one of his encouraging smiles and led the way.

The air-conditioner hummed while a pair of ceiling fans whirred frenetically. Lola's eyes took a moment to adjust to the relative lack of brightness. Next to McCann, Duncan looked very formal – his dress code made no concessions to the heat. He wouldn't dream of wearing a T-shirt anywhere but the gym. Weekends he swapped expensive Savile Row suits for pale corduroy trousers and casual shirts. He didn't even own a pair of jeans. She knew she was being stuffy, but McCann looked like he was going to a rock concert, not to work.

'Here's my card,' he said, handing them one each.

'That's odd,' said Lola, reading the card. '"Realtor" isn't a word we use in England.'

'Really?' said McCann.

'We say "estate agent".'

'Thanks for the English lesson,' he said, treating her to another full-frontal smile. It was impossible not to smile back but just as Lola began to warm to his eager exuberance, he turned away and addressed himself to Duncan.

'So, if you were thinking of investing in a vacation property, what kind of budget would we be talking about?'

This was not how Lola wanted to spend her time. She was usually more tolerant but the dull pain of her hangover still lingered and she craved coffee and carbs. It wasn't as if they had any intention of buying a property – vacation or otherwise. She was about to make light of the idea when Duncan spoke.

'Four hundred thousand,' he said, casually. 'Dollars.'

Lola stared at him, eyebrows raised. What was going on here? Why was Duncan humouring him? If he noticed her consternation, he didn't let on. Perhaps he was missing work and wanted a distraction. McCann put his hands in his pockets and shook his head.

'I don't have anything in that price range.'

'Nothing at all?' said Duncan.

'Don't think so,' said McCann.

He sat down at one of the desks and peered at a computer screen.

'No,' he said. 'Only thing is a little fixer-upper at the bottom of Spring Mountain. Been empty for a couple of years. Before that it was rented.'

'How much is it?' asked Duncan.

McCann hit the keyboard with a decisive click.

'They're asking four-fifty but it's been listed for a while so they'll probably take an offer.'

A printer at the far end of the office sprang into life.

'Great location,' said McCann, picking up the details. 'Just a mile from town.'

He handed a set to Duncan and then, as an after-thought, printed another set for Lola. As he leaned over her she noticed a slight bump on the bridge of his nose and the faintest hint of a scar. It blurred the bland perfection of his face.

'It needs remodelling,' he said, 'but for that price, you really can't go wrong.'

Lola looked at the picture – a square wooden struc-ture on four wooden stilts – and immediately thought of a tree house. She had one as a child – a precarious lop-sided thing her father built before he absconded with a woman half his age. When Lola wanted to escape her mother's lugubrious presence, or the many reminders of her father's absence, she retreated to the quiet solitude of her tree house.

'It looks interesting,' she said, studying the picture. 'Unusual.'

Now it was Duncan who raised his eyebrows.

'It's a beautiful spot,' said McCann. 'We could take a drive over there if you want.'

Despite her pique at having been railroaded into it, Lola was curious to see this odd little house. The setting looked gorgeous, and he did say it was close to town. They could have a quick look around and then find somewhere to eat.

At the very least it would give them an interesting topic of conversation over lunch.

She turned to Duncan. 'Why not?'

It was the sweet, comforting smell of warm wood that first struck her. The house, made entirely of timber, stood nestled among a cordon of tall, spindly pines and shorter, thicker firs. There appeared to be just a single room – a fireplace at one end, the shell of a kitchen at the other – with a ceiling that sloped upwards to a height of maybe twenty feet. Fiery June sunshine bombarded the filthy windows, imbuing the air with a soft amber glow. A mesh of silvery cobwebs fanned out from every crevice. Dust sat thick and languid, disturbed only by resident vermin as they scurried about their business.

'Is this it?' asked Duncan.

'There are two bedrooms at the back,' said McCann. He pointed to an opening – a doorframe, but no door. 'And a small bathroom.'

Lola touched Duncan's arm, signalling that she wanted to explore. He appeared surprised but followed anyway. McCann said he had to make a phone call, that he'd be right outside if they needed him. Duncan pulled a pristine white handkerchief from his pocket and wiped a film of sweat from his brow.

'No wonder the particulars only showed a picture of the outside,' he said, looking around. 'You don't get much for your money.'

Lola peered into the tiny bathroom that led off the tiny bedroom and decided not to venture further.

'How much is it in sterling?' she asked.

Duncan thought for a moment.

'Around three hundred thousand,' he said. 'Why? You don't actually like it, do you?'

It made no sense at all, but she did. Something about the neglected house defied her grief-soaked indifference. It was as though those few momentary flashes of pleasure – the view from the window, the taste of champagne, the magnificent Golden Gate – had gathered momentum and released something inside of her, allowed it to break free.

She took Duncan's arm and led him onto the rickety wooden deck. A canopy of leaves offered shade from the sun and a soft breeze carried the scent of cut grass and rosemary. She looked out at the trees and vineyards, birds she'd never seen before, butterflies as big as her hand.

'You seem enthralled,' he said.

'I am,' she said, 'but don't ask me to explain why.'

How could she explain the ludicrous notion that bringing this house back to life might somehow bring her back to life?